Corrupted Protector

Strangers to Lovers Dark Mafia Romance

Kiana Hettinger

This book is an original production of Hardmoon Press.

HARDMOON PRESS

By Kiana Hettinger

Corrupted Protector is the third book in the <u>Mafia Kings: Corrupted Series.</u>

Mafia Kings: Corrupted Series
#0 Cruel Inception
#1 Corrupted Heir
#2 Corrupted Temptation
#3 Corrupted Protector
#4 Corrupted Obsession

Your Exclusive Access

Thanks a million for being here. Your support means so much to me.

The best way to keep in touch with me is by signing up for my newsletter – sendfox.com/authorkianah (I promise I won't spam you!) and by joining my readers' group, Kiana's Kittens – facebook.com/groups/KianasKittens

You'll receive bonus chapters, inside scoop, discounts, first access to cover reveals and rough drafts, exclusive material, and so much more!

See you on the inside,
Kiana Hettinger

Author's Note

It was very difficult for me to write Leo and Ella's story because it contains a lot of triggering topics. It took a lot out of me to tell Ella's tragic story, but I wrote it with hope in my heart. Ella found hers in Leo.

I hope you find your *hope*.

K

Table of Contents

Prologue

Moonlight slipped through the part in the bedroom's curtains, shining dimly across the man lying in the middle of the four-poster bed. Salt-and-pepper hair. Clean-shaven. His eyes were closed, and he'd kicked off the thick burgundy comforter some time ago, revealing a body lightly sprinkled with the same combination of black and graying hair.

For a man in his early sixties, he was still in good shape. No flab, a bit of muscle, no deep wrinkles except for the crow's-feet at the corners of his eyes and the furrow lines across his brow.

Reasonably attractive, but I hated the man.

I hated him with every fiber of my being.

If I was braver, I would have searched the room for a letter opener or slipped the curtain from its rod and used it to stab the vile creature in the heart.

But I was a coward.

I was weak.

And sore.

And dirty.

It had been four days since he'd let me shower.

My dark hair hung matted and oily down my back. The chafe marks around my wrists were red and swollen. I'd been awake so long, my eyes stung and my eyelids felt like leaden weights.

He sighed in his sleep and rolled onto his side.

I'd been watching him from the floor for hours, waiting for the perfect moment that never came.

He could wake up at any second.

He could catch me.

Punish me.

Maybe even kill me.

I took one deep, steadying breath and stood up.

My knees were stiff from hours on the Persian carpet, but there was no time to unstiffen them.

I crept toward the bedroom door, glancing back over and over again, watching for a flinch, listening for a hitch in his breathing— anything at all that signaled my escape was over before it had even begun.

He remained motionless aside from the steady rise and fall of his chest.

I kept going until the cool metal of the door handle laid beneath my fingers. I grabbed the key from the gray boxer shorts I'd stolen after he fell asleep.

My hand shook so hard, it would be nearly impossible to unlock the door without waking him up.

But I'd come this far.

I had to try.

Willing my hands to be still, I glanced back once more, then held my breath as I slipped the old-fashioned skeleton key into the lock.

The scrape of metal against metal blared like a siren.

The man didn't make a sound. His chest continued to rise and fall in the same steady rhythm.

With a turn of the handle, I tiptoed out of the room and closed the door quietly behind me.

The hallway was dark, but I could hear voices coming from the main floor. Two voices—that's how many men were supposed to be posted at the front door.

"He's late," one of the voices barked. It was Johnny. He was about as well-tempered as a wolverine.

"Just relax. He'll be here," Riccardo said—the nice one. At least as close to nice as a thug could get.

Riccardo wasn't like the other guards; though I held no illusions about him. He'd stop me just as quickly as all the others.

"Don't fucking tell me to relax," Johnny seethed as I crept along the hallway to the top of the tall, spiral staircase.

The chandelier's light from the marble-floored foyer shone across the stairs, making it impossible to remain in the shadows. The moment I set foot on them, I'd be exposed. Out in the open.

I glanced back at the bedroom door.

It stood there motionless, as doors tended to do.

I closed my eyes and listened, trying to listen to their footsteps, their breathing.

They weren't at their posts like they should have been, so where were they? In the living room? In front of the locked door that led to the basement?

A shiver ghosted down my spine just thinking of that wretched place.

I'd almost given up when the clank of a glass against the granite countertop gave them away.

They were in the kitchen.

It was past the parlor and dining room, so the kitchen had no clear view of the front door.

This was my chance!

As quietly as I could, I crept down the stairs. I'd traveled up and down them so many times, I knew exactly which part of the seventh and twelfth steps to avoid to keep from making them squeak.

One step, and then another, while my heart pounded like a drum in my chest. The blood whooshing past my ears was so loud it drowned out the bickering coming from the kitchen. I could barely hear them now.

What if they'd stopped arguing? What if Johnny or Riccardo was already on their way back to their post by the front door?

I glanced back up the stairs.

I could still turn around.

I could still run back to the bedroom and the man I loathed.

I could return his clothes to where I'd found them. Lie down on the floor like an obedient pet. Let myself be used, abused, tossed, turned, as if I was a rag doll.

It had only been by chance the skeleton key had slipped from his pants pocket.

What were the chances the opportunity to escape would present itself again anytime soon? Or ever?

You can do this, I tried to pep-talk myself into motion since it seemed my feet had frozen and glued itself to the stairs. But I could do this. I had to do this.

Even if it meant I died trying.

I forced my feet to move, descending the final four steps.

So far, no Johnny or Riccardo. Maybe they'd be too busy tearing each other's throats out to notice me slipping past them.

I crossed the foyer to the keypad by the front door without a backward glance.

It was too late to turn back now.

All I could do was move forward.

As quickly as I could, I punched the six-digit code into the keypad.

Through my lashes, I'd watched the men here punch in the same code over and over again. Why the code never changed, I had no idea, but I wasn't about to look a gift horse in the mouth.

With a quiet click, the electronic locks on the door disengaged. Still not daring to look back, I darted for the door, turned the handle, and yanked it open.

The cool night air slipped through the thin, oversized dress shirt I'd stolen, but I didn't care.

I'd rather be cold and frozen to the bone than trapped for one second longer.

The petrichor scent of the earth after a fresh rain assailed my nostrils—this was what freedom smelled like.

I breathed in deep as I closed the door behind me.

Then I saw a dark sliver of movement right before the door clicked shut.

Damn it.

I turned and dashed down the front stairs, leaping from the fourth step to the ground. The impact slammed through my bare feet, but I had no time to let them recover.

Fortunately, I'd planned the route I would take if ever I made it out of this godforsaken place, so I veered off the main drive and into the hedges down the side.

Beyond them, an open expanse of lawn would leave me out in the open, but the bushes amid the maples and pines at the property's edge would swallow me up and keep me hidden from other guards.

I dove into the hedges, ignoring the sting of torn flesh as the branches fought my intrusion. Footsteps sounded close behind me, but I took no time to look back as I burst out the other side and ran through the open yard.

The ground was wet, making the grass so slippery beneath my bare feet, I slipped and slid over and over again.

Faster, damn it.

I could hear the rustle of leaves behind me, and then the heavy thud of footsteps as my pursuer gained ground.

He was close.

Too close.

I'd never be able to outrun him.

A hand grabbed my shirt from behind, yanking me to a stop.

Terror and misery coursed through my veins in equal measures. And yet, I wasn't ready to give in. I wasn't ready to accept that this was all my life would ever be.

I used the momentum of him yanking me back to spin around and plant a fist in his jaw as hard as I could.

Johnny's head shot back as pain exploded across my fist and shot up my arm.

I tried to pull away, but he still had a handful of my shirt in his meaty hand. Just as I tried to slip out of the shirt, he grabbed hold of my arm with his free hand, wrapping around my bicep in an iron grip.

"You stupid whore," Johnny hissed. "You're going to pay for that." He turned, pulling me with him and making my feet slide precariously beneath me.

I looked everywhere, searching for something. Anything. But there was nothing to grab onto. Nothing I could use to try to defend myself.

There was nothing.

I glanced around once more, not searching this time, just trying to take it all in.

I was outside, of my own volition, for the first time in so long.

I breathed in deep, committing every layer of the earthy musk smell to memory. Etching the feel of the cool breeze against my cold skin into my mind. Memorizing the craggy surfaces of the tree bark at the property's edge, taking careful note of every brown in its ridges, from rich chestnut to deep mahogany. And the taste.

It was everything and nothing at the same time.

It was freedom.

And it had slipped just out of my grasp.

A loud crack sounded in the distance—like the sound of lightning striking a tree or concrete exploding in winter.

Or a gunshot.

Johnny stumbled back, loosening his grip on my arm.

I waited to feel it.

A tearing pain through my abdomen. A searing agony in my chest.

I had no idea what to expect; I'd never been shot before.

But I couldn't feel anything. Maybe I was in shock? I glanced down to see where the bullet had entered me.

Then I saw the thick, red rivulet running down Johnny's chest.

He staggered back further as I glanced around, searching for the shooter.

Riccardo stood in front of the hedges with a gun in his hands. "Go," he hollered, waving his empty hand at the trees beyond me.

I took one last look at Johnny as he dropped to his knees.

I could have tried to help him.

I knew enough about first aid to apply pressure to the wound to try to staunch the bleeding.

But I didn't.

Maybe it was born from years of trying to keep as much distance from him as possible. Or maybe, sometime during my stay in hell, I'd lost the ability to care.

Either way, I turned away and sprinted toward the towering maple trees ten yards in front of me.

Away from Johnny.

Away from Riccardo.

Away from the place that would star in my nightmares for the rest of my life.

Chapter One

Leo Luca

We crept through the dark run-down parking lot.

The streetlights were all burned out or smashed to pieces, and the cloud cover overhead meant we could move undetected.

We were like ghosts with nothing but the occasional crunch of gravel underfoot to give us away.

Twenty yards.

Ten yards.

I could see the dull haze of light coming from the windows of the building up ahead—an old, ramshackle warehouse on the outskirts of the city.

Nobody had paid it much attention until we'd learned about the stolen product inside. Stolen product that belonged to the Lucas.

It wasn't much, really; no more than a hundred thousand dollars' worth, but they'd killed two of our men to get it.

"Nice night for a stroll?" I whispered to Dante as he came up on my left.

Dante shook his head, barely visible in the darkness. "I still can't believe I let you talk me into this. We could have sent Marco and some men to shoot up this place hours ago."

Corrupted Protector

"What? And miss this brother-bonding experience?" I quipped.

"Right." Dante laughed under his breath. "Leo, if I'm going to spend this much time with you, I prefer it when there's a hot woman's body between us."

"The night's still young, *fratello.*"

And a hot woman's body—or two or three—didn't sound like a bad idea at all.

We reached the outskirts of the building. Every man with us fanned out around the building, just like we'd instructed them to do.

I could hear the quiet *glug glug* of the fuel as they poured it on the ground in a circle around the warehouse—Brute's idea, of course. The crazy leader of the Old Dogs had a thing for fire.

Thirty seconds passed.

Then sixty seconds.

It was time.

I struck a match and tossed it onto the ground in front of me, watching as the flame caught and spread out like a blazing halo around the building.

The light of the fire lit up the faces of the men standing nearby, some of them dressed in black like Dante and me, and others in leather and the signature cuts of the Old Dogs.

"What the hell?" someone shouted from inside the building.

"What the fuck's going on?" another voice hollered.

And then it was a dozen voices, all yelling while heavy footsteps thudded from inside toward the warehouse's only door.

I raised my gun as the door flew open and men stuttered to a stop, colliding into one another in the confusion.

"What the hell?" one of them shouted, trying to backpedal, but the men behind him gave him nowhere to go.

He wasn't what I'd expected. At least sixty years old, the man at the front was pockmarked and scarred, with gray tufts of hair standing up on the top of his head. The others weren't much younger, and they all wore the scars and weathered skin of a life that had been hard-lived.

"You stole from the Lucas, Giuseppe, and you killed two of our men," Dante said matter-of-factly to the ringleader.

Giuseppe could try to deny it, but our intel had been concrete.

"No, we didn't. We didn't steal from no one," old man Giuseppe yelled back while his eyes darted around, squinting to see beyond the flames to take stock of what he was up against: Five Luca men and five Old Dogs. The odds were stacked against him.

"There's no sense in lying," I said, stepping through the ring of fire, impervious to the flames. The gear we had on was fire-resistant, and let's face it, I'd always wanted to do that.

Giuseppe's eyes bulged at the feat, and I stifled a laugh.

Who knew this type of work could be so much fun?

"We'll... we'll give it back," Giuseppe offered with his hands up in supplication.

Unlike his men, who were armed and glaring daggers at me, this man was no monster. Desperate, maybe, and more than a little stupid, but not evil.

"Hey, Leo?" Brute called from somewhere behind me.

"Yeah?"

"If you're done chatting, you maybe want to get back here so we can get to the show without lighting your ass up too?"

"Sure thing," I said, backstepping through the flames—*fuck, that was cool*—while keeping my gun trained on Giuseppe.

The man's hands shook, and his eyes were wide and pleading. This guy had nothing on Bullet.

"Dante?" I said, nodding at the scared mutt.

Dante eyed Giuseppe from head to toe.

The Lucas needed to make a statement. Stealing from us would never be tolerated, and murdering our men was a one-way ticket to hell.

When Dante nodded back in agreement, I offered the man the only mercy I could.

I shot him dead center between the eyes.

Giuseppe fell to the ground as his comrades took aim, but it was too late for them.

Every one of my men and the Old Dogs fired at them, hitting knees, shoulders, elbows—anything that wasn't vital—until they were wounded on the ground.

The Molotov cocktails flew through the night sky like meteorites. Dom had said it was one hell of a sight to see, and he'd been right.

The blazing fireflies crashed to the ground inside the ring and exploded, one after another.

The dying men screamed, but I tuned them out until everything within the ring of flames was alight and the screaming had dissipated.

"What do you think, my young friend?" Brute asked, coming to stand beside me and crossing his arms over his chest. He reminded me of an artist, stepping back from his masterpiece to take it all in.

"You've done well, *amico*."

"That's just what your brother said the first time he came out with us." He laughed, clapping me on the back.

If you asked my father, he'd say we were getting a little too close to the Old Dogs and their crazy leader. But if you asked me, there was nothing wrong with having allies you could count on.

And maybe, just a little, I wanted to see what it was that made the Old Dogs tick. Because while Dom was busy with his wife and new baby, and making the Luca name a fortune with his casino, and Dante was busy doing—well, who knew what Dante did for kicks and giggles—I was searching for something else.

Not something more, necessarily.

What kind of spoiled asshole would I have been to bitch about my lot in life?

A good family. Lots of money. Women available around the clock.

I had everything a man could desire, but something was missing. Something I never could seem to put my finger on.

"So, did it scratch the itch?" Dante asked as Brute headed back to his bike with the Old Dogs.

"It was one hell of a show," I hedged.

I stared at the flames, ignoring the rancid odor of charred hair and flesh, whatever was missing was just as elusive as it had ever been.

***

It seemed Dante had gotten his fill of Old Dogs and Molotov cocktails for one evening.

He played the responsible older brother card and headed home to report back to our father when the deed was done.

I, on the other hand, followed Brute and his Old Dogs back to his bar for a round of celebratory drinks.

"To the men we sent to hell tonight," Brute toasted with his beer held high in the air. "May they keep the place warm and toasty for when we get there."

The Old Dogs cheered and tossed back beers and shots of whiskey.

"I'll be sure to bring the sunscreen," the gray-haired Old Dog parked at the bar said, smiling and stretching the long, jagged scar that ran along his jaw.

"That's awfully kind of you, Mike," another one joined in, wrapping his beefy arm around one of the waitresses. "Since your ancient ass will get there before the rest of us, I'll be sure to send down your pretty whore to slather it on for you."

"Fuck, no!" the Old Dog with the shaved head and a black goatee objected boisterously. "Those heavenly thighs don't belong in hell."

The whole bar roared with laughter. Even the waitresses were jovial tonight, handing out kisses like they were going out of style.

All of the waitresses but one.

I'd seen her both of the times I'd been in here with Dom—it was hard to miss her.

She was drop-dead gorgeous. Long, dark hair that shimmered even in the bar's low lighting. Big green eyes that were narrowed and upturned just enough at the outer corners to give her an almost feline look, and lips that had to have every man who saw her thinking the same thing. She was an inch or two taller than the other waitresses with curves in all the right places and long legs that just didn't quit.

It was more than her appearance that had me watching every move she made. Maybe it was the way she seemed to shy away from the men like she was an innocent, and yet, the haunted look in her eyes said she'd lived three lifetimes in the dark underworld.

"What's gotten your attention, my friend?" Brute asked, sitting down across from me. He followed my gaze and smiled, but something about his demeanor changed, and a possessive gleam shone in his pale blue eyes. "She's as skittish as a stray kitten, but damn pretty," he said, watching as she smiled shyly at a fellow waitress, then set about filling fresh glasses. "Hell, most of the men in here would pay just to look at her."

"Is that so?" I scrubbed my chin.

Brute nodded absentmindedly. "She didn't strike me as the waitressing type, but she sure seemed to need the job." He sat up straighter in his seat. "I've kind of taken to looking out for her, if you know what I mean?" he said, looking me dead in the eye.

Message received. Hands off. Not that I cared about Brute's messages, but Dom wouldn't like it much if I messed up the relationship here. Besides, I'd come to like Brute, and more than that, I respected him.

The gray-haired Old Dog, Mike, with the scar across his jaw had sauntered over, following our gazes back in the girl's direction. "Looking out for her? Is that what you call it?" he drawled. "Don't let him fool you, Mr. Luca. Brute doesn't let anyone near that girl. He won't admit it, but he was a papa bear in his last life."

"A bear, huh?" I grinned.

"Well, either a bear or a forest fire." Mike shrugged.

Brute glared good-naturedly at him. "So long as you keep your hands off her, Mike, I won't have to maul you to death or set your ass on fire."

"Message received, boss." Mike clapped Brute on the back and sauntered back to the bar, taking a wide berth around the knockout waitress who was apparently under Brute's protection.

"I really appreciated your help tonight, Brute," I told him earnestly, even if working with the Old Dogs hadn't shed any light on whatever it was I was looking for. "It was quite the show."

"Anything for the Lucas, my friend. You know that. We're always up for raising a little hell." He did seem to have a knack for it.

"I'll come around with the money tomorrow," I told him.

"If I'm not six feet under, I'll be here."

I stood up and took a last look around, hoping for one more glimpse of the gorgeous waitress, but she was nowhere to be seen. Probably in the back room. *Damn.* I couldn't help laughing to myself. Brute was right. The men here would probably pay just to look at the girl—myself included.

Shaking off the disappointment, I left the bar, slid behind the wheel of my jet-black Lamborghini Urus—the only four-wheeled vehicle in the lot—and pulled out onto the near-empty road.

Right away, something didn't feel right. There was a strange sensation of walking into a dark room but knowing it wasn't empty, that someone else was there.

I pulled the Glock out from inside my jacket.

"You might as well come out," I said lazily, hoping there wasn't an Old Dog gone rogue lurking behind my seat.

Brute might be pissed if I shot one of his men—rogue or not.

This was the problem with tinted windows. Sure, they kept up the mystery aura, but it was impossible to see a goddamned thing in the back seat.

"The bullet will go right through the seat," I said casually, pointing the barrel of the gun against the leather.

A head popped up in the rearview mirror.

The gorgeous waitress.

Her lips were pressed tightly shut, but her feline eyes were as wide as saucers. It was possible she could have been an assassin in disguise, but somehow, I didn't think so.

She looked more like a… well, a skittish kitten.

I holstered my gun. *"Ciao, gattina."*

Kitten. It seemed fitting.

She stared back at me, her emerald eyes gleaming in the moonlight.

"If you were looking for a free ride, all you had to do was ask." I flashed her a grin in the rearview mirror.

She was so quiet, I wasn't sure she was even breathing.

"Not much for small talk, are you?"

She shook her head.

"All right then, do you have a destination in mind?"

She looked out the windows, left and then right. As I slowed to a stop at a red light, she opened the back door and darted out, making a mad dash for the dumpy three-story walk-up across the road.

She was strange and skittish, but she had amazing legs. I'd let her wrap those thighs around me any day of the week.

She ran up the first set of stairs and disappeared inside the door on the second floor, slamming the door shut so hard I could hear it over the car's engine.

I watched, waiting to see the light turn on inside, but it didn't.

The stoplight turned green.

I shifted gears and pushed down on the gas. As I drove away, I couldn't help but think that was the strangest encounter I'd ever had.

For a Luca—who'd taken a stroll through fire just hours ago—that was saying something.

Chapter Two

Ella Taylor

I pushed the blue checked curtain aside just enough to peek out the window.

The street was empty, but would he come back?

Was he just waiting for me to let my guard down?

A minute passed, and then several more.

Still, there was no sign of him.

Letting the curtain fall back into place, I breathed a tentative sigh of relief, then checked each of the locks on the front door, unlocking then locking each of the dead bolts.

There was nothing saying the guy was actually gone.

The suit, the Italian accent, the suave, confident stride; I would have recognized it anywhere. The guy was mafia-made. And boy, was he *made.*

The body, the model-perfect face, the dark hair that was just a little too long but somehow managed to fall in perfectly ordered disarray; the guy looked like he'd been sculpted by the gods. A favorite of the gods, if you will.

The sound of splashing from the bathroom drew my attention away from the ridiculously handsome mafia man.

My knees were still shaking, but I managed to stay upright, crossing the short distance to the olive green cubicle of a bathroom. As I pushed the door open all the way, the splashing intensified. It sounded like there was a whole flock of birds in my bathtub.

"*¿Qué haces?*" I asked the bathtub's only occupant as Duck clambered out of the tub and waddled across the floor, adding to the watery mess he'd made.

Duck quacked excitedly until I grabbed a towel from the rusty rack and wrapped him up, holding him close against my chest.

"*C'est bien,*" I crooned as he nuzzled his green-feathered head against me.

Was it strange that I was proud Duck understood at least a few words in five different languages?

Probably.

"You need a bigger bathtub," I observed, backstepping carefully out of the wet room.

Duck quacked—perhaps in agreement—as I returned to the checkered curtains and peered outside.

How could I have been so stupid? Hiding in the back of a mafia guy's car?

That was just asking to get caught.

It wasn't like I could have hidden behind any of the motorcycles that had been parked in the lot, and I had to get out of there.

The man who'd strode into the bar just before the mafia man left could have been anyone. He was clad in leather and a cut, just like Brute's men, but I'd never seen him in the bar in all the time I'd been working there.

That made him too much of a risk.

Looking outside now, the mafia man's car hadn't returned. No sign of his souped-up sports car or the six-foot-something broad-shouldered Adonis who drove it. Nothing but the occasional old Ford Escort or Dodge truck cruising down the street.

It wasn't a popular area in town. A run-down convenience store, a family-owned diner, and a repair shop sat side by side across the street, but they were all closed. All the lights had been turned off, and thick metal bars had been pulled down over the windows and doors.

"I think we dodged a bullet tonight," I said, stroking Duck's head, just behind his eyes, the way he liked.

Maybe I was being paranoid, and there'd been no bullet to dodge. It still seemed like a sign to me that I'd overstayed my welcome.

It was time to move on.

Duck yawned and nestled closer as I glanced around the tiny apartment.

The plank flooring was cracked and stained. The old floral print wallpaper in the hallway had curled up at all its edges, and the plaster in the living room was crumbling. All just like it had been when I moved in. Aside from the few groceries in the fridge and the water on the bathroom floor, there weren't many signs I'd ever been here.

Moving on would have been easy if it weren't for Brute. And maybe Mrs. Abernathy.

Just like me, Mrs. Abernathy had no family.

I glanced up at the digital clock on the stove in the kitchen—it was a wonder a stove so old even had a clock. It was three in the morning.

Mrs. Abernathy didn't sleep any better than me. I'd spent more than one late night in her apartment, listening to her talk about the farm where she'd grown up, the bakery where she'd worked when she was younger, and the man she'd married the day she turned eighteen, only to lose him in a car accident two years later. She'd never married again. *"That was it for me,"* she'd told me. *"I gave my heart once, and what I've got left of it, I'm keeping to myself."*

Duck was already asleep, both eyes closed. He used to sleep with one eye open—as ducks did when they were wary of predators—but he didn't do that anymore.

I plunked him down gently in the straw bed I'd made for him in the living room and stroked his bronze-brown wings.

Since it felt like sleep would be a long time coming, I left him to his rest and unlocked the door.

I peeked outside—just to be safe—and then scurried down the steps to Mrs. Abernathy's door.

For just a brief moment, I listened for footsteps rustling through the grass behind me or thudding along the sidewalk.

Nothing.

No sound aside from the distant hum of car engines.

I knocked on the paint-chipped door then whipped my head around to be sure the sound hadn't drawn anyone out from the untamed bushes that dotted the property.

No one was around, but there was no sound coming from inside the apartment either.

A prickle of unease ghosted down my spine.

I reached beneath the hem of my skirt and felt for the knife in the holster around my thigh. With one hand on the hilt, I knocked again.

I could see the slivers of light from inside slipping out through the edges of the orange-and-blue checkered curtains. I tried to peer inside through the window, but the curtains were thick, and the slivers were too thin to make out any detail.

If it had been anyone else, I would have scurried back up to my apartment, but what if Mrs. Abernathy had fallen and broken her hip? What if she was having a heart attack right this very moment?

I didn't know how old the woman was exactly, but old enough I didn't think the possibilities were outlandish at all.

Or maybe whatever happened to her had been no accident? Images of knife and gunshot wounds flashed through my mind, turning my stomach.

She probably just fell asleep in her chair, I told myself as I tried to slow my breathing.

Yet, I gripped the hilt of my knife tighter as I reached for the door handle.

The door was seldom locked.

Mrs. Abernathy always worried she'd go out and forget her key, so she'd gotten in the habit of leaving it unlocked.

I tested the handle, unable to keep the images from flashing through my mind. Blood. Gaping flesh. Faces contorted in pain.

The handle turned easily beneath my fingers, and I pushed it open slowly and peeked inside.

On my left, the kitchen, which was an exact replica of mine, was empty.

On my right, Mrs. Abernathy had a small dining room with the orange-and-blue checkered curtains on the window. It was empty, too.

The notes of an old classical piece of music played quietly from somewhere further inside.

"The music you kids listen to these days is just awful, dear," she'd said when she introduced me to her collection of classical records that had been passed down from her grandfather.

I never told her, but thanks to my father, I'd grown up listening to classical Russian composers like Stravinsky, Medtner, and Tchaikovsky.

I'd kind of fallen in love with them.

I tiptoed down the hall, but my heart beat faster and goosebumps raised across my flesh despite the heat.

Mrs. Abernathy's apartment always smelled faintly of the old potpourri she must have put out years ago and hadn't changed since.

I could barely smell it now, not over the pungent, metallic scent that grew stronger with every step I took. A scent I knew all too well thanks to the whips that had left my back flayed open and weeping blood more times than I could count.

With my heart in my throat and knife in hand, I peered past the doorway into the living room where Mrs. Abernathy sat in her ancient beige recliner with her head tipped back and black-red blood saturating the front of her broad chest.

I dropped the knife.

It barely made a sound as it landed on the brown carpet.

Her neck had been sliced open, so deep I could see the severed edges of her trachea.

This wasn't the first dead body I'd seen, but I knew this woman.

I'd sat in this living room with her, drinking tea and listening to the bright, rich sounds of Tchaikovsky's concertos.

Now, she was dead. I stumbled back, slamming into the bedroom door behind me.

Murdered.

They'd killed an old woman to punish me.

My chest felt cold, like my lungs were filled with frost.

It spread out more with every second I stared at Mrs. Abernathy until all the way to the tips of my fingers.

I couldn't make my eyes to move, willing her to get up.

For the blood to go away.

For all this to go away.

But no matter how much I wished it, Mrs. Abernathy didn't move and her blood stayed there, saturating her olive green dress.

My teeth chattered, and my fingers felt numb with ice as I leaned down to retrieve my knife.

They could still be here, waiting for me.

"I'm sorry," I whispered to the woman who could no longer hear me.

The floor seemed to shift beneath my feet as I ran back to the door and darted up the steps to my pathetic excuse for a hiding place.

But it didn't matter where I ran.

It would never be far enough.

I shut my door and slammed the locks into place. My legs were too shaky to stand. I slid to the floor, looking around to see if they were here.

But I couldn't see.

I couldn't see anything but Mrs. Abernathy's slit throat and so much blood. The image had been burned onto my retinas, and no matter how hard I squeezed my eyes shut, it wouldn't go away.

The coldness inside me stretched all the way to my toes, making me shiver.

They'd always find me, and now they were murdering innocent, old women.

Mrs. Abernathy was dead because of them.

Because of me.

The commotion had woken Duck. He waddled over and climbed onto my thighs. It was ridiculous to cling to a bird, but that's what I did. I wrapped my arms around him and held him close like he could keep me safe.

If I was brave, I would have run out into the street and screamed at the top of my lungs.

"Come and get me, you assholes," I would have hollered.

I sat on the floor with my arms around Duck, waiting for them to come.

Chapter Three

Leo

I slid the Lambo into park next to the long row of bikes in front of Brute's bar and shut off the engine.

It had been a long day of making arrangements to replace the product that had been stolen, but it was finally done. All I had to do now was drop off the money we owed to Brute, and then I could call it a night.

Inside the bar, drinks were flowing, though there wasn't quite the same jovial air about the place tonight.

I suppose there was nothing quite like a fresh job well done to keep the spirits high, but I had no doubt Brute would have the Old Dogs celebrating again in no time. There seemed to be no shortage of fires that needed setting or men who needed killing.

I sat down at the same table where Brute and I had sat the night before, watching the men drink while the waitresses kept the beers topped up.

Not *my* waitress though.

Not the crazy, sexy stowaway I'd kind of been hoping to see when I walked in.

Brute sauntered out from the back room behind the long, wooden bar, and it was clear something was up.

It wasn't anything overt, just the worry lines around his eyes I'd never seen before and the slight furrow between his eyebrows. Not to mention that the vitality and exuberance that radiated from the man was subdued tonight.

"You look like your imaginary friend is running around with scissors, *amico,*" I said as he sat down across from me.

Brute barked a dry laugh with a barely-there grin. "And good evening to you, my friend."

I nodded but didn't respond.

Something was wrong, and it had to be something pretty damn major to ruffle Brute's feathers.

Brute sighed, resting his elbows against the table. "It's nothing for you to worry about, though, I appreciate your concern. That's what I always liked about you Lucas—you're good men."

"Maybe I can help?" I heard myself saying.

Brute let out another heavy sigh while he scrubbed his fingers through his short hair. "That girl you were looking at last night, her name's Ella, she took off before her shift ended and didn't show up for work today. It's probably nothing. It just has me concerned, that's all."

I kept my face blank, contemplating my next move. "Why don't you just send someone to check on her if you're worried?"

He laughed, though there was no humor in it. "I would, but the thing is, I don't quite know where that is."

Oh. That was a problem—for Brute.

I had a feeling I knew precisely where the girl lived.

As her employer, shouldn't he have known that too?

I eyed Brute suspiciously, wondering if we'd judged him wrong.

The Luca family had their hands in plenty of illegal pies, but one thing we'd always prided ourselves on was how we treated our women. Our wives. Our daughters. Even our whores.

I guess this meant I was making a house call. Why I had any interest in checking on the waitress, I had no idea. Maybe it helped that she was beautiful, and crazy, and one hundred percent mystery.

"Sorry, Brute, I wish I could help," I lied.

If it turned out Brute was treating her badly, I'd see that the Lucas found out about it.

"No worries, my friend. I'm sure she'll turn up." Brute smiled weakly, looking more rattled than I'd ever seen him.

Brute's mental health wasn't my problem, so I gave the guy the money we owed him, said my goodbyes, and hightailed it out of there.

It wasn't a long drive to the girl's dingy three-story walk-up, though there was more traffic than there'd been the night prior. And the cars parked along the road narrowed the street to one lane at some points.

Soon enough, I slid into an empty stretch of road in front of the walk-up. It looked no better this evening than it had last night, though I hadn't noticed the tiny, neatly pruned garden right next to the first-floor entry door—which happened to be hanging wide open. A little strange given this wasn't exactly Mister Rogers' Neighborhood.

Ignoring the door for now, I started up the steps to the second floor.

A prickle of apprehension was ghosting down my spine by the time I made it to the top.

The door was closed, curtains drawn, just like they'd been last night.

Instead of knocking, I leaned against the door and listened.

It was silent.

No noise at all.

Maybe the girl had just skipped out on work and gone shopping for the day, or whatever it was gorgeous girls did when they didn't feel like working.

I kept my ear against the door, listening.

Seconds passed, and just when I decided I'd looked like the neighborhood's creepy stalker for long enough, a thud sounded from somewhere inside.

It could have been nothing.

The girl could have stubbed her toe or slammed a jar down on the counter.

There were countless possibilities.

Yet, I grabbed my Glock from its holster and tested the door handle.

It turned freely.

I clenched my jaw.

Skittish girls didn't leave their doors unlocked.

I pushed the door open quietly, just enough to slip inside.

Before I'd taken another step into the apartment, another thud sounded from down the short hallway.

This time, it was followed by a girl's quiet whimper.

"You're in big trouble this time, *puttana*," a man's gruff voice hissed from the vicinity of the thud.

I tread across the old wood floor silently and peered around the doorway into what must have passed for the living room.

The girl was on her knees on the floor.

That's what the thud had been.

There was a nasty-looking bruise on her bicep and a bright red palm print on her cheek.

She wasn't crying.

She didn't make a sound.

She didn't beg.

She didn't plead with the man to let her go.

She just stared halfway across the room to where her assailant stood with a wicked leer on his face.

She didn't try to get up.

She didn't try to flee.

She just kneeled there, staring at the man while the most miserable, hopeless resignation radiated from her.

A fist clenched hard around my heart, not just because of the bruises she wore or her silence.

It was the hopelessness radiating from her.

"Stupid whore," the man spat. "I can't wait to see what he's going to—"

I raised my gun, which caught the guy's attention from out of the corner of his eye.

I squared my shoulders.

The man's head swung in my direction. His beady, gray eyes widened. "What the fuck are you doing here? Did your brother let you off the leash?"

I shrugged. "What can I say? I started chewing the furniture and he kicked my ass out of the house."

"So, which one of the brothers are you?" he seethed while his eyes darted back and forth between me and the girl.

"I'm the Easter Bunny," I said with a shrug.

The guy really should have been less concerned about who I was and more about what I was going to do to him.

"Smart-ass, are you?" he scoffed.

I laughed. "I've been called a dumbass before, so I'll take that as a compliment."

The man scowled. "If you've got any brain cells, you'll turn around and walk out of here right now. This doesn't concern you, boy," he said, edging in my direction while his empty hand moved slowly toward the holster on his hip.

I raised an eyebrow. *Boy?* The guy couldn't have been more than two or three years older than me. "It seems to me you're picking on a girl who's half your size, and that does concern me... *Boy.*"

"She's not your whore," he snarled as his hand settled on the grip of his gun.

"As of now, she's not your whore either, so I suggest you take your hand off that piss-poor excuse for a gun and get your ass out of here."

"Fuck you," he spat, yanking the gun out of its holster.

"No thanks." I fired two shots before the guy could get his finger on the trigger, one straight through his hand and the other one into his kneecap—because anyone who could elicit the kind of misery that radiated from the girl deserved a special kind of hell.

The guy screamed as he collapsed to the ground, but he was too stupid to give up.

He grabbed for the gun he'd dropped when he fell.

I shot him dead center between the eyes.

The girl didn't scream.

She didn't move.

She continued to kneel there, staring at the now dead man.

It wasn't until I'd walked right into the room that she seemed to notice I was there at all.

The waitress looked up at me with confused eyes, though none of the hopeless resignation had seeped away. It was still there, radiating from every pore in her body like she expected me to...

"I'm not going to hurt you," I assured her, holstering my gun and crouching down a few feet from her to give her some breathing room.

She didn't relax or draw further away.

"Can you stand up?" I asked.

Maybe she'd been injured worse than I'd thought.

She was silent for a moment, but then she nodded.

Instead of standing, she shifted a little, wincing like I was probably right and she'd sustained more injuries than those I could see.

"I can take you to the hospital," I offered since I figured she wasn't about to let me look her over.

The waitress stared at me without answering for a long, silent moment.

"Leave," she whispered eventually.

It came out harsh, but her eyes were pleading with me.

If I'd been a smart man, I would have done just that.

If Brute caught word that I'd been here, or I got tangled up in a police investigation, it was going to make a few people none too happy.

But Brute could kiss my ass at the moment, and it wasn't like the Lucas had anything to worry about from the cops.

Besides, there was something else, too. A strange feeling fluttering around in my chest.

"I want to help. Let me help you," I told her, surprising myself.

I wasn't quite the hard-ass some of my family was, but rescuing the damsel in distress? That wasn't exactly my thing.

She was silent for so long.

Was she thinking?

Was she in shock?

Maybe I should have been wrapping blankets around her.

"They killed her because of me," she said finally.

"Who are they?" I asked her.

At the very least, "they" were people who had no problem beating a girl in her own home, and that put them pretty high up on my hit list.

"You're coming with me," I said with finality because I didn't have time to cajole and sweet-talk her into leaving with me.

Obviously, her apartment—if the dilapidated place could be called an apartment—wasn't safe.

Whoever "they" were, more of them could show up at any minute.

My brother, Dom—eldest and next-in-command behind our father—would probably appreciate it if I kept the killing spree to a minimum.

I stood up and reached down to help her up, but it kind of took me by surprise when she took the proffered hand and let me help her onto her feet. Instead of heading for the door, though, she headed in the opposite direction and opened what might have been the bathroom door.

"Where are you—"

Something quacked.

Seriously, it fucking quacked.

Ignoring me, she disappeared into the bathroom while I tried to figure out what was making the strange noises coming from inside.

Then the girl reappeared with a duck.

A real, live quacking, swimming, waddling duck.

It was wrapped in a towel, cradled in one arm against her chest, its jewel-green head bright against the backdrop of the girl's torn cream-colored shirt.

"What is that?" I asked. Not my most brilliant moment.

I could see very well what it was; the better question would have been why the gorgeous girl had a duck in her arms.

She deposited the bird in an animal carrier, looked down at the wet feathered bundle, then back at me.

"The duck stays here," I said—not something I ever thought I'd have to say.

She didn't say a word, but for a girl who didn't say much, the jut of her heart-shaped chin and the way her feline eyes tightened at the corners spoke volumes.

Maybe crazy was contagious because rather than insisting there was no way we were bringing a duck on our speedy getaway, I just squeezed my eyes shut and pressed on. "Pack your stuff, and let's go, *gattina.*"

She walked halfway across the room, leaned down, and grabbed a knife off the floor. Holding the duck in one arm, she hitched up the hem of her skirt with the knife and slid it into a holster around her thigh.

Fuck me if that wasn't the sexiest thing I'd ever seen. *Lucky holster.*

Then she remained where she was, her eyes downcast.

"You don't have any other stuff, do you?" I asked.

The girl nodded to a satchel on the floor by the front door.

All this young woman had fit inside that thing?

The girl had to have been raking in the tips at Brute's, so where had it all gone?

I looked at her arms—what wasn't obscured by the bird.

No track marks. She'd also looked healthy the times I'd seen her. There'd been none of the telltale pallor or heavy bags under her eyes that were indicative of a drug problem.

In fact, she looked more than healthy; she looked like a supermodel.

Now, though, her cheek was puffy beneath the reddened handprint and the way she held her free arm across her ribs confirmed she had more injuries than I could see.

If that motherfucker had broken any bones, I'd bring him back to life just to kill him all over again.

Chapter Four

Ella

The strange man opened my front door and looked out.

He was so tall, I couldn't see over his shoulder, but the way he stood there, surveying the street made me nervous.

What did he see?

Were there others outside right now, waiting for me?

"Just stay close," he said, glancing back at me.

Then he turned back toward the open doorway.

He'd pulled the gun from his holster, and he held it in front of him now as he stepped outside. His spine was straight, and the way he kept glancing back and forth said he was alert, but there was a certain lack of stiffness in his broad shoulders that told me he was no stranger to confrontation.

I, on the other hand, was doing my damnedest not to hyperventilate.

It wasn't like the night I'd escaped.

Back then, I could taste the freedom that had hovered just outside my reach.

Now, I had no idea where this man intended to take me.

And yet, I mirrored his steps as he started down the stairs.

I couldn't stay in that apartment anyway.

If there weren't already more men coming for me, they would be soon.

We reached the bottom of the stairs.

I looked around, searching the cars and the shop windows across the street for familiar faces, but the light from the streetlamps glimmered off the windows, making it impossible to see inside.

Then I saw them; one tall, the other short, both of them burly and clad in near-identical suits.

They stepped out of the diner and looked right at me.

I didn't recognize them—hadn't seen them before in my life—but I knew the predatory look in their eyes.

I didn't need to see the guns in their hands to know these men had come for me.

My strange rescuer saw them, too.

He grabbed hold of my arm and pushed me behind him as a gunshot rang out and a bullet whizzed by somewhere on my left.

"Don't move, *gattina*," he said.

There was none of the tension in his voice that would usually have come from being shot at.

The strange man had his gun raised, and he fired a shot.

I couldn't see what it hit, but one of the men screamed, and his gun clattered to the pavement.

Duck quacked and wriggled around in his carrier.

"That girl doesn't belong to you," one of the men hissed in Italian from across the street.

"The girl doesn't belong to anyone," the strange man in front of me called back. "Twenty-first century, and all that shit, *stronzo*."

I flinched.

Under what rock had this guy been hiding? Twelfth century or twenty-first century, it was all the same; men with enough power could buy whatever or whomever they wanted.

"She's valuable property," another voice called. "I'm afraid I'm going to have to insist she come with us. But we're all businessmen here. I'm sure we can come to an understanding."

"The girl stays with me," my strange savior said. "Besides, you've got bigger problems than getting your property back at the moment, *amico*. You can take your chances and try to kill me before I get another shot off. Who knows? Maybe you'll get lucky. But you better have a deep, dark hole to hide in for the rest of your life because that's the only hope you've got of surviving what'll come at you."

Silence.

I peered past the broad shoulders in front of me.

Two beefy men, one of them scowling while he gripped his bleeding hand to his chest.

"Have it your way," the man without a bullet hole in his hand said, holstering his gun.

The bleeding man scowled and bent down to retrieve his gun with his uninjured hand.

I stared at the hand, the long fingers curling around the black steel, waiting to see one slip toward the trigger.

He holstered his gun, glaring in my direction as the two of them took a step back, then turned toward the diner.

"Open the car door, and get in," the man shielding me said, his eyes still fixed in front of him and his gun half-raised.

I did as he said and climbed into the back seat, behind the driver's seat, just like I had the night prior.

Duck flared his wings, ready to make a ruckus, but I cooed to him quietly, fumbled a treat out of my bag for him, and slipped it into his carrier.

"Okay, so, the crazy hot girl doesn't like riding in the front seat," the strange man muttered to himself, loud enough I could hear him, then closed the car door.

The front seat? I hadn't ridden in the front seat of a car in years.

He slid into the driver's seat a moment later and revved the engine. "What do you say we get out of here before the cops show up and we have to answer a lot of sticky questions?" he asked, turning in his seat to smile at me.

I nodded, and the man turned back around.

"I'm Leo, by the way," he said, looking at me in the rearview mirror.

As we drove away, I looked at Leo in the mirror, trying to study him. To see past the sculpted jaw, straight nose, and deep-set blue eyes.

Leo had shot two men—just like that.

How good of a man could he be?

I couldn't afford to take that kind of risk. As soon as we got to wherever he was taking us, I'd find a way to sneak away before he could lock me up or hand me over, or do any of the countless things I'd learned men were capable of doing.

"Brute sure was worried about you today," he said, casually glancing back at me.

I got the feeling he was gauging my response.

I nodded.

Was Leo one of Brute's men? That didn't seem right. Leo had come in with the Old Dogs last night, and I'd seen him in the bar before, but the clothing and his mannerisms were wrong for a rough and tough biker.

Though, Brute had been nice to me from the moment I met him—not at all like his namesake, in my opinion.

"Is there something I can do for you, pretty girl?" Brute had asked when I'd worked up the nerve to approach him outside his bar—it had taken me three days.

Three days of watching him, assessing the risk.

God, I was starving.

"I need a job," I forced the words out, squeezing my hands together behind my back.

They were the first words I'd spoken since escaping hell.

"Can you cook?" he asked, crossing his big arms over his chest.

I shook my head.

"Can you mix drinks?"

Another shake. This wasn't going well.

He was silent then, assessing me back with kind, pale blue eyes. "Can you start tonight?"

Finally, something I could do. "Yes."

"Well then, pretty girl," he said, looking me over with a flicker of concern in his eyes. "Why don't we get one of the girls to fix us something to eat, and then we'll get you started."

Brute held out his hand, and I shook it.

It was the first time I'd touched another human being of my own volition in years.

Months later, I still couldn't cook, but I could serve up beer and whiskey just as well as the rest of the waitresses.

This man though, he was much more of a mystery than Brute.

The first mystery I'd encountered in a long time.

The way Leo carried himself and his confident stride said he was an important man and well aware of it, but his easygoing manner and the respect he showed Brute said he wasn't arrogant. He was quick to pull a gun and a good shot, which suggested plenty of exposure to violence, but he'd been quite gentle with me.

"Those men, they're the reason you don't talk very much?" Leo asked, jumping subjects.

Not exactly. They were just lackeys. Mean, heavy-handed lackeys, no doubt, but mindless drones, nonetheless.

"Are you hungry?" he asked, jumping subjects again.

I pursed my lips.

What difference did it make to him what Brute worried about, or why I didn't talk much, or whether I was hungry?

"A simple yes or no, and I'll shut up," Leo said with a goofy grin that was, hands down, the sexiest smile I'd ever seen.

But what he was asking was never that simple.

A yes meant I wanted something from this man, and a no? Well, that word just wasn't allowed in my vocabulary.

Still, I searched for words that would put this man's need for answers to rest.

"I'm… not hungry," I said eventually.

It was the best I could come up with.

"There, that wasn't so hard," he said, smiling at me in the rearview mirror.

He had a nice smile. Not just sexy, but pure somehow, like there was nothing evil behind it.

And that scared me because it just wasn't possible.

My palms grew sweaty.

I needed to escape.

I spotted a stoplight ahead. Green... yellow...

This was my chance.

Leave now.

Run away.

Find a new place to hide.

The car rolled to a stop, but I didn't move.

Maybe the best time to do it was right before the light turned green.

A moment passed, and the light turned green.

The car started forward.

I continued to sit.

What was wrong with me?

Stoplight after stoplight, I didn't move.

Chance after chance, I let slip right by me.

Maybe I really had gone crazy.

Chapter Five

Ella

The car slowed as we drove past a tall, ritzy-looking hotel.

I was startled when he turned into the underground parking lot next to it.

It would be dark in there.

Nobody around.

Leo could do whatever he wanted to me, but still I sat, waiting as he maneuvered the car into a parking spot and slid the key out of the ignition.

"I didn't know where else to take you," he said, staring at me in the rearview mirror for a long moment.

Leo got out of the car and opened my door. He held out his hand again, and instead of brushing it off and making a run for it—like I should have—I grabbed the handle of Duck's carrier and took his hand. A big hand; it enveloped mine. His fingers weren't rough like sandpaper, but they weren't completely smooth.

I could tell he used his hands, but he didn't work with them, not in a plumber or construction worker-type job. Leo was strong, and he kept himself in impeccable shape, which was evident by the way he filled out the custom-tailored suit. But the sleeves weren't bulging awkwardly around his arms like I imagined they would have been if Brute tried to dress up in fancy clothing.

Outside the car, Leo dropped my hand, leaving me to follow him to an elevator. Once we were inside, he pressed the button for the top floor. The penthouse suite.

Maybe the girl I'd once been would have been impressed, but I'd seen plenty of penthouse suites.

They didn't impress me.

In fact, they made my stomach turn, and it was all I could do when he opened the door not to backpedal my way to the basement when he motioned for me to go inside.

This was what he'd wanted.

It was pathetic the way something crumpled a little inside me.

Of course, *this* was what he wanted.

It's what they always wanted.

"We have the suite reserved for business associates and that sort of stuff," Leo explained when I didn't move.

With Leo at my back, I had no choice but to move forward and step inside.

Once there, Duck picked up his ruckus, so I lifted him out of the carrier and stood awkwardly in the foyer, curling my toes in the soft, pale gray carpet.

"There's a washroom down that hall if you want to freshen up," he offered, closing the door behind us and motioning toward the hall on the left of the enormous living area.

I couldn't exactly freshen up with Duck in my arms.

I chewed on my bottom lip, trying to figure out what to do with Duck. He wasn't going to go back into the carrier nicely.

"I don't actually have a clue what to do with a duck. I'm generally the only quack around, but I guess I can hold him for a minute." He flashed a lopsided grin and held out his arms a little uncertainly.

Give Duck to this man?

Duck and I had only ever had each other. What if he… all right, it seemed unlikely he'd try to hurt a defenseless bird. What would be the point?

As carefully as I could, I shifted Duck from my arms to his, right away feeling the loss of the warmth against my chest. Duck ruffled his feathers but then nestled contentedly against Leo's much broader chest.

Traitor.

I glared at my feathered friend but quickly tamped down the thought, grabbed Duck's treats from my bag and handed them to Leo before scurrying to the bathroom.

When I returned to the main living area, he wasn't here.

Should I leave?

I eyed the door, but I couldn't leave without Duck.

"Hey, *gattina*," Leo said, coming up from behind and nearly making me jump out of my skin.

I spun around to face him.

Apparently, he'd been down the same hall. I hadn't heard him go by.

Duck was still perched on one arm, nestled against Leo's chest.

"How about something to eat?" he offered, but there it was again; more questions.

More questions that required the kind of answers I didn't want to give.

When I didn't answer him, he motioned toward the kitchen then started in that direction.

I fell into step behind him, glancing longingly at the door just once.

"Have a seat," Leo instructed in the kitchen, motioning to the black granite-topped breakfast bar that extended from the compact L of the cupboards.

Instructions, those were good.

Those, I understood.

I sat down obediently, and Leo transferred Duck back into my arms, brushing his fingers against my wrist in the process and making my skin tingle where he'd touched me. I discreetly rubbed my wrist against Duck's feathered side, trying to wipe away the disconcerting sensation.

And then Leo went to work, cracking eggs into a large metal bowl, chopping up onions, garlic, and spinach, and adding them to the eggs. He added a few spices I didn't recognize, whisked them altogether, then set a skillet on the stove to heat up. When the food was done cooking, he served it up onto two plates on the breakfast bar.

"*Mangia!*" he said with another goofy grin that had the same effect on my insides as his touch had on my skin.

I couldn't wipe the feeling away.

It tingled in the core of me, stoking a warmth I couldn't ever remember feeling.

Part of me wanted to refuse the food as he sat down across from me. I didn't want to be any more indebted to this man. But I'd survived on cereal and sandwiches for the past several months. The only time I'd eaten anything else was whenever Brute pushed plates of food at me at the bar. *"If you get any skinnier,"* he'd said, *"my guys here are going to start accusing me of not paying you enough to keep you fed."*

It was a lie. The men at the bar never had anything bad to say about Brute. If one was to believe some of the chatter, they'd be inclined to think the sun rose and set around the rough and tough leader of the Old Dogs. A strange man, indeed. Kind of like the enigma eating eggs across from me now.

"All right," he said, setting down his fork. "I suppose dinner conversation is out of the question," he mused aloud with a grin. "What do you say I take a few guesses, and you just nod if I get something right?"

This again? Why did he care? I wasn't good at conversing with people. Duck had been my primary companion since I found him as a duckling, wounded on the side of the road the day I escaped.

"Seems only fair, doesn't it?" Leo said, nodding at the untouched food in front of me.

Of course. Payment. A strange kind of payment—not the kind with which I was familiar, but I recognized it nonetheless. Maybe I should have just been grateful it was the only kind of payment he was demanding at the moment. So, I nodded.

"Good. Okay, let's see. You look awfully young, but something in your eyes says you're no child. I'm guessing really early twenties, am I right?"

I nodded. Twenty, precisely.

"And you got tangled up with some bad people, thanks to a boyfriend who turned out to be a scumbag?" Leo posed.

I shook my head.

I'd never had a boyfriend. The foster homes I'd lived in had been pretty strict about that, which was funny in a sick sort of way given that it had been my last foster father who'd sold me.

"Okay, no scumbag boyfriend then." Leo picked up his fork and delved back into his eggs, but I could see in his eyes the wheels turning in his head. "Look, I need to know who those guys were— who they're associated with and why they're after you. I can help you, but I need to know what I'm up against here. My family, we're… okay, we're not *good* people," he said with a grin, "but we don't like it when bad things happen to good people, if you know what I mean?"

Leo was nice—at least, he seemed it—but there was nothing saying he wouldn't hand me over the minute he learned *"who those guys were"*. And if he figured out I hadn't just been kept for entertainment purposes, the result could be even worse. There were a lot of secrets floating around in my head that people would go to great lengths to get, and there was nothing saying he wasn't one of those people.

He sighed as an air of agitation crept up around him.

It was time to get out before that agitation found an outlet.

"I should go," I said and moved to stand, clutching Duck close.

He stood up too but didn't block me. "You don't have to leave, *gattina*. You're safe here."

Safe was an illusion, or a carefully constructed fortress of cards, at best, that could be toppled by a gentle breeze.

And yet, I didn't move.

I stared at him, searching his blue eyes for answers. They were the most perfect shade of blue, like the sky, just before twilight, but what I saw was more than that. It was a look in them that was both kind and hard at the same time. How was that even possible?

"What do you say we call it a night?" he said, and his easy grin made a reappearance, warming and tingling in the core of me while his words sent a chill down my spine.

I'd never felt this kind of conflict before.

I'd never wondered what a kiss would feel like.

Would his lips feel as warm and firm as they looked?

What would happen when he touched me again? Would he invoke the same tingling sensation everywhere he touched?

Would I still feel those sensations when the charming façade he wore gave way to the baser animal underneath?

Because it would give way.

It *always* did.

"I mean, let's get some sleep and go from there, *gattina*," Leo hurried to add.

Oh.

I breathed a small sigh of relief and nodded.

"There's a spare bedroom down the hall, across from the bathroom. Go get some rest."

I nodded, and before he could say anything else or ask any more questions, I hurried out of the kitchen with Duck in my arms, down the hall, and through the open door across from the bathroom.

The room was nice. Light tan walls and dark wood floors that matched the queen-size bed and the dressers perfectly. Ivory bedspread and curtains, but it was the artwork that drew my attention most. All but one of the prints were ordinary hotel finds— a lovely meadow scene, a grape orchard. It was the print beside the window that stood out from the others—a young woman, naked beneath an apple tree, a snake wrapped itself around the tree's trunk. There was no apple in her hand. Not yet, at least.

Poor Eve.

If only she'd known what that viper would do.

Chapter Six

Leo

Okay, so I'd just brought a crazy woman into my life—not that any man with eyes in his head would ever blame me for it.

A crazy woman with some kind of tie to mafia or cartel—if the vibe of the guys who'd come after her were any indicator. Not good. Plain stupid if you asked any member of my family.

Dad was going to be pissed. Dante was going to go through the roof. And Dom... well, maybe Dom wouldn't freak out. He was still the hard-ass he'd always been, but something had been different about him since he'd married Fallon and became a father.

But it sure would have helped if Ella had given me more to go on. She didn't have much in the way of material goods, so it was unlikely she was anyone's mistress, and a daughter seemed even more unlikely. There was too much effort being put into retrieving her for her to be a random whore.

Pinpointing exactly what role she played didn't matter at the moment. Really, I was just delaying the inevitable.

It was time to face the music.

I pulled out my cell phone and pressed the screen to call home. Not one of them was going to be impressed, but so long as it wasn't—

"Leo?"

Merda. Of course, it was Dante.

"Leo? You there?"

I pinched the bridge of my nose and prepared myself for the reaming out of a lifetime. "*Si, fratello,* I'm here."

"Everything okay?" Dante asked.

No, and it certainly wasn't going to get any better over the next several minutes. But better to just bite the bullet and get it over with.

"I ran into a problem," I told him and then proceeded to fill him in on all the gory details he'd missed while silence rang in my ear from the other end of the line.

"What the hell, Leo?" Dante barked the moment I was finished. In his defense, he'd let me get it all out before going off on me. That was an improvement for my brother. "You think after all the shit this family has gone through, we needed you to throw us knee-deep in more?"

"No, Dante," I seethed. Maybe I'd known his rant was coming, but that didn't mean I had to like it. "What I was thinking was that there was no way in hell I could have just left her there."

"Why the hell not?"

"Because…" I slammed my mouth shut.

I had no logical answer to that question. If it had been anyone else, wouldn't I have just handed over the information to Brute at the bar and then forgotten all about it?

Dante sighed, though it came across more like a growl. "Let me guess, the girl's hot?"

Hot was an understatement, but was that really all there was to it? It wasn't like I was hard up for women.

"That fact is we're in the middle of this, Dante—whatever the fuck this is—whether you like it or not." I was done with this conversation.

The girl had me riled up in about a hundred different ways. I'd said what needed to be said. The rest could wait until the morning.

"I damn well don't like it, and you know it. But there's nothing I can do about that now, is there?" Dante snapped.

"No, there isn't."

"Then sit tight—no more killing people tonight—and I'll see if I can find out anything about the girl—not that you've given me much to go on. I'll get back to you when I know something."

"*Grazie*, Dante," I said, and I meant it.

As pissed off as he might have been, I knew I could count on him. That's what being a Luca was all about.

"*Buona notte, fratello*," he said, and I was just about to hang up the phone when I heard his voice again. "Leo?"

"*Sì?*" I ground my teeth.

"We'll get through this. We always do."

I paused. "*Grazie.* I appreciate it."

I hung up the phone, slid it back into my jacket, and flipped off the living room lights before heading to the master bedroom.

Staring at the bed though, there was no way I could sleep.

It bothered me a little to know the reason wasn't the men I'd killed or the dangerous situation I'd walked into, or even concern for the girl who'd obviously been traumatized.

It was her legs—toned as much as any supermodel's—and her ass, and her amazing tits. And her eyes, and her lips.

That girl was a walking, talking—okay, maybe not talking—fantasy.

I headed for the glass-walled walk-in shower in the en suite.

Ella might have been a damsel in distress, but I was no knight in shining armor.

It had taken everything in me to keep my eyes to myself. My thoughts… well, there was no stopping them from wandering where they wanted. And what they wanted was that damsel in every conceivable position known to man.

I turned on the shower, stripped off my clothes, and stepped beneath the hot spray. I could have tried a cold shower, but I had a feeling it wasn't going to douse a single thing.

I wrapped my hand around my cock, leaned my free hand against the shower wall, and let my mind take me wherever it wanted to go as hot water sluiced down my overheated body.

Ella, naked, with her long legs spread for me, staring up at me with those green eyes, and her hair spread out like a dark halo all around her.

On her hands and knees, with her toned, tight ass up in the air, begging me to take her in every hole she had.

I gripped my cock harder, pumping slow as the sensation began to build at the base of my spine.

Ella, stretched out spread-eagle on my bed while I licked, sucked, and sunk my teeth into every inch of her body. I could imagine her breathy sighs turning to moans, louder and louder, until her whole body shook, and she screamed her release while her back bucked clear off the bed.

I'd have my tongue buried deep in her pussy when I made her come so I could lap up every drop.

My hand sped up of its own volition as my mind took me deeper and darker.

Would she let me tie her up?

I'd fasten her hands behind her back, thrusting her full, round breasts out at me. Then I'd spin her around, bend her over the bed, and drill my dick into her senseless.

I swallowed back a groan as the sensation at the base of my spine grew stronger, tightening my balls, and making my hand work faster.

I wanted to hear my name on her cupid bow lips as she begged me to let her come. I'd bring her to the brink, over and over again, pulling back at the last moment every time until she was a wet trembling mess.

I was so close.

Image after image flashed through my mind. Every way I wanted to have her. Everything I wanted to do to her.

I wanted to squeeze her tits together and shove my cock between them.

I wanted to see her lips wrapped around my cock. She'd take me all in, working me into the back of her throat just long enough for me to feel the intense spasm of her muscles around the tip of me.

The image did me in.

I groaned as the most exquisite electricity shot through my body and ribbons of come shot onto the shower floor.

I leaned harder against the wall to let the sensation wash over me for a minute longer, letting the hot water pound away at my shoulders.

I shut off the faucet, wrapped a towel around my hips, and padded barefoot back into the bedroom.

Just as I was about to collapse onto the bed, a thought prickled from the back of my mind.

The girl had been traumatized by something—there was no way for her to see what I'd just been imagining—but what if whatever had happened to her had left her a little off her rocker?

Dante would be none too pleased with me in the morning if we now had to explain away why some girl had hanged herself by the bedsheets or taken a dive out the window.

That was the logical reason why I abandoned sleep for the time being and went to check on her.

I knocked lightly, but there was no sound of stirring coming from inside.

I opened the door slowly and peeked in as the light from the hallway spilled across the empty bed.

It took a moment of glancing around in the dark to find her curled up on the floor at the far side of the bed.

I scrunched my eyebrows together.

It looked like she'd fallen off the bed.

I crept across the room, intending to pick her up and lay her back down on the bed, but I stopped halfway across the room.

Brute had said she was as skittish as a kitten, and what I'd seen of her thus far confirmed it. I had a feeling this girl didn't like to be touched. Too bad, though, because every inch of her looked one hundred percent touchable to me.

Corrupted Protector

Chapter Seven

Leo

I'd tossed and turned the entire night.

When the morning sun streamed through the master bedroom window, I was ready to abandon any attempt at a decent night's sleep.

Ella's door was still closed. Presumably, she was still in there, so I set the coffee to brew for two, and then made breakfast.

She still hadn't emerged from the bedroom.

It was probably ten different kinds of crazy that I wanted to see her.

Did she look just as good first thing in the morning?

Were her eyes bleary with sleep and her hair mussed up?

Had a good night's rest done anything to make her any less skittish? Any more talkative?

I tapped lightly on her door, listening for any indication of movement inside.

A loud *quack* was the only response.

I smiled.

A duck for a pet. *Could the girl possibly have been any more interesting?*

I knocked again, louder this time, but the duck was the only one to respond.

If she'd been asleep, she was awake now.

I opened the door.

Nobody could sleep through that much quacking.

In the room, the floor where I'd found her sleeping last night was empty, but the door to the en suite was open and plenty of quacking and splashing was coming from inside it.

An image of Ella, naked in the deep oval bathtub sprung to mind—with or without the duck.

I wasn't picky. But I buried the image—with great effort—before my hardening cock could give me away.

"Ella, are you in there?" I stayed in the doorway, waiting.

Of course, she was in there—possibly naked. *Merde*, this gentleman shit was for the birds.

Ella peeked her head out of the en suite door. She was on the floor, currently on her hands and knees, and while she wasn't naked, the top buttons of my shirt she wore were undone, revealing the entirety of the upper swells of her breasts in her position.

"*Buongiorno, gattina,*" I said, forcing my gaze to meet hers.

"Good morning." Ella sat back on her heels as I approached.

Some of the damp fabric of the shirt clung to her skin, outlining one perfect breast. Apparently, she'd been in the duck's splash zone.

"You know, you don't have to stay in here?" I asked her, because I wasn't entirely sure she did know that.

Ella nodded, though she made no move to stand up.

"I made us breakfast," I said, turning away because looking at her any longer was a bad idea.

Regardless of why she was on her knees, I dared any man not to picture all the ways he could put that position to good use.

At the door, I paused.

She hadn't moved.

"Come eat," I said, quickly realizing that she seemed to respond to commands easily. Requests, not so much.

I turned and left the room without waiting to see what she would do, but it didn't surprise me to hear her quiet footsteps following a moment later, the duck waddling behind her.

When I motioned for her to take a seat like last night while I went and retrieved the eggs and sausage wraps I'd made, she slid right onto the stool.

The duck was now diapered.

Seriously, there was a duck in my hotel suite wearing a diaper. The duck continued on, waddling past her, presumably to explore his new surroundings.

"Coffee?" I offered, retrieving the carafe.

When she didn't answer, I poured it into the two mugs I'd set on the bar anyway, added cream and sugar to my own, then held each one out questioningly.

Ella shrugged this time.

A nod, I could understand, but what did a shrug mean? Only one thought came to mind. "You've never had coffee before?"

She shook her head.

Where had she been hiding from whoever was after her? On the moon?

I sweetened her coffee with a little cream and sugar then slid it in front of her. In hindsight, maybe shoving caffeine down an already skittish girl's throat wasn't the best idea.

Nevertheless, she took a cautious sip then immediately wrinkled her nose.

It looked like it was taking everything she had to not spit it back out.

I laughed. "Not a coffee lover, huh? So, let's see," I said, taking the same seat across from her as last night. "I already know your name is Ella. We've established you're in your early twenties, and you don't like coffee." I flashed her a grin and was rewarded with a flicker of a smile. "Anything else important I should know, like maybe a passionate hatred of clowns, one-ply toilet paper, or the month of March?" I teased, making the corners of her lips turn up in another small smile.

"I like March. It means spring is right around the corner," Ella said quietly.

"Good, because my birthday is in March, so if you hated it, we might have had problems."

Another smile.

Again, it felt like a reward.

Strange.

"All right, it seems we're on a roll." I flashed her a grin.

Maybe if I could get her talking on safe subjects, I'd be able to branch further without her really noticing. This game should have been frustrating as hell, but it wasn't.

Ella was like a million puzzle pieces, and apparently, I had a thing for beautiful puzzles.

The duck waddled back to her just then, nudging her leg with its beak. He was, presumably, a safe subject, and definitely an interesting piece to the puzzle.

"What made you decide on a duck for a pet?" I asked while she bent down to retrieve it and placed it on her lap.

Lucky duck!

Ella shrugged, and I started to think that was all I was going to get.

"I found him. He was injured and alone, so I brought him with me," she said, stroking the duck's green head.

Well, that was more words than I'd gotten out of her thus far. "And you knew how to take care of an injured duck?"

She nodded. "A little bit. I grew up on a farm."

Ella, a farm girl? I hadn't figured that. I'd have to tell Dante to extend his search beyond the city.

"Did you spend your whole childhood there, on a farm, I mean?"

Ella shook her head, and the small smile she'd been wearing disappeared.

Clearly, that was a topic that would send her running back into her shell.

Time for some damage control.

"My dad used to take me, my sister, and brothers to a park that had a duck pond. We'd sit there eating ice cream, talking about stupid kid shit while all four of us raced to finish the ice cream and be the first one to feed the cone to the ducks."

Ella laughed. Not a keel-over-and-laugh-until-your-gut-hurt kind of laugh. A light tinkling sound that might have just been the best damn thing I'd ever heard.

When it seemed she was done with food for the time being, I steered the conversation into the living room. She stood at the room's edge until I motioned for her to take a seat on the chocolate-brown leather sofa.

I wanted to sit right next to her. Hell, I wanted to sit down and drag her onto my lap, but instead I kept the middle cushion of the sofa between us and took a seat on the opposite end, silently envying the duck who was once again nestled comfortably on her thighs.

"The only animal we had growing up was a dog," I said, trying to focus on something other than Ella's thighs. "His name's Bullet. My dad got him for my sister when she was ten."

Maybe learning about me would put her more at ease. How bad could a guy who talked about puppies and baby sisters be, right?

"I had a brother," she said, but the look on her face said there was absolutely no point in prying into that topic.

It didn't escape my notice that she'd referred to her brother in the past tense.

I steered the conversation back onto neutral ground and headed back to the drawing board.

The answers I needed were in her head. I just had to find a way to lull her into letting her guard down to get to them.

How difficult could that be?

Chapter Eight

Ella

For two and a half days, I existed in a bubble of relative peace, listening to Leo recount stories from his childhood, answering what questions I could, and deflecting those I couldn't.

The bubble felt foreign, and it seemed to fit stiffly around me, but with every passing moment, it settled into my grooves and curves a little more.

And then it burst.

The phone on the coffee table in front of us started to ring, injecting the outside world and stretching the bubble too thin.

Leo's shoulders grew taut, and tension crept up in his movements as he stood up and answered the phone.

"*Ciao, fratello*," he spoke into the phone and wandered toward the kitchen.

I couldn't hear what was being said on the other end of the line, but the tension in Leo's shoulders grew tauter, creeping down and stiffening his spine. He let out a breath and combed his fingers through his hair, but he didn't speak.

A moment later, he hung up the phone without saying a word, but the agitation clung to him.

I wished like hell I could have heard what the caller had been saying.

"That was my brother," Leo said, standing at the end of the sofa. "I asked him to see if he could figure out who you are and who's after you because without that information, there's no clear plan I can come up with. Information is power, and right now, you hold all the power, *gattina.*"

A plan? A plan to send me back?

Signore's basement flashed through my mind, the place he'd chained me whenever I displeased him. Dear god, how *displeased* would he be when he gets me back?

I might never see sunlight again.

My lungs worked harder, chasing oxygen that had suddenly been sucked out of the air.

Leo seemed nice. He seemed safe. But those things were just illusions, bubbles that could burst at any second.

"You're worried I'd hand you back to whoever you're running from if I knew?" Leo tilted his head to the right.

It came out like a question, but it didn't feel like one.

He sat down on the sofa, keeping the same distance from me as before. "You don't know me, I get that. But I don't know you either. For all I know, you were sent to bait me into a trap."

My jaw dropped. "You're right, Leo. You don't know me," I said, feeling a flicker of something hot and uncomfortable, so much like anger that I tamped it down fast. It wouldn't be the first time my temper got me into trouble. But if Leo knew what I'd done for *Signore,* he'd know the accusation was preposterous. "Baiting" wasn't my specialty. My only purpose was to listen with all my senses, to memorize every word and gesture, every subtle nuance of a man's body language. But I couldn't tell Leo that; it was too dangerous. "I'll understand if you want me to go," I said, swallowing back every bubble of emotion that tried to rise to the surface.

"Do you want to leave, Ella?" he asked, though there was no anger in his tone. A little hurt, perhaps, but that made no sense.

What difference did it make to him?

Of course, I wanted to leave—I *needed* to leave.

And yet, I found myself shaking my head.

It seemed my body had developed a mind of its own.

"Good," he said, "because I don't want you to leave either."

My gaze shot up to meet his. "Why not?"

Leo laughed. "The truth?"

I nodded.

"The truth is, I don't know." He shrugged his broad shoulders.

If he was telling the truth, it probably meant he had no immediate intentions of hurting me.

"Do you want to call it a night, *gattina*?"

I'd go stir-crazy in that room.

I shook my head tentatively, just a little, leaving room to deny it if it made him angry.

"Do you want to just sit here with me?" He smiled a lopsided grin then added, "Quietly."

A tingling warmth set off inside me, making me acutely aware of the shadow of stubble across his jaw, the molded outline of his shoulders beneath his shirt, and the long, sinewy muscle that ran down the length of his forearms.

I glanced at the door.

Leaving was the right thing to do, but it felt like there was an elastic around me, stretched taut, trying to draw me even closer to him.

Leo nodded after a moment then held out his hand. "Then come here."

There was only two feet of space between us; certainly, I could have navigated it on my own, but I took his hand because I wanted to take it.

Because I wanted to feel the warmth of his skin and the strange tingling sensation his touch created.

This time, it shot all the way up my arm.

Leo tugged me toward him, close enough that my thigh brushed against his. He let go of my hand then.

My attention was torn between the residual tingling sensation his touch had left behind and the heat of his thigh suffusing mine.

True to his word, Leo didn't speak.

I kept waiting for it.

In my experience, few people were comfortable with silence. They needed to break it as if the quiet was some terrible creature that needed to be destroyed. But if they would only listen, the silence wasn't quiet at all.

I watched Leo out the corner of my eye.

The way his hands rested loosely on his thighs said he wasn't on guard at the moment, not worried over his imminent safety. But the slightly deeper rise and fall of his chest screamed of the tension that was running through his body.

The strangest things began to happen as I followed the movement of his chest and stared at the hand that had enveloped mine and left my flesh tingling.

The tension in my shoulders began to loosen.

The ever-present tightness in my chest eased its grip.

I breathed in deep and let it out in a quiet, almost contented-sounding sigh.

My eyes grew heavy and the heat of the man sitting next to me drew me in.

I went willingly, resting my head against his shoulder and breathing him in.

The fresh, light sandalwood scent of him wrapped around me, and I let sleep pull me down, more at ease than I'd been in so very long.

Chapter Nine

Leo

I'd lived through gunfights and explosions.

I'd survived beatings and torture.

But *this* was going to kill me.

I'd been listening to the slow, rhythmic cadence of Ella's breathing for the past hour, painfully aware of her toned thigh against mine and her breast pressed against my arm.

Every fantasy I'd had of the girl since I first laid eyes on her was playing like a porn reel in my head.

To make matters worse, she'd wriggled in her sleep exactly twenty-two minutes ago, and her hand had ended up on my thigh, agonizingly close to my cock.

My fingers itched to touch her, and my cock had even more direct plans, but while Dante and I had done plenty of kinky shit with women, all in the pursuit of a good time, molesting a woman in her sleep didn't even make a blip on the Richter scale. The women we'd had were always active participants in our debauchery.

So, it was time to put some distance between me and Sleeping Beauty.

Gritting my teeth, I slid her weight onto my lap and stood up to carry her to her bedroom—despite the strong urge to take her to mine.

Ella shifted in my arms once as I stepped around the sleeping duck and strode down the hall. Her lips parted on a sigh when I laid her down on the bed, starting up the porn reel once again.

I was just about to leave when she rolled away onto her side.

The wide neckline of her shirt had slipped down, exposing her shoulder and part of her back.

I froze.

All I could do was stare as bile climbed up my throat.

Of all the ways I'd tried to put the puzzle pieces together, *this* had never occurred to me.

The thought hadn't crossed my mind once.

All across her back and shoulder, thin, white, pearly tendrils crept across her flesh—scars, most of them well-healed.

She'd been whipped. Repeatedly, by the looks of it.

Even more disturbing was the puckered scar on the back of her shoulder in the perfect shape of a five-petaled flower.

It wasn't just a scar.

It was a *brand*.

Somebody had pressed the hot iron shape to her unmarred flesh, branding her like cattle.

Combined with her near-constant silence and the ease with which she obeyed commands, Ella was no mistreated girlfriend. She wasn't the daughter of some asshole cartel man, or any of the other dozen possibilities that had flitted through my mind.

She'd been branded, and she'd been beaten.

Ella had been a slave.

I scrubbed my fingers through my hair when what I wanted to do was put my fist through a wall.

I had to get out of here.

Staring at her scars, I could imagine it too well.

I could hear her screams, see the fresh damage to her body. The lash of a whip was a special kind of torment. Not just the straightforward breaking of skin; it was like fire, burning so hot and so deep, it felt like the flames wrapped right around the bones.

I strode across the room and closed the door behind me then thought better of it and opened it a crack so that her duck could find her.

I was halfway to the front door when I realized I couldn't just leave.

I needed to hit something, beat the living shit out of something, but fuck only knew who was after Ella.

I pulled out my phone and dialed Marco's number—a loyal Luca man, I could count on him even in the middle of the night.

"*Signor* Luca?" Marco answered on the first ring. Either he was wide awake or he hid the grogginess in his voice well.

"I need you here, Marco. I'm at the Four Seasons."

"*Si, Signore.* I'll be there in twenty minutes."

I hung up the phone and paced back and forth across the living room carpet, remembering in vivid detail every pale scar across Ella's back and picturing all I was going to do to whoever had put them there.

No wonder she was skittish. It was a wonder she wasn't batshit crazy.

It felt like it took hours for Marco to knock on the front door. The second he did, I flung open the door, keys in hand, ready to fly.

"*Buona sera, Signor* Luca," Marco said, his hand on his gun inside his jacket, ready for whatever emergency had brought him here.

I shook my head. "It's not that kind of emergency. I need you to guard this door until I get back."

Marco looked at the open door. "It's a fine door, *Signor* Luca. I'll guard it with my life." He spoke with such a straight face, most people would have missed the spark of humor in his dark eyes.

I clapped him on the back. "If anyone tries to get through it, feel free to stop them in whatever way flicks your switch. So long as they end up dead, I'm not picky."

"*Si, Signor* Luca. I'll be sure to get creative."

"*Grazie,* Marco."

***

It could have been seconds or minutes later when I reached the parking garage and squealed out of the lot, but it felt like an eternity before I was pulling into the long, winding drive that led home.

Inside, all the lights were out; it shouldn't have surprised me.

It was past one in the morning, so Dante was probably out getting laid, and Dom, Fallon, and my father had likely gone to bed.

I flipped on the foyer light at the same time the office door down the hall opened, spilling light out into the hallway and illuminating the two figures who walked out.

"Well, speak of the devil…" Dante said when he saw me.

Dom smiled grimly and nodded his head in agreement as they came toward me.

I shrugged. "What can I say? My ears were burning."

Now that I'd gotten here, I wasn't sure I wanted to talk to either of them about Ella.

I just wanted to hit something, and the punching bag in the basement seemed like a more sensible option than some poor random guy on the street.

"Did you cut the girl loose, Leo?" Dom crossed his arms over his chest.

I glanced at Dante—the knowing look in his eyes said the question was just a formality.

"No, I didn't," I admitted, bristling. But I let it out in a long, slow breath. I wasn't looking for a fight, not with them, and definitely not right now.

"Why not?" Dom persisted. He didn't look angry, exactly, but he wasn't wearing his happy face either.

Usually, I was good at keeping my cool.

I'd learned to roll with life's punches and seek out the good—whether that was the good things life had to offer or just a good time.

But tonight, I could feel my heart pumping hard in my chest and the heat rising up the back of my neck.

"Because whoever had her, treated her like a fucking slave," I ground out, "and there's no goddamn way in hell I'm handing her back."

My brothers stared at me.

They'd seen me happy, sad, injured—all seven colors of the rainbow, except for one.

"You're angry," Dante stated, his eyes narrowed like he couldn't quite believe it.

I exhaled sharply. "A slave, Dante, like—"

"I heard you," he snapped, and I realized my slip.

Dante had been discreetly trying to track down a missing girl as a favor to a friend. Discreetly as in Dom didn't know anything about it.

"She told you she was in hiding, I presume. Did she tell you who she escaped from?" Dom asked, clearly on a fact-finding mission.

I couldn't really blame Dom. Our father had the final word in all family business, but it was Dom who was in charge of most things these days.

I shook my head. I loved my brother; I'd take a bullet for him in a heartbeat. But no matter what Dom thought, there was no way I was handing Ella back to whoever had put those scars on her body.

"She didn't tell me anything," I said. While I wouldn't back down to Dom, I wouldn't lie to him either.

"Then how do you know, Leo?"

"I just know." I pressed my lips into a straight line.

Dom sighed, the dark bags under his eyes coming off as gray and blue under the fluorescent lights. "I get you've got a thing for this girl, Leo, but you have to admit there could be more going on here than you know," he said, speaking carefully. "The girl shows up out of nowhere, and in a few days' time, has you pretty riled up about defending her. It would be a great way to lay a trap…"

"She didn't '*show up out of nowhere*'. She's been working at Brute's bar for quite a while. The dark-haired girl every one of his guys drools over. Does that ring a bell?" I corrected.

Recognition flashed in Dom's gray eyes. He was loyal to a fault to Fallon, but no man with eyes in his head hadn't noticed Ella.

"Your mystery girl works for Brute?" Dom furrowed his brows together.

I cursed inwardly. "I need to talk to him. He's got to be going batshit crazy by now."

Now that I was certain Brute hadn't hurt Ella, the guy deserved to know she was okay.

Dom flicked up a doubting brow. "Brute? Crazy… with *worry?*"

"You didn't see him, *fratello*. He was trying to hide it, but he was seriously losing his shit when she didn't show up for her shift."

"Then how did you…" Dom shook his head. "Never mind. If you think you can fill Brute in without starting a war with the Old Dogs, then, by all means, go have a talk with him tomorrow. I still want to talk to your mystery girl, though. Maybe I'll come by while you talk to Brute," Dom said then glanced at his watch with a furrow between his brow.

He and I both knew he didn't have time for a casual meet and greet.

"I'll go," Dante jumped in. "I'll babysit the girl while Leo's out."

Dom shot Dante a look of disbelief.

Dante wasn't usually quick to volunteer for babysitting duty.

"What? You've both had a look at her. It's my turn," Dante said with a wicked grin.

"What on earth are you boys up to?" Fallon appeared at the top of the stairs, glaring down at us in mock-sternness.

Unfortunately, it lost its effect when the bundle in her arms started to fuss and she cooed to it while making kissy faces.

"It's nothing, *limone,*" Dom called up to her in an overloud whisper. "Go back to bed, and I'll be there soon."

"Back to bed?" she said, looking like he'd just proposed that she go take a stroll on the moon. "You do remember that we have a month-old daughter, right? I'm not sure I remember what a bed looks like."

"Me neither," Dom muttered under his breath.

I smirked. I had a feeling they had two different purposes for said bed in mind.

Fallon blew Dom a kiss and turned to go back down the hall, her long, silk gown billowing behind her.

"Fallon? That shopper you had get your clothes for you, do you know her number?" I asked when she paused.

Fallon looked me over from head to toe. "I suppose you've got the long legs for dresses, Leo, but I'm not sure you'll enjoy the waxing they'll require to pull them off."

"Damn," I cursed. "But I'd look pretty hot in a pair of thigh-highs, don't you think?"

Hiding her smile against her daughter's head, she nodded. "I'll make you a deal, dear brother-in-law: you take your niece, and I'll go look for the number—I know the woman left me a business card."

"Deal," I said then climbed the stairs to retrieve my niece who was currently gnawing on her pudgy fist with great voracity.

"Planning on revitalizing your wardrobe at one in the morning?" Dante asked with a knowing grin when I reached the bottom of the stairs.

I glared at Dante, then turned my attention to the semiswaddled infant in my arms. "Your Uncle Dante knows damn well what I'm planning, doesn't he, Maria?"

One-month-old Maria gurgled in agreement—at least, that was my interpretation of it.

Fallon reappeared at the top of the stairs, but when I went to climb up, she waved me off.

"You're lucky, Leo," she said as she reached the bottom of the stairs. "I passed by the bed on my way to get the number and almost decided to take a nap first."

"That kind of thoughtfulness should be rewarded, dear sister-in-law," I said, taking the business card from her. I flashed her a conspiratorial smile when she held out her arms for her daughter. "Run," I whispered and promptly deposited Maria into her father's arms. "It looks like it's your shift, Dom," I said then made a quick escape while Fallon laughed and hightailed it back up the stairs.

"I'll see you in the morning, Leo," Dante called, laughing over Dom's misfortune.

"Absolutely. Oh, and don't be surprised by the duck," I called back.

"The what?" I heard him ask, dumbfounded, as I closed the heavy oak front door behind me.

Nothing had been resolved.

I could still see Ella's scars in the back of my mind, and I still had the strong urge to hit something, but I felt better than when I'd walked in.

That was the great thing about family—my family, at least.

Now, all I had to do was figure out how to tell Brute Hastings that I had his missing girl and had no intention of giving her back.

Easy as pie, right?

Chapter Ten

Ella

There were two voices coming from somewhere beyond the bedroom door.

Two voices—one familiar, one not.

I recognized the warm, deep timbre of Leo's voice, but the other one, I'd never heard before.

I crept toward the door, wishing now that I hadn't decided to close it when I'd woken up last night.

I'd woken up on the bed—a strange enough occurrence on its own—with the door half open and Duck quacking in circles on the floor.

A knock sounded on the door.

"Ella?" Leo's voice called.

I looked wildly around the room like an escape might materialize out of nowhere, but up on the top floor, the suite's front door was the only way out.

There was no point in staying silent. "Yes?"

The handle turned, and the door opened slowly.

"You're safe here," he'd said, and I clung to the illusion as he appeared in the doorway.

"*Buongiorno, gattina.*"

At first glance, he looked no different today, aside from the morning stubble that only served to accentuate his chiseled jawline. But looking closer, there was a tightness in his eyes and tension in his jaw.

"What's wrong, Leo?" I asked while Duck ran circles around my feet.

I hadn't fed him yet, and he wasn't impressed.

"Nothing's wrong, Ella. I have to go out, and I didn't want to leave you alone, so I asked my brother to come stay with you for a while. I thought you might want to meet him before I go," Leo explained.

"Stay with me... like a babysitter?"

Is that how Leo saw me? Like a little girl?

He laughed. "No, *gattina*. Trust me, if anyone is in need of supervision, it's my brother. I just thought..." He blew out a frustrated breath. "I said you were safe here, I'm just keeping that promise."

His words flooded my chest with warmth.

I couldn't remember the last time someone had cared about keeping a promise or keeping me safe—well, aside from Brute, I supposed.

It seemed Leo and Brute were alike in many ways.

Leo's brother, though... that was yet to be seen.

"Okay. Thank you," I said a little awkwardly. And then, because I had no idea what else to say, I grabbed Duck's food and poured out his breakfast into a bowl Leo had given me from the kitchen.

Duck delved in with fervor while I squared my shoulders and followed Leo down the hall, ignoring the way my legs were shaking.

I missed our two-and-a-half-day bubble in which nothing outside this hotel suite had existed.

The man standing in the kitchen turned around as me and Leo entered the living room.

He bore a strong resemblance to Leo. The same dark hair and jawline, and he held himself with the same sense of self-assuredness. But while their eyes were the same color, there wasn't much more than a flicker of humor in this man's eyes, not like Leo's, which seemed to be perpetually brighter, like he was always ready to laugh.

"Whoa. Leo wasn't kidding, was he?" the man said, looking me over from head to toe in one swoop.

When his gaze settled on mine, I looked away, taking in the brewing coffee, the mugs on the counter, the polished Oxfords on the man's feet.

Leo was shaking his head, his lips pressed together in consternation, though amusement danced in his eyes. "Ella, this is my ill-mannered brother who wouldn't recognize chivalry if it bit him in the ass. Dante, this is Ella."

Dante laughed. "All I'm saying is that you're beautiful, Ella, and it's nice to meet you."

"It's nice to meet you too," I forced the lie out.

There wasn't anything wrong with Dante. I just missed the bubble.

"I'll be back as soon as I can," Leo said.

Turning to me, he leaned in and kissed my forehead.

Just the whisper of his lips against my skin, and then they were gone.

It was a chaste kiss. So chaste, not a single warning signal went off in my head.

And yet, the sensation rippled across my body like the faintest touch of electricity all over my skin, so much more potent than the tingling from the brief moments of contact before.

"Behave," he chastened his brother with a lopsided grin.

And then Leo left.

The walls moved in closer, and the ceiling hung lower.

It felt like Leo had taken half the oxygen in the room with him, making my lungs work harder to get enough.

"I don't know what you take in your coffee," Dante said, nodding to the two empty mugs on the counter.

I resisted the urge to shudder.

Coffee was awful, I'd discovered my first morning here.

"Cream?" he offered. "Sugar?"

Neither, thank you very much.

There was nothing that could improve that god-awful drink.

Duck waddled around the corner, stopping to tap my leg with his bill before moving on—in search of more food, if I had to guess.

"And apparently, Leo wasn't joking about the duck either." Dante chuckled to himself. "Yours?"

What difference did it make to him who Duck belonged to?

When I didn't respond, he chuckled again, shaking his head. "Okay, when a duck in a diaper appears out of nowhere, I say that's justification to go straight to the good stuff."

Dante reached for a whiskey bottle from the top shelf beside the sink then poured the liquor in each of the mugs, topped them up with coffee, and carried them to the breakfast bar.

He took a seat in the same spot Leo had sat and tipped back a healthy swig from one of the mugs.

"I don't bite, Ella. Well, I do, but I promise you're safe for the time being." He motioned to the seat across from him and smiled, one corner of his lips a little higher than the other, making him look even more like Leo.

I crossed the room and sat down on the stool, perched on the edge.

Now that he'd reeled me in, the smile vanished as he crossed his arms over his chest. "We need to talk."

That's what you think.

I'd spent four years seldom allowed to speak. I'd gotten very good at it.

This man wasn't Leo.

I felt none of the compulsion to talk to him about *anything.*

"What game were you playing, hiding out in Leo's car?" Dante asked bluntly, one eyebrow cocked.

Games are for children, you arrogant jerk.

But that wasn't fair. Nothing about this man screamed arrogant.

The slight tightening at the outer corners of his eyes, the thickness in his voice; he was concerned, hiding it behind a mask of haughtiness.

I kept my mouth pressed into a straight line, not saying a single word.

"You know, usually when I'm interrogating somebody, there's a whole lot more blood and screaming involved."

I looked at Dante, meeting his gaze.

Go ahead, I fumed inwardly.

There wasn't anything he could do to me that hadn't been done before.

Dante kept looking.

I felt like a book he was trying to read, but the words were written in a foreign language.

Eventually, he sighed, and the mask fell away. The forbidding glare gave way to an earnest face.

"If you're putting on an act, you're one hell of an actress, but I'm not so sure you are," he said aloud.

It seemed he was mulling the words over to himself.

I couldn't fathom why he'd think I was acting, never mind what had made him consider that I wasn't.

"It doesn't matter what you say—or don't say. It's the look in your eyes, Ella," Dante continued like he'd read my mind. "I've seen it before, and I'm not sure it's something anyone could fake."

I looked away, staring down at the full mug of whiskey-coffee in front of me.

I much preferred thinking he couldn't read me at all.

"Look, Leo's got good intentions, for sure, but if you want the Luca family to keep your hot ass safe, you've got to do more than bat those sexy eyelashes at me." Dante quirked a small grin.

The Luca family?

Leo was a *Luca?*

Leo… Dante…

The names scrolled through my head like the opening sequence of *The Shining.*

My hands turned clammy.

I clenched them together and hid them in my lap, trying to hide any sign that my heart was pounding like a drum in my chest.

I'd seen Leo in Brute's bar before, but I'd had no idea who he was.

I'd had no idea.

Dear god, what have I done?

"I don't want you to keep me safe," I finally said, hating how choked my voice sounded.

Dante looked fazed but not suspicious. "Then what is it you do want?"

I wanted a lot of things.

1. *To not be here.*
2. *To never have gotten into the back seat of Leo's car.*
3. *To never have heard the name Luca in my life.*
4. "I just want to be free," I said instead.

I half-expected Dante to laugh.

Men like this man had no idea what it was like to be anything but free.

They took it for granted because it came to them as easily as breathing.

Dante didn't laugh. He was silent for a moment then nodded. "We can help, Ella, but to do that, you've got to help us."

It was my turn to laugh, but I resisted the urge.

Dante couldn't help me.

No one could stop what was coming for me.

I could help him, though.

I could save him and the rest of the Luca family.

But the moment I did, he'd know about the secrets in my head, and I'd cease to be a stray that needed rescuing.

I'd be nothing more than a resource to be tapped.

Chapter Eleven

Leo

Brute sat down across from me, carrying a glass of something in one hand.

The man looked like he hadn't slept since I'd last seen him and was about ready to lose his shit.

The few men already in the bar kept glancing over at him, a wary look in their eyes like they were waiting for him to go off any second like a grenade with a rusty pin.

"To what do I owe the pleasure, my friend?" Brute asked then drained his glass.

"I've got Ella," I said without preamble.

The look in his tired eyes turned lethal.

I'd never seen Brute Hastings without some light of humor in the back of his eyes.

Yet now, it was gone, snuffed out in an instant, his eyes blue flames ready to combus at any moment.

In its place was a craving for violence, burning hotter than his Molotov cocktails.

Any other man would have been shaking in his boots.

It wasn't like I was totally immune, but no one—not even a six-foot-five crazy-ass biker—was going to make me quake.

"I didn't hurt her, if that's what you're thinking," I told him, less to placate the snarling beast and more to put it out of its misery.

Whatever Ella had done to him, she'd dug in deep. The guy really cared.

"Where is she?" Brute snarled.

"Take it easy, Brute. You know better than to think I would have hurt her. You good now, *amico?*"

I was more than willing to share what information I could with the man, but not until he'd collected himself.

Brute let out one slow breath, and some of the rage that had been rolling off him fell away.

"She popped up in my car the night we took care of Giuseppe. When I stopped the car, she bolted—straight into a three-story walk-up. I thought that was the end of it, but when you said she hadn't shown up for work the next day, I decided to check it out." I summed up the events from then until now, and while I hadn't intended to tell him about the scars I'd seen, it felt like the right move. "The brand was in the shape of an ordinary flower. I know I've seen the fucking thing before, but I can't think of where."

Brute was silent, eerily still.

If his men were wondering what it looked like when Brute Hastings detonated, they were about to find out.

He shot to his feet, roaring, and chucked the table across the room.

The wooden table splintered impressively against the wall next to the door.

I couldn't blame the guy. I hadn't managed to put a finger on exactly what it was about Ella, but she had a way of getting under a guy's skin. Fast.

The Old Dogs in the bar had all gotten to their feet, eyeing the scene warily.

"It's all right, boys," Brute said when the wave of rage had passed. "Just some bad news."

He sat back down as his men returned to their seats. "Fuck, I knew there was something," he said, rubbing the furrow between his brows. "Of course, I knew. You don't spend a lifetime in this life without recognizing the signs."

I nodded in agreement, though, I'd missed the signs too, or maybe I hadn't wanted to see them.

"I don't suppose you have any idea who had her?" A violent gleam shone in his eyes.

I could well imagine what he'd do to whoever it was, but he'd have to get in line.

"All I've got to go on is the brand. She'll talk about plenty of other stuff, but as soon as I get anywhere close to the subject, she shuts down."

He raised both brows. "She talks, huh? She didn't do much of that here."

A ripple of satisfaction ran through me, knowing she'd talked to me but not to Brute. Maybe next, I'd challenge him to a fight on the playground after school.

I swallowed a healthy mouthful of whiskey. I wasn't usually in the habit of drinking before noon, but today seemed like a reasonable exception.

"We'll keep her safe, Brute," I said, committing my family even more than I had already.

"Why?" he asked, looking at me, baffled. "Why are you and your family willing to go to bat for a girl you didn't even know a week ago?"

I didn't have an answer for him, not one I could put into words.

Brute nodded with a fleeting trace of a smile. "She has that effect, doesn't she?"

"Can't argue with you there." I shrugged.

"I'd like to see her," Brute stated.

He wasn't asking. He wasn't demanding either. He was just a guy who was used to getting what he wanted. Like me.

"After you, *amico*," I said, motioning toward the door and downing the rest of my whiskey.

"Hold down the fort, boys," Brute said as he got to his feet.

Here and there, heads bobbed in acknowledgement as we left the bar.

"She's at the Four Seasons. I'll meet you in the underground parking lot," I said then got in my car while Brute climbed onto the Black Beast—his nickname for the bike, not mine.

Not a full minute out on the road, I noticed the tail.

He was on a bike, a few cars back, but he wasn't wearing the Old Dogs' cut.

Brute pulled up beside me as the light in front of us turned red. He was already signaling to turn right.

Perfect—or maybe a little disturbing that the crazy leader of the Old Dogs and I were of the same mind.

Either way, we needed to separate to figure out which one of us the mystery biker was after.

When the light turned green, Brute turned right, but the tail didn't move to follow. He kept the same distance behind me, following a moment later as I turned left off the main street.

Didn't I feel special?

I led the guy further and further away from congested traffic, down one side street and then another.

The guy was smart, keeping his distance, skipping the occasional turn, but he kept ending up behind me.

Five minutes out, I caught sight of Brute rolling through the intersection a street over. Clearly, he wanted in on whatever I was planning.

Two more turns, and I led the tail onto a narrow street, lined with old rental buildings.

There was no delay this time; the guy followed my turn and picked up his speed.

I almost chortled.

The dumbass thought he'd been wrangling me all this time.

I was just about to hit my brakes when Brute appeared at the top of the street, riding at full speed in my direction.

This time, I did laugh because *this* could certainly be interesting.

I kept right on going, heading straight for him, waiting until the last possible second to swerve.

The crazy Old Dog didn't even flinch.

With me out of the way, Brute kept going, playing a two-second game of chicken before my tail lost the round and swerved right into a hydro pole.

Ouch! That looked painful.

I got out of the car and pulled out my gun at the same time, pointing it at the mystery biker's chest.

His left leg was bent at an ungodly angle, the fractured tibia snapped and protruding through a tear in his pants.

I clicked my tongue. Despite not being squeamish, I had to admit that was gross.

Aside from the broken leg, he looked relatively unscathed, which was really too bad.

If he'd been more injured, perhaps he wouldn't have been so quick to draw his gun.

"Put it down, *stronzo*," I warned him once because he'd be more useful alive.

Dead guys generally didn't say much when you tried to torture information out of them.

To no one's surprise, he was too stupid to listen.

He raised his gun. The visor on his helmet had fallen back; I could see his eyes. They were heavily etched with wrinkles and wide with fear, but he'd made up his mind: This was kill or be killed.

There was no convincing him otherwise.

I pulled the trigger, firing two bullets into his chest, cursing the son of a bitch for leaving me no choice.

Brute chuckled as he sauntered over. "You're my kind of man, Leo."

I cocked an eyebrow in his direction.

"The kill-first, ask-questions-later kind of man," he explained.

I laughed, though it wasn't an entirely fair assessment. I would much rather have asked questions first *then* sent the guy to the Great Beyond.

"Do you recognize him?" I asked as I leaned down and pulled off the guy's helmet.

His eyes stared sightlessly up at me; light gray eyes I was quite certain I'd never seen before.

Who the hell was this guy?

"Can't say I've had the pleasure of making his acquaintance." Brute kneeled down on the other side of the guy, grabbed his head, and turned him for a better look.

If he hadn't, I might never have seen the tattoo that crept up the guy's neck. It was a spider in its web—a tattoo I recognized.

I tore open the dead guy's shirt.

There was a sun on his chest with seventeen rays around it. And on his knuckles, there were three crosses. The spider indicated he was a thief, the sun's rays meant he'd spent seventeen years in prison, and the crosses meant he'd been imprisoned three times.

All useless information on its own, but put together, it all added up to one thing.

"He's Russian," I told Brute, who was kind of looking at me like I'd lost my mind since I started stripping down the dead guy. "More than likely Bratva." I shuddered with revulsion.

Every one of them could burn in hell as far as I was concerned. But what were they doing tailing me now?

"Well, my friend, it looks like you've got a new nationality after you. Glad to see you're keeping it multicultural. Very PC, and all that shit," he said, clapping me on the back.

I laughed. "Yeah, that's me, Mr. Diversity."

But the Russians weren't new, and God help them if I ever got my hands on them.

Brute stood up. "Unless you want to bring him home and hang him on the wall, I say we get a move on before Spider-Man's friends start showing up."

It wasn't like Brute to pass up an opportunity for a fight, but I had a feeling he had more pressing issues on his mind—like the gorgeous brunette in my hotel room.

*   *   *

"Hey, pretty girl," Brute said as we walked into the hotel room. Ella hopped off the stool while he crossed the living room in four long strides.

I'd never been a jealous man.

I had no problem sharing women—and had done so, quite literally, on countless occasions.

However, I felt the ugly green beast on my shoulder now. It wasn't like she'd ignored me completely; there was no mistaking the lust that had shone in her eyes. But the smile she wore for him was enough to make the beast start to snarl.

He wrapped his enormous arms around her, but Brute Hastings was so much bigger than Ella, she seemed to disappear inside his embrace.

"You sure had me worried," he said when he eventually released her.

"Sorry, Brute," she said, looking chagrined.

Looking at the two of them, the beast on my shoulder settled down, tucking its tail between its legs.

The dynamic between them were pretty clear.

This was a father-daughter-type thing they had going on here.

Brute shook his head. "Don't be sorry, pretty girl. Are these boys taking good care of you?"

"Yes," she said while a light blush suffused her cheeks.

"All right then." Brute looked at me then at Dante who was watching on with an amused look on his face. "But I want you to take this," he said, pulling a cell phone from his pocket. Ella tried to refuse it, but Brute wasn't having any part of that. "Day or night. If you need anything, you call me, understand?"

Ella nodded. "Thank you, Brute."

Flicking the chagrined green beast off my shoulder, I signaled to Dante, and he followed me toward the front door, giving Brute and Ella a moment's semiprivacy.

It also seemed pertinent to have a conversation with my brother about what had transpired on the way over.

"We have a problem," I told Dante, ripping off the Band-Aid all at once.

"More problems? Are you collecting them now, *fratello*?" Dante cocked an eyebrow.

I shrugged. "Got bored with my erotic stamp collection."

Dante rolled his eyes, putting on his disapproving big-brother face, but the corners of his lips twitched upward. "All right, what new trouble have you gotten us into now?"

I wasn't the one sneaking around behind Dom's back—like there weren't a hundred and one ways that could blow up in our faces, but that was a problem for another time.

"Bratva," I said simply.

His eyes widened, and he shook his head. "We killed every one of the Sokolovs, Leo. You know that."

"I didn't recognize him. There's nothing saying he came from the same family, but he was following me for some reason."

Dante sighed, scrubbing a hand over his face. "It's her, Leo."

I shook my head. "The men who came for her at her apartment weren't Russian."

But they could have very well been working for the Russians.

"Well, boys, it was good to see you," Brute said, crossing the room.

Dante nodded to him warily.

While Dante had never objected to the Old Dogs, he hadn't had the opportunity—or inclination—to get to know Brute.

"Leo, I appreciate you coming by." Brute held out his hand, and I shook it. "It seems I have some digging to do," he said a little quieter. "I'll let you know if I figure out who it is we need to kill. I trust you'll do the same."

"I will," I agreed.

Brute left, and Dante followed him out a minute later. "Work your magic on the girl, Leo, because we need answers," he said from the hotel hallway, almost pulling off the serious big-brother face this time.

"No problem. What do you think? Fairy dust? Magic wand?"

Dante peered over my shoulder toward the kitchen. "Not the equipment I'd use on the girl, but whatever floats your boat, *fratello*."

Chapter Twelve

Ella

Leo closed the suite's front door and turned in my direction.

I sighed, trying not to feel the sting of bitter regret.

The man was beautiful—not that there was anything feminine about him.

Handsome just didn't do him justice.

Leo was beautiful, and kind, and funny.

But he was a *Luca*.

It was time to get my butt out of here and never look back.

Maybe *he* wouldn't flay me open to get to the things inside my head, but the rest of his family might.

"Sit down, *gattina*," Leo said before I'd taken a step, motioning to the seat I'd vacated.

I sat—it was just written in my bones to obey—while he crossed the living room and sat down across from me.

Leo didn't speak.

He sat staring at his hands, laid flat on the countertop.

With every second that passed, the knot in my stomach twisted up tighter.

This wasn't the Leo who'd found me in the back seat of his car.

This Leo radiated tension from every pore of his body.

I was too late.

Somehow, he already knew about my secrets.

I swallowed hard as my whole body started to tremble. I tried to anticipate his next move, but I couldn't see it.

I could not imagine this man scaring me, hurting me, torturing me until I'd handed them all up.

"How long?" Leo asked, but I'd been so caught up in thought, the sound jolted through me.

"I don't know what you're talking about," I lied out loud.

Please don't do this, I silently begged.

He shook his head. "*Sì,* you do, *gattina.* I saw the mark on the back of your shoulder. How long were you... there?"

My heart skipped a beat.

Leo was asking about *Signore's* mark on my shoulder?

How had he seen it? When? Had he been spying on me?

Not prepared for the question, I reached for a lie.

"The brand, it's worse than the other stuff, right?" he continued, stilling the untrue words in my throat.

He was still sitting right in front of me, staring at me intently, but his voice seemed to be coming from further away.

My heart was pounding so hard I had to strain to hear him.

"It's like the other stuff hurts and leaves marks on your skin, but that kind of thing leaves its mark on your soul," Leo said, his eyes never wavering.

My breath caught in my throat.

How could Leo know that? *That* was exactly what it felt like.

He stood up and grabbed the hem of his shirt, yanking it off over his head.

There were no warning signals going off in my head, no voice screaming at me to run, to hide.

All I could do was stare at him, following the hard planes of his chest to the chiseled ripples of his abdomen. Perfectly tapered hips, half-hidden by the waist of his pants. The man was ripped.

My breath should have been coming faster, but it wasn't. It was slower and deeper. My limbs felt like they'd been suffused with warmth instead of ice-cold dread.

Leo turned around.

A gasp slipped out, but I wished it hadn't.

It wasn't that what I saw was repulsive, not at all.

Just like the rest of him, the jacked muscles across his back looked like they had been hand-carved by the gods.

He looked powerful, magnificent, *scarred*.

Long-healed whip marks crisscrossed his back. There were at least a half dozen pearly puckered circles in a straight line beneath his left ribs—cigarette burns. On the back of his left shoulder was the kind of scar I knew all too well. The kind that might have healed years before, but somehow still burned like it was fresh.

Though the mark wasn't the same as mine, its purpose was.

The men who had done it had sought to cut deep, to burn away his identity.

They'd tried to make him less than human.

It shouldn't have surprised me.

The moment I'd discovered Leo was a Luca, I knew.

I knew that while the mark on the back of his shoulder looked like an obscure bird of prey, it was a falcon, burned into his flesh by a man of the Sokolov family.

"How?" I asked, unable to tear my gaze away.

Knowing how, and hearing it from Leo's lips weren't the same thing.

"My first year working with my family, I was cocky as hell. Fuck, I thought I was untouchable. I wasn't watching my back when I should have been." He shrugged, but he didn't turn around, allowing me to look my fill. "They messed me up pretty good trying to get what they could out of me. I held up all right—if I do say so myself." He turned then and smiled at me, but the smile was gone as soon as it appeared. "When he put that iron to my back, fuck, it hurt, but it burned a whole lot deeper than skin, if you know what I mean."

I nodded then stood up without making the conscious decision to do so.

I could feel the elastic again.

It was drawing me closer, and closer, until I stood directly behind him. I ran my finger lightly over the falcon on the back of his shoulder, tracing it over and over again.

It was the first time I'd touched a man other than Brute of my own volition, and this was different.

My hands were shaking, but I didn't care.

Leo understood what I felt. He understood why the mark on my shoulder was a thousand times worse than the worst of the beatings I'd ever gotten. It was worse than whippings, than broken bones, than any of the vile things they'd done to me.

The elastic pulled tighter, and I went with it, letting it tug me up onto tiptoes to place my lips against the mark on the back of his shoulder. I could feel the bumpy texture against my flesh, so much in contrast to the smoothness around it.

I kissed every millimeter of the scar as if my lips could somehow wash it away.

Leo was holding himself still. I could feel the muscles taut across his back.

I should have stopped, but I didn't.

Heat radiated from him, and my lips tingled from the contact, making me want to press harder to make it stop and make it tingle more at the same time.

He spun around and grabbed hold of my biceps. He held me firmly, but not painfully; at least, I didn't think so.

I couldn't feel anything but the scorching heat in his gaze.

He swallowed, and I followed the movements of his throat as the muscles there contracted. Further down, his bare chest rose and fell with slow, deep breaths.

Aside from breathing, he wasn't moving, and though I couldn't explain how I knew it, I hadn't a doubt in my mind what he was waiting for, what it was he needed me to give him.

Could I do it?

I'd sworn never to want this.

I'd vowed to myself the night I escaped that I would never let a man touch me again.

And yet, here I was.

The word trembled on the tip of my tongue.

"Yes," I whispered. It slipped unbidden past my lips.

The heat in his eyes flared hotter.

I could almost see blue flames leaping in his irises as he leaned in until there was no more than a hair's breadth of space between us and his warm breath grazed across my cheek.

Maybe I had gone crazy because I shouldn't have wanted this.

After all that I'd lived through, this was the last thing I should have wanted. If he knew half of the vile things that had been done to this body, I wouldn't be what he wanted either.

When his lips touched mine, I felt none of the revulsion I'd always felt. The languid heat that had been pumping through my veins sped up. His lips were warm and firm as they pressed harder against mine. Not just tingling now; the touch of him set off sparks in the core of me, starting a fire that spread through my whole body, settling at last low in my abdomen.

His tongue grazed along the seam of my lips. I supposed it shouldn't have surprised me that I could understand what he was saying; I'd always been more attuned to silence than to words.

Open for me, his tongue whispered. *Let me in,* something deeper in him demanded, not on threat of violence, but with the promise of pleasure.

I obeyed, parting my lips, and his tongue swept in, grazing along mine and making the fire in my core blaze brighter. I wanted to touch him, to feel his flesh beneath my fingers and the play of his muscles underneath, but I kept my hands at my sides. I wasn't afraid; I felt… shy, which was perhaps the most absurd thing I'd ever felt. I knew how to pleasure a man's body; it was a skill in which I was well-versed, but I felt like a trembling virgin.

He leaned away, breaking the kiss, but his eyes were intent on mine as his hands moved to the buttons of my shirt. One at a time, he unfastened them. He moved so slowly, the message was clear.

You can stop me, he told me without speaking.

Maybe I should have.

I barely knew this man.

The things he was making me feel were equally as foreign.

110

But Leo wasn't a stranger, not in some ways, at least.

In some ways, Leo understood me more than any person ever had.

He pulled the shirt's hem from my skirt and continued until all the buttons were undone.

"Turn around," he said, and I did.

His fingers brushed my skin as he took hold of my shirt and slipped it off my shoulders. The fabric tickled as it slid down my body, pooling in a heap on the floor. The clasp of my bra sprang free next with a deft flick of his fingers.

Instead of feeling his hands on my body like I expected, his lips touched the back of my shoulder once, and then again, and again, as if he could kiss away the scar like I'd tried to do for him.

Leo didn't stop there. His lips grazed across my back from shoulder blade to shoulder blade, every touch rippling through me.

Still, he didn't stop. He laid a trail of featherlight kisses back the way he'd come, and it was only then I realized what he was doing.

They weren't random kisses.

His lips were following the paths of the scars across my back.

Again and again, lower each time. My whole body was covered in gooseflesh, but I didn't feel cold. I'd never felt so warm.

When Leo reached halfway down my back, he kneeled behind me, continuing the trail.

It should have repulsed me to follow lash mark after lash mark on my body, but it didn't. It didn't bring into focus the times I'd screamed in agony, but instead, his lips were like a soothing balm that couldn't wipe the memories away. They muffled them, creating a thin, opaque film between me and them.

There was nothing but the feel of his lips against my flesh and his fingers digging lightly into my hips, holding me steady. He reached the low waist of my skirt, and I held my breath, waiting.

Would he stop?

Or tug off the skirt, giving his lips access to more?

My insides clenched at the thought of him moving lower, but not all of it was in trepidation.

I wanted *more*.

A phone rang.

It wasn't the phone Brute had given me.

It was Leo's.

"Fuck," he cursed, but he kept one hand on my hip, holding me still while he retrieved the phone from his pocket. "What?" he barked into the phone, making me jolt. "Fuck, fine," he said with a heavy sigh a moment later. "I'll be there shortly."

Leo hung up the phone, but he didn't stand up.

His lips touched my flesh, just above the back waistline of my skirt, blazing another path from hip to hip.

And then his lips were gone.

His hands fell away.

He stood up.

I felt the foreign urge to whimper at the loss.

"Turn around, Ella."

I obeyed.

As I did, the bra that had been perched loosely on my nipples slipped off and fell to the ground.

Leo sucked in his breath while his scorching gaze traveled over my body, tightening my nipples and making my breasts feel heavier.

Kiana Hettinger

"God, you're fucking beautiful," he groaned, running his fingers through his hair.

A shimmer of something good rippled through me. Pride, perhaps but it wasn't a feeling I was accustomed to.

I liked the way he looked at me and the almost reverent tone in his voice. The way he'd kissed me... the way my skin heated as his lips had traveled across my back...

"I have to go," he said, but it came out hard and bitter like a curse. "But I'll be back, and there'll be one of our men outside the hotel door the whole time I'm gone."

His gaze stayed fixed on my body while he reached for his shirt and tugged it back on.

I watched his movements, following his hands down his pecs and his abdomen. Then my gaze traveled lower, and there was no mistaking the thick bulge in his pants.

A hot shiver rippled down my spine, and arousal pumped through my veins.

There was no point in pretending I hadn't seen plenty of men, but this was different.

I'd never wanted them, but I wanted Leo, and the proof of his own arousal made me heady with desire.

I tore my gaze away and forced it back up.

Leo was looking at me with a wicked smile. "Like what you see?"

"Yes," I whispered, though there'd been no real question in his voice. Confident. Cocky. He knew what a desirable man he was.

Leo only touched me once more, grazing his finger down the center of me from my neck to my abdomen and then he turned and strode out of the suite with a tortured groan.

Chapter Thirteen

Leo

I turned toward the docks and pulled into the lot in front of our warehouses.

Aside from two other cars, the lot was empty.

Our men had just finished clearing out a fresh shipment, so there wasn't much activity going on at the moment.

"There's a problem. Meet me at the warehouse." That was all Dante had said.

It had better be an emergency—like the sky is falling, the oceans are boiling, or every-woman-on-earth-has-gone-lesbian kind of emergency.

Inside, the main warehouse floor was empty.

I followed the muffled noises coming from the office in the back, left corner. It wasn't much of an office—an old desk and a few chairs—but the room seldom served an administrative purpose. Plenty of work got done here, but it was the kind of work Marco liked to conduct with a bat.

Marco had it with him now, holding it in one hand while a dark-haired guy in his midthirties sat in the rickety old chair in front of him, screaming bloody murder.

Dante stood on the other side of the room, his shoulder propped against the wall and his arms crossed over his chest.

"Are you ready to tell me why you've been spreading lies, *stronzo*?" Dante asked the guy who was looking rather worse for wear.

It seemed Marco had already taken care of one of the guy's legs and the right side of his face wasn't a pretty picture. The guy wasn't winning any beauty pageants anytime soon, and given the scowl on his face, Miss Congeniality was out of the question, too.

"Not lies," the guy panted. "You took the girl."

Dante looked at me, cocking an eyebrow.

So, *this* was the problem.

This was about Ella.

"It's you who lies," the guy said then spat a mouthful of blood onto the floor.

Marco grabbed the guy by the back of his neck and jerked him off the chair and onto his knees. "You'll show *Signor* Luca respect, or you'll never stand again. *Capisce*?"

The guy gritted his teeth but didn't make a sound, which was impressive, since Marco had dropped him down onto his injured leg. After a moment, he nodded, and Marco yanked him back up onto the chair.

"We didn't take anything that wasn't running around free, did we, Leo?" Dante said, looking unperturbed.

"As free as a duck."

Dante laughed, but the guy, completely missing the joke, shook his head. "Not free, *escaped*. *Signor* Avalone will never set that whore free, and if you don't return her…"

Signor Avalone.

Blood pounded in my ears, blocking out the rest of his words. Only one word mattered.

Fiorenzo Avalone.

"Why won't he set her free?" Dante asked.

That should have been my question. Ella was seriously messing with my zen.

The guy looked up, shock registering on his face for just a moment before he tucked it away. "She was a top-rate whore. The *puttana* couldn't get enough."

"Marco, hold him, *per favore,*" I said, crossing the room as Marco stepped behind the guy.

Ella might have rendered me zen-less, but not blind. That single fleeting moment of shock on the guy's face was like a flashing neon sign.

I drew my knife and pressed the tip to the center of the man's chest. "What aren't you telling us?" I seethed, digging the knife in just a little.

I'd always hated this part of the job. To kill a man in the midst of combat, sure, sign me up. To defend the people I cared about, I'd tear a man apart with my bare hands. To torture some asshole? Usually, it just hit too close to home, I supposed. But not this time.

This time, I was going to enjoy every second of it.

The guy shook his head. "If I come back without her, I'm a dead man anyway, so go ahead and kill me."

"Kill you?" I chuckled. "You don't really think that's what I'm here for, do you?" I dragged the knife down the left side of his chest, cutting deep enough that blood welled over and dripped a steady cascade to the waist of his pants.

The guy screamed, but the sound didn't bother me.

It drowned out the sounds of Ella's screams I'd conjured in my head.

"What do you know about the girl?" I asked, and when he didn't answer, I sliced him again.

Three quick slashes that transformed the wound down his chest into the letter *E*. It seemed fitting to carve Ella's name into one of Avalone's men. I was halfway through the second *L* when his eyes turned pleading.

I paused, the tip of the knife hovering over his scarred flesh.

"He... passes her around... when she's needed," he panted.

My stomach turned.

It wasn't like I hadn't imagined all that "slave" entailed. Nobody branded and whipped a woman just to keep her locked up like a princess in a tower. But what vague knowledge I had had just been transformed into concrete images.

"Needed for what?" I clenched my jaw.

That same fleeting pause. "A good fuck, of course. What do you think I mean?"

I shook my head.

Avalone had plenty of whores he could pass around, and it would be no great loss to him if one of them up and disappeared. No, there was more going on here, so it was back to the drawing board.

I completed the second *L* and the *A*.

I could see Dante's amused expression out the corner of my eye while Marco looked on with wholehearted approval.

Time for another round. There were at least three pints of blood on the floor, so the guy didn't have many rounds left. "Why does Avalone want her back so badly?"

He shook his head, his eyes going a little cross-eyed as he did. "You really don't know, do you? The whore never told you?" He smiled, making his swollen right eye close completely. "She's *Signor* Avalone's most valuable possession, *stronzo*. And she's going to destroy every one of you."

He lunged at me, breaking free of Marco's grip for a fraction of a second. But the dumbass hadn't been thinking clearly. He'd no sooner put pressure on his broken leg when he cried out and collapsed, slamming the back of his head into the corner of the desk with a sickening thud.

I didn't need to see the dead eyes staring up at me when he hit the ground to know the guy was on his way to hell.

The problem was he'd taken whatever he knew about Ella with him.

"We have a problem, Leo," Dante said, waving off Marco's apology the moment he opened his mouth.

Not much point in crying over spilled milk at this point.

"Global warming?" I quipped, still staring at the dead guy.

Dante scoffed, cracking half a smile. "If Avalone knows we have her, then it's only a matter of time before he knows *where* we've got her."

"And the hotel isn't exactly locked up like Fort Knox." It would have been great if that was the only problem. "But bringing a girl who could 'destroy every one of us' into our home might not be the genius move of the century."

Dante grabbed the jacket he'd left folded over one of the empty chairs. "You've been pretty damn insistent about this girl. What is it you want to do now?"

I scrubbed my fingers through my hair—though a genie's lamp would have been a whole lot more useful at the moment. "The right answer is to cut her loose."

For the Luca family as a whole, it was the smartest move.

"Maybe," Dante said, shrugging into his jacket.

I shot my head up.

"I think you're right about the way Avalone treated her. To send her back to that just doesn't sit right," Dante continued.

I pressed experimentally on Dante's shoulder.

"What the fuck are you doing?" Dante grimaced.

"Just looking for your soft spot, *fratello*. I didn't know you had one." I grinned.

"*Stronzo*," he muttered under his breath, cracking a smile. "How about you stop poking me and go see what you can get out of her? You need to get her to the house, too. There's no way Avalone's getting to her there. I'll try to find out just how much Avalone already knows."

"I can do that." At least, I could try. A chatterbox, the girl was not. "I'll let you know if I make any progress," I said, turning to leave.

"Leo?" Dante called as I left the room.

"*Sì?*"

"Remember, I said to see what you can get out of her—not what you can put in her."

I shrugged. "Tomato-tomahto, *fratello*."

***

I'd never wanted to kick my own ass before.

Until now.

It was a very strange feeling.

Ella was standing in front of the bed in her room, rummaging through her satchel. She had her back to me, and the duck was quacking bloody murder, so she hadn't heard me come in. Her hair was wet. The occasional bead of water dripped onto the back of her shirt—the only clothing she was wearing—and her skin still shimmered with moisture. She'd taken a shower recently. She'd been naked, with her hands gliding over those curves, her fingers slipping across her nipples, making them harden beneath her touch.

She was a slave, you asshole, my conscience tried to intervene. It tried, it really did, but the image of Ella with her hands on her breasts wasn't budging. I seriously needed to stock up on sunscreen because I was definitely going to hell.

I hadn't realized I'd crossed the threshold until Ella spun around and stared up at me.

Her eyes were wide, and her lips had parted on a gasp before she realized it was me and closed her mouth. Too late, though. My mind had conjured plenty of things to do with those parted lips.

"I didn't hear you come in," Ella said sheepishly.

"Why didn't you tell me it was Fiorenzo Avalone?" I asked her, maybe to keep myself from doing the things my mind was conjuring, the very things that son of a bitch had done to her. It came out a little more blunt than I'd intended. The way she flinched, it was like I'd struck her.

"I didn't... I mean, I don't know what you're talking about." She'd abandoned the satchel entirely. Her gaze flitted to the duck, then back to me, but I saw it in her eyes a split second too late.

Ella ran past me in a flash and out the bedroom door—the girl was *fast*. Her muffled footsteps sounded down the hallway before it hit me what she was up to.

"Ella, wait," I shouted at the same time the hotel suite's front door slammed closed behind her.

If she made it outside, God only knew how long it would take me to find her.

I ran after Ella, out the hotel suite and down the hallway.

Ella was already in the stairwell by the time I caught up with her—she'd never told me she was an Olympic sprinter.

"Stop," I barked, only realizing after that the sound was just going to make her run faster.

She put on a burst of speed, but as fast as she was, I was faster.

I leaped the four steps between us and grabbed her arm.

"Let me go," Ella cried.

She wriggled against my hold on her so much she was going to dislocate her own arm if she kept it up.

"Just calm down, *gattina*." I pushed her up against the wall, using my weight to limit her ability to wriggle and injure herself. At least, that was my intention. Little did I know, Ella was an octopus. The moment I'd subdued one arm, another seemed to snake out of nowhere. Thank Christ she didn't have her knife in her hand. "What the hell are you doing?" I said as yet another wrist slipped out of my grasp.

Ella was slick with sweat, making it impossible to stop her flailing without hurting her.

"Let me go," she cried, raking her fingernails down my cheek. "I'm not going back there. I'm—"

"What are you talking about?" I tilted my head at her.

Ella hesitated for just a moment as confusion furrowed her brow.

It was enough to get hold of her wrists and pin them against the wall, reining in the kitten's claws. At the same time, what had her so spooked finally clicked. "You think I'd give you back to him?"

That stung, but I couldn't really blame her.

"You're not?" she asked, the furrow deepening.

I shook my head. "No, I'm not. You can trust me, Ella." It was true—to an extent. I had no intention of handing her over to Avalone, but the dead guy with her name carved into his chest hadn't been lying. For some reason, he genuinely believed she held an awful lot of power. "*...She's going to destroy every one of you,*" he'd said. Now, it was up to me to figure out what that meant. "But I need you to tell me why he wants you back so badly."

Ella looked away, staring at some spot past my shoulder. "*Signore* doesn't like it when his things go missing."

I eyed her closely. "Try again, *gattina,*" I said, doing my damnedest to ignore the toned body pinned against mine.

I'd wedged a thigh between her legs to keep her from kicking, but now, I could feel the heat at the apex of her thighs. Her hair was mussed from the struggle, her lips were parted, and I had her wrists pinned above her head. *Christ, she looks like she just walked out of every man's fantasy.*

Her throat worked as she swallowed hard and forced her gaze to meet mine. "He never bothered to censor his conversations in front of me."

The words were careful, measured; it wasn't the whole story. I could feel the way she was holding back, but at least it was a start.

I should have kept prodding, pushing for more, but at the moment, her eyes were locked on mine, and with every passing second, the furrow between her brows faded as some of the tension subsided.

She was softer against me, making me painfully aware of her breasts pressed against my chest.

I breathed in deep, trying to will the blood that was pounding in my cock to make its way back into my veins. I wasn't some horny teenager who had no grasp of self-control.

"Leo?" Ella asked in a voice that stroked my cock.

Her eyes had darkened to limpid pools of emeralds, and her breathing was deeper, making her breasts press harder against my chest with every inhale. None of which was helping to send my blood back to the rest of my body.

The way Ella's brows knitted together bespoke her confusion. And if that wasn't enough to make my conscience scream, the lost look in her eyes told the story of the hell she'd lived through. No matter what she'd been forced to do in the past, this was foreign territory to her.

What was even stranger was that it felt foreign to me, too.

This—whatever *this* was—appealed to more than just my cock. And that was just a whole barrel of monkeys full of crazy.

"I want you, *gattina,* but you're not ready. And I'm sure as hell not going to fuck you in some hotel stairwell."

It didn't stop me from grabbing her hip with my free hand and pulling her toward me, pushing her pussy harder against my thigh.

Her thighs squeezed mine, and her tongue darted out to lick her lips.

It nearly cut right through every ounce of the tenuous restraint I'd managed to muster.

I kissed her once; I couldn't resist. Her lips were soft and pliant, opening for me as I sought out the moist heat of her mouth.

Ella tasted like oranges, but her freshly-washed hair smelled like coconuts and tropical flowers. Both sweet, but the exotic edge conjured images of dark, erotic fantasies that I forced away before they could take root.

I was so going to hell.

"Now, Ella. Go," I said, ignoring the way every fiber of my being screamed in protest as I took a step back.

Ella obeyed, which did wickedly wonderful things to my head while at the same time, it made me cringe.

She was a slave, you twisted fuck, my conscience screamed at me over and over again.

My cock didn't care; it had no qualms about following the perfectly-toned legs in front of me and the tantalizing sway of her hips.

Whatever else *this* was, it was a recipe for disaster because I was no monk.

For the time being, though, it was time to get Ella out of this hotel and safe in our home. At least until I discovered how she was going to destroy every one of us. Then all I had to do was figure out a way to neutralize the threat.

Easy as pie, right?

Chapter Fourteen

Ella

I followed Leo obediently to the elevator, ignoring the thrumming and pulsing in my body.

Truth be told, my insides felt like a hot quivering mess.

Leo had me get dressed and hurried me back out of the hotel room, so focused on getting out of the hotel that he barely looked at me.

Would he kiss me again?

Did I want him to?

Part of me screamed yes.

A part I'd never heard before.

It wasn't like I'd never experienced physical pleasure from sex—sometimes, it had been *Signore's* greatest weapon—but this was different.

It was more than carnal, and it wasn't ambivalent in its direction.

It all focused on Leo.

Inside the elevator, Duck wriggled around in his carrier, but I couldn't look at him. Not an hour ago, I'd run from the hotel suite and left him there.

At the mention of *Signore's* name, the whole world had disappeared. There had only been pain, and fear, and blood. My blood. Lashes that had barely begun to heal before he'd use me and rip them open again.

"You thought you didn't have a choice, *gattina,*" Leo said like he'd read my mind.

Did I really have such a glass face?

"And admit it, I'm practically a duck whisperer. You knew I'd take good care of him." Leo flashed me a boyish grin, marred only by the scratch marks down his cheek. They seemed to stand out in more vivid contrast now.

"I'm sorry," I said, motioning in their general direction.

The smile didn't waver. He pressed the palm of his hand to his cheek. "*...'Tis not so deep as a well, nor so wide as a church door,*" he quoted.

"Romeo and Juliet?" I smiled despite myself.

He bowed overdramatically. "The lady doth know her old, boring stories."

"You find Shakespeare boring?"

Signore hadn't let me read books, but I'd remembered a few from school like *Romeo and Juliet* and *The Chrysalids.* Memories of the stories had been my only companions for a long time.

Leo shrugged. "He gave Venus an occasional redeeming line. *'Graze on my lips, and if those hills be dry, stray lower where the pleasant fountains lie,'*" he quoted, waggling his eyebrows.

A laugh slipped out.

How on earth could he do that?

Leo was dangerous, indeed.

The elevator door opened to the parking level.

Leo withdrew his gun from its holster as he stepped out, looking left, then right, making fear tingle down my spine.

He was alert, but while there was a quiet tension radiating from him, it was subdued, and his shoulders were relaxed.

After a moment, he reached back for my hand, leading me in the same direction we'd come from the night he brought me here.

The overhead lights cast long shadows across the concrete floor.

I watched them, my eyes darting from one to the next, looking for signs of movement. I tried to listen for footsteps but could barely hear anything over my own heartbeat.

I spotted Leo's black car—*God, it was pretty.*

It was just a few feet in front of us.

He towed me toward the front passenger side door and opened it.

The gunshot went off like a thousand fireworks all at once in the confined underground space.

"Get in," Leo barked, loud enough to hear over the ringing in my ears. He pushed me in and slammed the door closed behind me.

Duck quacked as I tried to right myself in the seat, the sound drowned out as more gunshots went off.

My breath was caught in my throat.

Leo was behind the car; I couldn't see him.

If he'd been shot…

The driver's side door opened, and Leo slid in, gun in one hand and key in the other. He shoved it into the ignition, revving the car to life, and closed the door at the same time.

The tires squealed.

The car shot forward.

The crack of another gunshot sounded behind us.

It didn't hit anything, but I could almost imagine the agonizing pierce of a bullet; the fear so vivid, I could smell the coppery scent of blood.

"Put on your seat belt, *gattina*," Leo said, his voice unruffled, unlike Duck's feathers.

Duck looked ready to launch at the ceiling if he could.

I scrambled for my bag to find his treats, but there was no bag.

I'd forgotten it. *Damn it.*

All I could do was clutch the carrier tight to my chest with one arm, using the other to wrap the seat belt around us both.

I could see the street. It was right in front of us.

"The hotel service is great, but I have to say the parking attendants suck," Leo joked. He sounded a little breathless.

I chanced a glance back, but there were no cars in pursuit.

Leo shot out of the underground parking, narrowly avoiding a black BMW that swerved, then righted itself directly behind us.

The black BMW stayed right behind us as an identical car merged into traffic beside it. They were close. Too close. So close, I could see the eyes of the man in the passenger seat as he rolled down his window and leaned out.

He had a gun.

"Leo?"

"Get down, *gattina*," he said, his voice too calm.

I obeyed, sinking down in the seat, but now I couldn't see.

It was like being blindfolded. No way to know when it would strike; only knowing that it would.

I wanted to be in the driver's seat, speeding away, outrunning whoever was chasing us.

Leo swerved at the same moment the man fired.

My head knocked against the side panel, but I barely felt it.

I felt useless.

Trapped.

My heart raced as my lungs chased air.

I'd spent four years feeling this way. No control. No say over whether I lived or died.

But I'm not alone, I reminded myself.

For the first time, I wasn't alone and the man in the driver's seat didn't look out of control.

He wasn't panicking. There was no fear in his gaze; just a single-minded focus on whatever was in front of him.

I fixed my eyes on Leo's hand on the gearshift, watching the play of muscle and tendon.

I watched him through every sharp turn and squeal of the brakes.

His movements were smooth and methodical, and I grasped onto his composure with every fiber of my being.

And then there were no more sharp turns. The brakes were silent.

"They're gone," Leo said after a long moment of watching the rearview and side mirrors.

I breathed a sigh of relief and sat up.

It was over... at least for now.

Chapter Fifteen

Ella

Leo groaned and switched hands on the steering wheel, drawing my attention up.

I gasped. It hadn't been my imagination. The smell of blood, it was real. "You've been shot," I whispered, my voice trapped in the crushing grip of something in my chest.

There was blood on his neck. It had saturated the shoulder of his jacket.

Leo shook his head, wincing as he did. "Just a scratch, *gattina*." He smiled an extra goofy grin like he was trying to prove it.

The back of my throat burned.

I tried to swallow the feeling away, but it didn't help.

Leo had been shot because of *me*.

"Really, I'm okay," he said, the grin gone. "It's just a flesh wound. See?" He unfastened the top button of his shirt and pulled it aside to show me.

He was right; it was a flesh wound, just where the neck and shoulder met, but seeing it did nothing to loosen the painfully tight feeling in my chest.

"It could have been more," I said, my voice barely above a whisper.

An inch over, and he could have been dead because of me.

"Sure, plenty of things 'could have been', *gattina*. It *could have been* worse. I *could have been* a trapeze artist or an underwear model." He winked at me.

I wasn't sure about the trapeze artist, but he definitely could have been an underwear model.

"What matters is we're both *alive*—and I don't have to swing from the circus ceiling in a unitard."

Leo had been shot because of me; he was *still* in danger because of me.

"You should let me out." They were the right words, but even I could hear the lack of conviction in them. I didn't want to go back to running and hiding on my own. Always alone.

I wanted Leo.

"No," he said without a moment's thought.

"You've helped me enough, Leo. If *Signore's* men find me alone, they'll have no reason to pursue you. It just makes sense." I shrugged, trying to convince him by feigning nonchalance.

"It's not an option, *gattina*. For now, you're stuck with me whether you like it or not." He was smiling, but this wasn't a joke.

"You don't understand. Enough people have been hurt because of me, and you…" I slammed my lips shut because I wasn't entirely sure what I was trying to say, except, "You matter, Leo. It would matter to me if something happened to you." The revelation left me with a strange, uncomfortable sensation in my chest. "I thought there was nothing, but now there isn't," I said, only realizing once the words were out how little sense they made.

His smile was gone. "You matter, too, Ella. So, don't fight me on this, *per favore*."

I should have fought more, but unless I was going to jump out of a moving car, I settled for what I *could* do.

Shifting Duck's carrier onto the back seat, I grabbed hold of the hem of my shirt, intending to tear a strip to staunch the bleeding.

Leo put a hand over mine. "I like the less clothing idea, but open the glove box," he said, nodding toward it.

I obeyed and found a pile of sterile bandages inside beneath a black handgun. There was medical tape too and other emergency-type things I didn't recognize.

While Leo drove, I cleaned the wound as best I could with one of the bandages. He was right; it wasn't nearly as bad as I'd first feared.

"Can I ask you something?" Leo was staring straight ahead, and I got the uncomfortable feeling the question had nothing to do with how he'd look in a unitard.

I nodded, trying to keep my attention on arranging a clean bandage over the wound and fiddling with the medical tape.

"What did you mean when you said *'there was nothing'*, Ella?" Leo briefly glanced over at me.

"I meant I thought I couldn't…" I shook my head, frustrated because every explanation that came to mind made me sound worse. "I saw a man bleeding to death, and I felt nothing. When you shot those men before, there was nothing. Even when I found Mrs. Abernathy—the old woman who lived in the apartment below me—it scared me, but I didn't feel sad. I just felt… *cold*. I thought I'd lost those things. I thought maybe I couldn't feel *anything* anymore."

"And now?"

I smoothed the last piece of medical tape into place and sat back. "Now, it's different. It's like before, but I want that numbness back."

The numbness was better than the crushing pain I'd felt in my chest.

Leo was silent, and I let the quiet suck me in, listening to all it had to say.

He was tense; his shoulders were taut and the line of his spine was straight. He was watching the road, and yet, the faraway look in his eyes said his mind was caught up in thought, so much I could almost hear the sound coming from inside his head.

I didn't know how much time had passed when he turned into a gas station on the outskirts of the city.

As Leo pulled up to a pump, I looked around, searching for any car that might have been following us.

There were no black BMWs in sight, and no other car turned into the gas station's lot behind us.

"Are you sure it's safe?" I asked, just for good measure.

He laughed. "There's precious cargo on board, *gattina*. I wouldn't have stopped if it wasn't safe."

Warmth rippled through my veins, and I followed him out of the car to stretch my legs.

Duck was in a cantankerous mood, but there was little I could do for him at the moment.

"We'll check inside to see if there's anything he can eat," Leo said, reading my face.

It turned out, there wasn't anything but junk food and sugary drinks on the shelves inside, but the guy on shift happened to have raw broccoli florets inside his paper bag, late-night lunch. Leo offered him twenty dollars for them; the guy thought it was a worthwhile trade.

Back at the car, I opened the back door and slipped some of the florets into Duck's carrier—magically transforming his cantankerous mood.

When Leo opened the front passenger door for me, I paused, looking at the sleek black body of his Lamborghini.

It really was such a pretty car.

"Ella?" he asked, putting his hand on my shoulder.

A week ago, I would have kept my mouth shut.

I never would have asked, would never have even *considered* it.

"Can I drive?"

His eyes widened. "Do you know how to drive?"

I shrugged and did my best to hide my smile. "A little."

Leo looked dubious but nodded.

I could feel the uncertainty radiating from him as he handed me the key.

He stood watching while I circled the car and slipped into the driver's seat.

God, it felt good.

My fingers shook in both fear and excitement—mostly excitement as I slid in the key then looked around the console for just a moment, familiarizing myself with its layout.

Leo sat in the passenger seat, still watching me as I pressed down on the brake and hit the button to turn on the engine.

The car revved to life beneath me, all around me, the vibrations purging the worry from my veins.

Leo pointed toward the steering wheel. "You have to—"

I pulled the paddle on the back of the steering wheel then hit the button to switch the car to manual mode.

"It seems you know what you're doing, *gattina*," he observed with an inquisitive brow cocked.

You have no idea.

I wrapped my fingers around the steering wheel, the leather cool beneath my touch, then took it nice and easy around and out of the parking lot.

I kept to the speed limit all the way to the highway's on-ramp.

Then I stretched my wings.

That's the way it had always felt, like if I could get enough speed, I'd fly right up to the sky.

It had been years since I'd sat behind the steering wheel of a car, but I didn't feel rusty.

There was no relearning curve.

There was only the blur of the scenery at my sides and the wide open stretch of road in front of me.

Out the corner of my eye, I saw Leo grin as he let his head fall back against the headrest.

"It seems you've been holding out on me, *gattina*," he said as I swerved around the vehicle in front of me and flew right by.

I smiled, letting myself get caught up in the speed, the vibrations, the blur of the world all around us.

"So, are you going to tell me the story?"

I shrugged. "The girl I shared a room with in my first foster home kind of had a thing for cars." The words spilled out; I couldn't say whether it was the car or the man making them flow so easily. Probably both. "Her dad stole cars, taught her how to hot-wire one when she was seven, and that was it for her—love at first ride. She taught me, and I kind of…"

"Kind of what?"

I wasn't quite sure how to explain it. "I kind of fell in love with it, I guess. The speed, the thrill. The freedom. The first time I ran away, I didn't exactly run. *I drove.* I got halfway through New Jersey before the police caught me and brought me back. Not bad for a fourteen-year-old kid."

Leo chuckled. "Not bad? I'd say *this* is pretty damn impressive," he said, nodding in my general direction, but his eyes were fixed on my face. I could feel the heat of his gaze prickling my cheek. "You look like someone turned the lights on inside you. Your eyes are bright, your cheeks are flushed. Fuck, you're beautiful, Ella."

I smiled, feeling it all the way to the core of me.

It was maybe the nicest thing anyone had ever said to me.

It kind of felt like I was glowing on the inside.

With Leo and his Lambo, I could almost believe I was free. Free to go anywhere, to live any life I wanted.

But like all good things, it had to end.

Leo directed me onto the off-ramp a little while later.

"All right, my turn, Danica Patrick," he said as he directed me onto the shoulder of the road then switched places with me.

I did my best to hide my disappointment, but he saw it.

Of course, he did.

"We'll go out driving again soon, *gattina.* I promise."

I had a feeling Leo was the kind of man who kept his promises.

It wasn't long before he pulled into a winding drive that led up to a grand old house at the top. A house that looked rather similar to my prison. Not identical, but close enough, my insides started to tremble.

It didn't help that Leo's energy had changed. He radiated so much tension, I could probably cut it with my knife.

"Look, I hate what happened to you," Leo said as he shifted the car into park. "Hell, I want to kick my own ass for the things I want to do to you, Ella. But I need you to tell me about it." He reached out like he was reaching for my hand but stopped halfway there and put his hand back on the steering wheel.

I couldn't bring myself to say no.

The word hovered on the tip of my tongue, but it had been beaten back so many times, it wouldn't come out.

"I might not be able to relate to all of it, but I know what it's like to be trapped and terrified," Leo said while he stared at his hands in front of him.

"Did you want to talk about it, Leo? About what happened to you?" I forced the words out, though they felt dangerously similar to the word *no*.

He shook his head. "No, I didn't. I've never talked to anyone about what happened, but I'll talk about it with you, Ella, if that's what you want."

"Why me?" I asked, hating that all of a sudden, I could feel the seams of my determination coming loose.

Leo sighed. "Everyone else, even if you told them, they still wouldn't really *know*, if that makes any sense?"

"They'd know enough to pity you, but not enough to understand you don't want their pity?" I offered.

"Exactly." He did reach for my hand this time, but instead of enveloping it, he traced along each of my fingers, down to the pale veins that ran beneath the skin of my hand.

Not for the first time, I felt more connected to this man than to anyone I'd ever known, but it wasn't enough.

I couldn't let it be enough.

"Look, Ella, your memories, they belong to you and no one else. If you don't want to share them, I don't have any right to them. But I need to know why he wants you back so badly, and I know there's more to it than what you've told me." Leo held my gaze.

I fought the urge to turn away.

I willed my hands not to shake.

I cursed my stupid glass face because if he was asking, then he already suspected.

His eyes were intent on mine, staring like he could see deeper.

Could he?

"I don't know why," I lied, praying the truth wasn't written all over my face.

The secrets in my head belonged to me.

I'd paid for them with my body and my blood, and to let them out would only cost me more.

But what he didn't know—what I couldn't afford to let him find out—was that one of my secrets might cost Leo and his family everything.

Chapter Sixteen

Leo

I opened the passenger door, but Ella didn't budge.

Her hands were trembling, and her teeth dug into her bottom lip.

And she was lying.

That was going to be a problem.

"Come, *gattina,*" I said, holding out my hand to her.

She'd obey me, even if she was terrified.

I couldn't stop the grin from quirking my lips upward.

Ella took my hand and let me pull her up. "Where are we?"

I slapped my palm on my forehead.

I'd never seen Avalone's home, but I had a feeling it was a big, old estate, just like this one.

"It's my home, my family's home," I explained.

"Oh." The tension coming from her skyrocketed.

Nervous, I expected. This was something else. "Ella?"

She merely nodded.

"What's wrong?" I asked.

Ella kind of looked ready to detonate. The light in her eyes was gone, and instead of flushed cheeks, her face had gone three shades paler.

"Nothing, I'm okay."

"Uh-huh, and I'm the queen of France."

She almost cracked a smile, but it would have to do. Camping out on the front drive wasn't really on the agenda.

"All right then. Let's do this."

Keeping a tight hold on the duck's carrier and the plush bottom lip between her teeth, she squared her shoulders and let me lead her up the steps to the front door.

Inside, I could hear voices coming from the open war room door.

Dante had just come through it, walking toward us.

"*Ciao*, Leo. Ella," he said as his gaze grazed over her appreciatively then swung back to me. "It looks like Ella has quite an appetite," he said, glancing at the bandage on my neck and the blood on my jacket.

Dumbass. I'd already texted him to catch him up to speed.

"It's nothing," I said, shrugging it off.

If a guy couldn't handle being shot at occasionally, then the mafia was kind of the wrong life choice.

By force of habit, I was already heading toward the war room, but the second we got close, Ella stumbled back a step and froze.

There had to be at least a dozen men in the room, some of them seated around the table, others leaning against the walls. Lucas, Costas, Lucianos. Even Vito Agossi, the man who'd been my sister's caretaker for ten years. I'd seen them all before; even together, it wasn't such a strange sight.

But when I tried to envision what the room full of men looked like to Ella, suddenly, the war room wasn't a civilized space with mahogany tables and millions of dollars of knickknack shit on the walls.

It was a den of wolves with plenty of teeth that could tear her apart.

If the shell-shocked look on Ella's face was any indicator, that was exactly what she was seeing.

Way to go, Leo.

"It's not like Avalone's without connections," my uncle Enzo Luciano said, shaking his head. "If we go after him, has anyone even considered the broader fallout?"

"He's got connections, but not allies," Nico Costa argued. The new don of the Costa family—and fiancé to my baby sister—was not a man to ever back down from a fight.

Ella's whole body was shaking, but when I tried to tug her away surreptitiously, her feet wouldn't budge. Only her eyes moved, flitting from one man to the next.

"But we know he's got innocents on his property," Gabe Costa said—the second eldest of the Costa brothers. "His wife and kid. It's not as simple as throwing everything we've got at him, not unless we're prepared to take them out along with him. This isn't the right move."

"So, you're proposing we do nothing?" Dom asked, his arms crossed over his chest and the muscles twitching in his jaw. My brother was not impressed.

Gabe shook his head. "No, I'm saying we don't know enough to rain down hell on him and his family."

Zietto Enzo nodded. "I'm not sure we have enough reason—"

142

Nico growled. "Like hell we—"

"I'm the reason," Ella cried. Her voice was raw and shaking, but it rose above everyone else.

Her whole body was trembling as every eye turned to her, but she stood tall, staring back defiantly at the men in the room.

She swallowed hard. I could see the muscles in her throat working. "I'm the reason you're here, and I'm telling you," she said, pausing long enough for one deep breath, "whatever you're thinking, don't do it."

Ella shook her hand loose from mine and ran, fast as lightning.

Instead of heading for the front door, she veered down the closest hallway and kept going.

I looked back at the war room when she'd disappeared from sight. "Sometimes the fallout from doing nothing is worse, *Zietto*," I said with as much respect as I could muster then turned away and followed after her.

I found her in the open sitting room at the far end of the house.

Ella was sitting in the corner, her knees drawn up to her chest, the holster around her thigh peeking out from her skirt, and Duck in his carrier next to her.

She wasn't crying; it didn't seem to me that Ella was brought to tears easily.

She was just sitting, staring at the tops of her knees.

For once, I had no idea what to say.

"You sell drugs, right? Your family?" Ella asked, looking up from her knees.

I nodded, not sure where she was going with this.

"And you kill people?"

I nodded again. I never said I was a saint.

"So… so what makes any of you any different? And why put yourselves at risk because of me? I don't understand."

I clenched my fists.

How could she compare the Lucas to Avalone?

I swallowed it back and slid down the wall next to her, trying to see us from her perspective.

"You're right, my family, all the families in that room, we sell drugs. We make a lot of money selling things that are illegal, but we've never forced anyone to take them. We never once let our guys try to get kids on the streets hooked so they'd keep buying. The people who buy from us—it's their choice. And the people we kill, they aren't good people, Ella. They've murdered innocent people, or they've betrayed us, or they've tried to hurt us. They had every opportunity not to, but they did what they did, and sometimes there are consequences. But tell me this: What choice did you have?"

Her brow knitted, and she looked at me questioningly.

"Those scars on your back, did you ask for them?"

Ella shook her head just a little, like she was being careful not to commit to it.

"And what about all the other things that were done to you? Were they your choice?"

She shook her head incrementally again.

"That's the difference. No one under this roof would dare hurt you like that. *I* would never hurt you like that, and I would never take away your choice."

It was mostly true.

If it turned out she was a threat to my family, I'd have no option but to take away her choice.

"Thank you, Leo." The furrow between Ella's brows remained in place.

Yet, when she slipped her small hand into mine, I wasn't sure I ever wanted to let her go, dangerous or not.

I stared at where our hands were joined, trying to figure it out.

What did I really know about Ella? Except that she was gentle and soft. And despite what she'd been through, there was still a light in her eyes when she raced a Lamborghini down the highway and when she smiled at rough and tough men like Brute. And she still trembled beneath the reverent touch of a man she barely knew. And she still held my hand knowing I was a murdering criminal who made no apologies for what I did.

"Come on, *gattina*," I said, standing up and pulling her to her feet.

Ella reached back down for the duck but didn't ask where I was taking her.

I led her through the house, up the stairs, and down the hall.

When we'd left the hotel, I'd intended to show her to one of the guest rooms in the house, but not now.

Now, I wanted her in my room.

"I won't be gone long," I said once we were inside.

Ella stood stock-still as I leaned in and kissed her lips.

"Make yourself comfortable," I said. "There aren't many people who get a peek behind the curtain."

I motioned around the bedroom and sitting area, realizing how much she could learn about me from the quotes on the wall, the books on the bedside table, and all the odds and ends in the room.

She might just know me better than I knew myself by the time I came back.

It should have bothered me. But the girl's effect was utterly baffling. First Brute, then me; even Dante had softened up after spending an hour with her.

Whatever it was about this girl, if we could harness it, we could have the whole world bending to our will.

It was almost sad that Ella had so much power and didn't even know it.

"…She's going to destroy every one of you." The dead guy's words came back once again.

Maybe she did know it, and maybe I was the dumbass walking right into her trap.

Chapter Seventeen

Leo

The atmosphere in the war room had changed.

No longer crackling with tension, the air was subdued now, if not quite settled.

My father sat at the head of the table, a whiskey in one hand. He looked at me and nodded his head incrementally, his lips pressed together in a flat line.

"Enzo," my father said, getting to his feet. "We'll meet tomorrow evening, if you're amenable, to discuss the best course of action."

So, they'd agreed, had they? I couldn't help but wonder how much Ella had played a role in that.

The rest of the men at the table followed my father up, and *Zietto* Enzo nodded, shaking hands with my father.

The room began to clear out then, but Nico stayed where he was. "We'll gut the bastard, Leo," he said.

Though I didn't know the history, I knew Nico had a real thing about women being mistreated. There was a cold glint in his eyes now—eyes the same color green as Ella's, which made it strange to see them flash with steel.

While I appreciated the sentiment, if anyone was gutting Fiorenzo Avalone, it was going to be me.

"*Grazie*, Nico. I'll bring my gutting knife."

I wasn't joking. Ripping out Avalone's insides sounded like a good idea to me.

Within minutes, the house had cleared out, leaving me, my father, brothers, and Nico alone.

"The girl's effective, Leo. Well-played," Dante said, clapping me on the back as I joined them in the war room.

"I didn't exactly plan it, but I see your point."

It seemed Ella had gotten a lot of people all on the same side of the fence with a few words.

Impressive. And Dangerous.

Fallon passed by the war room's open door. She had Maria in her arms, who was squirming and whining.

If the bags under Fallon's eyes were any indication, Fallon looked in serious need of a break. And if that break happened to work to my benefit, well, that was just a happy coincidence.

"Fallon?" I called, following after her.

She paused and smiled wearily. Even tired, she was an attractive woman with a pretty smile.

"Do you think you'd be up to welcoming our new houseguest if I took Maria off your hands for a while?"

Fallon laughed. "Leo, if you're going to take my daughter, I will personally arrange the welcoming party of the century." Even as she joked, she held Maria tighter like she was loath to let her go.

"Hanging out with Ella for a while would be fine, but whatever floats your boat."

Kiana Hettinger

I could imagine Ella's horrified response to a welcoming party in her honor.

"Hanging out, I can do," she said, planting an extra long kiss on Maria's forehead and hugging her close once more.

I returned to the war room with Maria in my arms, making goofy faces at her.

She stared up at me with big, blue eyes, no longer whining.

What can I say? I had a way with the ladies.

"We all know Avalone is trouble," Dom said, smiling at his daughter despite the conversation. "We know he deals in girls, and *Zietto* Enzo has heard rumors that he's taken up his son's penchant for sewing strife. It's only a matter of time before that 'strife' ends up at our doorstep."

I dropped down in the closest chair.

It had been a long day, and while the bullet had only grazed me, it still hurt like a son of a bitch.

"Ella's definitely lying, and I don't know why," I said without preamble, scrubbing my fingers through my hair.

"Well, if the girl's going to destroy us all," Dante said, sitting back down in the chair across from me, "I doubt she's going to come out and say it—makes the destruction trickier, *si?*"

"But how?" Dom mused aloud. "Unless she's got a bomb strapped to her chest, I don't see the angle."

"No bomb strapped to her chest—I checked," I quipped.

Dom, Dante, and Nico laughed. Even my father cracked a smile.

"I've met with Avalone," Nico said, sobering. "He's a slimy motherfucker, but he's also smart. Without any real allies, he's still mysteriously managed to increase his family's empire exponentially

149

over the past several years. A man like that is smart enough to make sure a girl—even one who escaped—is too scared to spill whatever she's hiding."

I shook my head. "I don't think it's just Avalone that's got her scared."

"What do you mean?" Nico and Dom asked, almost in unison.

"It's like she's trying to figure out whether we're the good guys or more bad guys."

Nico nodded like he wasn't surprised. "So, whatever it is she's hiding, it could be used against her."

"*Sì.*" I nodded.

Of course, that meant she could be hiding anything up to and including the role she played in Avalone's quest for world domination—kind of a lot of wiggle room there.

"It's irrelevant," my father said with a decisive nod. "Enzo, Nico, and I are in agreement. Avalone should be stopped. And now that his men have shot at my son, we have clear justification to proceed."

Heads bobbed in agreement around the table.

"However," my father continued, "since the girl has drawn our family and others into a fight that was never our own, Leo, I would like to speak with her."

Dante laughed. "I think, *Papà*, you'll probably find it's more speaking *to* her rather than *with* her."

"Perhaps, my son, you just need to work on your skills with the ladies." My father smiled smugly.

I almost choked.

Humor was not my father's strong suit, but he'd nailed it.

"I'll see what I can do," Dante replied, repressing a Cheshire cat grin that bespoke his feelings on his repertoire of "skills with the ladies".

"If we're going after Avalone, the Old Dogs are going to want in on it," I noted, imagining Brute's reaction if he found out after-the-fact.

There'd be bar tables and Molotov cocktails flying everywhere.

Dom cocked an eyebrow while Dante gave me a wary look.

"You saw the way he was with her, *fratello*. Ella's like a daughter to him. Cut him out of this, and he'll remember that," I added.

Dante nodded, albeit reluctantly.

My father steepled his fingers on the table in front of him, considering. "The Lucas owe Brute Hastings and his men a great debt for the assistance they provided the night…" He stopped to clear his throat. "…the night the Novas attacked."

The silence in the room grew heavy, weighted with memories.

We all remembered that night very well.

It was the night a rival, Tony Nova, and his men came into our home with guns, trying to wipe us out.

The night Leandro—one of our men—died protecting Fallon.

The night our mother died, murdered in cold blood by Nova's men. She'd taken her last breath in Dom's arms.

I looked down at my niece, named in honor of my mother, Maria.

If Brute Hastings and his men hadn't come to our aid, how much more would we have lost that night?

Some of us would have survived. We were Lucas, that's what we did.

But baby Maria? Would she be here? Dom or Fallon? Me?

Dom was looking at Maria, too.

I could almost feel the need in him to reach for her, to reassure himself she was *here*, alive and unaffected by that night.

I stood up and laid Maria in her father's arms.

"She's here, *fratello*," I said under my breath, patting him on the shoulder.

Dominic nodded and settled Maria in the crook of his arm, smoothing back the thin wisps of dark hair on her forehead.

"We may not require Brute's assistance," I said to the room at large, "but we owe him this."

My father and Dom looked at each other then nodded and turned to Nico, waiting for him to ring in on the subject.

Nico shrugged. "This is your show. I'm just happy to come along for the ride," he said, though I didn't miss the steel in his eyes.

The guy definitely wasn't the poster boy for violence-free problem-solving.

Dom nodded, but he was wearing that smile older brothers got when making plans to torment their siblings. "Gabe was right that Avalone's got innocents under his roof, so what we're doing here isn't usually Brute's style. And since bringing him in was your brilliant idea, Leo," he said, the smile growing ominously, "you get to be the one to tell him he has to leave the Molotov cocktails at home."

Well, lucky fucking me.

Chapter Eighteen

Ella

I'd shuffled through the books on the nightstand.

Crime thrillers, the occasional horror, and a large number of classics that had been read many times. But there were no scribbles in the margins. No notes stuffed inside.

I placed them back on the stand, each one in the precise position it had been, and moved onto the nightstand drawer. A few bookmarks, a box of condoms, an old college ID card. Nothing out of the ordinary.

I wasn't going to give up that easily.

Signore had trained me for this.

I could tear apart a room and put it back together in a matter of minutes.

I dropped down and lifted the bed skirt. Nothing but a lone dust bunny underneath.

The tall dresser by the bed held promise, though.

I tiptoed to it, listening for the sound of footsteps from the hallway.

No footsteps, but the drawers were another dead end.

I slid open one after another, but there was only neatly folded clothing inside.

I closed the bottom drawer and moved onto the sitting area, searching between seat cushions and underneath the coffee table.

Sweat had begun to bead on my brow, but I wiped it away and stood up, looking for places I hadn't yet checked.

It had to be an act.

Leo couldn't possibly be the kind of man he seemed to be. His family, they couldn't be good people.

I just needed proof.

I pricked up my ears. *Silence.* I wasn't out of time yet.

I crossed the room and opened the closet door.

It was a walk-in closet with wall-to-wall clothing. Impeccable-looking suits. Dress shirts and ties in a hundred different colors and shades, jeans, T-shirts.

I slipped my hand behind each clothing rod, searching for shelves or hidden compartments.

There was nothing.

Until my fingers brushed against a cardboard box on a shelf behind Leo's T-shirts. My heart rate sped up like it was on an F1 race.

I pulled out the box, but my fingers shook.

It was an old shoebox. The kind of box in which old personal things were kept and secrets were hidden.

Leaning my head out of the closet, I held my breath and listened for footsteps, willing my heartbeat to quiet down.

Still no footsteps.

I turned back to the box, but my fingers hesitated on the lid.

This wasn't like all the other times I'd rummaged through people's belongings. Those people had been strangers. Horrible, despicable strangers, and I'd had no choice.

You have no choice now, the paranoid voice in my head whispered.

It was right.

Of course, it was right.

And yet, my cheeks flamed hot with shame as I flipped open the lid and peered inside. A child's drawing with the name *Sofia* scribbled in the bottom corner. A knife with an intricately carved hilt. A coiled whip.

It was a strange collection of memorabilia, but perhaps no stranger than my own box of memories had been.

I'd had to leave it behind with Foster Family Number Three, but without closing my eyes, I could still see it. Photos of my family. A handmade birthday card from my brother, my father's gold ring, my mother's silver bracelet, and an old horseshoe—from my first pony. And three crushed flowers from my family's funeral.

I blinked hard, trying to dislodge the image.

There was only one other thing in the box in front of me. A folded piece of paper. My heart skipped a beat. A hit list? A manifest from one of the ships I'd heard about—the ones that carried kidnapped women bound for sexual slavery?

Could this have been what I was looking for? Proof that Leo was just like all the others?

Please, don't be proof, a part of me cried as I unfolded the paper and stared at the page.

It was a hospital report from 2016. Multiple arm fractures, wrist fractures, a hairline skull fracture, second-degree burns to the feet and back, lacerations that required one hundred and seventy stitches, and infected lacerations across the back.

"They messed me up pretty good trying to get what they could out of me," he'd said.

My breath felt like it was frozen in my chest.

I already knew far more about Leo's kidnapping than I should, far more than even Leo knew, but I'd never imagined how much he'd endured, how much he'd suffered.

My stomach roiled uncomfortably and the scars across my back ached in empathy.

I could feel *Signore's* whip cutting into my flesh, my wrists trapped in cuffs above my head, my toes barely touching the ground.

The cold cement wall scraped my cheek, and my screams had turned my throat to sandpaper. Screams that were useless; they did nothing to stop the lashes of fire that blazed across my back.

The kind of fire Leo had suffered, too.

I dropped the piece of paper back into the box and slammed it shut. The child's drawing stuck out from one side.

If he saw it, he'd know I looked.

But at the moment, I didn't care.

My hands were shaking too much to fix it.

I shoved the box back behind the clothing and stumbled out of the closet, slamming it too hard behind me.

Duck started to quack, but when I tried to pick him up, he waddled away from me.

"Are you ashamed of me too?" I asked him in Russian, to which he responded with a loud quack that I interpreted to mean a resounding yes.

I'd sought out proof Leo was a villain to justify my silence.

I'd invaded his privacy.

And I'd found nothing.

"*¿Que voy a hacer*, Duck?" *What am I going to do?*

Duck had no answer for me. He waddled across the room like he was giving me the cold shoulder. *Or the cold flank.*

I sat down in the wingback chair next to the big window in Leo's sitting area, but it wasn't the landscaped grounds beyond the house I was seeing.

It was the posh condo of a man with salt-and-pepper hair, like *Signore*. Lines etched around his eyes and mouth. And a deep hatred for the Lucas in his black heart.

"Fiorenzo was right, my dear, you really are exceptional," Signor Belemonte had said, crooking a come-hither finger at me. He'd been in good shape for a man his age, unlike most of his companions, who had let their bodies go. I kneeled down in front of him, just like he wanted; eyes down, hands on my thighs. It hadn't taken long for his lips to loosen; it never did in the company of liquor and sex.

A knock sounded at the door.

The image disappeared, and the lush green grounds of the Luca estate came back into focus.

I sat up straighter in the chair and scooted back a little further in it.

It was probably Leo.

It had to be Leo.

What if it wasn't?

I waited with my heart pounding in my chest as the door swung open.

A woman stood in the open doorway.

An attractive blonde-haired woman, a little shorter than me. She was smiling, but I felt no relief.

The men I'd known had been cruel, but the women—whores, slaves, mistresses, and jealous wives—they were vindictive and conniving in the things they'd do to get ahead, to be spared from pain, to be showered with favors.

What was this woman to Leo?

"Hi, I'm Fallon," the woman said as she walked right in. "I'm Dominic's wife. Wow, can you believe we have a baby together, but it still feels so strange to say that?" She laughed. The sound seemed light and guileless. "Anyway, Leo thought... well, I'm not too sure what he thought, but he said you were up here, and you could probably use some company. So, here I am." She held out her arms in front of her like an offering.

I shifted in the chair, not sure how I was supposed to respond.

It was unlikely the wife of Leo's older brother was Leo's mistress, but I wasn't ready to rule out vindictive and conniving just yet.

Fallon's gaze traveled around the room, settling eventually on Duck.

She laughed. "I thought for sure Dante had been kidding," she said, shaking her head. "So... you and Leo, huh?" She waggled her eyebrows. "He's a really great guy. My friend, Corinne, she's seen him, and let me tell you, that boy had her drooling." Her eyes suddenly went wide. "Not that you have anything to worry about. Leo's not... well, he and Corinne could have hit it off, but they didn't." She shrugged. "Okay, so I'm going to stop putting my foot in my mouth. Why don't you tell me how you two crazy kids met?"

Fallon flounced down on the edge of the bed like the conversation—a conversation she'd basically had with herself—had exhausted her.

She wanted to know how I'd met Leo? Telling her I'd been hiding in the back of his car kind of made me sound crazy—which might not have been entirely untrue.

Still, I had some pride left, it seemed.

"Brute," I said instead.

"Oh? Oh, Dom told me about him. Biker, right? I hear he's a good guy."

I nodded.

"Okay, so I get the impression you're not really the talkative type. If I'm annoying you, just say the word, and I'll leave you alone." Fallon held up her hands as if in surrender, a sheepish grin on her face.

No, she wasn't annoying me.

I just didn't know what to say to her.

It had been nearly five years since I'd had a real conversation with another female.

It was clear Fallon was trying awfully hard, though.

"Thank you," I said. It was something.

Fallon smiled from ear to ear. "To be honest, it's kind of nice to have another woman to talk to—not that you do much talking." She chuckled. "Dom's sister, Raven, is awesome, but she works at the hospital, and they've got her working crazy hours at the moment, and I have a month-old daughter who has me working even crazier hours. So, other than my friend, Corinne, who has a new boyfriend—and you know how that goes—my girl-talk meter has been running kind of low."

I tried.

I really did.

But I had no idea what to say.

I could vaguely remember the last day I'd spent with a friend. We'd been studying in my bedroom for exams in Foster Family Number Four's house. Just studying, giggling a little over her latest crush.

"Leo's very nice," I said, trying to ignore the heat in my cheeks.

Fallon laughed, or maybe it was a giggle. "Really? Of all the words that could be used to describe Leo Luca, that's the best you can come up with?" She furrowed her brow exaggeratedly, but the effect was lost by the giant grin.

"He's very attractive," I confessed.

"Now, we're getting somewhere."

The door opened, and Leo walked in, holding a pink bundle in his arms.

Fallon laughed. "Speak of the devil, and he appears," she joked.

But no, Leo was no devil.

That was the problem.

If he was cruel, then keeping my secrets would be easy.

"Hey, Fallon," Leo said, smiling kindly, but there was no heat in his gaze, not until his eyes settled on me, and it flared to life.

I could feel my insides responding, heavier and hotter than they'd been the moment before.

Fallon pushed off the bed and stood up. "Well, if you've ever wondered what a third wheel looks like…" she said, pointing both thumbs toward herself.

"Thanks for keeping Ella company," Leo said, transferring the pink bundle into Fallon's outstretched arms.

I caught a glimpse of one tiny hand sticking out from the blanket.

I'd never seen a baby before—at least, not that I could recall. I must have seen my brother as an infant, but I was two years old when he was born. The hand sticking out from the pink blankets now was so small, it looked like a doll's hand, so pink and so perfect.

"Anytime, dear brother-in-law," Fallon said then she turned to me and winked. "More girl talk later," she said in an overloud whisper then left the room.

"Girl talk, huh?" Leo asked, crossing the room. He stopped right in front of me.

I nodded.

"So, did you rate us brothers on a scale of one to ten? Who came out on top? Never mind, the answer's obvious: Me." Leo smiled devilishly.

Well, I'd never met Dominic, but I had a feeling a hundred Luca brothers had nothing on Leo.

"Have you ever thought about leaving?" I asked, regretting the words the moment they spilled out.

This was foolish. Dangerous.

"Leaving? My home? My family?" Leo asked.

There was a furrow between his brows, but he looked confused, not angry.

"Yes," I ventured.

If I could save *him*, wouldn't that be enough?

"I've never considered it and never would, not in a million years. Why?" Leo tilted his head to the right.

I stood up, positioning myself for a clear path straight to the door.

If he tried to stop me, I'd run as fast and as far as I could.

My body shook with the adrenaline coursing through my veins.

What are you doing? the coward in my head cried, but I had to try.

I owe him this, I argued, but really, it was more than that. Leo *mattered.*

"What if I told you that I know things, Leo? Things I shouldn't know?"

His expression didn't change, but something in his eyes did. They were alert and distant at the same time. "If you told me that then I'd ask you to try to find a way to trust me, Ella."

Trust? It was a word people threw around like confetti.

I'd been like them once; I'd thrown it around too, thinking they were harmless little pieces of paper.

Not harmless, I discovered, but like tiny explosive devices that could wound in a thousand different ways.

But I had to give him something. I'd never be able to live with myself if I didn't.

"Harry Belemonte isn't a good man. You shouldn't—none of you—should have anything to do with him."

Leo laughed. "Belemonte is a piece of shit, *gattina,* but how do you know that?"

"Please don't ask me that, Leo," I said, taking a step toward the door while an image of the man with salt-and-pepper hair flashed through my mind.

"You don't have to run, Ella." He held out his hand but didn't grab me.

Trap! the coward cried, but I silenced it and slipped my hand into his. Only then did he close the distance between us.

"*Grazie,*" he said as he leaned in slowly.

His gaze stayed locked on mine until the last possible moment when he brushed my lips with his. He kept my hand in his and placed the other on my hip, pulling me closer.

It was warmth and electricity, and hot, molten lava in the core of me.

But despite the urge to melt right into Leo, guilt crept up my spine.

"Leo, I have to tell you something," I blurted out.

"By all means, *gattina,*" he said, though he kept his hold on me.

"I found the box in your closet," I confessed, feeling my cheeks flame hot. "I shouldn't have been snooping, but I needed to know if you're really the kind of man you seem to be, and so I did it, and I'm sorry."

You're going to regret that, the voice in my head whispered. *He's going to punish you.*

I silenced the voice.

At least, I tried.

Leo shrugged. "That's all?"

"I didn't just look in the closet. I looked everywhere," I said, not sure if he was looking for a more thorough confession.

"I told you to take a peek behind the curtain, remember?" He didn't seem the slightest bit perturbed. "Now, if you've damaged my old porn collection between the mattresses, then there'll be hell to pay." He smiled goofily.

I looked at the mattress.

I hadn't thought to check there.

How had it escaped my mind entirely?

Leo laughed. "I'm kidding, *gattina.* There are no naked women between the mattresses these days. Now… if you ask me if I'm desperate to get one on top of the mattress…" He returned to my lips, sampling them with a featherlight brush.

I could have remained passive.

I could have tried to ignore the arousal he sent coursing through my veins, but I didn't want to ignore it anymore.

Alone with Leo, it felt like the bubble was reforming, molding to my curves and his hard planes and pushing us together. Closer.

And closer.

I leaned up to meet him and parted my lips, welcoming him in as I raked the fingers of my free hand through the short hair at the nape of his neck.

A knock sounded at the door. "Leo?"

Leo groaned against my lips then leaned away. "Please tell me the world's just been taken over by an alien race of man-eating zombie rabbits," he called back through the closed door.

"What?" the voice responded. Dante, maybe?

"Never mind," he grumbled then released me and opened the door.

Dante stood in the hallway, his gaze traveling back and forth between Leo and me before his lips curved in a knowing grin.

"Is there something I can do for you, Dante?"

Dante's gaze shifted to me then back to Leo. "*Sì*, but for now, just checking to make sure you hadn't gotten distracted."

Leo exhaled deeply and rolled his eyes. "*Un minuto*," he said, shutting the door.

He turned to me, wearing an expression that was caught between annoyance and the ever-present humor always tugging at the corners of his lips. "One day soon, I'm taking you somewhere with no phones or doors for a thousand miles."

"The Antarctic?" I teased.

Leo chuckled. "If that's what it takes," he said, looking me over from head to toe. "You're worth a frostbitten ass, a thousand times over, *gattina.*"

Chapter Nineteen

Ella

As quietly as I could, I crept down the stairs.

I hadn't traveled up and down them enough to know which steps would creak, but it didn't matter.

Leo was right next to me, and he was doing nothing to silence the sounds of his footfalls on the stairs.

One step, and then another, while my heart pounded like a drumbeat in my chest. The blood whooshing past my ears was so loud it drowned out the handful of voices coming from somewhere down below.

I could barely hear them.

"My father just wants to meet you," Leo had said like it was no big deal.

Vincent Luca, the don of the Luca family.

This *was* a big deal.

And a bad idea.

Such a bad idea.

I followed Leo down the stairs, past the foyer, and toward the kitchen where half a dozen people were gathered, chatting amicably.

Dante, I recognized, as well as Fallon with the baby in her arms. Given the resemblance he bore to the others, it was reasonable to assume the dark-haired man standing next to Fallon was Dominic Luca, eldest son of Vincent Luca—the older man with graying hair standing near an attractive man who looked nothing like the Lucas.

"It's just family here, *gattina,*" Leo said, squeezing my hand.

I hadn't realized I'd stopped moving until he tugged me gently forward.

The scene in the kitchen didn't appear ominous.

To an unknowing eye, they looked like an ordinary family. Happy, relaxed. Even the infant looked content, lying peacefully in her mother's arms.

"Hi, Ella," Fallon said when she spotted me.

She crossed to where I stood, hovering on the kitchen's threshold, and thrust a crystal glass of something pale orange into my hand.

"Thank you," I said quietly, trying not to draw attention, but it was too late.

Every eye in the room had settled on me.

Except for Dominic Luca's, whose gaze seemed distracted, traveling back and forth between me and the man standing next to his father.

There was something about the look in Dominic's eyes, something like—

"You've met Fallon, Maria, and Dante already," Leo said. "This is my father, *Signor* Vincent Luca." He motioned to the older man. "And this is my brother, Dominic, and Nico Costa, my—"

The glass slipped out of my hand.

It smashed into a thousand crystal shards, each one of them picking up the light from overhead and glittering.

I took a step back. And then another.

Why on earth was Nico Costa here?

I'm too late.

The look in Dominic's eyes; I knew I'd recognized it.

"Ella?" Leo's voice seemed to come from far away.

I stared at Dominic as the conversation I'd overheard in the posh condo played in my head.

"I'll arrange it so he owes me a favor," Signor Belemonte had said to his companions in Italian as he pulled me up onto his lap. *"And then I'll let him burn himself and his fucking family to the ground."* He'd laughed, and the other men there had joined in.

I backed away from the kitchen.

They were all looking at me.

Leo, concerned. *Signor* Luca, perplexed. Nico Costa and Dante, like I'd perhaps dropped my marbles rather than a champagne flute on the floor.

I didn't bother running for the front door.

In my experience, front doors were locked up tighter than any cell.

I ran down the same hall I'd fled down earlier, stopping in the same sitting room, the same corner, the same soft Persian rug beneath me as I sank to the floor.

"He'll discreetly sabotage one of the Costas' casinos for me, thinking I just want the Costas brought down a peg," Signor Belemonte had said, still speaking Italian because he thought I couldn't understand him, while his hands wandered across my body distractedly. *"Then that cold motherfucker, Nico Costa, will wipe them out, and the Lucas' territory will belong to us."*

Leo appeared in the doorway. He didn't look angry; more perplexed. "Correct me if I'm wrong, but I have a feeling this isn't about a broken glass," he said, sliding down next to me like he had before and taking my hand in his.

Before I could answer him—not that I had any idea what to say—another figure appeared in the room's doorway.

"We seem to have gotten off on the wrong foot, *signorina,*" Dominic Luca said, crossing the room like he was approaching a cornered animal.

"Did you do it?" The words spilled out as I wondered if I was truly too late. But no, his body language said I wasn't. "But you know, don't you?" I pressed, though it wasn't a question.

I could almost taste the bitterness of guilt and obligation in the air around him, two equally heavy flavors that ate at one's insides.

Leo was silent, but the thigh pressed against mine was taut with tension.

"Know what, *signorina?*" Dominic asked.

There was nothing in his expression that gave him away; he was doing a good job of locking it all up, but not a perfect job. His stillness, combined with the new tension in his shoulders, spoke volumes.

Don't do it, the coward cried, but it wasn't as persuasive today.

Leo mattered, maybe too much.

"You've spoken with *Signor* Belemonte." I spat out the name, the slimy feel of it on my tongue as vile as his hands had been.

There was no turning back now.

Dominic covered it fast, but it was there for the most fleeting of seconds—the truth written plain across his features.

The kind of truth that put Leo in danger.

"What are you going to do?" My heart had started to pound, and my palms were slick with sweat.

Whatever this man chose to do would have a direct impact on Leo's life. And Fallon's and Maria's. And Dante's. I didn't know these people, but suddenly, their lives mattered, too.

Enough to jeopardize your own life? the coward cajoled.

Dominic's blank expression stayed in place for a moment longer, but then he dropped it. "*Non lo so,*" he admitted as his shoulders sagged. "I think the bigger question is how did you know?"

I closed my eyes, my stomach churning like all the butter in the world had ran out. "Please don't ask me that."

Dominic nodded, but his gray eyes stayed fixed in my direction; I could feel them boring into mine, trying to find the answer behind them.

He was an intuitive man—I could see it.

But I must have been written in a language that Leo had an easier time deciphering because, eventually, Dominic averted his gaze.

I kept my face turned away from Leo, certain he'd have me translated in three seconds flat. "What *Signor* Belemonte wants you to do, you can't do it," I said, still focused on Dominic.

"What is it Belemonte wants, Dom?" Leo asked.

Dominic shook his head at Leo then sighed and rubbed a hand over the stubble on his jaw. "I would rather kill that piece of scum than look at him, but I gave Belemonte my word. Breaking it isn't something I can take lightly."

"When I was sixteen," I said, not wanting to share any piece of me with this stranger but knowing I had no choice, "my foster father made a bet, and when he lost, he honored that bet."

Signor Luca had appeared in the room's doorway.

The three men were looking at me, the same confused furrow between their eyes.

I squeezed my hands into fists and forced myself to go on. "Me," I spat the word out. "I was the bet. Do you think what he did was honorable?" I asked, meeting Dominic's gaze. "Do you think I remember him as an honorable man because he didn't break his word?"

A fleeting expression of shock ghosted across Dominic's features, but he tucked it away fast. "Avalone? That's how he... *acquired* you?"

Leo gripped my hand tighter as I nodded, trying not to think about that day; about the hard, concrete floor, or the cold, heavy weight of the shackles around my wrists, or the cut of the whip across my back.

No matter how much I tried to block it out, it was always there in the back of my mind.

"I'm more sorry than you can know, Ella," Dominic's voice cut through the damp, dark basement, "but it's not the same."

"You're right," I snapped with more emotion than I'd intended. "It's not the same," I continued with a little less fervor. "When my foster father honored his word, I was the only one to suffer. If you honor yours..." I shook my head, trying to force thoughts of Leo away. "*Signor* Belemonte is not after the Costas. He's after *you*, Dominic. He's after the Lucas, and he'll lead Nico Costa right to you the minute you do it. Nico's father was still alive when *Signor*

Belemonte crafted his plan, but even then, he knew Nico was the key. Threaten his empire, his *family's* empire, the Costas' empire, and he'll burn the whole world to the ground."

It was all out there now.

Something inside me unclenched.

No pretending I'd overheard the deal in passing, feigning ignorance over *Signor* Belemonte's motives.

I hope you know what you're doing, the coward groaned, throwing her hands up in the air.

"What the hell, Dom?" Leo's head shot to Dominic.

"*Calmati*, Leovino," *Signor* Luca said, his hands behind his back. He glanced at Dominic, a meaningful look on his face.

The corners of Dominic's lips tightened as his jaw clenched, but he gave one clipped nod to *Signor* Luca then turned back to me. "I suspected that was a possibility. *Grazie,* Ella. I'll think about what you said."

"Dominic," I said, surging to my feet. "He'll... he'll burn Leo to the ground," I choked out then my cheeks flamed, remembering my audience. "And Dante, and everyone else," I covered too late.

Dominic's gaze flitted back and forth between me and Leo, who'd gotten to his feet too and now stood behind me.

"Leo will be fine, Ella." Dominic chuckled. "If anyone gets to set my brother's ass on fire, it'll be me."

No, it won't.

If not Nico Costa, then it would be *Signore*... except, it didn't have to be.

Leo scoffed. "I'd like to see you try, *fratello.*"

I looked up at *Signor* Luca and then at Dominic, an older, slightly less jocular version of the man who'd rescued me, who'd killed for me.

Whatever else this family was, they were good people.

Good people who were going to fight for me, die because of me.

Unless I found the courage to do what needed to be done to stop them.

Chapter Twenty

Leo

"Have a seat, *gattina*," I said, motioning to the grass at the edge of the pond near the back of the property.

The duck was wriggling like a worm in her arms.

Ella leaned down and relinquished her hold on him and sat down at the water's edge while the duck made a beeline for the water.

With every step we'd taken away from the house, the tension coming from Ella had diminished a little more. Her shoulders were just about relaxed now as she dipped her toes into the water.

I sat down next to her, ditching my shoes and socks and joining her.

"He's only ever been in the bathtub," she said, eyeing the duck while worry knitted her brow.

The duck dove, plunging all but his tail feathers beneath the water's surface "He seems to have the basics worked out."

The duck resurfaced, and the worry faded away.

Ella turned her attention to her toes as she dipped them into the water then lifted them up, watching the water droplets drip back into the pond.

"Is that why Avalone wants you back so badly? Because of the things you know?" I asked.

It wasn't the conversation I wanted to have, but I had a feeling *this* had something to do with what made her dangerous.

If knowledge was power, then just how much power did Ella have?

Ella nodded as her toes slipped beneath the water's surface again. "He had me... gather a lot of information," she said, her voice quiet and tentative like part of her wished she could pull the words back.

"Why you?" I asked stupidly.

The answer was staring me right in the face.

If anyone could entice the secrets out of a man, it was Ella, who took beautiful to a whole new level.

"*Signore* said I was young and desirable." She stared at her toes, the water droplets sliding down her flesh. "It made me the ideal thing for him to use, particularly when he discovered my easy grasp of languages."

"Languages?" I repeated.

"*Parlo molte lingue.*" Ella shrugged. "When *Signore* gave me to the men of his choosing, I was to act like I didn't understand them and only respond to English commands. I was just a thing," she said, keeping her eyes on her toes, "so it was never long before they were speaking more freely in their native languages, and I could report what they said to *Signore.*"

Something white-hot was pumping through my veins.

The urge to lash out at something, to tear it to shreds, had never been so potent.

"That's how you knew about Belemonte's plan? Avalone gave you to him?" I gritted my teeth.

She nodded.

I balled my hands into fists, my knuckles turning white.

They were both going to die slow, agonizing deaths.

I was already imagining just how I'd cut them up, starting with the least fatal pieces and working inward.

It would be messy work, but sometimes a man just needed to get his hands dirty.

"Leo, I… I don't want to talk."

I nodded.

"I mean, I've been thinking a lot about it, and I don't know why it's different with you, but it is." Ella looked around then stood up. Her fingers moved to the buttons of her shirt.

My brain seemed to short-circuit for half a breath.

It seemed pretty clear to me what she meant, and yet, I was having a difficult time making the leap from where we'd been to where it seemed she was going.

The moment she started unfastening her buttons, though, I caught up fast.

The rage gave way to something else, equally as hot but a fuck ton more pleasurable.

I was on my feet faster than a bolt of lightning and rock-hard in an instant, every fiber of my being screaming at me to take, to devour, to fuck until there was no telling where I ended and she began.

I grabbed hold of her hips and pulled her closer.

My cock rubbed against her abdomen, and the faintest tingling started at the base of my spine.

I lunged for her lips, savoring the sweet taste of her as she parted for me.

I swept in, gliding, caressing, sipping at the corners and nipping at the fullness of her bottom lip, but it wasn't enough.

My lips craved more.

I tasted her jaw, her neck, the upper swells of her breasts, kissing, suckling, and nipping every inch of flesh I could reach.

With every kiss, she molded her body more firmly against mine.

With every suckle and nip, more breathy moans fell from her lips.

Her fingers had hold of my shoulders, digging in deep, holding me close.

Every sound, every writhe of her hips was perfect as if she...

I froze.

Though my cock throbbed in protest, I leaned away.

"Is this what you really want, Ella?" I looked into her eyes, trying to see through and translate what swirled in her emerald orbs.

Was it an act?

A carefully choreographed routine she'd been forced to practice countless times?

But Ella nodded.

Was there a slight furrow of uncertainty between her brows?

My cock throbbed to the beat of full speed ahead, but I grit my teeth and kept the brakes on. "I need you to say it. I need to know this is what you want."

"Yes, Leo, I want this," she said.

There was a slight tremble in her voice, but at the same time, her eyes flared with desire and her hips writhed as she fitted herself impossibly closer.

Whatever part of my brain housed my conscience went quiet.

I'd wanted this girl from the moment I first saw her.

I hadn't even touched her yet, and I was halfway there.

This was going to take some monumental control.

Luckily, I had one hell of a fetish for control.

"Take off your clothes, *gattina*. I want to see all of you."

Her fingers were trembling a little, but she didn't hesitate.

One button after another; it seemed time had slowed down.

When she finally unfastened the last one, she wriggled her shoulders and her shirt fell to the ground as she hooked her fingers and dragged down her skirt with it.

I clenched my jaw.

No underwear; nothing but the holster with the knife around her thigh, smooth, bare skin, and curves any man could get lost in.

I'd let her leave the holster on; maybe it would give her an added sense of security, and it didn't hurt that it looked sexy as fuck.

My cock strained painfully against my pants. "You're perfect, Ella."

One corner of her lips tugged up in a smile, and she stepped toward me.

The light breeze brushed across her nipples, making them grow taut as her fingers moved to the buttons of my shirt.

Her eyes flicked up to mine, and I could see the question in them.

She was asking permission.

Didn't that do all kinds of crazy, wonderful things to my head.

"*Si, gattina,*" I said, keeping a hold on that depraved part of me I'd determined to keep under wraps.

I wasn't ashamed of it.

She deserved more.

Her fingers brushed against my skin as she unfastened one button and then another.

Maybe one of Ella's secrets was that she was a sadist at heart because it felt like we were in a slow-motion film.

With every button she undid, her lips followed the ever-widening *V*.

They were the softest lips I'd ever felt.

Inch after inch, she left no exposed flesh uncovered.

Halfway down, though, I'd just about reached my breaking point.

"Lay down," I told her, taking hold of her shoulders and maneuvering her around before I lost my shit and drove into her like a maniac.

The duck splashed merrily in the pond as she moved obediently, lying back on the grass with her hands above her head and her legs stretched out, parted just enough I could see her clit peeking out from her smooth pussy.

The girl knew what she was doing.

I refused to think about why, or how this was absolutely not what I was supposed to be doing.

Instead, I focused on finishing what she'd started, stripping off my shirt since it seemed to be about a hundred degrees outside all of a sudden.

Her eyes followed the movements of my hands.

A light blush stained her cheeks as I tossed my shirt to the ground.

"You look like an Adonis, all chiseled muscle and hard planes," she said as she licked her lips.

Resisting the urge to pounce, I stood still, letting her look her fill for as long as I could—which amounted to about three and a half seconds.

Then I kneeled between her thighs, nudging them open until I could see the wetness glistening on her slit.

My cock jerked at the sight of her.

Every fantasy I'd had of her came flooding back, but Ella deserved more. Or better. Or gentler.

She deserved everything I wasn't.

Rather than pinning her down and fucking her senseless, I leaned over her, bracing one arm next to her head as I forced myself to take her mouth gently.

Her fingers wound in the hair at the back of my neck as her lips parted for me.

I delved between them once more, sweeping, caressing, tasting, while my free hand sought out more, following the contours of her from neck to shoulder to her breast.

Her flesh overflowed my fingers; the girl had incredible tits. Her nipple was hard against the palm of my hand, growing tauter with every touch.

Drawn by the contrast of hard and soft, I kissed my way from her lips to her breast, swirling my tongue around her nipple before drawing the taut peak into my mouth.

No teeth. Don't suck too hard.

The warnings sounded in my head even as her back arched off the ground, pressing her breast more firmly against me.

Her fingers roamed over my back, tracing the outline of muscles with just enough pressure her fingernails scraped lightly over my flesh.

Still suckling one perfect nipple, my hand traveled lower, following the jut of her ribs, the concave dip of her stomach and then lower.

The moment my fingers brushed over her clit, Ella gasped.

Her hips jerked and her hands stilled on my shoulders, digging in just a little.

I moved lower, grazing a finger through her lips. "You're soaking wet, *gattina.*"

Warnings were still sounding in my head despite her body telling me otherwise.

Don't rush it. Be gentle.

This conscience shit sucked.

Instead of barreling forward, I laid back in the grass, pulling her with me and positioning her on top so that her thighs were straddling my face.

My mouth watered more as I breathed her in, staring at the deep pink of her engorged clit and slick lips.

"*Perfetta,*" I whispered then ran my tongue between them, tasting the honeyed musk flavor of her that might just have been the most addictive flavor I'd ever sampled.

The moment my tongue touched her, she jolted against me.

I grabbed hold of her hips to keep her right where I wanted her.

Not too hard.

I loosened my grip and flicked my tongue across her clit, eliciting a quiet moan from her that wrapped around my cock and made it throb painfully against the fly of my pants.

I lapped at her again and again, and her moans grew louder as her wetness saturated my tongue. Her hips were writhing, and her hands had migrated to her own body, cupping her breasts, her nipples caught and peeking out between her fingers—*a good old-fashioned lap dance had nothing on this!*

Wanting, *needing*, more of her, I suckled her clit into my mouth, careful to keep my teeth tucked away.

"Oh god, Leo," she panted.

Her hands worked more enthusiastically on her breasts while her moans grew even louder.

It was a shock to hear her make so much noise; a shock that went straight to my cock as another thread of restraint snapped.

I suckled harder and slid a hand down her ass and between her thighs until my fingers brushed along her wet slit.

With her clit in my mouth, I slid a finger inside her, the tight walls of her pussy clamping down and sucking me in.

She was *tight*.

Ella threw her head back and moaned.

She looked like the goddess of all things sex and sin with the moonlight spilling across her body.

"Eyes right here, *gattina*," I commanded, releasing her clit only to drag my tongue across the sensitive bundle of nerves when she obeyed.

I fucked her pussy with my finger, attacked her clit with my tongue.

Her eyes were like green fire in the moonlight; her cheeks flushed like before. Moans tumbled from her lips, and her body writhed, grinding her clit against my tongue and driving my finger deeper inside her.

I could feel the exquisite tension in her body as it hit its breaking point and her cry filled the night sky and wrapped around my cock.

In one smooth motion—a motion I might have practiced a time or two before—I had her back beneath me on the ground, my still-confined cock grinding against her pussy—my cock was not impressed with its confinement.

Her hands grazed over my shoulders and back. Her nails pressed just enough to leave a light tingling sensation in their wake, seriously messing with my self-restraint.

I kind of wished I could tie her up, but I didn't need my conscience to chime in to know that was a definite no-no.

"Leo, I want you," Ella said as her fingers dug in a little more.

I stood up long enough to ditch the clothes and sheath my cock.

In no time at all, I was on top of her, fisting my shaft as the tip of me pressed against her wet slit.

I couldn't remember ever wanting something so bad.

I grit my teeth and forced myself to go slow, penetrating her one hot tight inch at a time no matter how much it felt like her body was trying to draw me inward.

It didn't help when she wrapped her legs around me, tilting her hips and giving me full access.

I could drive right in, fill her up with every inch of me with one kick of my hips. But I fought the urge, resisting the temptation to use her body the way I wanted.

When I'd buried three quarters of my cock inside her, I stilled, giving her body time to adjust.

Her grip on my shoulders had tightened, and her quiet moans had turned to breathless panting, but with every passing moment, her fingers relaxed a little more until finally, it seemed safe to move.

I withdrew until only the head of my cock remained inside her then thrust back in slowly, clenching my jaw so hard it was a wonder my teeth didn't break.

Ella was indescribable, the tight walls of her pussy sucking me in deeper and deeper.

The last thing I wanted to do was take it slow, but what I wanted was too similar to the way she'd been treated.

I wouldn't do it.

Her lips parted as I thrust again, fresh moans spilling out.

I delved for her mouth and swept my tongue between her lips, which only served to drive my depraved mind crazier, knowing she could taste herself on my tongue.

Her fingers dug into my shoulders as I picked up my pace.

I left her mouth, leaning up enough so I could watch her and see the play of pleasure across her features.

Her lips were still parted, and her face was flushed with arousal. Her breasts bounced between us with my every thrust, and her moans grew louder, soon sending the tingling sensation at the base of my spine into overdrive.

Ella was *close*.

I could feel the urgency in the way her fingers dug in deeper and her legs wrapped tighter around me.

"You feel so good, Leo," she cried out, louder than I'd ever heard her.

It felt like there was something rattling inside me, a beast in its cage, desperate to break free.

When her moans turned to screams, and her back arched clear off the ground, it just about tore the bars right off the cage.

Her pussy spasmed around my cock, and I let the exquisite sensation take me over the edge, driving in as deep as I dared once more as shock waves ripped through my body.

Chapter Twenty-One

Ella

I'd gotten what I wanted.

Entirely for me.

It had been *incredible*.

Duck was preening at the side of the pond while I laid in the crook of Leo's shoulder, watching the slow and steady rise and fall of his chest.

He was impeccably made, the planes and grooves of his body chiseled to perfection.

I ran my fingers lightly over his chest, the tanned skin marred only by the faintest white line that wrapped across his ribs, beneath his nipple.

One hundred and seventy stitches, the report had said.

"Was it the same as me?" I asked, tracing the faded scar.

It wasn't the right time to ask, but I wanted to know more about the man who'd made me care again, who'd made me want things I'd never thought I *could* want.

"You're asking if they raped me?" Leo's tone was hesitant, *tentative*.

I nodded against his chest.

"No. It wasn't like that," he said as the arm around me pulled me closer.

I'd thought his answer would make me feel less connected to him, but all I felt was relief that he'd at least been spared that.

"At first, it was awful," I said, the words spilling out of their own volition, "and then it was lonely. I mean, it was always awful, but the loneliness was worse sometimes."

It seemed I didn't just want to learn all I could about him, I wanted him to know *me*.

"You're not alone now, *gattina.*"

True, but that was, perhaps, worse.

In hell, I'd cared about nothing.

No one.

All of my fears had been centered on myself.

Now, they weren't.

"My family died," I said, not sure where the words had come from.

This had to be the worst post-sex chitchat ever.

Leo hugged me closer. "How old were you?"

"I was twelve. My brother was ten. Victor," I said, and then it all came flowing out. "It was a car accident. My parents were in the front seat, and my brother and I were in the back. I don't remember the crash. Just waking up at the hospital. They said my parents had died right away, but my brother was there, in critical condition. They wouldn't let me see him."

"I'm sorry, Ella."

"I screamed at the nurses, and I fought them. I got away from them once, and I raced all over the emergency room, throwing back every curtain, searching for him. It didn't take them long to catch me. They sedated me. By the time I woke up, Victor was dead. My brother was gone."

"I can't even imagine how I would have felt."

I scoffed. "Angry. I was so angry. And guilty. All I had were a few cuts and bruises, three hairline fractures to my left arm, and a concussion." Not only had I survived when the rest of my family didn't, but I walked away with little more than a scratch. "And then, I took it out on all the wrong people—not that I had a lot of choices."

"Who?" he asked, tracing idle circles along my shoulder.

"My foster families. I went through three in three years— between arguing with them constantly and running away, they just hadn't signed up for that, you know?"

"And then what happened?" he asked, though, he already knew how this story ended.

"My last foster family was different, or maybe I was different, less standoffish? My foster mom, her name was Alice, she'd sit and talk to me, sometimes for hours. She'd tell me about her childhood, her grandparents' farm, her annoyingly perfect older sister. She never bugged me to talk, but she made me feel like I could, if I wanted to. I guess I wasn't much of a conversationalist, even back then," I said, trying to lighten the heavy mood I'd brought down around us.

I should have stopped.

This was stupid.

What difference did it make if Leo knew my life story when he wouldn't be in my life for much longer?

"Go on, *gattina,*" he urged, and I did, whether out of obedience or some ridiculous need, I couldn't say.

The truth probably laid somewhere in between.

"My last foster father seemed nice," I said, shrugging, not sure how else to describe him. "He wasn't around nearly as much as Alice, but he always asked me about school and whether I'd made any friends, that kind of thing.

"He came home from work late the evening of my last exam before summer break, and he told me he was taking me out for ice cream to celebrate. He'd never taken me out before, but he'd dropped me off at a friend's house to study. I didn't think anything of being alone with him." And it seemed, that was where my need for Leo to know me ended. None of the words about what happened after came. They stayed firmly lodged behind the lump that had formed at the back of my throat.

"He took you to Avalone's. To pay his debt," Leo concluded.

I nodded, ignoring the way my eyes started to sting. "Apparently, he'd had a gambling problem for a long time. Mortgaged the house, spent all of his and Alice's savings, borrowed money from dangerous people. He said explaining to Alice that I ran away was easier than explaining why men were coming to break his legs. And now, you know my life story," I said, shrugging against him like it was no big deal.

"Well, not the whole story, but it's a start. *Grazie, gattina.*"

I didn't know what to say to that, so I did what I did best and said nothing.

Leo leaned up long enough to kiss me then dropped his head back onto the ground.

"Being a dumbass is what got me caught," he confessed to the sky above us. "I was seventeen, which meant I basically thought I was invincible. I should have been sticking with Dom and our men, but I didn't need them. Hell, I was a *Luca*. I figured I could make any man quake in his boots. It turned out I couldn't."

It wasn't supposed to be you, I cried silently, knowing I could never say it aloud.

"It was one hell of a way to figure out I had an overinflated ego." Leo laughed, but I could feel the cracks that ran through it.

They were the fissures that never went away no matter how much time passed.

What happened to Leo was the kind of thing that left its scars permanently, and not just on the flesh.

"What happened after?" I asked.

The scars would never fade, but Leo seemed to have made peace with his past, and I couldn't help but wonder how he'd done it.

"A quick stay at the hospital, and then I was whisked off to the Luca Family safe house while my family killed the men who did it, Sokolov men." He spat the name out like it was something vile, making me wish I could wrap the blood in my veins in a dark shroud and keep it hidden forever. "They killed every one of them," he said with warring ripples of satisfaction and regret in his voice.

Maybe not every one.

"What's the 'Luca Family safe house'?" I asked.

Leo laughed again. "Well, if you're picturing a run-down cabin in the middle of the woods, it's not quite that. It's just what my mother called it. The 'safe house' is actually a private Caribbean island. And come to think of it, that's not a bad idea, *gattina,*" he said as his fingers began to branch out further, traveling down my arm and back up, and around to the upper swell of my breast.

"What isn't a bad idea?" I tilted my head to the right.

"There are no phones on the island and very few doors," he said, waggling his brows.

Something clenched painfully in my chest even as I forced an outward smile.

There would be no private Caribbean island getaways for me and Leo.

I leaned up on my elbow to look at him. "If we hadn't met, what would you be doing right now?" I asked, maybe wanting a snapshot of what his life had been like before, what it would be like *after*.

"The truth?" Leo met my gaze like he was trying to gauge my response.

I nodded.

"Dante and I probably would have had a nameless woman or two between us. Meaningless sex."

"And this isn't meaningless?" I said, nodding to where our bodies still touched.

It wasn't meaningless to me, but that was different.

Leo had been the first man I'd ever chosen on my own.

"No, Ella. Fuck, I don't know what to call it, but it sure as hell isn't meaningless, which, to tell you the truth, is fucking insane. I don't know what secrets you've got in your head. For all I know, you've got enough firepower in there to annihilate everything that's ever been important to me. And yet, whatever this is between us, I've never…"

For once, Leo was at a loss for words.

But I didn't need him to continue.

I understood him perfectly.

"Me neither," I said as my heart grew warmer.

It was selfish of me to want to matter to a man I couldn't possibly keep, but I wanted it nonetheless.

I reveled in it, basked in it like it was sunshine.

All the while, I pretended that the things I knew couldn't touch him.

Chapter Twenty-Two

Leo

I'd never been much of a morning person.

Today was an exception.

The woman in my bed had wriggled while she slept, kicking off the covers in the process.

Her long, dark lashes fanned across her cheeks and her lips were slightly parted. One arm stretched above her head while the other laid across her slim body, her hand resting in the concave dip of her abdomen. Her breasts rose with every deep rhythmic breath, and her thighs had drifted apart enough to leave me starving for the deep pink folds between them.

Fuck sunrises. *This* was a sight to behold.

After an hour of waiting for Sleeping Beauty to wake up, though, I was ready to go back to sunrises.

Not once had they given me a hard-on so painful, I had to start worrying about permanent damage.

It was time for Prince Blue Balls to wake the slumbering princess—though I had something much better in mind than a kiss.

I leaned over from the end of the bed, slowly sliding my hands up her thighs.

Ella was like silk, soft and pliant beneath my fingers… for a whole second and a half.

Then her body went rigid as her eyes flew open.

In hindsight, it probably wasn't the best thought-out plan I'd ever had, but I was committed now.

"*Buongiorno, gattina,*" I said while pushing her thighs open.

I leaned in closer, breathing her in. The familiar musk filled my nose, making my mouth water.

"What are you doing?" Her eyes quickly lost the cloudy vestiges of sleep, and her body began to relax beneath my hands.

I thought what I was doing was kind of clear, but I spread her thighs further and slid my tongue along her slit for good measure.

Her hands gripped the sheets, and she let out a quiet moan.

"All up to speed?" I flashed her a wicked grin then returned to the task at hand, teasing her clit with featherlight flicks of my tongue until her hips began to writhe beneath me.

It was crazy that every touch, every taste of her made me want to possess her more—her body, her mind, her soul.

I covered her clit with my lips and sucked her into my mouth like I could suckle the answer out of her.

Ella writhed against me.

Her moans grew louder as she abandoned her white-knuckled hold on the sheets and reached for me as best as she could, grazing her fingertips along my shoulders and up the back of my neck.

I wanted her legs open wider, stretched to the max, all of that tension circling the core of her, but I kept it reined in, gripping her silken thighs instead of pressing them further.

I lapped at her clit. Dragged my tongue along her slit. And when I suckled her clit back into my mouth, I slid a finger into her pussy, feeling the tight, slick walls of her sucking me in as her moans turned to cries.

Ella was dripping *wet*.

I'd already dropped a condom on the bed beside me.

With one last flick of my tongue on her clit, I leaned away, sheathed my cock, and climbed on top.

She wasn't the only one who was ready.

Her fingertips grazed along my sides as I gripped my cock and lined myself up to drive home.

Slow down, asshole, cried the conscience I'd come to loath over the past few days as I thrust in.

I jerked to a stop as her pussy gripped the head of my cock, then I made the necessary adjustments—which pretty much entailed gritting my teeth and clenching every muscle in my body.

I eased into her one slow inch at a time as her fingers traveled down my back. Halfway in, I withdrew then thrust again.

Even careful and controlled, she felt *incredible*.

On the next thrust, she wrapped her legs around my hips, and her fingernails dug in just a little as she grazed back up on either side of my spine, sending a tingling sensation back down it.

It did nothing for my self-control when she leaned up and her lips kissed a trail down my neck to my pecs.

I tried to ignore the urge to plunge deeper. To fuck harder.

Thrust after thrust, her moans grew louder.

Her lips and hands covered every inch of my body she could reach.

Ella was like fire, igniting everywhere she touched.

It was a wonder I didn't go up in flames.

I could see the fine sheen of sweat on her brow as she threw her head back against the pillow. Her eyes closed, her lips parted; she was unequivocally the most beautiful woman I'd ever seen.

"Leo..." My name fell from her lips like a plea as her fingers dug into my shoulders.

"Come for me, *gattina.*" It came out rough through my gritted teeth, more like a command than an invitation, but if I let go, I was done for.

Ella barely had time to nod once before her back arched off the bed. She cried out as her pussy spasmed around my cock and sent me headlong over the edge after her. One final thrust, and I stilled deep inside her, jaw clenched tight as wave upon wave of my orgasm overtook me.

It was a long time before I slipped out of her, reluctant to leave the warm sheath of her body, but eventually, I ditched the condom and flopped down beside her.

"I think you broke me," she said, wincing as she stretched out her long legs.

Not even close, the frustrated little voice in the back of my mind bitched.

I smacked him back into the hole he'd climbed out of.

I'd fucked her twice more last night before we'd collapsed in sweaty, sated bliss, but the truth was, I'd never taken it so easy, never been so careful in my whole life.

When our breathing had returned to something that resembled normal, Ella sat up, and I followed her up.

Her gaze darted around the room from one garment bag to the next.

I'd run them all up here while Sleeping Beauty slept.

It had been a pathetic attempt at distraction at the time, but now I was holding my breath, waiting to see how she'd respond—and didn't that prove just how seriously the girl was messing with my head.

The way she wriggled back further on the bed and went three shades paler wasn't quite the response I'd been anticipating.

Didn't women love clothes, and shopping, and shit? If not, I'd apparently missed that memo.

"They're yours, Ella," I said because all my dumbass brain could come up with was that she thought I'd bought them for someone else.

"Mine?" Her voice sounded strangled. "I… I didn't order those."

"I had a personal shopper drop them off. I wasn't sure if crowded stores were really your thing."

No smile. Maybe she didn't hear me?

Ella sidled back even further, eyeing the nearest garment bag with silver writing on the top left corner like it was a nest of vipers, ready to strike at any second.

"What's the matter, *gattina?*" I glanced at the bags. There were no venomous heads sticking out.

She licked her lips, still staring. "Why do you want me to dress up?"

"Fuck, no, that's not what I meant. They're just clothes." I held my hands up.

"No strings attached."

She didn't move, but she exhaled lightly. "Thank you, Leo, but I don't need all this," she said, still eyeing the bags.

"Well, maybe not," I said, reaching for the nearest garment bag, "but if you don't wear them, I'm going to have to." I unzipped the bag, revealing a pale yellow dress inside. "And I've been told I might not be able to pull them off, if you can believe it?" I waggled my eyebrows.

Despite her trepidation, she giggled. "I think you'd look great in it," she teased, surprising me.

I held up the dress—garment bag and all—in front of my bare chest and nodded decisively. "That's what I said." I dropped the garment bag back down and kissed her. "Want to try something on?"

She stared at the discarded bag, chewing on her bottom lip.

"Ella, you can say 'no' if you don't want to. I'm not going to punish you for it."

It didn't take a rocket scientist to figure out that was why she had a hard time with yes-no answers.

She bit her lip harder.

I should have let it go, and yet, it felt like she needed this—not that anyone would ever hold me up as the poster boy for good mental health. But weren't we all just one step away from a straitjacket and private accommodations in a padded room?

"No, thank you, Leo," she said, her whole body cringing, her wide feline eyes fixed on mine.

It was a simple thing—a two-letter word, but I could only imagine the kind of courage it had taken for her to force it out.

I hopped out of bed and didn't mind at all the way her gaze followed my body across the room to the last of the packages I'd carried up.

I had a feeling she'd be far more impressed with these.

"I also figured we needed to get more stuff for the duck, so…" I held out two oversized shopping bags, one filled with duck diapers, the other with duck food.

Ella sat up more and wriggled closer, her trepidation seemingly forgotten, replaced with a smile that made me think of sunshine and rainbows.

And as if he was aware he'd become the topic of conversation, the duck waddled out of the bathroom—clad in a fresh diaper I'd managed to wrangle onto him all by myself, thank you very much.

"You changed him?" Ella's eyes widened, suddenly brighter with a sheen of tears, but the smile was still firmly in place. Talk about a girl who was easy to please—and what man in his right mind would complain about that?

"I told you," I said, pointing my thumbs at my chest, "Duck Whisperer."

"Thank you," she said so sweetly then hopped out of bed and wrapped her arms around me, still naked.

I tried to think about baseball—I really did—but a naked Ella in my arms just wasn't conducive to anything but one chain of thought.

"Let's go, lover boy," Dante called through the door three seconds before he started banging on it. "Duty calls."

I groaned, which was an improvement over the string of expletives that came to mind—most of which centered around creative euphemisms for my brother.

I pulled Ella closer, reluctant to relinquish the heat of her bare breasts against my chest. It didn't help that my cock had decided that, next to the tight, slick heat of her pussy, pressed against her abdomen was pretty much its favorite place to be.

Unfortunately, Leo junior, like me, had little say in the matter at the moment.

"Apparently, duty calls, *gattina,*" I said, leaning away before I couldn't. "I have work to do, and then I'm going to grab your stuff from the hotel, but I'll be back as soon as I can."

I didn't bother to hide the way my eyes grazed over her from head to toe, imagining all I could do with that nimble flesh when I got back.

Her brow furrowed in consternation. "Are you sure it's safe to go there?"

I shrugged. "Dante's coming along. If we run into any trouble, I'll just use him as a human shield."

Her lips turned up in a nervous smile. "I… I got the feeling he's kind of good at lectures. If you run into trouble, you could just have him talk them to death."

I barked out a laugh, caught completely off guard.

It seemed my kitten's sense of humor was making its way to the surface.

It was completely egotistical of me to think I'd had anything to do with that, but I was okay with being an egotistical son of a bitch.

Her smile grew, but she tried to hide it against my chest as she pressed her lips to my pec, just above my nipple.

She lingered long enough I was about ready to tell all responsibilities outside this room to go screw themselves, but then she turned and started to rummage through the sheets on the bed until she'd found her shirt.

I fought the urge to laugh this time.

All these new clothes, and she wasn't going to wear any of them, was she?

I grabbed my own clothes from the closet and dressed as quickly as a man with a fresh hard-on could.

"Feel free to venture downstairs if you want," I said when I'd completed the task with relatively little damage. "It's just family down there at the moment."

Ella nodded.

I had a feeling the clothes and the girl would be right where I'd left them when I returned.

Chapter Twenty-Three

Ella

"Leo offered to watch over me, that's how we first met," Fallon explained as she laid Maria down on the sofa between us in Leo's sitting room. The infant seemed to be content blowing milk bubbles, having just finished eating. "Dom was worried about this asshole, Tony Nova, and I was worried I'd strangle Dom if he tried to keep me from working," she said as she buttoned her shirt. "I'm a veterinarian, by the way. So, Leo offered to play bodyguard, which kind of made him my favorite person in the whole world. Following me around a five-room office all day had to be the most boring thing the poor guy had ever done."

Maria flailed her arms around until one tiny hand brushed her lips, and she thrust the hand into her mouth.

"What's it like? Being a veterinarian, I mean." I could see how, perhaps, following a person around an office all day could get boring, but working with animals sounded kind of amazing. Maybe that was because I'd spent my childhood around animals on my parents' small farm.

Fallon's lips turned up in one of those smiles of real contentment. "Overall, it's awesome. The cliché's true, though. It can be frustrating at times working with patients who can't tell me what's wrong, not in words, anyway. But at the end of the day, I always get to go home knowing I helped. I really made a difference, you know?"

I nodded, though my agreement was entirely theoretical.

I hadn't done anything in my life thus far that made a difference.

Fallon was married with a child and had a satisfying career. The things I'd done would never be engraved on a plaque on the wall.

I kind of felt small sitting next to her.

Signor Berlusconi's vicious fingers dug into my scalp, yanking my head from between his muscled thighs by the hair at the back of my head.

"Is it true you can't understand me, whore?" the dark-haired thirty-something man asked in Italian, meeting my gaze, searching for signs of understanding on my face.

I kept my expression blank, a perfect mask of incomprehension.

"Answer me," he barked in Italian, then he slapped me so hard, black spots danced across my vision.

He laughed, and the men around him joined in, though his eyes never left mine. "I'm going to ram my dick so far up your ass, you'll taste me when I come," he continued in Italian, still testing me. "Nice and dry, just the way you like it."

I tamped down the urge to shudder.

I commanded my eyes to remain dry.

No emotion. No understanding.

"You're fucking perfect, aren't you, whore?" he asked in English before shoving himself back into my mouth. "My bastard of a father will have no idea what hit him when I come at him," he told his companions in Italian while I gagged and listened, gathering secrets.

Corrupted Protector

That night was the epitome of the difference I'd made in my life.

I was a whore with a head full of secrets. Secrets that would make Leo and his family sick.

Maria's hand slipped from her lips, and she let out a sound that was somewhere between a coo and a whine before finding it again and thrusting it back into her mouth.

"You can hold her if you want," Fallon said, nodding to Maria.

I hadn't taken my eyes off Maria since Fallon laid her down, I realized. But suddenly, the infant looked like she'd been crafted from the most delicate glass known to man.

I shook my head. "I've never…"

"It's easy," Fallon persisted. "That is, unless it's three in the morning, and you've been holding her so long it feels like your arms are going to fall off. For such a tiny thing, she sure seems to weigh a lot after a while." All the time she talked, she was busy slipping her hands beneath her daughter and scooping her up into her arms. "Here," she said, moving in front of me and leaning forward.

Trapped, I tried to arrange my arms in the way I'd seen both her and Leo hold Maria, and Fallon placed the baby in them, showing me how to keep her head supported.

"She's so small," I said, kind of awestruck. At least, I think I said it out loud. She was warm and tiny, and she smelled like baby powder and fresh, sweet milk. A perfect, tiny human in *my* arms. "*Signore* had a baby," I blurted out. "Even from the other end of the house, I could hear him sometimes. I never saw him, though." I stroked a finger along Maria's hand. Her fingers curled in then stretched out again as her lips parted in a yawn.

"You're talking about Fiorenzo Avalone?" Fallon clarified.

204

I nodded.

"Why do you call him that?" Fallon held up her hands and made air quotes. "'*Signore*'."

I hadn't always.

Once upon a time, I'd been stubborn and defiant.

I'd screamed, and I'd fought, but I never won.

Well, except I almost did one day.

The day he'd taken my virginity. How I'd managed to get a hand loose, I couldn't say, but I'd raked it down his face so hard and so deep, his blood trickled off his chin and onto my naked body.

I could still feel remnants of the feral thrill that had run through me. I'd wanted nothing more than to do it again and again until there was no blood left in him.

In the end, though, it hadn't been worth it.

He'd made me bleed far worse.

"It's what I was expected to call him," I said, thrusting the memory far back in my mind. It seemed like a terrible thing to think about with an innocent child in my arms.

"Prick!" Fallon hissed.

My heart skipped a beat as my gaze shot around the room, half-expecting him to materialize out of thin air.

"Sorry," Fallon said, laying a hand on mine, "but it's true. And you can call him anything you want now, Ella. I know Leo, and I know the rest of the Lucas. Fiorenzo Avalone will never lay a hand on you ever again. They'll go to hell and back for the people they care about, so taking out one slimy bastard is nothing."

Nobody was going to hell for me.

They didn't understand what *Signore* was capable of.

A long time had passed, but the memory of what he did to people who tried to help me had been seared into my brain.

The blood. The ear-piercing screams. The maimed and broken heap of flesh and bones at my feet. He'd left the decimated carcass of my would-be savior with me for two days as a reminder, but *Signore* had failed. The part of me that cared what he did to the man had died in that room.

"Ella?" Fallon's hand still rested on mine, and she squeezed gently.

I stared at Maria as her eyes fluttered closed. So perfect, untouched by all the vileness beyond the walls of her home. And Leo? My mind tried to superimpose his image on the remnants of the man who'd tried to help me, but my stomach roiled and something clenched painfully in my chest even as I forced an outward smile.

"Thank you," I said, but I didn't mean it.

I wanted to curse her, not thank her. And Leo and Brute and everyone else who had played a role in reviving the part of me I'd long thought was dead.

They'd made me care.

And damn it all to hell, I cursed silently, because I could think of only one way to keep them safe.

Chapter Twenty-Four

Leo

Something wasn't right.

Looking around, there was nothing out of the ordinary.

The same mix of average and high-end cars in the lot, the same flickering light at the opposite end of the parking garage, the same muted smells of concrete and humid air.

I shook it off and headed for the elevator while Dante and Marco waited for me in the Escalade.

It was probably just remnants of the last time I'd been here, which explained why the sense of wrongness clung to me, prickling at the back of my neck as the elevator glided up to the top floor and opened to an empty hallway.

No longer the cocky kid, I pulled out my Glock as I opened the hotel suite door.

Standing in front of the living room sofa was a black-haired burly goon with a white jagged scar across his neck and arms the size of soccer balls. Seriously, someone could cut them off and have a good old-fashioned game of European football with them.

"I'm not usually opposed to meeting strangers in my hotel room, but you're not really my type, *amico*," I said, my gun aimed between the soccer balls, at the guy's chest.

He cracked a smile. "Then I guess that means we can skip the foreplay and get down to business."

Finally! A goon with a sense of humor. They usually just stared straight-faced with their barrel chests thrust out, trying to look intimidating. Hell, even if he was here to kill me, this guy was a breath of fresh air.

"You show me yours, I'll show you mine?" I quipped because, really, I had no clue what he was doing here.

If he'd come to try to collect Ella, he was a little late. Maybe someone needed to tell him that slow and steady didn't always win the race.

"You know why I'm here, *Signor* Luca. *Signor* Avalone wants Ella, and he said if you were a wise man, you'd hand her back gladly."

"You see, that's your first mistake," I said, leaning against the doorjamb. "I told one of your comrades—right before I killed him—that I was fairly well-known as a dumbass. So, 'wise man' isn't really my thing." I shrugged.

"You think she's a poor, innocent victim?" he asked, cocking an eyebrow. "Are you certain about that?"

I tightened my grip on my Glock.

"She told you *Signor* Avalone abused her? Beat her, even? That he forced her to offer herself up to the men he chose?"

"Let me guess: You're going to tell me Avalone was the epitome of gentlemanly behavior?"

The goon laughed. "*Signor* Avalone never forced the girl to do anything she didn't want to do. Not that it's for me to judge, but in my opinion, he always treated her more than fairly."

It seemed the goon and I put what was *fair* at grossly different ends of the good-behavior spectrum. "She wears his scars, and scars don't lie," I said, shrugging.

He scoffed. "The scars weren't *Signor* Avalone's work. He rescued her from her monster of a foster father—killed him for what he did to the girl. She was grateful enough she chose to work for *Signor* Avalone."

"Work for him?" I cocked an eyebrow, hiding a sneer of disgust. "Is that what you crazy kids are calling it these days?"

"Not all men are fortunate enough to have powerful alliances," he said, shrugging. "Some men must rely on their cunning and wit. Ella was useful in spreading lies and collecting secrets, and she loved every second of it."

"If she loved it so much, then why the fuck did she leave?" I was running out of patience.

"Did she really 'leave', *Signor* Luca? Or has she just decided to venture out on her own? Think about it—she's become an expert at what she does, and her business partner—*Signor* Avalone—is all that stands in the way of her reaping the benefits entirely for herself. If she feeds you a sob story, and you come after him… well, that solves her little problem now, doesn't it?"

"You're lying." I clenched my jaw.

Pull the trigger.

But it wasn't the goon with a future in stand-up that I wanted to kill.

It was Avalone.

"*Signor* Avalone didn't send me to threaten or harm you, *Signor* Luca."

"Well, that's good to know. Otherwise, I'd be quaking in my boots, really," I said, trying not to laugh.

"He instructed me to come to reason with you. Why would he do that if there was no truth to what I'm saying?"

"I can think of a reason or two." It was kind of obvious, wasn't it? "Avalone's smart—smart enough to know there's no chance he'll ever make it through the Lucas' front door, and no fucking way he'd make it off our property with her." The night the Novas attacked our home had taken more than my mother from us. It took our deep-seated arrogance, our belief that we were untouchable. It was a mistake we'd never make again. The Lucas had gone to great lengths to make our home an impenetrable fortress. "All he can do is send you to try to peddle his bullshit, but I'm afraid I'm not buying."

The goon looked about as irritated as I felt, but to his credit, he kept it under wraps. "All *Signor* Avalone is asking is that when you return to her—as I'm sure you will—you ask her two things."

I cocked an eyebrow, waiting, wondering what bullshit he was going to spout off next.

"Ask Ella what she knows about your... tragic past, *Signor* Luca, and while you're at it, ask her how *Signor* Avalone happened to know you'd be here at this hotel, not just today, but right now."

I barked out a forced laugh. It hadn't escaped my notice that he couldn't possibly have guessed when I'd show up here. "I'll be sure to do that just as soon as hell freezes over or unicorns fly out of your ass." Because who the hell wouldn't love to see a unicorn?

"Then I suppose we have nothing further to discuss," he said, standing up straighter as his gaze flicked from the gun in my hand to the doorway behind me.

"Wondering if you're going to leave here with more holes than you came with?"

His hand had been slowly working its way to his jacket, but he paused. He looked down at himself then back at me, cracking another smile. "To tell you the truth, I'm a little more concerned about the suit."

Admittedly, for a goon, it *was* a nice suit.

While it went against the grain to let the guy walk out of here, killing him served no purpose.

"Get out of my hotel room," I said, taking a step to the side to let him pass. "And tell Avalone that the next time one of his goons shows up unannounced, I'll turn him into a human sieve."

"Creative," he said, wiping his hand across his mouth to cover the smile.

"What can I say? I've always had a flair for inventive gastronomy."

The goon stepped past me into the hall and pressed the button for the elevator.

Taut seconds passed before the door opened, revealing a half dozen goons with guns standing inside. The soccer-ball goon stepped on, shifting the men and revealing the man at their center.

It wasn't a man; it was a monster in a navy blue three-piece suit. A beating, whipping, raping, sadistic monster. The son of a bitch looked like an ordinary, kempt man in his early sixties. More dark hair than gray, just a few deep-set wrinkles around his eyes and mouth.

Life had treated him kindly. Too kindly.

"Avalone," I growled, the sound rumbling deep in my chest.

Avalone smiled at me, and I could see the flames of hell in his dark, dead eyes.

My finger vibrated against the trigger of my gun.

One shot, and the son of a bitch would be dead.

Gone.

Never able to touch her ever again.

But it was a trap, a *game*.

Every man on the elevator had a gun in his hand, ready to fill me with bullets.

Who cares? Kill him, a reckless voice seethed in my head.

All my blood rushed to my finger sitting atop the trigger.

There was nothing saying I'd hit my mark before I wound up bleeding like a stuck pig on the floor.

To protect Ella, I had to stay alive, even if it meant letting Avalone walk away.

"Tell Ella I hope to see her soon, Leo," Avalone said, nodding to me before turning to the goon with the soccer ball arms. "Time to go, Riccardo," he said and nodded toward the panel on the elevator door.

Three seconds later, the elevator door slid shut.

My insides shook with the potent urge to go after him, to throw caution to the wind and chase him all the way to hell.

But I'd been reckless once, and I'd paid for it.

I wouldn't make the same mistake twice.

I'd rather make a new one.

I holstered my Glock, called for the service elevator, and did my damnedest to tamp down the raving lunatic who wanted to set fire to the whole building just to watch Avalone burn.

One day soon, I was sending Avalone to hell where a nice bed of flames awaited him.

***

Dante was waiting outside the elevator when I reached the parking level.

He had his arms crossed over his chest, his jaw clenched tight. "What the hell were you doing up there?" he snapped the moment I stepped out.

I'd gotten myself under wraps on my way down.

That didn't mean I had an endless supply of self-control at the moment.

I took a deep, calming breath and arranged my face into a mask of cool waters. I peered past Dante for a glimpse outside as we started walking toward the car, Ella's satchel slung over my shoulder. "I don't see any snow, but is it Christmas already?"

"What?"

"You look as impatient as you did the Christmas that Dom broke his arm, and we had to wait to open presents until he got back from the hospital."

"Ha! If I recall, it was you who was so impatient, you convinced our baby sister to sneak in and start opening them."

"Not *opening* them, just *inspecting* them," I corrected him, "and that was just good recon, *fratello.*"

"All right," Dante said, rolling his eyes. "Do you want to tell me what 'recon' was going on up there?" he said, nodding back at the elevator.

"No recon. I was just having a chat with Avalone and one of his men."

Dante stopped walking. "What?"

Underneath cool and calm waters always lurked sharks.

No matter how pissed I was, it was always so much fun to throw him for a loop.

I shrugged and kept walking.

Dante pulled out his gun and phone.

I shook my head. "Even if he's got men waiting outside, the Escalade's bulletproof. But I didn't get the feeling he came here to kill me. He just wanted to fuck with me." *Or to be here to snatch Ella if she'd come with me.*

Avalone wasn't going to risk what would come at him if he killed a Luca when the prize he was after was still out of his reach.

"His man, though, tried to convince me Ella had been working for Avalone of her own free will all this time. According to him, she only left because she wants to take him out and keep the secrets and lies 'business' all to herself," I said.

We'd reached the Escalade.

Marco opened the rear passenger door, and I slid in smoothly, leaving Dante to process.

Dante got in a minute later. "That's one hell of a story, but it's bullshit."

"*Sì,* it has to be, but…"

"But, what?"

"He said something I'm having a hard time figuring out," I said as Marco got in the driver's seat and revved the engine.

"And that would be…?" Dante prompted.

"He told me to ask Ella how Avalone knew I'd be at the hotel today. I mean, it's possible the guy had been camping out there since Ella and I left, but that doesn't sit right."

I kept my eyes open, watching out the windows as Marco pulled out of the lot and onto the street.

"So, you're wondering who the hell could have tipped him off and whether Ella had anything to do with it?" Dante asked, sitting back in his seat as we drove away unscathed.

My gut said she had no part in it, but I couldn't say the possibility hadn't crossed my mind. I told her I'd be swinging by the hotel today.

"But what would be the point? I don't see what she'd have to gain by forcing a confrontation between Avalone and me. If she wanted him dead, then it wasn't a smart move on her end to let me walk in unprepared." I kept my eyes out the window as we drove past sky-high buildings.

"Speaking of which, you don't look any worse for wear. Do we have any dead bodies to clean up in the penthouse suite?"

"No bodies, no blood," I said a little smugly.

Dante's expression seemed to flicker back and forth between impressed and disappointed. "How'd you manage that?"

"Would you believe I managed it with my irresistible personality?" I said, donning my most charming smile.

"No, I wouldn't," he said flatly, though the corners of his lips quivered as he fought a smile.

I shrugged. "The guy really just seemed to want to peddle Avalone's bullshit."

Dante was silent for a moment, then he nodded. "*Bene*," he said, reaching for two bottles of *Peroni Nastro Azzurro* from the refrigerated console and handed me one.

"*Bene?*" I hadn't realized Dante was such a fan of bullshit peddlers.

"It means Avalone's not confident he can take her back by force. But we still have to figure out who tipped him off."

"I'll talk to Ella."

I wanted to trust my gut, but there was no denying my cock had spent a fair amount of time in charge since I'd met her.

Dante nodded. "I'll have Moore get us phone records for the house and for all our men at the warehouses today."

The same warehouse where we'd spent two hours overseeing the latest shipment.

With nothing more I could do for the time being, I dropped my head back onto the leather headrest and closed my eyes.

Ella and I hadn't done much sleeping last night—not that I was complaining.

"By the way," Dante began just as I'd started to drift off. "While you were busy making friends with Avalone's lackey, we heard back from Douglas about the Russian that you and Brute… ran into."

The tendrils of sleep that had been trying to pull me under vanished as fresh adrenaline pumped through my veins. "What about him? What did Moore say?"

Dante shook his head. "He's Bratva, but not *them*, Leo. He wasn't a Sokolov. I told you we killed every one of those motherfuckers."

My brother seemed to be under the impression that something about the Sokolovs scared me.

I'd never bothered to correct him. But fear had nothing to do with it.

I wanted revenge—vengeance that my family had sought on my behalf while I'd laid half-comatose on a sunny island.

I'd healed just fine, and I'd gotten on board the accept-the-things-you-cannot-change train. But what I wouldn't give to get my hands on one of the Sokolovs now.

"But if he's not a Sokolov, then what the fuck was he doing tailing me?" I knitted a brow.

"I don't know for sure, but I still think it has something to do with Ella. The timing's just too coincidental, *sì?*"

The possibility didn't make sense before, but it was starting to now.

"If she's got information on them, they might not be too happy with that," I mused, scrubbing my fingers through my hair.

Dante chuckled. "I sure hope she's worth it, *fratello*," he said, waggling his brows. "Because now we've got the Bratva to worry about, too."

"Wouldn't you like to know." I smiled then dropped my head back and closed my eyes.

I had a feeling the drive home was all the rest I was going to get for a while.

Chapter Twenty-Five

Ella

Our clothes were drenched.

The en suite floor was soaked.

I hung up the phone Brute had given me; he'd called three times just to check up on me.

This time, Brute had insisted I put him on speakerphone, laughing with me and Fallon as Duck did his best to soak the bathroom from floor to ceiling.

The moment the doorknob turned, Duck waddle-flew out of the bathroom with single-minded determination.

"Duck!" I cried as the door swung open.

Leo dropped into a crouch, reaching for his gun at the same time Duck plowed into his leg.

Fallon burst out laughing as Leo got his hands around Duck and snagged him up before he could circumvent his obstacle and make a beeline out of the room.

"Sorry, I didn't mean that kind of 'duck'," I said, my lips pressed into a flat line, trying not to smile.

"Yeah, I got that," Leo said with a grin as he got back to his feet and shut the door.

"It's good to know… your reflexes are as fast as ever," Fallon choked out.

It looked like she might have been trying to get her laughter under control, but she was failing miserably, and apparently, laughter was contagious.

I covered my mouth and turned away.

My eyes stung with tears in the effort to swallow it back, but after a moment, I'd composed myself enough to turn back around.

"When Dominic came to get Maria, Duck seemed to remember there was more house to explore. I tried filling the bathtub for him, but…" I nodded down at the wet clothes sticking to my body as evidence of Duck's discontent, but Leo's gaze was already there.

"You two kind of look like you've been in a wet T-shirt contest," Leo commented, his eyes fixed on my breasts, poorly covered by the now-transparent material.

Fallon's clothing had fared a little better.

While it clung to her body, her dark burgundy shirt had maintained its opacity. She was a little curvier than me—she'd just given birth a month ago—but she was no less attractive than any of the women I'd been with.

"If you're open to suggestions for the next event," Leo said, waggling his brows and wearing a lascivious grin, "can I recommend Jell-O wrestling?"

Fallon scoffed. "Oh, yeah, I bet Dom would be real impressed to hear about that."

Leo shrugged. "Hey, what happens in the Jell-O pool stays in the Jell-O pool."

Fallon shook her head dramatically while she reached for a towel. "You're going to have to get your head out of the gutter one of these days, Leo."

"Why? It's so much fun down here," Leo quipped as he placed Duck back down on the ground and placated him with a handful of treats.

Fallon shook her head while she laughed. With her hair no longer dripping, she dried off her feet then wrapped the towel around her and made her way carefully out of the wet bathroom to the bedroom's door. "Have fun playing in the gutter," she said, waggling her fingers in a wave at Leo then winking at me before she disappeared out into the hallway.

Leo and I were alone again.

If there'd been sexual tension sparking in the room a moment ago, it was going off like fireworks now.

But Leo's body language was all wrong, his shoulders tense, his jaw set in a hard line.

Old fears bubbled to the surface.

What did I do wrong?

What does he know?

How do I fix it?

And inevitably, *how much is it going to hurt?*

Like too many times before, no answers came to me.

I dug my teeth into my bottom lip and stared at the floor until Leo tilted my chin up.

"I need to ask you something, and I need you to be honest with me," he said, running his fingers along my lower lip until I stopped biting it. "Have you been in contact with Avalone or any of his men?"

My heart started to pound as my lungs struggled to draw a full breath. I tried. Faster and faster.

I told you this was a bad idea, the coward inside me gloated. *He's coming.*

I glanced at the door, expecting it to swing open any second.

"No, Leo, I haven't," I clipped.

"Ella, are you certain?" he asked, meeting my gaze, staring intently into my eyes.

I had to swallow back the fear climbing up my throat. It was like a scream, scraping and clawing its way up.

"Yes," I said, trying to force my breathing under control. "He's here?" I glanced at the door again, still waiting for it to fly open.

"What?" His brow furrowed. "No, *gattina.* No, of course not."

I hated the way the coward sighed in my head and my shoulders sagged with relief.

"I just needed to be sure, that's all," he said, though he remained still like he had more to say.

"What is it?" I asked when the silence had grown painful to my ears.

It had never done that before.

Leo bit his bottom lip—not something I'd seen him do. "Do you know anything about my past, Ella?"

My heart, only just slowing to a beat that resembled normal, picked up its pace.

I could feel his eyes boring into mine, and like an idiot, I looked away as if that could keep him from seeing the truth.

"What haven't you told me?" He leaned away just a little as he spoke.

Don't do it, the coward cried.

But even if I had the nerve to refuse him, he deserved this, didn't he?

This small piece I could give him.

The knot in my stomach twisted painfully as I opened my mouth. "When the Sokolovs took you, it wasn't supposed to be you."

Leo was eerily still. I wasn't sure he was even breathing.

"What do you mean? Who was it supposed to be?" His voice was quiet.

There was a fist around the name in my head, clinging tight.

It felt like I had to pry each finger loose until it was finally free to slip down onto my tongue.

"Dominic," I whispered.

Leo didn't move. He didn't speak.

I could feel the warm brush of each breath against my cheek, but otherwise, he might have been a statue.

Seconds passed, and then minutes.

I'd never hated the silence so much.

"Leo?"

All at once, he came back to life. "All this time, I'd thought it was for nothing," he said, sitting down on the edge of the bed.

I stayed in place, not saying a word.

"You saw the report. All that... and for what?" He gestured around him. "There was never an answer—not a good one, not one that justified what those motherfuckers did."

I continued to watch him, his every movement.

"Now there's a reason." Leo nodded like the matter was finally settled for him. "What I went through meant Dominic didn't."

It was that simple for him. It brought him comfort to know his suffering meant his brother had been spared.

I hated that my respect—not just respect, but admiration—for him grew tenfold in that moment.

"How did you know, Ella?"

"You know how," I said. The lie tasted bitter in my mouth.

"I guess what I mean is who? Who did you overhear?"

"I don't know their names," I lied again.

In truth, I knew the name of the man who'd unknowingly offered up the secret while I'd hidden behind a tall weatherworn gravestone.

"This is your fault, you son of a bitch," the tall, dark shadow of a man had spat the words at a marble headstone half a dozen yards away. *"That kid didn't deserve what you sent at him, and I'm glad I killed you. I just wish I could do it again."* He'd slammed his fist into the headstone, and I'd held my breath, terrified he'd discover me at any moment. But he seemed thoroughly engrossed as he poured out half a bottle of whiskey on the grave. *"Here's to you, daddy dearest,"* he'd said, his voice rough with emotion for the first time. He downed the last sip from the bottle, smashed it on the headstone, then turned and walked away, leaving a dotted trail of blood in his wake from the wounds across his knuckles.

Leo was nodding again, but the expression on his face was conflicted. "If I hadn't asked, you would never have told me, would you?" He looked up at me, and while he didn't look angry, exactly, the emotion couldn't have been far from it.

The guilt grew.

It always did.

Guilt over the secrets in my head, over the blood that ran through my veins.

The heavy weight laid like lead in my stomach, but something else wrapped itself around it this time.

Something uncomfortable and hot that I hadn't been allowed to feel in a very long time.

"Do you think I want them?" I hissed, unable to stop myself.

"Want what, Ella?" Leo furrowed his brows together.

"All the things in my head." I lifted my hand, pointing upward. "You don't think I wish I could get rid of them? All of them?"

He startled, his eyes widening as if in surprise. "Do you know how much power—"

"Power?" I cried. "If you had no choice but to offer up your body over and over again, would you feel powerful, Leo?" The words spilled out, filled with venom that Leo didn't deserve, but for once, I couldn't stop them. "Would you not trade in every bit of that 'power' to have yourself back, to undo everything that was done to you, everything *you* did and won't ever forget." The uncomfortable heat had spread into my limbs, making them tremble.

"I'm sorry, *gattina*. I shouldn't have—" He put up his hands, palms facing me.

"I have spent years playing with secrets, Leo, balancing truths and half-truths and lies—what to hand over to *Signore* and what to hold back. Never—not once—have I felt powerful." I was breathing heavily, my chest retracting up and down.

Memories of all the times I'd gotten the balancing act wrong hit me like a sucker punch.

I plopped down on the edge of the bed, out of breath.

Tired.

Exhausted to the bone.

I'd been fighting against this moment.

Ever since Dante had said the Luca name, I'd been dreading it, burying it, but I had no fight left.

Leo deserved the truth, at least one of them.

A truth that had nearly cost his family dearly.

A truth that was all my fault.

"I knew about *Signore's* son's plan to take down his father for a long time," I confessed. I just didn't have the energy to hold it in anymore. *Signore* hadn't known Diego Berlusconi existed until Diego showed up at his doorstep a decade ago. When *Signore* sent his own son away, plans for revenge had kindled inside Diego's mind. Plans to murder his father and throw every family in New York into chaos. "I thought if Diego could do it, then I'd..."

"...then you'd be free," he finished the selfish words I couldn't say. "But how could you have known? Avalone wanted nothing to do with his son. He wouldn't have let you—"

"He didn't."

His brow furrowed.

"He gave me to *Signor* Belemonte. None of *Signore's* thugs knew what Diego looked like, so they thought nothing of the dark-haired stranger with *Signor* Belemonte."

"You're saying Harry Belemonte knew what Berlusconi was planning?"

"Yes, Leo, and so did I. I knew, and I wanted him to do it. But I was wrong, and your sister..." I trailed off.

Diego had kidnapped and nearly killed Leo's sister.

If I'd spoken up, if I'd told *Signore* my secret, Diego would never have gotten his hands on her.

It was only because the Costas and the Lucas had teamed up to rescue her that she hadn't died by Diego's hand.

Understanding had dawned in Leo's eyes.

I waited for the anger to follow.

Maybe, I even wanted it.

Maybe it's what I'd been after from the moment he'd walked into the room.

If I could paint a clear enough picture, I wouldn't have to find the will to leave to keep him safe.

He'd shove me out the front door all on his own.

"You couldn't have known," Leo finally said, shaking his head.

I turned my head away. "You're right. I didn't know who would suffer, but Leo, I didn't care." I whipped my head back to look at him. "You, your sister, the whole world. I didn't care. It was me or them, and I was done giving a damn about a world that didn't give a damn about me."

"And now?" he asked, meeting my gaze and leaving me with nowhere to hide.

"Now it's worse because I *do* care. I care about what happens to you. I care whether people like Fallon and Maria get hurt because of me."

Leo placed his hand over mine and squeezed.

I yanked it back and shot off the bed, backing away across the room.

"I don't want to care, damn it," I cried.

It felt like someone else had taken control of my vocal cords. Someone who was allowed to get angry. Someone who'd never been beaten for fighting back.

Someone who wasn't *broken*.

"And you think I do?" he said, his voice a quiet rumble I could barely hear over my pounding heartbeat. "It would have been so much easier to walk away, *gattina,* to not care what happened to you."

Leo stood up and moved toward me. "But I do care."

The way he moved, closer and closer, his gaze fixed on mine; the predatory light I'd never seen in his eyes before made it feel like he was stalking me.

I tried to stand my ground, I really did, but my feet moved of their own volition until my back pressed up against the wall.

"I care enough that I walked you right into my family's home, not giving a flying fuck what repercussions would come from it," he said as he placed his hands against the wall on either side of me.

He wasn't touching me, but I felt trapped nonetheless.

"It turns out that you knew about Dom's 'deal' with Belemonte. You knew that it wasn't supposed to be me the Russian fuckers took. Hell, you knew about Diego Berlusconi. You could have stopped the man who almost killed my sister." Leo leaned in closer until his lips were a hair's breadth from mine, but the predatory light still shone in his blue eyes. "And you know what?"

I opened my mouth to respond, but my throat felt like a desert, scorched and dry.

"I still don't give a flying fuck, Ella. Those people out there," he said, pointing toward the door, "they've been here for me my entire life. We have history. We have loyalty. Every one of them would take a bullet for me, and me for them. You should mean nothing to me in comparison to them, and yet, I'd take a bullet for you without a moment's hesitation whether I want to feel that way or not. So, I know exactly how it feels to not want to care and to have no fucking say in the matter."

His lips crushed mine, hard and demanding.

His body pressed against me, molding all my curves to his jacked frame.

I could feel it in the firm sweep of his tongue along the seam of my lips.

Leo wasn't asking, he was *commanding*.

This was not pure lust.

It was the lust for control that fueled him.

I waited for the familiar twist of fear in my stomach as I parted for him obediently and his tongue delved in.

I waited for the repulsion that would make bile rise in the back of my throat as he grinded his cock hard against my abdomen.

My veins only flooded with red-hot desire unlike anything I'd experienced before, even with Leo.

My lungs worked harder, mimicking his deep, ragged breaths.

Maybe I really was broken because the power I could feel pulsing in his veins didn't scare me.

It challenged me.

It *ignited* me.

It made me want to feel.

To fuck.

It made me want to *fight*.

To battle for control over me, over him, over anything, or maybe everything.

I dug my fingers into the back of his neck and pulled him closer.

For every millimeter he pushed against me, I pushed back until not a hair's breadth of space remained between us.

Leo grabbed my hips, and his fingers dug in as I sunk my fingernails into his shoulders. He tore his lips away and sunk his teeth into my neck as I dragged my nails down his arms and hooked my leg around his thighs.

So close, and yet I was painfully aware of every bit of fabric between us, every zipper and every button that separated us.

I wanted flesh.

I wanted *him*.

I leaned away despite the warning sound that rumbled in his throat.

Before I'd managed to unfasten the first button of his shirt, he had my wet shirt bunched in his hands.

With one hard jerk of his arms, the buttons flew free.

I grabbed hold of his shirt and mimicked him, destroying his shirt while baring the ripped planes of his chest.

My head swam, giddy with lust, the thrill of the battle, not one I was destined to lose this time.

I reached for the fly of his pants, but he thrust me back against the wall and had my skirt pooled at my feet so fast, I barely saw his hands move.

Leo paused, trying to look his fill.

I gave him all but three seconds.

I lunged for him, nipping at his bottom lip to draw his mouth open for me while I fumbled blindly with his fly. It didn't take long. His pants and boxer briefs hit the floor as our tongues battled. His cock pressed hard against my bare abdomen, leaking precum and making my skin slick.

I writhed against him, creating a ghost of the friction his body craved and making him groan with need.

But even as I won, I lost.

The sound of him against my lips sent fresh ripples of lava swirling low in my abdomen.

I dragged in breath, but the air was tainted by the battle, heavy with the musky scent of sex.

"What the fuck are you doing to me, *gattina*?" he whispered, his breath hot against my cheek.

Building you up and destroying you with every touch.

Punishing and worshipping you in equal measures, just as you've done to me from the moment I first saw you.

I would never say the words aloud, but I didn't have to.

Leo could see them; he could feel them in the sex-laden air between us because they were the same words he wasn't saying to me.

He shoved my thighs apart with his knee, forcing me open and slipping a hand between us.

The moment his finger slid inside me, he groaned. "You're so fucking wet." He pressed his forehead hard against mine.

"And you're as hard as steel," I whispered as I wrapped my hand around his cock.

I was delirious with lust, and so was he.

I gripped him harder, sliding down the long, thick length of his erection. He crooked his finger, stroking the ultrasensitive patch of flesh inside me.

The pressure was exquisite.

He withdrew his finger, and I stifled the whimper that tried to sneak out while he sheathed his cock, grabbed my ass, and lifted me.

The wall was cold against my heated back, the contrast sending goose bumps chasing across my flesh.

Leo settled me over the top of him, lining himself up. The tip of his cock teased my slit for just a second, and then there was no wall, no floor, no ceiling.

Nothing but the hard, thick length of him as he drove in, filling me until the tip of his cock kissed my cervix.

I wrapped my legs around his hips and used the wall at my back as leverage.

I wasn't a passive recipient in this game, this battle.

I sunk my fingernails into his shoulders as he kicked his hips and thrust in hard and deep. Over and over again, the head of his cock pounded against my cervix, the veiny skin of the length of his cock sliding in and out of my slick walls.

It felt like my world was just him, all of him propelling inside me.

Pain was just another facet of sex, and it twisted up inside me, spinning the coil at the core of me faster and faster.

My nails sunk in deeper.

He fucked me harder.

I dug my heel into the small of his back.

He nipped at my neck, leaving my flesh stinging sweetly.

Pain for pain, pleasure for pleasure.

We gave, and we took.

"I never wanted to care about you," I confessed as he drove my body higher.

"I never wanted a stranger full of secrets in my home," he ground out, then delved for my lips, punishing them with brutal pressure, then worshipping them with the gentle sweep of his tongue.

Leo drove me toward a foreign edge.

It was jagged and sharp, so steep I couldn't see the ground below.

If I fell, if he drove me over the precipice, would I be smashed into a million pieces? Shatter irrevocably? Did I care?

"Don't stop," I cried.

"Come for me, *gattina*. I want to feel you coming around my cock. Now," he commanded, his voice drunk with lust for me, for control, *for control over me.*

I was helpless to resist, but I wasn't going to fall alone.

"Come with me," I said as the coil wound up so tight, it ached, and it pulsed, until finally, it sprung free.

I screamed as it threw me over the edge.

But instead of plummeting, I soared on shock waves of exquisite bliss as Leo drove in deep and stilled inside me. He came with me as the quakes tore a groan clear out of his chest.

I'd won, I'd lost.

I'd punished and worshipped.

I had never felt so much all at once, I realized, as he lowered my feet to the ground.

Leo was silent—*too* silent.

His hands held my hips, but the way his fingers curled inward, it was like he was resisting the urge to ball them into fists.

"Leo?"

"Fuck, I'm sorry, Ella."

Leo took a staggering step back.

His face was a canvas of guilt.

There was no light, no flicker of humor dancing in his eyes as they grazed over me, taking in the aftermath of what we'd just done.

I reached for him before he could withdraw completely.

Even if for just a little while, I'd felt alive. Whole.

Unshackled from my past and unburdened by my future.

I'd been *free*.

"Please don't be sorry, Leo. I'm not." I caressed his cheek, letting my knuckles brush his cheek slick with sweat.

How could I tell him that of all the memories I could have made to take with me, to cherish, to remember even after he'd forgotten the girl who'd hidden in the back of his car, this was *it*.

He'd given me something no man ever had.

Freedom.

Chapter Twenty-Six

Ella

This was it.

The moment I'd been dreading since I'd held Maria in my arms two days ago and realized what had to come next.

The room was full again with many of the same men that had been here before.

It didn't look like a room I wanted to enter.

The knickknacks looked harmless enough, but the men sitting around the mahogany table looked capable of all types of harm. And they were. Every one of the men in the room had killed before.

I could see it in their eyes, though, there was no clear way to describe it.

Taking a man's life didn't make their eyes darker, exactly, but it left a smudge of black on their souls.

If the eyes really were the windows to the soul, then I think that blackness stopped the light from reflecting in their eyes the way it once did.

Could they see it in my eyes? I wondered.

It was there.

I could feel the black smudge like thick grime on my soul.

Signore had seen it.

I'd been careful to wash the blood from my body, every last drop, but even before his men had told him what I did, he'd known.

"Hey, pretty girl," Brute said.

He'd been standing inside the room next to the door with two of his men, so I hadn't seen him, but he stepped out into the doorway, his broad frame blocking the view of the men beyond him.

It was more difficult to see the proof of *it* in Brute's eyes.

Like Leo's, they were always dancing with humor, which gave the illusion of light and hid the blackness.

Brute smiled and pulled me into a one-armed hug.

Though he never wore the Old Dogs' cut, he smelled like leather and the warm, caramel richness of whiskey.

My father had drunk whiskey, but not often, only every New Year—the biggest celebration in our home. According to him, it was bigger than Christmas in Russia since Christmas had been nearly nonexistent until the Soviet Union collapsed. We'd toast in the New Year, and he'd tuck me into bed not long after. When he leaned down to kiss my forehead, the rich, sweet scent of his breath brushed across my face and heralded in another year.

I rested my cheek against Brute's chest for just a moment, holding onto the ghost of a memory a little longer.

Too soon, I pulled away, but it was for the best.

Soon, Brute would be nothing but a memory to me, too.

Old Mike and Tate Sanchez smiled at me. The room's light glinted off Tate's shaved head while making his goatee shine almost blue-black. They'd always been nice to me, kind of like a crusty old grandfather and a slightly scary older brother.

"Come, sit, *signorina*," *Signor* Luca said kindly from the head of the table, motioning to an empty chair at the opposite end.

My insides shook.

Every eye in the room followed me as I crossed the short distance.

I recognized many of them.

Enzo Luciano, who'd quietly made arrangements for his daughter's marriage. She was going to be none too happy to discover it.

Gabe Costa, who'd been digging around in some dangerous men's business.

My mental survey of secrets ceased as I reached the table.

There, laid out on it was a giant unrolled sheet of paper.

At first, it seemed to be covered in lines and shapes—rectangles and squares. But as I stared at it, the lines transformed into something much more. The marble front foyer with the security system that required a code to get in and out. The master bedroom with its king-size bed and the Persian carpet where I'd slept most nights. The stairs that led to the basement…

A cold shiver shot down my spine.

I reached out to touch the blueprint with trembling fingers but hesitated at the last second, my fingertips a hair's breadth from the spiral staircase I'd crept down.

"Why do you have these?" I asked no one in particular, my voice little more than a whisper.

Nico Costa smiled grimly. "It's not what you know. It's *who* you know, *signorina*."

I glanced from Nico to Dominic, whose countenance was different today, no longer boggled down by the weight of guilt.

He's decided against Signor Belemonte's favor. I breathed a small sigh of relief.

"We were hoping," *Signor* Luca said, drawing my attention back to the head of the table, "that you might be able to fill in some blanks for us. Any information you have could be useful." He nodded to the blueprint.

They were planning to go through with it.

The certainty in their eyes and the determined set of their shoulders said there was no way I was talking them out of this.

Six months ago, I wouldn't have cared.

If there had been people willing to help me then, I would have let them no matter the consequences.

Now, I had to stop them no matter the consequences.

I turned to Brute, a man with secrets that could destroy him if they ever got out, a man who'd looked out for me, watched over me like a father. He smiled, though the corners of his eyes were creased with concern.

My father would have forgiven me for what I was about to do, but would Brute?

I resisted the urge to look at Leo, who was standing behind me.

I'd already committed every part of him to memory, and giving in to the urge now only threatened to topple my resolve.

Don't do this, the coward cried, but as much as I wanted to listen to her, she'd lost her power. I shoved her away and squared my shoulders.

"I lied," I said, looking *Signor* Luca right in the eyes.

The room was silent, like they were collectively holding their breath.

"You lied about what, *cara mia?*" *Signor* Luca asked, his voice kind, but his expression guarded.

"All of it," I said without equivocation.

Signore had taught me to act well, and for once, I was grateful.

All I had to do was keep my eyes trained straight ahead, avoiding turning my head to look behind me.

Eyebrows arched around the room. Shoulders tensed. Bodies shifted in the chairs.

But *Signor* Luca didn't move. His expression didn't change.

"*Signor* Avalone is no more of a villain than anyone in this room." The words tried to stick in my throat. Lumping people like Leo and Brute and Dominic into the same category as *Signore* felt so wrong. "I was angry with him, but I was wrong," I said, feigning chagrin and forcing myself into the role of jilted mistress.

I paused for just a moment, testing the atmosphere.

Already, it had begun to grow heavier with doubt and indecision.

"I'm sorry for the trouble I caused," I said, meeting every pair of eyes through downcast lashes.

I had no doubt I appeared the epitome of contrition and embarrassment.

This was an act I'd had no choice but to feign many times before.

The atmosphere prickled with sparks of annoyance, even anger, but none so much as the rage that rolled off the man who stood behind me.

I could feel the heat of Leo's anger undulating up my back.

"I'll... I'll go now." I stood up, the sound of my chair scraping across the floor seemed to reverberate around the room.

I didn't need to fake the tremble in my voice or the way my hands shook.

It hadn't escaped my notice for a second that I confessed my supposed sins to a room filled with mafia men, all of them lethal.

Worse than that, I confessed them to the man who'd taken possession of a piece of my heart.

Chapter Twenty-Seven

Leo

Ella was leaning over the bed when I walked into my bedroom, shoving her old clothes into her satchel.

Her hair fell in long, loose waves down her back, and the pale yellow dress she wore skimmed her curves. So beautiful. So sexy. The girl of my dreams. The girl of *any* man's dreams.

And I was going to wring her neck.

"What the hell was that?" I barked, slamming the bedroom door shut behind me. "I tell you that I care about you, and you try to sabotage everything I'm trying to do to keep you safe?"

She turned around slowly, her eyes downcast, her expression a perfect mask of chagrin. "I'm sorry, Leo, but I'm not trying to sabotage anything. I wasn't lying when I said I cared about you. That's why this has to stop."

"You forget that there's a difference between me and them," I said, nodding at the door that separated us from the people beyond it. "I can see right through your act—"

"Can you?" Ella asked, looking up at me, her green eyes resembled a dark forest. "Or is that what I wanted you to believe all along? I made you feel like you were the only person in the world

240

who could understand me, who could see 'me', didn't I? What better way to turn a man into my own knight in shining armor? You've killed for me, and you'd do it again. You think I've played no part in that?"

I clenched my jaw.

It certainly sounded like a clever ploy.

I didn't even want to contemplate what kind of idiot that made me if I'd fallen for it.

"You do realize you're confusing as hell?" I said, scrubbing my fingers through my hair.

A genie's lamp would definitely have been a whole hell of a lot more useful.

"I was *Signore's* mistress, Leo, and we had an argument. I wanted him to suffer for being unfaithful, and I took it too far." Her voice was hard.

"'*Signore*'? Is that what mistresses are calling their lovers these days?"

The determined set of her jaw never faltered.

Ella slung her satchel over her shoulder and started for the door, taking a wide circle around me.

"What are you doing?" I asked stupidly.

"I'm leaving." Ella tilted her chin a little higher.

"Like hell you are." I grabbed her arm when she tried to circumvent me and reach for the door.

"Let me go." She tugged against my hold on her, glaring daggers at me.

I pulled her closer. "You're right, I've killed for you. So tell me, was that fucker beating you part of the act? Were the scars on your back another hoax?"

Ella didn't answer.

She just kept trying to wrestle her way free, but no matter how angry she got, she'd never be able to out-strength me.

She really was one hell of an octopus, though.

I wedged her body between me and the wall.

"You're not his mistress, Ella. His own goon told me as much."

She froze for a fraction of a second as cracks began to form in the façade she wore. Cracks that revealed the kind of pain and humiliation Avalone had made her feel. Cracks that made me want to rip Avalone's heart out of his chest so he could watch as I sliced it up in front of his dying eyes.

"You're lying, Leo. Stop lying, and let me go," she seethed as she yanked one hand out of my grasp. Her green eyes flashed with determination. "I don't want to be here anymore. I want to leave, damn it!"

"Hate me if you want to, but you're not leaving, Ella, and I'm not buying your bullshit story."

I grabbed her hand back and pinned both of them above her head.

I had to hand it to her; for all Avalone had tried to tear her down, there was one hell of a fighter still inside her. Fighting and cursing at a mafia man—even one as charming as me—that wasn't a move for the weak and cowardly. Not to mention the way she'd stood in a room full of mafia men and lied her ass off.

"What difference does it make?" she cried when she couldn't break free. "I don't need your protection. I don't want it."

"I get that you're scared, *gattina*, but have I really not proven I'll do whatever it takes to keep you safe?"

Her arms stopped flailing, though it felt like there was no less fight in her.

I tentatively let her hands go, ready to grab them back if the need arose.

"You still don't get it, do you? I'm not scared for me," she cried, thumping her fists against my chest. Her eyes filled with tears, but she seemed to hold them there out of sheer will. "I'm scared for you and your family, all of you, all because of your stupid plan. I'm... I'm scared for *Signore's* child even though I've never seen the kid, for Christ's sake. And for girls who would serve me up in a heartbeat if it spared them one ounce of pain. And it's all your fault, goddamn it." She hit my chest again, but some of the fire behind it had fizzled out of her.

"My fault?" I tilted my head to the left.

"Why couldn't you just leave it alone?" she whispered. "If I'd never met you... if you'd never..." She shook her head. "I didn't used to care, Leo. I didn't care what happened to a child I'd never met or to the girls *Signore* locked in the basement until their buyers came for them. When they were gone, I never thought about them again. I didn't care. The truth is I would have served them up to save myself one ounce of pain too."

"So what?" I brought her hand to my lips and kissed the inside of her wrist where our struggle had left its mark. "It's natural to want to protect yourself, *gattina*. You don't think there was a time when I would have handed up just about anything?"

Ella shook her head, and I could feel the way she was struggling for words, opening her mouth, then closing it.

"I killed a man, Leo," she said and nodded minutely like she'd found the right fit. "He had me on his dining table, and I got hold of a steak knife. I dragged it across his throat." There was no emotion in her voice like she was reading from a textbook. "I can still remember the way the tearing sensation vibrated up my arm, the sticky warmth of his blood as it spurted all over my body. The metallic scent was all I could smell, but do you know what I felt?"

I didn't respond.

"Nothing. Absolutely nothing. I sat there until *Signore's* men came for me. Riccardo thought I was in shock, but I wasn't. I wasn't... *anything.*" She was standing right in front of me, but her eyes were far away.

I felt the strange need to pull her back, so I did the only thing I could think of and pressed my lips to hers.

Her lips were warm, but for a moment, it was like kissing an empty vessel.

Ella wasn't here with me.

She was sitting in a room, covered in someone else's blood with a bloody steak knife in her hand.

I could feel it the moment she came back, her lips pliant and the blood long gone.

Ella pulled away, the absence immediately leaving a coldness in my mouth. "It would be so much easier to be numb again. I could hide away in this room and let you and your family and Brute risk your lives for me. I wouldn't even have to try to convince myself that you'll all be safe, because I wouldn't care."

"This is what we do, *gattina.*" I tried to lean in again, desperate to replace the chill with her warmth.

Ella shook her head and put a finger over my lips. "I've tried to get that numbness back, but it's gone. You took it away from me, so, if you care about me at all, Leo, you won't do this. You won't let your family, the people you care about, do this."

"He's just a man, Ella—"

"No, he isn't. He's a monster. You think people like Fallon and Maria have nothing to do with this, but there is no limit to the lengths *Signore* will go to for revenge. If you fail, everyone you've ever cared about will suffer for it. They'll suffer because of me," she said as an errant tear slipped free and slid down her cheek.

I'd never seen Ella cry.

Not when I'd found her injured on the floor of her dumpy apartment.

Not any of the times she'd spoken about her past or the hell she'd lived through.

"I'm begging you, please don't make me live with that, Leo." She met my gaze as she spoke.

Even more than the pleading look in her eyes, it was the determined set of her jaw that told me she wasn't going to let this go.

If I was a better man, I would have listened to her.

But there was no way the Lucas were backing down from Fiorenzo Avalone.

I was going to rip his heart from his chest and lay it at her feet.

Then she could curse me.

Then she could stay or go where she pleased.

"I'm sorry, *gattina*," I said, pressing my forehead to hers, savoring the feel of her against me for one more moment because it could very well be the last time she touched me willingly. "I wasn't lying when I said I didn't give a flying fuck about what anyone thinks, and that includes you, when it comes to keeping you safe."

Her breath caught in her throat, and her body went rigid as I took a step back.

One more step, and I reached for the door handle.

Her eyes were empty husks.

Guilt twisted my gut as I slipped out of the room, slammed the door shut behind me, and shoved a key in the lock.

The great thing about big, old houses was that they came with big, old skeleton keys.

With one turn of the key, Ella had just become my prisoner.

Chapter Twenty-Eight

Leo

The scene in the war room hadn't changed much since I'd stormed out after Ella.

The air was still heavy with uncertainty—not an aroma that suited the men here.

A week ago, I would have walked right by and gotten my shit together before heading back in there.

Not today.

I could clearly hear the heavy, frantic thuds of Ella's fists banging on my bedroom door.

I could still hear her screaming my name. Her voice echoed down the stairs and jackhammered in my chest, right into my heart.

I slammed the war room door shut, trying to block it out.

"I want to know where the fuck the wife and kid are and anyone else Avalone's got in that house against their will," I barked, banging my hands down on the mahogany table.

I didn't miss the incredulous looks from my father and brothers. I wasn't generally the one prone to irrational outbursts.

"You think she was lying about being Avalone's mistress?" *Zietto* Enzo's son, Amadeo, asked.

I liked the guy, but even for a mafia man, Amadeo was one skeptical son of a bitch.

"Of course, she was lying. She's scared," I ground out, analyzing the blueprints on the table, searching for answers.

Out the corner of my eye, I watched as Amadeo looked around at all the mafia and biker men in the room. "Seriously? She's scared we can't handle one pathetic fucker?"

I laughed, but there was no humor in it. "No, she's afraid one of us fuckers are going to get our asses shot full of lead."

"She's afraid... *for us?*" *Zietto* Enzo asked. The expression on his face said he wasn't buying it.

Zietto Enzo was family—my mother's brother—but that didn't stop me from wanting to smack the disbelieving look right off his face.

"Look," I said, scrubbing my fingers through my hair rather than taking a shot at my uncle. "Avalone kept her prisoner for four fucking years, and now I've got her locked upstairs..." I paused, looking around the room. "So, forgive me if I'm not in the mood for chitchat. I want the fucker dead. Now, if you don't want to help, that's fine. I'll do it myself."

"I'm with you, my friend," Brute said, stepping up next to me.

Not surprisingly, the two Old Dogs, Old Mike and Tate, with him followed suit.

"Leo," my father said, his voice full of restraint, his face a thinly veiled mask of agitation.

I exhaled a long, slow breath. "I mean no disrespect, Papà, but you know it's the right thing to do. And until Avalone's six feet under, I've got her locked up, no better than—"

"Bullshit," Dante cursed. "You're nothing like him, Leo. You're trying to keep her safe. Somehow, I doubt that was Avalone's intentions."

Zietto Enzo cleared his throat. "That's assuming Avalone had any 'intentions' at all."

I balled my hands into fists, my pulse rising.

"Son of a bitch," Gabe cursed under his breath.

The second eldest of the Costas hadn't said a word since I'd first walked in with Ella, but given his previous thoughts on the subject, I was fairly certain I could tell him where he could shove his thoughts now.

"Leo's right," Gabe said, sighing heavily. "Avalone is neck-deep in human trafficking, and lately, he's been bringing it right into the damn docks." Anger flashed in his green eyes. Eyes the same color as Nico's. Eyes so much like Ella's. Hers were probably snapping with the same anger at the moment.

"How do you know that?" Dom asked, but my gaze swung to Nico, who had the same question in his eyes.

However Gabe had come by the information, Nico hadn't known about it.

"It doesn't matter how I know." Gabe shook his head. "All that matters is there might not be fuck all we can do about it."

"Why the hell not?" I snapped, forgetting about everyone else in the room.

Gabe sighed. "Bulletproof glass, proximity alarms," he said, counting off each obstacle on his fingers. "A security system that can only be disabled from the inside, guards crawling all over the property. The fucker's place is just about impenetrable. And in case you were hoping to fall back on a public hit, Avalone seldom leaves his home. The occasional time he does, there's nothing predictable about it. To hit the ships or the vans carrying the girls—it's possible. But to take out Avalone is going to be a challenge of monolithic proportions."

My mouth tightened. "I want Avalone, not one of his scumbag drivers."

"Then we'll get him," Dante said, exchanging glances with Dom.

Gabe shook his head, scrubbing a hand over his face. "If I didn't know better, Leo, I'd say you must spend a lot of time running into brick walls."

"Nah, my head's harder than any brick, *amico*. I run right through them."

Chuckles sounded around the room, but the atmosphere sobered quickly.

"I can take Leo out and give him a firsthand look at the obstacles," Gabe said, his gaze swinging back and forth between Nico and my father.

Nico nodded once. "I'll be coming too," he said in a voice that brooked no refusal.

My father wasn't as easily convinced. "If Avalone is untouchable as you say, I'm not sure I see the point."

"It's possible that I missed something," Gabe admitted, but his voice was full of doubt. "A fresh set of eyes couldn't hurt."

Dom was nodding, but he looked unsettled. "Don't you think you might be a little too close to the situation to be objective, Leo?"

"Tell me you would have given a damn about objectivity when it came to keeping Fallon safe, *fratello*. Besides, I'm younger than the rest of you—my eyes are as fresh as they get." It wasn't often being the youngest guy in the room proved beneficial.

"All right." My father nodded. "Recon only, and you'll report back to me by morning."

"I'm coming," Brute said.

Gabe shook his head. "We need to be discreet about this," he said, eyeing Brute's massive frame, "and I'm afraid there's nothing discreet about you, *Signor* Hastings." Understatement of the century.

"I'll be as discreet as a politician's mistress." Brute crossed his big arms over his chest, his eyes gleaming as he stared Gabe down.

Gabe could argue all he wanted; nothing shy of a bullet between the eyes was stopping Brute.

***

I'd never given it a whole lot of thought over the years, but it turned out, I was a man of action.

I needed forward momentum, a purpose. Something productive.

Because I sure as hell wasn't built to crouch in the dirt for hours with a pair of binoculars in my hands.

Avalone's estate was right there, five hundred yards away, and here I was, sitting around like a garden gnome.

Brute looked like the biggest garden gnome ever made, and Nico… well, Nico kind of looked like he was ready to come out of his skin. The man was made for action, not recon. I could sympathize.

"So, you want to get all chatty and tell us how you came across information on Avalone?" I asked Gabe who was crouching perfectly still next to me.

"He found it on countless hours of video surveillance, isn't that right?" Nico asked, one eyebrow cocked and his eyes on Gabe.

"Video surveillance?" Brute repeated.

Nico nodded. "We were trying to track down Avalone's son, Diego Berlusconi."

The name sent rage racing through my veins.

The name of the man who'd kidnapped my sister. One of the men who'd raped Ella—didn't matter if he'd had to hold her down or not; not one second of it had been her choice.

Gabe shrugged. "I have my own reasons for looking into men like Avalone, Leo. And to be honest, if I'd thought I could have handled him on my own, I would have kept my mouth shut. If we blow this—"

"We won't." I raised the binoculars and tracked across Avalone's estate from one hidden guard to the next.

Gabe laughed under his breath. "Pretty damn sure of yourself, aren't you?"

"That's me, one cocky son of a bitch."

There were at least eighteen guards on the property, all of them armed. It reminded me more of a South American cartel compound than a nineteenth-century estate in New York. Most of the guards were situated a fair distance from the house. The proximity alarms Gabe mentioned must have been positioned somewhere inside their perimeter.

"I sure as hell hope you've got more than bravado to back you up here, *amico*," Gabe muttered.

Me too.

"We'll need to cut the power," Brute observed.

A night assault was the obvious choice, but the grounds outside were too well-lit, and it would be better to kill the lights inside as well.

"No can do." Gabe was shaking his head. "The inside of the house, security system included, is on its own power. All of it, internal. There's no way we can access it from the outside."

I'd known Avalone was smart, but I certainly hadn't given him enough credit.

Brute took one more look around the grounds. "All right. We cut the power to the outside. That's on the hydro grid?"

Gabe nodded.

It was a start. "If we cut that," I began, "it at least puts the guards outside in the dark. If we're ready with night vision or infrared, we can see and move around unimpeded."

"Great," Gabe said, rolling his eyes, "we can decorate Avalone's lawn with bodies, but I'm not sure that gets us any closer to the goal. We still can't get through the security system or the bulletproof glass."

"You're sure about the glass?" Nico asked his brother.

"B-six polycarbonate. Forty-one millimeters thick. Not even high-power rifles can get through it," Gabe answered.

I stared at the bulletproof glass windows through the binoculars like my eyes were laser beams that could burn right through them. Sure, it wasn't the coolest superpower ever, but it would have been useful right now.

"Fuck the glass. I'll go through the wall," I blurted out.

Brute put down his binoculars to look at me.

Gabe laughed. "I'm assuming you don't mean you and your hard head are going to ram right through it?"

It was my turn to laugh. "I mean explosives—C-four. Walls… windows… even if the glass is blast-resistant, C-four up close will blast right through it."

Years ago, I'd had a lot of time to plot my revenge, recovering at my family's island. Revenge that had involved knives and whips and a *lot* of explosives. Revenge that had come to nothing. It had been sought on my behalf, leaving me with a whole lot of plans and fuck all I could do with them.

Gabe was already nodding. "Not bad. It'll draw a lot of attention, which would have been a problem for *me*, but if there's enough of us, it could work. I assume you can get your hands on it?"

"It'll take a couple of phone calls, but we'll get it." I smirked.

"The explosion will draw every guard inside, but a few flash grenades will fuck with their vision and balance," Gabe added.

"Not bad. I assume you can get your hands on those?" I asked, turning his question around on him.

Nico smiled. "Already got them, *amico*."

"Impressive."

The plan was already coming together, but I couldn't help but wonder what Gabe had gotten himself into that he knew all about Avalone—right down to the type of bulletproof glass he used—and kept a stock of flash grenades?

"The wife and kid keep to the west wing," Gabe said, pointing to the left side of the house.

"So, we set the C-four on the right." I closed my eyes and called up an image of the blueprints we'd left on the mahogany table in the war room. "The parlor's right there?" I said, pointing to the large bay windows about fifteen feet to the right of the front door.

Gabe nodded. "But if Avalone's smart, he'll make a beeline for the basement if he can't get out of the house."

"Why?" the three of us asked in unison.

"That's where he keeps them," Gabe said. He spoke lightly, but the dark expression on his face stood out in stark contrast.

"The girls?" I asked, my vision narrowing.

Gabe nodded. "Not many of them end up here. They usually go straight to buyers or whorehouses—but if he's got any when we come at him, I have no doubt the asshole will use them as a shield."

"All right," I said, seeing the plan take shape in my mind. "So, we get in and cut him off before he can get there. Barricade all access to the basement until we've finished with the guards. But no one kills Avalone. I want him alive."

I looked over at Brute, making sure he was clear on this point as well.

Avalone was mine.

Gabe put down his binoculars and cracked his knuckles. "Are you sure that's what you want, Leo?" he asked, staring at his fingers.

"*Sí.*"

Ella didn't know it, but I'd made her a vow when I'd transformed myself into her captor.

She'd have Avalone's heart—and any other pieces of the fucker she wanted. She'd probably want all my pieces served up on a silver platter too for turning her into a prisoner. But one dismemberment at a time.

Gabe hadn't moved. "It's one thing to kill when you have to," he said, still staring at his fingers like they were a book he was trying to read. "But to take delight in it... It changes you. For a long time, I didn't really understand what it did to Nico. I understand now." He shrugged then grabbed his binoculars again.

"It made me into the calm, levelheaded man I am today," Nico said with a smile that wasn't quite stable.

I didn't know the gory details about Nico and Gabe's childhood, but I did know that their father had forced Nico to torture people ever since he was a teenager. Nico got so good at it, he'd earned quite a reputation for his morbid skill with a knife.

A black van turned off the street and started up the long, winding drive toward Avalone's estate. It moved so slowly, it was no difficult task to track it with the binoculars. As it rolled along, I looked for words or markings on the van's exterior, but there was nothing. A plain, black cube van. It reached the top of the drive, meandered toward the right side of the house, and slowed to a stop.

"Watch," Gabe said, adjusting his position for a better view.

The van sat there idling. Small puffs of exhaust escaped from the muffler into the cool evening air, but there was no other movement.

Then a door at the side of the house opened, and two goons stepped out.

They were so big, I didn't see her at first; the thin, scantily clad woman the goons held between them. Long, dark hair hung over her slumped shoulders and blew into her face. Her feet were bare, and her hands were bound behind her back. She put up no struggle, her small feet trudging along in a blur to keep up with the goons' steps.

I blinked hard.

It's not her. It's not her.

My heart pounded, pumping rage instead of blood through my veins.

All I could see was Ella.

Starved. Beaten and bound.

"Fuck," I cursed under my breath, gripping the binoculars so tight, it was a wonder they didn't break.

I was already calculating the time it would take to get there.

"Don't do anything stupid, Leo," Gabe cautioned, placing his binoculars back down on the ground.

I shot my head to look at Gabe. "*This* is fucking stupid. Why the fuck are we just sitting here?"

Nico had dropped his binoculars, reaching for his gun when Gabe put a hand on his arm and shook his head.

I couldn't tear my gaze away as one of the goons opened the rear door and shoved the girl inside.

Don't close it. Don't close the fucking door.

It was as if she was safe so long as I could still see her.

Had someone watched on when Avalone had Ella brought here?

Could someone have done something to stop him but sat in the bushes instead?

A low growl rumbled out of Brute's throat.

"Everyone just cool it," Gabe whisper-barked at us. "We're sitting here because the job is to figure out a way around the obstacles of taking that fucker out for good. This isn't a rescue mission."

But whether we took down Avalone or not, the moment the van drove away, that girl's life was over.

How could I face Ella if I let this happen?

One of the goons slammed the van door closed.

She was gone. Trapped inside.

"You're about three seconds from doing something stupid, aren't you, *amico*?" Gabe said to me, sitting his ass down in the dirt, wiping a half-smile off his face. "Since when did all mafia men get a hard-on for rescuing damsels in distress?" he muttered under his breath.

I kept my gaze on Gabe. I hadn't known him long. There was no doubt that he was lethal, all the rest of us were. I just didn't expect him to be heartless.

The van circled around in the drive and headed back the way it had come.

"You've got to trust me, Leo, and keep your eye on the long game. We end that fucker, or we die trying." The vehemence in Gabe's voice spoke volumes. Whatever had set him on a collision course with Avalone, it was personal.

I shook my head. "This had better fucking work, or that girl just died for nothing."

Gabe gathered up his binoculars and sidled back the way we'd come. "The girl is far from dead, *amico*."

There were things a whole lot worse than being dead.

Chapter Twenty-Nine

Leo

"Ten days," Gabe said as he slid into the passenger seat of my Lambo.

Brute revved his bike's engine, and Nico got into his Porsche, headed for some unrelated meeting.

I didn't envy the don of a mafia family. It seemed someone was always in need of a piece of their time.

We'd left our vehicles parked five miles from Avalone's, so it had been one hell of a hike back.

Suddenly, though, I had more pent-up energy than I knew what to do with.

"You expect me to sit around twiddling my thumbs for ten fucking days?" I barked, standing outside the driver's side door.

Gabe laughed. "You forget that I've seen your 'captive', *amico*. If you can't figure out ways to keep yourself occupied for the next week and a half, then you seriously need to get your hands on a copy of the *Kama Sutra*. Hell, *Cosmo* might even have a few useful tips for you."

I blew out a breath. "I'm more of a *Playboy* man myself, for the articles, of course," I joked, getting behind the wheel. I revved the engine and pulled out onto the dirt road that led back to civilization. "But seriously, ten days? Why?"

"Avalone has a shipment coming in eleven days from now. If we hit him too early, they'll get word of it, and it'll spook them. If we wait until they've made the delivery, then he'll have more collateral in the house. So, ten days."

Just days ago, "shipment" had meant drugs. Weapons, maybe. And because my family made a shit-ton of money off them, the word had never been a derogatory term.

But Gabe wasn't referring to a shipment of cocaine or assault rifles. He meant a shipment of human beings; girls like Ella. Girls who would be beaten, raped, and eventually, murdered, whether by weapon, drug, or disease.

"All right. Ten days," I agreed as I slowed the car to a stop at the end of the road and turned onto a paved street.

Ten days felt like an eternity.

Ten days of keeping Ella confined to the house, under constant watch.

Ten days of Ella feeling like she'd never escaped at all.

I turned onto the next street, merging with traffic easily.

There weren't many cars on the road this early in the morning.

The sun had barely begun to peek above the horizon, turning the sky a mottled gray.

If there'd been more traffic, I might not have noticed the two black BMWs that turned onto the street a few cars back.

I passed a few more side streets, and another black BMW merged into the strung out traffic behind us. Two side streets up, another one turned onto the street and fell into the growing line of cars that I was fairly certain weren't out for a pleasure cruise.

"You might want to buckle up," I told Gabe while I visualized the next few minutes.

"I see them. You got a plan?" he asked a little doubtfully, fastening his seat belt.

"Always, *amico*. There should be a frequent-flyer program here. Pay for three high-speed pursuits, get the fourth one free," I said, flashing him a grin.

I grabbed my Glock from my jacket as I considered and dismissed the next three side streets. Too wide or too narrow, and what I had in mind wasn't going to work. The four-way stop up ahead; that was perfect.

I waited until the last possible second then took the corner hard and fast. The binoculars and other shit in the trunk slammed against the trunk wall.

A little distance; that was all I needed. I hit the gas, speeding ahead as the first black BMW turned after me.

We zipped by buildings and early morning joggers, swerved around an old Ford Escort that was crawling up the street.

All four cars had turned onto the street, speeding along behind me. I had to let them get close.

I hit the brakes and spun the car, turning it sideways and blocking the road. At the same time, I aimed the Glock and shot out the lead car's right tire then put a bullet through the driver.

The BMW in the lead swerved. Its horn blared. The crack of a gunshot rang out, and fire sliced through my arm. *Motherfucker.*

Gabe had half his body out the passenger window, firing at the black cars as the lead BMW slammed into a parked car, thrusting it sideways. It crunched loudly as the one behind plowed right into it, blocking the rest of their convoy.

I maneuvered back around and kept going while a volley of gunshots flew from behind us, doing no damage to us but seriously messing with the Lambo's paint job.

"Well, that was… interesting," Gabe said, smothering a smile as we left the four trapped cars far behind us. "Frequent-flyer program, huh? This happens often?"

"More often than it used to," I griped, taking my eyes off the road long enough to look at my arm.

It hurt like a son of a bitch, but the bleeding seemed to be coming from both the front and the back, which meant the bullet went clean through at least. *Lucky fucking me.*

"Any idea who it was? It didn't look like Avalone's men to me."

"Fucking Russians," I muttered under my breath.

I hadn't gotten a good look at the tattoos on the hand of the guy who'd shot me, but they'd been there. I would have recognized them a mile away.

"Russians?"

"I had a run-in with one a few days ago. I'm guessing his friends were hoping to repay the favor." Friends who seemed awfully determined. But who were they, and what did Ella have on them?

Gabe laughed. "I'm guessing they might feel like they owe you a whole lot of favors now."

"Ain't that fucking wonderful? I think the bullet in my arm is *favor* enough for now." It wasn't the worst pain I'd ever endured, but the fire blazing in my arm didn't feel like a tickle. "Do you want to pass me the medical shit in the glove box?"

"Why don't you let me drive so you can tend to that?" he offered, nodding at my bleeding arm, "before you end up decorating the whole front seat in blood. It isn't a good look on the black leather."

I gritted my way past a few more streets, just to make sure my Russian friends wouldn't be catching up anytime soon, then pulled up to the curb and got out.

Gabe had already retrieved the emergency supplies from the glove box—gauze and bandages were already laid out on the dashboard.

"*Grazie, amico*," I said, clapping him on the back as we rounded the hood of the car and switched places.

After removing my jacket and yanking up my shirt sleeve, it was a simple matter to cover the wounds just above my bicep with gauze—fortunately, it looked like the bullet had missed the muscle. It was a less simple matter to stick the gauze there with medical tape that was just never meant to be operated one-handed.

By the time I was finished, it looked like a three-year-old had been using the tape for art class, but the job was done, and the bleeding had slowed, barely saturating the gauze.

The sun was well up in the sky by the time Gabe turned into the driveway of the Luca estate.

I'd shot off a text message when I'd finished with my preschool bandaging job, so it wasn't a surprise to find Dom and Dante waiting in the open doorway as Gabe parked the car and got out.

"Are you trying to see just how many times you can get shot before we put your ass on the bench?" Dante asked, coming down the front steps as I maneuvered out of the passenger seat.

"There's no benching me, *fratello*. I was born to be in the game," I joked. "Do you suppose I could borrow your wife?" I turned to Dom, waggling my eyebrows.

His eyebrows just about hit his hairline. *Priceless!*

"To suture my arm, dumbass," I explained, holding out the suture kit from the emergency supplies in the car.

"Are they—" I heard Fallon's voice right before she appeared in the doorway, and her jaw slammed shut.

I laughed. It wasn't often something could render Fallon speechless. "I look that bad, do I?" I asked, climbing the stairs.

"What the hell did you do?" Fallon snapped.

"Me?" I asked, a hand over my heart in mock-offense. "You think I did this?"

"First, you lock Ella in your room like she's a kid on time-out, and then you go and get yourself shot? What the hell, Leo?" She crossed her arms over her chest and glared daggers at me.

Apparently, I'd misjudged the speed at which female solidarity developed between two women.

I turned to Dom, but he had his eyes carefully averted, hiding a smile behind his hand.

"Do you suppose you could deal with this while I explain?" I asked Fallon, holding out my arm, which seemed to have gotten stiffer every minute.

She huffed but motioned for me to follow her. "You do realize I'm a veterinarian, Leo. I treat animals—"

"And since when have you thought of me as anything other than a jackass?" I grinned goofily at her.

"True enough, but just so you know, I don't have any anesthetic," Fallon warned.

"Then you're probably going to enjoy this more than me, aren't you?"

She tried to keep a straight face, but a smile tugged at the corners of her lips right before she burst out laughing. "Yeah, I will."

I swayed a little as we reached the dining table. I sat my ass down on one of the hard-backed chairs before I face-planted on the ground.

"Are you okay, Leo?" Fallon came around to inspect my injured arm with concerned eyes.

"Depends on your definition of okay. I've been shot, chased by Russians, sat there and watched Avalone's men lead a girl off to a life of slavery, and when you're finished with my arm, I get to go tell Ella she's going to be a 'guest' here for at least another ten days. So, yeah, I'm pretty great. You?"

She'd paused with one hand on the tape around my arm. "Fuck, Leo, I'm sorry. I didn't know. I had no idea..." She squeezed her lips shut. "Dom was pretty vague about why Ella was here. Avalone was going to *sell* her?" Her face screwed up like she'd just eaten a lemon.

"Not exactly. He preferred to keep Ella *close*," I said, not sure I could elaborate without vomiting in my mouth.

She nodded and turned her attention back to my arm, unfastening the tape and cleaning up the entry and exit wounds before prepping the suture needle.

I'd seen Fallon work at her clinic; she was never this quiet.

She flashed me an apologetic smile as she lined the tip of the suture needle at the edge of the wound, then dug in.

I gritted my teeth and held myself rigid.

One suture, then another. Like I'd learned to do long ago, I let my mind take me elsewhere. This time, between the silken thighs of the dark-haired beauty locked in my room. Her breathy moans. Her vivid green eyes. Her round, perfectly full tits.

Sweat beaded along my brow and dripped down the back of my neck, but I remained still as Fallon moved to the wound in the back of my arm.

In my mind, Ella's thighs were wrapping around me, pulling me closer, enabling me to thrust deeper.

"You do seem to have an amazing pain tolerance—or enough brain damage that your pain receptors aren't firing," Fallon mused as she tied the last stitch.

"Trust me, they're firing just fine."

She turned her attention back to the task at hand, silent as she covered the sutured wounds with fresh gauze and taped it in place.

"That's what this is about?" she asked as she laid the tape down on the table. "You're going to kill him? Avalone?"

I nodded.

"Good."

I cocked an eyebrow. "I seem to recall a woman who wasn't so fond of the violence of this life. Has Dom been warping you?"

She shook her head. "I think about what Ella must have gone through. And then I think of Maria... If anyone ever..."

I patted her hand. "We'll kill him, Fallon. And if anyone ever tried to lay a finger on Maria, I promise you we'd rip him apart and lay his bones at your feet."

Chapter Thirty

Leo

I turned the key in the lock, not quite sure what I'd find on the other side.

Ella was sitting on the floor in the corner of the room, her arms wrapped around her knees and her gaze fixed on the wall next to my head.

Everything in the room was how I'd left it.

There were no tears in her eyes.

There was nothing in them. Vacant, like her mind was far away.

The phone Brute had given her was on the floor next to her. Maybe she'd tried to talk Brute into kicking my ass into kingdom come.

"Ella?"

Her mind came back, but she looked down before I could read the look in her eyes, now staring at her toes.

"Why are you sitting on the floor, *gattina*?" I said, running the fingers of my good arm through my hair.

Ella didn't answer right away. She wriggled her bare toes, wrapped her arms tighter around her knees.

"*Signore* never let me on the furniture. Only his bed," she said, turning her gaze to my bed.

I exhaled sharply. "Ella, look at me."

Ella tore her gaze from the bed and looked up at me. There was sadness in her eyes, but something else too.

Whatever Avalone had done to her, he'd never managed to break her. She'd been there all along, stewing beneath the surface.

Wasn't it just crazy that it made me hard to think of all that fight and vibrancy bursting through the surface?

"I didn't do this to hurt you. I'm trying to protect you."

Rage flashed in her eyes. "It's for my own good? Is that what you're saying?" She pushed herself off the floor and stood up in one eerily graceful movement. "Do you think that you know better than me? That you know what's best for me?"

I had a feeling there was no good answer here, so for once, I kept my mouth shut.

"Do you have any idea how many times I heard those words from *Signore*?"

Something cold and slimy slithered down my spine at the comparsion.

"You know damn well I have no interest in hurting you," I seethed, my pulse rising.

"Are you sure about that?" Ella closed the distance between us, her hands balled into fists at her sides. "If I disobey you, will you lock me in the basement too, Leo? Whip me? Starve me? Will you tie me up and take whatever you want from me just because you can?"

Ella was goading me, taunting me, trying to see how far she could push me.

More slugs slithering down my spine.

"If I'd wanted you locked up, you'd be in cuffs," I said, grabbing hold of her wrists. "If I'd wanted to mark your body, I would have." I spun her around and backed her into the post at the foot of the bed. "And if I'd wanted to tie you to this bed and fuck you raw, there isn't a goddamned thing you could have done to stop me."

The image of Ella restrained, her hands stretched high over her head, jolted through me like a live wire. The thought of marking her body, covering up every one of her scars with my own marks was like a shot of pure adrenaline through my veins. Imagining having her tied spread-eagle on my bed, completely at my mercy, was just about enough to make me come without contact.

Maybe I hated her comparing me to Avalone because the comparison was more apt than I wanted to admit.

But Ella had taken something from me: *control.*

I sought it every day, from the minute my eyes open in the morning to my last waking second.

I sought it when shaking men's hands for business deals.

I sought it when my finger is on the trigger of my gun, just a regular day's work for a Luca.

I sought it when downing my whiskey at the end of a long day.

I sought it in bed when one woman is sucking me while the other's tits are in my mouth.

Control is what makes my heart pump, it's the electricity that flows through my veins.

Ella had taken that away from me.

It was like she'd used it to jump-start her cold heart, to fill the emptiness inside her.

I watched the muscles of her throat work as she swallowed hard. "Then let me go. I didn't ask for your help. I don't want it." She tried to yank her wrists out of my grip as her eyes flashed. "And I sure as hell don't want to be locked in your goddamned house like a prisoner." She tried to kick me, but I was too close for her to do any damage.

The green flame in her eyes blazed, a mesmerizing dance that captivated me, made me drunk with desire.

"Too bad," I said, shrugging despite my injury.

"Too bad? You lock me in here all night, and all I get is 'too bad'?" Her chest heaved with every breath. Her body had heated from the struggle, and the scent of her wrapped around me.

"I locked you in here because you refuse to see reason."

"Reason? I gave you my reasons, Leo, and you completely ignored them. But you don't get to decide for me," she hissed.

"While you were safe, locked in here, do you want to take a guess at what I was doing?" I asked, pressing closer to her despite the conscience that was screaming at me to back off.

No control.

Helpless to resist the pull of her.

The absence of the very thing that made me feel alive ate at my brain like a parasite.

"I got to sit by and watch Avalone sell off a girl like she was a fucking *thing*. A girl with long, dark hair, just like you." I paused, my voice quieter this time. "All I could think about was you." I pressed my forehead hard against hers, trying to banish the image. "She didn't do a damn thing, Ella. She didn't lift a goddamned finger to fight for her survival. And if you're not going to fight for yours, then I'll damn well do it for you."

"Why?" she cried, throwing her head back against the post. There was so much in her eyes. Too much. Anger. Hurt. Hope.

Fire and ice.

It ripped the truth right out of my throat. "I don't know," I hollered, clenching my teeth.

Her chest heaved. I couldn't help but follow the rise and fall of her breasts.

"I want to hate you for locking me in here," she spat, but there was no venom in it.

"And do you?"

She stared at me, meeting my gaze like she was searching for something. But while she searched, I could read every emotion in her green kaleidoscope eyes.

Whirls of sadness.

Bright splotches of anger.

Hot sparks of desire.

I delved for her lips.

I wanted to taste her sadness, drink in her anger, and binge on her desire, no matter how much I should have been backing away.

I was *delirious*. One minute angry, the next, I wanted to bury my cock hilt-deep inside her and never leave.

I released her wrists and reached for her hips, pulling her closer.

Her hands pressed against my chest like she was going to push me away, but then she fisted her hands in the fabric and pulled me closer.

"I want to hate you," she said against my lips.

"But you don't."

The way her body molded against mine, the way her tongue met me glide for glide—not *all* of her hated me.

The part of her that was needy, crazy, and *delirious* was winning, matching my insanity.

"You locked me up," she hissed right before nipping at my bottom lip with her teeth.

"To keep you safe." I nipped her back then worked my way down her neck, suckling and nipping.

"I don't want to be a prisoner." One of her hands moved to the back of my head, fingers tunneling through my hair and holding me closer.

"Prisoner or not, you're mine," I said, sinking my teeth in, just above the hollow of her throat.

Mine.

The word had crept up from the dark recesses of my mind like a confession, imploring me like a whispered prayer.

Its primitive lure wrapped around my tongue, its sweet taste reminding me of my first sample of Ella—her honeyed musk scent, her mouth tasting like oranges, her hair smelling of coconuts.

"Yours," she whispered, feeding my obsession like serving bourbon at an AA meeting.

"I lied when I told you I didn't want your secrets. I lied when I said I didn't want to tie you up. I want every part of you, Ella. Your body, your secrets, your pain and your pleasure. I want all of it."

She shivered.

Back the fuck off, my conscience screamed.

I reached between us for the hem of her dress and yanked it off over her head. My arm flamed in protest, but it had no say here either.

No bra, no panties; I palmed her breasts while my eyes greedily took in every naked inch of her. One hand traveled lower, spearing a finger into her tight, wet heat. She was so ready. All I had to do was unzip and—

My eyes met hers, and I stilled my finger inside her.

"Tell me if you want me to stop." I forced the words out before I couldn't.

Her breasts heaved against my chest with her heavy breaths. She dug her teeth into her bottom lip as confusion swirled in her gaze.

"Stop," she whispered, the word barely more than a breath like she was testing it on her tongue.

I held my breath, my cock twitching.

Inch by inch, I withdrew from her, doing my damnedest to ignore the wetness leaking from her pussy, the scent of her filling my head like a drug. And the hard-on that was making vicious promises that I was going to pay for this.

"You stopped," she said when I'd managed to lower my hand to my side when what I really wanted to do was paint her lips with my finger soaked in her wetness and then lick off every drop.

I nodded, jaw clenched.

"Why did you stop?" she asked, her eyes squinting a little like she was searching my face for the answer while she took hold of my hand at my side.

"Because you asked me to, *gattina,*" I forced out between gritted teeth.

Ella raised my hand to her lips and glided her tongue along the finger I'd had buried in her pussy just seconds ago.

She flicked and licked down to the last knuckle then wrapped her lips around it and sucked my finger into her mouth until she'd slurped every last drop of her own juice.

My cock strained painfully against the fly of my pants.

"You'll lock me in here, but you won't do what you want with me?" Her expression flickered with confusion, but it didn't stop her from grazing my hand down the center of her, from neck to pussy. She pressed my hand hard against her; my fingers itched to sink back in.

"I want every part of you, *gattina,* but I don't want to take it. I want you to offer it up."

"And the part of me that doesn't want to stay here? You *took* that. Are you going to keep taking it?" She let go of my hand, leaving it against her sensitive, wet flesh, while her hands grazed up my thighs, skimmed my hips, and met together between my pecs before she sank to her knees in front of me.

She had my pants undone and my cock unleashed in a flash, fisted in her slim hand as her tongue lapped up the bead of precum at the tip then flicked along the sensitive ridge.

Seconds later, her lips wrapped around me and took me into the moist heat of her mouth.

The beast rattled in its cage, threatening to burst free, to grab her hair and force every inch of my cock into that beautiful mouth. But I fisted my hands at my sides, watching as she swallowed every inch all on her own, taking me in to the back of her throat where the muscles contracted and damn near sent me over the edge embarrassingly fast.

I held on as she worked her way back to the tip before taking me all in again. Over and over again.

Ella, naked on her knees; the moist heat of her mouth; the exquisite clench of her throat muscles. It was the best fucking blow job of my life.

Don't let her do this, my conscience screamed, refusing to shut up. It knew as well as I did there was something else going on here.

I wanted to be pissed. She was using the skills Avalone had taught her, had beaten into her on me.

I tore her mouth away and dragged her up onto her feet. "This isn't going to work, Ella. You can't seduce me or fuck me into letting you go. I'm not keeping you here because I want you available around the clock. I'm keeping you here because if anything happened to you, I'd…"

"You'd what?"

"I don't know. And not knowing scares the fucking hell out of me," I confessed.

Her face was turned up to me, the kaleidoscope swirling in her gaze. Despite the raging hard-on, I leaned in and kissed her lips gently, a whisper-light touch at first. And then another.

Ella sighed as her fingers slipped up to my shoulders, pressing her breasts against my chest, the taut peaks scorching my skin through my shirt. Everything but the girl in front of me disappeared. No past, no future. Just Ella.

In the end, I couldn't say who seduced who. Neither. Both. All that mattered was the moment I slid into her body, I was home.

Chapter Thirty-One

Ella

It felt like someone had reached inside me and rearranged all my pieces.

Some of them fit better than before, some worse.

All of them felt new, unsettled.

I hated him for locking me up, and I kind of loved him for it too.

"How long?" I asked, keeping my eyes fixed on the grass beneath my feet as we wandered in the direction of the pond.

Signore had seldom let me outside. It was the best part of being free. The wind against my face, the sun warm on my skin, the sounds of birds during the day and crickets at night.

At least, Leo hadn't taken that away, too.

"How long, what?" he asked, turning to look at me.

"How long are you going to keep me here?" I held his gaze.

Leo sighed and scrubbed a hand through his hair. "Ten days. Once Avalone is dead, then you'll be free to go where you please."

My stomach roiled uncomfortably.

Free.

It was just an illusion, a mirage that could vanish at any moment. My throat burned with tears, but I was so tired of feeling. One minute angry, the next, aroused, and straight into sadness. It had been so much easier when there was nothing.

"I wish I could tell you I'm sorry, but I'm not, *gattina*. I won't apologize for wanting to keep you safe." Leo shook his head.

"I know."

If he was keeping me captive for his own selfish purposes, I could hate him. I could loath his touch and despise the very sight of him. But he wasn't.

Neither of us spoke as we followed the path we'd taken to the pond not long ago, side by side, but not touching. It was like Leo was trying to give me some space.

I counted at least four men guarding the front of the property, which meant escaping down the front drive was out of the question—not that I'd thought it would be that easy.

Leo stopped as we reached the pond, but I continued walking. I needed to see more.

"What's the matter, *gattina*?"

Aside from being kept here against my will? "I just don't feel like sitting still. Do you think... Would it be okay..." I mentally rolled my eyes at myself. I hated some of the things that had been ingrained in me.

"What would you like?" Leo pressed.

"Do you think we could just walk for a while?"

He nodded, but it seemed he was done giving me space.

He took my hand and led me past the pond and around a thick growth of wild blueberry bushes. Far beyond the bushes, trees bordered the property in a sweeping half-circle. What laid beyond them? More trees? How long would it take to reach some sign of civilization if I escaped that way?

"I know secrets are a prickly topic," he said after a few more quiet moments, "but I need to know what you have on the Russians."

My heart started to pound, and my throat tried to clamp down the moment he said the word. "I don't *have* anything on the Russians."

Not unless DNA counted.

I hadn't even known my father had been Bratva when I was a child. Not until I got older and began recognizing his tattoos. *Signore* had refused to tell me where I came from, but he knew. I know he did.

Out the corner of my eye, I watched Leo shake his head and run his fingers through his hair restlessly. His movements were stiff, and he seemed to be favoring his left arm.

"They've come after me twice, possibly three times, since we met. It can't be coincidence, Ella."

I looked him over from head to toe, searching for injuries. "What happened?" I reached out, starting at his shoulder and working downward, searching for the telltale proof. He hadn't taken the time to strip down when he'd fucked me; I'd just assumed he'd been in a hurry.

He laughed. "If you're trying to distract me, it's working." Then he unbuttoned his shirt and shrugged his shoulder out of it, revealing a swath of bandage all the way around, just above his bicep.

Bile rose in the back of my throat.

"It's no big deal. I was getting tired of my arm the way it was. This punches it up a bit, don't you think?"

"I'm sorry, Leo. I don't know why this happened to you."

Even if there was Sokolov blood in my veins, there were no other Sokolovs left. The Lucas had wiped them out... except maybe one.

"I guess it's back to the drawing board," he said dismissively, shrugging his shoulder back into his shirt.

Leo was quiet as we walked on, further and further away from the house until it was just a small square in the distance.

He stopped walking all of a sudden and turned to me, his gaze grazing from up to down.

"What are you doing?" I asked.

"Just looking to see if you've got any blunt objects."

"Why?"

He looked back at the distance we'd traveled. "In case you were planning on hitting me over the head and making a run for it while I was unconscious." He grinned like it was a joke, but there was an assessing look in his eyes.

"Tempting," I muttered.

One hit over the head, and it would be over. He'd recover just fine, and this would be over.

"Don't even bother," he said, watching my thoughts like they were written across my face.

"Wouldn't you?" I asked, wondering if he'd answer honestly.

"Yes," he admitted without hesitation. "I get why you want to run. I really do, Ella. And if I thought Avalone posed the kind of risk you think he does, I'd..." He shook his head. "Well, fuck, I don't know what I'd do. Hit our guards over the head and run off with you, maybe."

We'd have to run forever.

Always hiding.

Leo could never see his family again.

As angry as I was for him trapping me here, I wouldn't let that happen.

"But he's just a man, Ella," he said, tilting my chin up to meet his gaze, "and I'm going to kill him. Then this will be over. I know it's hard to believe, but when I locked that door on you, I felt just as trapped as you. You put me in a position where I had no choice. And for a man who isn't keen on having control taken away from him…" He let the thought trail off, but I could see the inner struggle on his face.

He was a strong, confident man who was used to being in control. Maybe it was how he'd dealt with the hell he'd gone through. Part of me wanted to give in, to do whatever he wanted me to if it erased the furrow that had formed between his brows, but I couldn't.

"I get it, Leo. Whether you want to or not, you can't stop fighting to keep me safe in the only way you know how. But don't think for a moment that I'll stop fighting to keep you safe in the only way I know how."

The more I'd thought about it, the more I'd come to realize there was only one way to make sure Leo and his family was safe.

I'm going to take care of it, Leo, I promised him silently as I squeezed his hand and headed back toward the house.

Chapter Thirty-Two

Leo

The heavy scents of grease and burnt meat hit me like an oily sledgehammer as I walked into the Main Street Diner.

Dom and Fallon followed close on my heels with Maria tucked in the crook of Fallon's arm. It was the same diner where Dom had met with the chief of police for years. The same dirty checkered floors. The same crude collection of rickety tables and metal chairs. But the man who sat alone at a table for four at the far side of the diner was barely recognizable as the man Dom had met with for years. The four stars embedded on his collar twinkled beneath the fluorescent lighting, like a neon sign driving attention to some badge of honor pinned beneath them. The man had done what he could to earn the honor attached to his uniform.

His fork moved around his plate, chasing the last plump cherry tomato in his chicken salad—a far cry from the greasy burgers he used to scarf back. The gut wasn't gone, but he'd lost weight. His hair was groomed, his shoes shined, and he wore a smile that stretched from ear to ear when he looked up and caught sight of his daughter.

I wasn't prone to the belief that a leopard could change its spots, but the chief of police had proved himself an exception to that rule.

"Hi, Daddy," Fallon said, as Douglas Moore stood and opened his arms wide and she stepped into his embrace, Maria snuggled between them.

The night the Novas attacked our home had been a turning point for Fallon and her father. He'd come roaring through the house, gun in hand, and screaming for his daughter. It was only thanks to Brute that none of our men put a bullet in him. Brute could be one hell of a shield when he wanted to be.

"Dominic, Leo," the chief said, nodding to each of us as he took a step back and pulled out a chair for Fallon.

Instead of a folder full of papers, he opened a compact laptop on the table next to his food as Dom and I sat down across from them.

"I pulled all the phone records you mentioned, but there was nothing out of the ordinary. I've got them here if you want to take a look," he said, spinning the laptop around for me and Dom to see.

We scrolled through the long list, and there were no incoming or outgoing calls to any phone numbers we didn't recognize. Nothing to suggest either Ella or any of our men had made a call to Avalone or his men.

"*Grazie*, Douglas," Dom said, turning the laptop back around.

"There was something else. Maybe," Douglas said, his brow furrowing. "I'm not sure. It could be nothing."

"Any information you've got could be useful," Dom said, and I had to hand it to my brother; his manners had definitely improved.

"It's that Russian fellow who had a… motorcycle accident a few days ago."

"What about him?" Dom and I asked in unison.

"Well, there was no good reason to go digging, but I thought I'd look around—city surveillance in places I thought worth looking, that sort of thing. I found this," he said, clicking on the screen and turning it back to face us.

A whole lot of random cars parked in front of a restaurant across town… and a whole lot of black BMWs with them. The snapshot had caught two men outside one of the BMWs, the tattoos on their necks and hands blurry, but visible.

"Like I said, it could be nothing. But maybe… maybe if there could be a problem, Fallon and Maria should come stay with me for a little while…" Douglas cleared his throat. "You know, just until things settle down."

"You think you can do a better job taking care of them?" Dom asked, his hackles rising.

"I think I don't know what I'd do if anything ever happened to them, Dominic. I treated Fallon wrong for so long after her mother died. I just want the chance to treat her and Maria right." He smiled at his daughter, and Fallon covered his hand with hers, squeezing tight.

Dom rolled his shoulders and cracked his neck, the less well-mannered version of my brother threatening to emerge. "Fallon and Maria are my whole world. I won't let anything happen to them. Ever."

"All right. If we could lower the testosterone level in the room just a little bit," Fallon said, cocking an eyebrow at her father, then

Dom. "I think *Fallon* is a big girl who can make decisions for herself, thank you very much."

"You go, girl," I joked.

"And besides, I think you three had reasons for being here other than discussing my living arrangements?"

Dom's shoulders relaxed a bit, and he nodded. "What made you decide to look around?" he asked Douglas.

I turned to Douglas, equally as eager for the answer. One lone Bratva guy showing up in a city hardly seemed like reason to scour how many hours of surveillance footage.

"I wouldn't have thought anything of it except the dead guy was a bratok of the Volkov family. There haven't been any rumors of that family making waves in this area for a long time—not since they had a big blowout with the Moretti family a little over twenty years ago. I remembered because it was the same time Moretti's daughter went missing—presumed dead, murdered by the Volkovs. They haven't been in the area ever since."

Douglas typed something on the keyboard then spun the laptop back around.

Tension coiled in my gut as my eyes landed on the screen. The woman in the photo staring back at us could almost have been Ella's twin—the same dark hair, high cheekbones, and heart-shaped chin. The same feline-like green eyes, but the woman's jaw was a little wider, her forehead, a little taller.

I wasn't the only one seeing the uncanny resemblance. Fallon and Dom's eyes were glued to the screen. Dom's expression was hidden behind a mask, but Fallon's mouth had fallen open.

Douglas cleared his throat. "That's Gabriella Moretti. When Dante brought me a photo of the girl, I knew she looked familiar, but I just couldn't place from where. Until I started looking into the Volkov family."

"Ella's a Moretti?" Fallon spoke first.

"I guess so," I said, but if that was true, then Ella wasn't just a Moretti.

Victoria Costa—Nico and Gabe's mother—had been a Moretti before she'd married Lorenzo, and that meant Ella was Victoria Costa's niece. She was cousin to the Costas, to Nico, Gabe, Sandro, and Caio.

Something warm exploded in my chest.

Ella thought she had lost her entire family in a car accident several years ago, but she had an aunt and at least a few cousins. She was part of the Morretti family who was a huge clan on their own.

"Did Ella ever mention her mother?" Dom asked me.

I nodded. "She said she died in a car accident, along with her father and only brother, eight years ago."

"Damn, that poor girl," Fallon said, her blue eyes brighter with tears.

Dom was shaking his head, his eyes caught up in thought. "But if Ella's mother died eight years ago, not twenty-something years ago, where had she been all that time?"

"Maybe she ran away?" I ventured a guess—a reasonable one, in my opinion. "If Nico's grandfather had been willing to marry Victoria off to a mean asshole like Lorenzo Costa, then who the hell had he lined up for Ella's mother?"

Dom nodded. "Definitely possible, but—"

"But what does that have to do with the Bratva?" I filled in. "Good question."

Douglas rubbed his knuckles across the five-o-clock shadow along his chin. "It isn't often the Bratva and the mafia mix blood, but maybe *Signor* Moretti had promised his daughter to a Volkov man for some reason? If Gabriella Moretti didn't think much of that arrangement, she might have decided to take matters into her own hands."

Not to mention, a little more than twenty years ago, she would have been pregnant with Ella.

"Good for her," Fallon piped up, glaring back and forth between Dom and her father.

There was a time when Fallon had been none too pleased about her own arranged marriage. Of course, that might have been because it was sprung on her at the age of twenty-eight, and Dom had been kind of a dick back then.

"You wish you'd taken matters into your own hands?" Dom asked, though the smile he was wearing said he wasn't really worried.

"Not for a minute," she said, smiling affectionately at her husband before her expression turned sober. "But if you think for a minute I'm going to let you tell Maria who she's going to marry, then you, my dear husband, are delusional."

"But that doesn't explain why the Bratva would be coming after her now unless they want—" My lips slammed shut. "If they think they're going to force Ella to marry—" I was on my feet, hands clenched, muscles shaking. I was more than ready to murder any Bratva who tried to get near her.

"Calm down, Leo," Dom said.

I sat back down, ignoring Douglas' wide-eyed stare and Fallon's concerned smile.

Dom laughed. Like full-gut, body-shaking laughter.

"Something funny?" I quipped.

"It's just been entertaining to see you lose your shit, *fratello*. The girl has seriously messed with that level head of yours."

"Anything to keep you amused, *fratello*."

My level head had good reason to be messed up.

Between Avalone, the Bratva, and keeping Ella from running off, it felt like I wouldn't see a good night's rest for the next decade.

Chapter Thirty-Three

Ella

"You can pet him, if you'd like," I said to the man sitting on the floor across the room with his knees bent and elbows perched on them. I sat cross-legged on the rug with my back against the bed while Duck meandered indiscriminately around the room.

"That's all right, *Signorina*," the man said, though he followed Duck with his eyes while the faintest hint of a smile tugged up one corner of his mouth.

When he'd opened the door half an hour ago with a tray full of food balanced on one big hand, I'd tripped backward across the whole width of the room, slamming my spine into the wall. The man was huge, like Riccardo and the countless other thugs *Signore* had used to transport me wherever he wanted me to go.

This man didn't seem quite so scary now—not that I'd relaxed enough to even contemplate eating.

"Why are you staying with me?" I asked him, less frazzled by his presence with every passing moment.

He shrugged. "I know what it's like to be alone." His voice was gruff and terrifying, just like his appearance, but there was something in his eyes that tempered the chill his presence evoked.

Not gentleness, exactly, but there was a rugged honesty in his gaze. If he'd wanted to hurt me, he wasn't the kind of man who would have bothered to hide his intentions.

"How do you know what it's like?" I asked, a little surprised by my own chattiness.

"I was an only child. My mamma worked in a brothel to keep me fed, but the boss wasn't a man like *Signor* Luca. Worked her into an early grave." He spoke matter-of-factly, not a flicker of self-pity in his tone, nor did I get the feeling he'd appreciate any pity from me now.

"You made him pay for that," I said, just as matter-of-factly. It was there in his eyes, what satisfaction he'd managed to glean from his retribution.

"*Sì, Signorina,* I did." He nodded.

"What made you come to work for the—"

The bedroom door swung open, and my heart skipped a beat, though, not in fear this time.

Leo was the most breathtaking man I'd ever seen. He smiled at me, and my heart pounded a little harder—such a stupid response.

The man who'd been sitting with me surged to his feet, his hands clasped in front of him, but there was no fear in his eyes.

The Lucas didn't rule their men with violence and threats. They commanded respect, and this man had a boatload of it for Leo and the other Lucas.

"*Buongiorno, Signor* Luca. I brought the *signorina* her lunch," he said, nodding to the untouched tray of food on the coffee table in front of the sofa.

"*Grazie*, Marco," Leo said with a nod of dismissal.

Marco left the room, but he paused for just a moment outside the door. He glanced back and nodded to me with what might have passed for a smile on his rugged face.

Leo was smiling, rubbing a hand over his mouth like he was trying to wipe it away.

"It seems there isn't anyone you don't have an effect on, *gattina,*" he said, turning to look across the room, out the window.

It wasn't the first time he'd said something to that effect, but with his face turned away, I couldn't read whether it bothered him or not.

"I need to tell you something," he said, turning to face me.

There was a furrow between his brows, and his arms were stiff at his sides, a file folder in one hand. He seemed agitated, but not angry, but nothing about his body language gave anything away.

"What is it?"

"Your mother, did you know anything about her?" Leo asked, making the back of my neck prickle uncomfortably.

This was dangerous territory. It wasn't a far leap from my mother to my father. I can feel my heart start to beat in my chest.

"I knew a lot about her. I don't know what you mean," I said quietly.

Leo closed the distance between us and took my hand in his, clasping it a little too tightly. "What was her name?"

"Ella Ricci. I was named after her. Why?" My mouth tightened.

Leo shook his head. "I don't think that was her real name," he said gently like he was breaking bad news. "I believe your mother's name was Gabriella. Gabriella Moretti."

Gabriella.

I tested the name on my tongue.

It still had my name in it, but it didn't fit right, not when I envisioned my mother as I'd last seen her.

Her long, dark hair that felt like silk when I played with it, and the tiny crinkles at the edges of her green eyes that I could only see when she smiled. But as much as it didn't fit, Leo's revelation wasn't entirely surprising.

If my father had lied about his identity, why not my mother too?

"Why were you researching my mother?" I asked.

"I wasn't, not directly. It came up after I ran into a problem a few days ago."

"A problem?" I raised a brow.

Leo shook his head. "It doesn't matter. What's important is I think you have a right to know who she really was."

He opened the folder he'd been holding and handed me the two pieces of paper inside it.

The first page was a photo of my mother, but not quite the way I remembered her. She was younger here, not much older than me. The other piece of paper was a photocopy of a young woman's driver's license, a woman who looked just like my mother, but the name on the license read *Gabriella Moretti*.

I tried to shrug it off, tried to ignore the thin tendril of my mother being torn from my chest. She'd been my mother, no matter her name.

"I just don't see why it matters. Whatever my mother's name was, she's gone, Leo. I don't get to have her back again."

I couldn't tear my gaze away from the photo. It was more of my mother than I'd had in a long time.

"No, and I wish I could change that," he said, pulling me closer, "but I might be able to give you something else."

"You found out more?" I asked, trying to steady my voice.

Leo grazed his fingers along my jaw. "Not exactly, but I know some things about your mother's family, and I thought it might help to patch up the hole a little."

I didn't know what to say. Telling him the holes inside me were wide and gaping and could never be patched felt melancholic and self-indulgent.

"Your mother had a sister, *gattina.* Victoria Moretti... now Victoria Costa."

My pulse rose.

"Nico and Gabe Costa are your cousins, along with two others, Caio and Sandro."

I had an aunt. Four cousins.

My stomach started to churn, a small whirl spinning in on itself until it destroyed everything in its path.

"Ella?"

I sat down hard on the edge of the bed as a cold sweat broke out across my brow. "I have family."

Five more people who could be hurt because of me.

"That's a good thing, *gattina,*" Leo said, sitting down next to me. "They're downstairs, and would very much like to meet you. You've seen Nico and Gabe, but Victoria..." He shrugged. "...she's a very nice woman."

Nice or not, I didn't want to meet them.

They were just more people I could end up caring about. More people I was going to have to leave behind.

"All right," I said.

I stood up and smoothed down my dress. It was a pretty dress—sage green and wrap-style, it fell past midthigh, but I felt underdressed. Underwhelming.

What would they think of me now that they knew who I was?

More importantly, what would *she* think of me? My mother's sister—the closest I would get to my mother ever again.

"You look beautiful, Ella," Leo said, stilling my hands.

While it may have looked like they were fidgeting with my dress, they were busy trying to smooth out and cover up the blemishes of the girl underneath.

He kept hold of my hands and tilted my chin up with his free hand to look at him.

"I meant, you look beautiful inside and out," he said, reading me too well.

"Thank you."

***

From the top of the stairs, I saw her.

She was tall and slim, and very beautiful. Her silver and chestnut hair was knotted intricately at the crown of her head, and she looked up at me with green eyes that were just like mine. Just like my mother's.

I wasn't sure if I walked down the stairs, or maybe floated; I couldn't remember getting to the bottom landing, but suddenly, I was there, staring into green tear-filled eyes. Eyes, that were fixed on mine, looking hard.

Before the panic could take hold, the woman pulled me into her arms, squeezing tight.

"You look just like your mother," she whispered against my cheek.

Out of nowhere, my body started to tremble and sobs tried to wrack free from my chest.

No woman had hugged me since I was twelve years old. I'd had no idea how much I missed it. But more than that, this wasn't just any woman. She was my mother's sister, and when I hugged her back, I could almost feel my mother wrapping her arms around the both of us.

Too soon, she let me go, but she grabbed my hand and held it tight. "I can't tell you how happy I am to meet you, *cara mia,*" she said and kissed my cheek.

"I'm happy to meet you too."

I realized it was true.

At the same time, I was aware of four other pairs of eyes on me.

"These are my sons, Nico, Gabe, Caio, and Sandro." She motioned toward each one as she spoke.

Nico and Gabe, I recognized; I'd seen them already.

Caio and Sandro were twins, only differing in haircut—one short, one long, as if they'd done it to be sure people could tell them apart.

"It's nice to meet you, Ella," the twins said nearly in tandem and stepped toward me, but Leo and Gabe stepped into their path while Nico shook his head at the twins.

My skin crawled, and my cheeks warmed, imagining all the sordid details of my life painted across my skin for them to see. All the fidgeting and smoothing in the world couldn't wipe that away.

I could either cower in shame… or not, and with Leo at my side, it didn't seem quite so difficult to stand tall and meet their eyes.

Eyes that were all green like mine, but that was where the similarity ended.

Sandro's eyes were guarded, taking in his surroundings like he hadn't been here often, if ever. Caio's eyes were open and inquisitive, and Nico's were like sharpened steel. It was Gabe's eyes, though, that helped me find my voice. There was something in them that reminded me of Leo and Brute; not something soft, but warm.

"It's okay," I said.

I was grateful when Gabe held out his hand instead of hugging me. It wasn't a handshake, exactly. He held my hand in his and smiled, setting the example for his brothers to follow.

It was Nico who clasped my hand last. "Welcome to the family, Ella," he said, but beneath the cordial words, there was a promise hidden in his steely gaze. *Nobody fucks with my family and gets away with it, and that family includes you.*

I squeezed his hand and stared right back.

Thanks to Leo, I'd found family, people with the same blood running through their veins as me. And thanks to Leo, I'd found the strength in me to meet Nico's gaze and make him a silent promise in return.

Nobody fucks with my family, I told him and then mentally prepared myself for what came next.

Chapter Thirty-Four

Ella

I stared at Leo as he filled Duck's food bowl.

I'd spent countless hours since we met looking at him, memorizing the lines of his body, the way he moved, the play of expressions across his features.

But it seemed more important now.

The barely-there crinkles at the corners of his eyes when he smiled. The way he tunneled his fingers through his hair when he was frustrated. The way his pupils dilated, narrowing the ring of twilight blue around them when he looked at me, just like he was doing now.

"What are you thinking, *gattina?*"

"I'm thinking I could look at you forever and never get bored."

Every other thought and feeling, I'd buried down deep, too deep for even Leo to find it.

I plastered a seductive smile on my face as he put down the bag of food and crossed the room to where I sat at the edge of the bed.

Any words I could say to him tonight would be lies, half-truths that hid what was really going on in my head.

But in this, I could be honest.

I could give him everything, holding nothing back.

I stood up and reached for the hem of my dress, watching heat flare in his eyes before I drew the dress up over my head and tossed it on the bed behind me.

"*Bored* certainly isn't the word that comes to mind when I look at you," he said, grazing a finger down the center of me from my neck to my navel.

Goose bumps rose across my flesh, but my body felt warmer, a languid heat already pumping through my veins.

As Leo leaned in closer, I took a step back, bumping the backs of my knees against the mattress, creating just enough room between us for me to sink to my knees in front of him.

I kept my gaze locked on his, so there was no missing the flare of heat in his eyes as I slid my hands up his thighs to his waist.

His cock jerked behind his fly as I worked the zipper of his pants down. Heat coiled low in my abdomen as I hooked my fingers in the waist of his pants and pulled them down along with the black boxer briefs beneath.

His cock sprung free, already rock hard and weeping precum from the tip.

My tongue darted out, lapping it up and making his cock jerk as his fingers wound in the hair at the back of my head.

I teased the sensitive ridge with the tip of my tongue, feeling the tension in his body grow.

Leo was fighting the urge to thrust forward into my mouth, and I knew he'd go on resisting, no matter how much he wanted it. He wouldn't force me, and knowing that made me hungrier. It made my mouth water with the desire to take him in, to wring every drop of pleasure from his body.

I opened my mouth and took him in, all the way to the back of my throat, relaxing the muscles there like I'd been taught.

But for the first time, I *wanted* this.

"Fucking Christ," he cursed as his hips jerked and his grip tightened in my hair. "Your mouth is fucking perfect, *gattina*."

His voice sent ripples of pleasure coursing through me as I worked my way back to the tip, sweeping my tongue along the ridge as I went before taking him back in. I reached for the base of his cock and worked my hand in rhythm with my mouth, knowing I'd never be able to take every inch of him. He was too big, but I tried, swallowing every inch of him I could. Faster. Humming, wrapping his cock in vibrations.

Without warning, he yanked himself away and dragged me up.

"Hands above your head, *gattina*," he ordered, pressing my back up against the post of the bed. "Hold on to the post and don't let go."

I obeyed, gripping the cool wood tight as his mouth paved a blazing path down my throat and then further, covering every inch of my body with his lips until his teeth joined in, nipping at the upper swell of my breast, my nipple, the flesh between my ribs, making my body sting sweetly.

By the time his breath brushed across my clit, I was a panting sparked-up mess.

"Leo," I moaned, throwing my head back as his tongue flicked across my clit in a featherlight touch.

"Look at me, *gattina*," he demanded, stilling until my gaze met his.

Without looking away, he raised my foot to his shoulder, spreading me before him, his warm breath touching me everywhere.

Then his mouth was on me, his lips suckling my clit, his tongue grazing along my slit, spearing me and lapping up every drop of my wetness. Driving me higher. His teeth grazed my clit, and the light sting spun the coil inside me tighter.

I gripped the post harder as his tongue flicked back and forth.

Leo pulled away, and I cried out, desperate to chase the orgasm that hovered just out of reach. But he lowered my foot to the ground and stood up, wearing a smile that said he knew exactly how close I'd been.

"Turn around, hands on the bed," he said, taking my hips and pulling them back toward him as I complied. "I've fantasized about fucking every part of you," he said as his fingers trailed between my cheeks, "but for now…"

His cock pressed against my slit, and he drove in.

"Oh god, yes," I panted as he filled me up, sending the coil spinning faster.

No easing in; no slowing to give my body time to adjust. I held on tight to the mattress, as his hips pistoned, fucking me harder. Faster.

"Look at me, *gattina.*" He grabbed my hair and turned my head.

My breath hitched.

Leo was an *incredible* sight—his body glistening with a light sheen of sweat, his jaw clenched, pleasure written across his face.

"You are the sexiest woman I've ever seen."

"You feel so good, Leo, so—"

His hips jolted, driving deeper, making me delirious, my eyes almost rolled to the back of my head.

His fingers stayed wrapped in my hair, holding me there, but I couldn't have looked away if my life had depended on it. Harder.

Faster. I drove my hips back to meet him, taking every inch of him inside me.

So deep. So close.

"Come for me, Ella," he ground out.

I fought the urge to close my eyes as I reached the precipice.

My scream filled the room as I shot headlong over the edge and shattered into a million shards of bliss.

"Fuck, I'm going to come," he groaned as my pussy spasmed around him, milking him, taking him with me. Eyes wide open. Never looking away.

It felt like his orgasm tore right through me, laying open my soul and claiming it.

Exposed.

One hundred percent his.

Always his, no matter what.

Chapter Thirty-Five

Ella

Moonlight slipped through the part in the bedroom's curtains, shining dimly across the man lying in the middle of the four-poster bed. Dark hair. Clean-shaven. His eyes were closed, and we'd managed to kick the comforter onto the floor some time during the night, leaving every hard plane and sinewy muscle on display.

God, he was beautiful.

Whatever laid at the core of Leo Luca was stubborn, and cocky, and the most beautiful thing I'd ever seen.

We hadn't known each other long, but it had felt like we were old souls, long-separated and finally reunited.

Yet here I was ripping us apart again.

He sighed in his sleep and flung an arm out to his side. It would have been so easy to crawl back into bed, nestle up against all that chiseled flesh, and feel the beat of his heart against my cheek.

So easy.

I'd been watching him for the past hour, waiting for the perfect moment to sneak away, but that moment never came.

He could wake up at any second. He could catch me. Stop me. Tie me up and banish any hope of escape.

Was it a thousand kinds of crazy that part of me wanted him to catch me, to take away my ability to leave?

I shook my head and forced the coward deep down. She had no say here.

She couldn't.

I took one deep, steadying breath, slung my bag over my shoulder, and forced my feet to move toward the bedroom door, glancing back over and over again, watching for a flinch, listening for a hitch in his breathing. Anything at all that signaled my escape was over before it had begun.

Leo remained motionless aside from the steady rise and fall of his chest.

So many similarities to the last time I'd escaped, and yet, so different.

The elastic inside my chest felt stretched to the max.

Every step, I struggled against its pull.

Damn it.

It shouldn't have to be this hard.

I kept going until the cool metal of the doorknob laid beneath my fingers. In my other hand, I held two coat hangers I'd been hiding under the bed, the ends bent straight to fit into the skeleton keyhole.

My hands shook so hard, it would be nearly impossible to unlock the door without waking him up.

But I'd come this far.

I had to try.

Willing my hands to be still, I glanced back once more, then held my breath as I slipped the hanger ends into the lock, hoping to catch the lever and dead bolt at the same time.

I'd managed it twice in *Signore's* room before he'd removed all the clothes hangers and anything else that could be fashioned into a pick for the lock.

The scrape of metal against metal blared like a siren, but Leo didn't make a sound.

His chest continued to rise and fall in the same steady rhythm.

I held my breath.

With a turn of the handle, I tiptoed out of the room and closed the door quietly behind me.

I crept along the hallway to the top of the staircase then closed my eyes and listened for any sound from downstairs.

Silence.

Unlike *Signore*, the Lucas trusted their men. They weren't worried about an attack from within, so all of their protective focus was directed outward, watching for incoming threats.

As quietly as I could, I crept down the stairs.

One step, and then another, while my heart pounded like a drum in my chest, blood whooshing past my ears, and the elastic pulled so taut, it ached through my whole chest.

You have to do this.

It wasn't a pep talk.

It was the truth.

The only way to keep Leo and his family safe.

I forced my feet to move, descending the final steps and crossing the foyer to the front door without a backward glance.

It was too late to turn back now.

All I could do was move forward, so I opened the door, just enough to slip out. No freedom this time. No relief. Just an empty, gut-wrenching ache in my chest.

The cool night air slipped through the thin dress I wore, but I couldn't feel it. There was nothing but the ache. So potent, so deep.

Maybe there would never be anything else.

I kept to the shadows of the house, staying out of sight of the men posted around the property. The few I could see were all standing alert, their backs straight, eyes outward, watching for threats.

It was the first time I'd considered that if they saw me, it might not end in a thwarted escape attempt. All these men were armed.

The crack of the gunshot I heard the night I'd escaped *Signore's* reverberated in my head. I'd waited to feel it, even wondered what it would be like. A burning pain? Stabbing? Hot or cold? If these men saw me, I could very well find out any moment.

I kept going, waiting until the last possible second to branch away from the house, swerving toward the pond. It was an aggravatingly slow progression, keeping to the bushes, hiding behind trees long enough to listen for any sign I'd been discovered.

While I'd planned the route, I hadn't figured out just how long I'd have to stay hidden before I could stretch my legs and run.

Past clusters of white lilies that looked gray in the moonlight.

Around wild blueberry bushes that blended with the night's blackness and scratched at my bare legs.

When the lights of the house were little more than specks in the distance, I crouched close to the ground and listened. Waiting for the crunch of twigs. A rustling of leaves. Anything that would give away a guard on approach.

Nothing.

I waited one more moment, staring at the specks of light and allowed myself to try to imagine what could have been if I'd been an ordinary girl.

What would that even have looked like? Dinner dates? Movie nights curled up on the sofa?

I laughed under my breath.

The truth was I had no idea what ordinary looked like.

I had a feeling that a life with Leo would have been anything but ordinary.

I stood up and turned away.

If I let myself think about it any longer, I wouldn't have the strength to keep pulling against the elastic.

It was time to let it go.

I ran.

I ran as fast as I could over the uneven terrain, made even more difficult by the canopy of leaves above that filtered out the moonlight.

I bashed my shoulder into a tree.

Caught my hair on a low-lying branch.

Scuffed my shin on a cluster of rocks.

I had no idea how long I ran. It was like the woods behind the Luca's estate went on forever.

My lungs burned. My legs ached. But I kept going, keeping my hands out in front of me to keep from running into more branches I couldn't see.

Then the trees were gone. Without warning, the woods gave way to a flat stretch of grass, maybe twenty yards wide. No more tree roots underfoot. No more branches snagging my clothes. It was an abrupt enough difference, it threatened my balance, and I had to throw my arms out at my sides to stay upright.

And then the long grass gave way to smooth asphalt.

I doubled over in relief, catching my hands on my knees and gulping one great lungful of air after another. Sweat trickled down my brow and the back of my dress was stuck to my body with sweat, but I'd done it.

Relief mixed with something bitter. Something that tasted an awful lot like the life I could have had with Leo, all of it coated in the black vile sludge of my reality.

I put one foot in front of the other, walking south along the road to put as much distance between me and Leo as I could while catching my breath.

Once my breathing had returned to normal, I stopped.

I pulled out the cell phone I'd stashed in my bag—the one Brute had given me. I'd taken Leo's too and left it in the blueberry bushes. It wouldn't slow him down for long, but it would stop any pestering phone calls from waking him up.

I turned on Brute's phone, dialed his number, and held the phone up to my ear.

I needed to hear his voice one last time.

It had barely finished ringing once when Brute's voice sounded on the other end of the line.

"Ella?" he barked, his voice caught somewhere between grogginess and panic.

The corners of my mouth tugged upward. The rough and tough biker was one hell of a softy at heart. "Hi, Brute."

"Is everything okay?" he asked, the grogginess giving way to panic.

"Yes, everything's fine," I lied. "I was just hoping... Would... would you do me a favor?" I finally managed to spit out.

There was a lump burning at the back of my throat, making it difficult to speak.

"Of course, pretty girl. Anything. What's wrong?"

I could picture him pacing back and forth across his bedroom, his worry forming creases at the corners of his eyes. I shouldn't have called.

It was selfish.

"N-nothing," I stuttered and cursed myself for it. I closed my eyes. "Would you just tell Leo for me that I didn't have a choice, I had to do the right thing, and that... that he needs to think about people like Maria and not do anything stupid."

"Ella, what's going on?"

I swallowed back the burning in my throat, shoving it down with the ache in my chest. "I love you, Brute. I should have told you that before, but I had to tell you now because... because I have to leave. I have to go back to hiding, and I couldn't do that without saying goodbye." I choked out the words then ended the call.

Tears gathered in my eyes, blurring the dark landscape around me, but I couldn't fall to pieces.

Not yet.

I stared at the phone in my hand.

It was almost done.

My fingers were frozen.

I couldn't make them move on the keypad.

"*No matter what comes at you in life,*" my father's voice echoed in my ears, "*you face it head-on, solnyshka.*" *Little sun.* He'd been talking about the vase I'd broken and tried to hide from him, but the lesson was just as relevant here, now.

I squared my shoulders.

I dialed the last number I needed to call.

It was funny that, to an outsider, it would look like I'd taken the coward's route.

I'd caved.

I'd given up.

But this was me fighting. Maybe not with guns and fists, but with every breath in my lungs and every drop of blood in my body to keep the man I loved safe from harm.

Loved.

I loved him with every piece of my shattered heart.

Damn the world and anyone in it who would label me a coward for what I was about to do.

The phone rang, rattling my brain.

Again and again.

I held it pressed tight against my ear, gritting my teeth.

The phone stopped ringing.

"*Sì?*" a deep voice spoke, sending shivers down my spine and making my whole body shake.

I took a deep breath, one inhale, one long exhale.

I opened my mouth then slammed it shut when no sound came out.

I counted one long second before opening my mouth again.

I gripped the hilt of the knife hidden against my thigh.

"I'm ready to come home, *Signore.*"

Chapter Thirty-Six

Leo

Duck's loud quacking woke me up.

No smooth transition.

No easing into consciousness.

He just might have been the most effective alarm clock known to man.

If only the duck could figure out morning from nighttime.

As I sat up, it didn't escape my bleary eyes' notice that the room was still shrouded in black, not even the faintest hint of dawn on the horizon.

I flopped back down, reaching for Ella.

The space on the mattress beside me was cold—the kind of cold that permeated my skin and wrapped around my spine.

I shot out of bed, narrowly avoiding the duck.

The sliver of light shining in through the window was just enough to make his green head stand out from the backdrop of black around him.

I swerved and hit the light switch.

The sofa was empty.

I spun around and spotted the closed bathroom door.

I knocked and waited with bated breath.

When there was no response, I opened the door, praying to every deity up in the clouds.

I found a folded piece of paper on the vanity next to the duck's carrier.

"I know I couldn't have left him in better hands," the note read.

I grabbed my pants from next to the bed and checked the pocket as I dragged them on, feeling for the familiar outline of the key.

"She picked the lock," I said aloud.

White-hot heat began pumping through my veins.

Ella had escaped from Avalone, after all. It's not like he opened the door and let her walk out.

I fought the urge to slam my fist into something and stormed across the room.

I jiggled the doorknob, and it swung freely in my hand.

I slammed the door closed behind me and started down the hall.

Dante's bedroom door cracked open, and he walked out, rubbing sleep from his eyes. "What the hell's going—" His eyes found me, and he stopped talking.

"I should have tied her to the fucking bed," I hollered.

"Calm down, *fratello*. What happened?"

I scoffed at the same time Dom's door opened.

Dom had a deep furrow between his brows and was holding his phone out in front of him like it was radioactive.

"I don't know what you did to piss off Brute," he said, holding out the phone to me, "but I suggest you fix it, Leo. And where the hell is your phone?"

Fuck. How could Brute know Ella was missing already?

Reluctantly, I held the phone up to my ear. "Brute?"

"Where the hell is she, Leo?" Brute barked from the other end of the line, his voice roaring over the sound of a loud engine. The crazy fucker was on his bike.

"I don't know, Brute. I'm trying to find out," I ground out, doing my damnedest to remember Brute wasn't the enemy here.

"I'll be there in ten minutes," he said, then the line went dead.

"Fucking wonderful." I scowled at the phone and handed it back to Dom.

I didn't have to wonder where my phone was. She'd taken it— one less thing to wake me up before she managed to slip away, but she wouldn't have kept it on her, knowing I'd track it.

"Ella's gone?" Dom asked, his gaze flying back and forth between me and Dante.

"She couldn't have gone far," Dante jumped in. "We'll find her, Leo."

I scoffed. "Do you think we're going to find her waltzing along the highway, thumbing a ride?" I shook my head. Ella wasn't just running away. She was hiding. She'd managed to hide from Avalone for a long time before his men found her, which meant she was damn good at it. "Avalone found her once, Dante. It's only a matter of time before he finds her again. If I don't find her first…"

Too many possibilities flooded my mind. Would he kill her? Beat her? Rape her? With the secrets in her head, he wouldn't sell her, but there was nothing stopping him from turning her into a lifeless, broken shell himself.

"Then we'll find her first," Dom said with more conviction than I felt.

"I need every available man out looking for her. Now. She can't have been gone more than four hours," I spat.

Four *fucking* hours. Four hours ago, she'd been in my bed, her bare legs twined with mine, her body slick with sweat.

"Marco, organize it," Dom barked.

"*Sì*, Signor Luca." Marco nodded from where he stood at the bottom of the stairs. His features were arranged in an emotionless mask, but his hands, curled into fists at his sides, belied his indifference. "The *signorina* could have maintained a maximum speed of no more than six miles an hour for four hours. I'll organize a search twenty-four miles from the house in all directions."

It was a lot of ground to cover, but we'd do it. "I'll head out twenty-four miles due east and work my way back toward the house."

Dom nodded—not that I was looking for his permission—then he sighed. "I'll apprise Nico of the situation."

I didn't envy him that job.

I was already heading down the steps, three at a time, when Dante fell into step beside me. "Your eyes might be the youngest here, but it never hurts to have another set," he said, clapping me on the back as he turned toward the door to the garage.

"*Grazie, fratello.*"

As much as I wasn't fit for company at the moment, he was right. And maybe having someone to vent at wasn't a terrible idea because I wasn't sure if I was going to hug Ella or strangle her when we found her.

If we find her.

Chapter Thirty-Seven

Leo

Twenty-four miles out, I parked the car on the shoulder of the highway and got out.

If Ella had wanted to head back toward civilization to get lost amid the crowd, this was the fastest route. But something niggled at the back of my mind.

I closed the door and circled around to the passenger side as Dante shut the door behind him, a flashlight in one hand.

No gun, no knife; my brother was armed with a *flashlight*. If I wasn't busy trying to keep all the crazy in my head from spewing out, I would have been laughing my ass off.

"Let's go," I said, hopping over the ditch at the side of the road and heading for the wooded expanse beyond it.

All we had to do was check every rock, bush, and tree from here to the estate.

A thousand-and-one bushes in, we'd found no sign of her.

The niggling grew stronger with every step, wrapping around my brain like rough fabric and making me itch.

I ran through every conversation I'd had with her in my head, searching for an answer, even a hint at which route she would have taken or where she planned to hide.

One conversation stood out from all the others.

"*...don't think for a moment that I'll stop fighting to keep you safe in the only way I know how.*"

My feet stumbled to a stop.

My chest turned ice cold.

"Leo?" Dante stopped beside me, swinging his flashlight in my direction.

"We need to get back to the house. Now."

I turned and ran.

We had to have covered at least a mile.

A mile of backtracking.

A mile of time wasted.

My mind turned into a sick son of a bitch as I ran, imagining where she was now and what was happening to her. It was like a nightmare, only I wasn't asleep. No hope of waking up to escape it.

I sprinted out of the trees and headed for the Lambo on the highway's shoulder, Dante following close on my heels.

He'd barely made it into the passenger seat when I revved the engine and turned the car around, darting across the highway, daring any late-night driver to try getting in my way.

"Do you want to tell me what the hell we're doing?" Dante barked as he chucked the flashlight onto the floor.

"She's not out there," I said quietly.

I could feel Dante cocking an eyebrow, impatiently waiting for an explanation.

I ground my teeth, not wanting to put a name to my nightmare, as if speaking it out loud would make it true. "She didn't run away, Dante."

"There's no fucking way anyone took her from our house, Leo. You know that."

I shook my head. "I had to lock her in the house, not because she didn't want to be there, but because she didn't want to put us at risk."

"Okay. So, what does that mean?"

"What's the only sure way to eliminate the risk? To make sure Avalone lost interest in us?"

I could see it in his expression the moment he figured it out, the corners of his eyes tightening, his teeth clenched together.

He nodded once, slowly. "She'd have to——"

"Don't say it. Just don't fucking say it."

I floored it down the highway and onto the exit ramp. The tires squealed around the corner as I turned onto the road, but I didn't slow down.

"Please call Dom," I told Dante. "Just tell him I need Gabe at the house fast."

I appreciated that Dante made the call without question, even though he wasn't usually the type to take orders from his younger brother without question.

It took fifteen minutes to get back to the house. Fifteen wasted minutes.

By the time the tires screeched to a stop at the top of the driveway, I had a plan. Not a great one. Hell, it wasn't even a good one. Just one of the reasons I was relieved to see a Costa standing on the front porch. All right, two Costas and a Luca, but I only needed Gabe at the moment.

Nico and Gabe both nodded in my direction as Raven, my baby sister, flew down the front steps. She ran into Dante first, catching him in a quick hug before circling the hood of the car and wrapping her arms around me.

It wasn't that long ago the Lucas and Costas had slaughtered their way through countless men to get to her when Diego Berlusconi had kidnapped her. Aside from a flesh wound in her arm from a bullet, Raven had walked away relatively unscathed from that nightmare. What were the chances Ella would walk away similarly intact?

"Dom called us right away and sort of filled us in on what's going on. Tell us how we can help." It wasn't an empty offer. I could feel the holster of the gun on her hip. After our mother had hidden her at the age of ten to protect her from a future she hadn't wanted for her daughter, Raven had been raised by Vito Agossi to be a strong, independent woman. She did not subscribe to the archaic notion that mafia work was men's work. Unfortunately, there was nothing she could do to help, not right now.

"I need to talk to Gabe," I told her, kissing the top of her head, trying to soften the blow.

Raven drew back, her brow furrowed. "To Gabe?"

Since she was engaged to the don of the Costa family, she was probably used to Nico being the one in highest demand, but not today. Not for this. There was only one Costa who had a hope in hell of helping me get to Ella.

"Dom said all of you were out looking for a girl that's important to you—a girl who's related to Nico—but suddenly you're back, and I don't see her," she said, cautiously peering into the car's front window. "What's going on, Leo?" She put her hand on my chest like she was bracing us both for the worst.

"She's not dead," I said, choking on the word. "She's just not out there." I motioned back the way we'd come.

Ella wasn't hiding in a tree or a bush. She wasn't hitchhiking her way back to the city. She wasn't on a bus bound out of state.

"Avalone's got her," I said, turning to Gabe who'd followed Raven down the steps. "I'm going to get her back."

"Fuck," Gabe roared. His hands were bunched in fists, and he seriously looked like he needed to hit something. Ella was no longer just a pretty face; she was blood. But at the same time, a literal boatload of girls was on the line too. "Damn it, I knew something was up."

"How?" I tilted my head to the side.

"Nico and your father have had men watching Avalone's estate ever since we decided to take him down. And up until two hours ago, there'd been nothing out of the ordinary happening."

My mouth tightened. "What happened two hours ago?"

"Two SUVs pulled into the garage, and twenty minutes later, all the guards headed into the house. They haven't come out since, and I don't know what the fuck they're doing in there."

"Fuck it," I said. Fuck caution. Fuck control. "I don't care how many men he's got in there." I balled my hands into fists so hard my knuckles turned bone-white. "I'm going to get her back without alerting the ship."

It was the only option.

I could hear Ella in my head, and no matter how much she cared for me, at least a part of her would never forgive me, would always despise me, if I condemned a ship full of girls to sexual slavery to save her.

"I'm listening," Gabe said, cracking his knuckles like he was gearing up for the fight.

"That black van we saw, was there anything remarkable about it? Anything that would stand out?"

"Nope." He shook his head, but the flash of understanding in his green eyes said he was catching onto the plan already. "Fake licence plate and no markings on the vehicle."

"Perfect. We need one," I said, turning to Dante, hoping his willingness to help first, ask questions later would hold.

I could tell he was still listening with half an ear as he pulled out his phone and made a call, securing the kind of vehicle we needed.

"We pack the back of the van with our men. If there are no guards out, then it won't be a problem getting close to the house. If they're back at their posts, then with the van, we should be able to get past the guards and make it to the top of the drive. Once there, all we have to do is make it twenty feet to the side door and tackle whatever comes at us from the house. But we do it quietly."

It wasn't a foolproof plan. Avalone could have instructed his men not to let anyone in, scheduled or not. Or we could make it up to the house only to be swarmed by his men. And even if we made it inside, we were going in blind with no idea what would come at us in there. A lot of opportunities for things to fall to shit.

Gabe was silent, the wheels clearly turning behind his green eyes. Eyes the same color as Ella's. "There're no guarantees, but it's a decent plan. Except for one thing. Assuming we make it up the driveway, if they don't have a girl coming out, then they're going to expect us to have a girl going in."

"So, you're going to need a girl," Raven chimed in, fisting her hands on her hips and standing up taller.

"Oh, hell no," I said in unison with Nico, Dom, and Dante.

She huffed and shook her head. "So, I suppose one of you is going to wax your legs and put on a pretty wig?" she said, looking from one of us to the next. "I'm sorry, boys, but I don't think any of you would be able to pull off a desirable girl—which is what I'm assuming we're going after here?" She cocked an eyebrow, clearly feeling like she had us trapped—which wasn't entirely untrue.

But since my sister looked about ready to kick every one of us in the balls, it seemed prudent to step in.

"It's not a sexist thing, Raven," I said, looking her in the eyes and hoping she'd see the truth in what I was saying. "You're strong and skilled as fuck, but you've had very little experience in combat situations. If you end up captured, or worse, none of us are going to be able to keep our heads on straight. I need to get Ella back. I need you to let me do this the way I know it needs to be done, *si?*"

Her hands slipped from her hips, and her shoulders deflated. "I'm sorry, Leo. I wish I could—"

"Don't be sorry. I know you'd do this if you could."

Raven might have spent a decade away from her family, but the minute she found her way back to us, she was a Luca through and through. She'd take a bullet for us in a heartbeat, just like we would for her.

"I'll do it," the tall blonde said from the top of the steps, her arms crossed over her chest and staring us each down.

Greta Agossi, Raven's best friend, and a force to be reckoned with. Greta didn't have the same combat experience the rest of us did, but she had some, and she'd been right there with her uncle, Vito, when we rescued Raven, slitting throats just like the rest of us.

It wasn't a bad plan; Greta was skilled with a knife and as cool as her steel blade under pressure.

Raven was shaking her head. "Are you crazy, Greta? Do you think *Zietto* Vito is going to let you do this?"

Greta laughed. "I think I was twelve years old the last time he tried to tell me what to do." She waltzed down the steps like some kind of warrior princess gearing up for battle. Any idiot who thought women were weak just needed to take one look at this girl.

"I don't like this, Leo," Dom said, his arms crossed. "There are a hell of a lot of unknowns here."

"I don't like it either." There was no sense in denying it. This was a fucked-up plan. A fucked-up plan that could go wrong in at least a hundred different ways. "If the ship gets wind of trouble at Avalone's, it'll cruise right on by, Dom. They'll unload the girls somewhere else. If that happens, you know we'll never find them."

"Since when were you in the business of rescuing girls you've never even met?" The open look in his eyes said he was more curious than critical.

I paused.

I had an itch I'd been wanting to scratch for a long time, something I couldn't figure out, never been able to define.

"It's just something I've got to do, Dom," I said, knowing he'd understand.

I didn't have to pull out the Fallon card. If it were Fallon in Ella's place, we both knew he'd be in my shoes, ready to do whatever it took to get her back.

Dom nodded, his lips pressed flat together.

"The van will be at the warehouse in ten minutes," Dante announced, finally hanging up his phone.

"Sounds like it's time for us to go, boys," Greta said, clapping me and Gabe on the back. "I'll be back in a flash." She darted into the house without an explanation but reappeared in the doorway a minute later, her jeans hacked off to short shorts and her T-shirt ripped and mangled.

"All right, it's time to make this look authentic," she said, hopping down the stairs and turning to my sister.

"Raven? Do you remember the role I played in keeping you in the dark all those years?" Greta asked.

Greta had spent ten years as my sister's best friend without telling her she'd been charged with keeping an eye on her.

Raven nodded slowly, not certain where Greta was going with this, but I had a feeling I did.

I cringed, but there was no denying it would help us pull this off.

"I need you to remember how pissed off you were when you found out," Greta said, smiling a little too brightly.

"Why?" Raven asked.

"Because somebody's got to give me a couple of bruises, and I'd rather it be you than them," she said, waggling her eyebrows at me and Gabe.

"Greta! You don't—"

"Yeah, I do, hon. Now, rile up some of that old anger and let it—"

Raven threw a punch, landing on the right side of Greta's jaw.

Greta stumbled back, her eyes watering, but she was smiling. "Feel better?" she said, laughing and rubbing her jaw.

"No! I think you're insane. If you were asking me to do this for any other—" She swung again, connecting with Greta's left eye. Raven might not have had any combat experience, but she was quick.

Greta, on the other hand, might just have been a little insane. Though her eyes were tearing up, she was still smiling. "What do you think, Gabe?" she asked, turning her full attention on him. "Will I pass inspection, do you think?" She looked down at herself, then back up at him, her face transformed into a mask of fear and abuse.

The easy rapport between the two of them didn't escape my notice, and Greta seemed to have substantial knowledge of just what she needed to do to pull this off. She looked just like a blonde version of the girl I'd seen outside Avalone's the other night.

Gabe nodded. "You've still got weapons, right?"

Greta laughed and patted various places around her hips and chest like she was counting them off, then she winked at Gabe. "You know I never leave home without them, hon."

I watched the two exchange knowing glances.

Greta sighed, and all of her laughter died away. "All right, boys. Let's go get your girlfriend back, Leo, and see if we can't bury that asshole, Avalone, six feet under in the process."

Chapter Thirty-Eight

Leo

What the fuck?

Gabe drove the black van slowly up Avalone's long drive. Not a guard in sight. No lights. No proximity alarm blaring. Absolutely nothing.

"Something's not right," Gabe said, shifting in his seat.

No shit. "Have you ever seen this place so dark?" I asked, hoping this wasn't a first.

The occasional rock crunched beneath the van's tires, but there was no other sound.

The three of us held our breath, listening, peering in every direction for some sign of life.

There was nothing.

"Does this feel like a trap to anybody else?" Greta asked, leaning past me for a better look outside.

A trap didn't make sense. It would have been a lot less effort for Avalone to have had his men hide around the entrance to the driveway and take us out right there.

We made it all the way up to the side door without incident, but the side door was open.

Gabe shifted the van into park and we got out, not bothering to wait for the welcoming committee.

I had a feeling there wasn't one coming.

Our men—comprised of three different families and two Old Dogs—swarmed out of the back of the van, moving like shadows toward the open door, all of us listening for sounds from inside and out. The thud of a footstep. The crunch of leaves. The dying cry of the woman who'd run off with my heart.

Complete silence.

I stepped inside, still listening.

We followed the plan we'd finalized on the way over; Greta leading a team toward the spiral staircase that led to the second floor; Gabe and the others weaving their way through the main floor, searching for any sign of life.

I headed for the basement with Brute and Tate close on my heels.

If Avalone had brought her here, she could still be down there.

Past the kitchen, I found the door. It was wide open, a dead hulk of a man blocking the upper landing with two bullet holes in his meaty head.

I'm too late.

Something withered inside me as I stepped over the body and descended the stairs. My legs felt heavy, heavier with each splatter of blood that marred the wood stairs. I tried to step around the splatters—what if it was Ella's blood? I couldn't just step on it; it felt wrong. But there was so much blood. I couldn't avoid it. It squelched beneath my shoes as the basement came into view.

My breath caught in my throat. My stomach roiled violently. And though there was no fresh blood down here, the whole room turned red. It was like a haze, pumping through my veins and distorting my vision.

Shackles attached to the walls and ceiling. Old, rust-colored blood stains and O-rings bolted to the floor with short chains and collars attached to them. The left wall was covered in shit straight out of nightmares; whips, riding crops, and canes, gags and rope, and a whole lot of other things I'd never be able to unsee. Dog cages in the right corner and a long, narrow metal table.

The back of my throat burned, and my hands shook.

I was just about to leave when something in the far right concrete wall caught my eye.

Ella was here had been etched into the concrete, and what I'd thought were random marks all around it, I realized were notches. A tally, arranged in groups of seven. Ten groups, twenty, thirty, forty.

There were at least a year's worth of notches carved into the wall.

She'd spent at least a year of her life in this basement, this *dungeon*.

I could imagine the sixteen-year-old girl she'd been, frightened, huddled against the wall.

I could hear her screams, feel her terror.

I could see her painstakingly carving the letters of her name into the wall, determined to leave some mark, some proof that she'd existed.

That she'd lived.

Bile was starting climb up my throat.

"Leo?" Brute said from beside me, his voice raw, ragged, like something had torn his insides apart. His eyes had followed mine to the notches on the wall.

I turned away just in time to avoid vomiting all over him, retching onto the concrete bloodstained floor.

"I don't know how to find her," I whispered, wiping my hand across my mouth when my stomach had finished revolting.

Greta appeared at the top of the stairs, followed by Gabe. She descended a few steps and then stopped, looking around. Her face was blank, but it had gone pale, and her chest heaved with deep breaths.

"The family's dead. Avalone's wife, his kid... They're both dead. Single gunshots to the head," she said, her voice thready.

Gabe nodded. "All the men on the main floor are dead, too. No sign of Ella."

His gaze continued around the room like he was looking for clues, but there was nothing useful here.

I'd seen it all, every square inch of this hell burned indelibly into my brain.

Think. Just fucking think.

I didn't have time to worry about shit I'd never forget.

Someone had killed Avalone's men and his family.

It looked like whoever had done this had killed everybody.

"It's personal," I said, connecting the dots. This wasn't a strategic hit. This was somebody seriously fucking pissed off. Someone who had no scruples about murdering a kid. Somebody who relied on his cunning and wit.

And I knew exactly who it was.

Chapter Thirty-Nine

Ella

There was a marching band inside my head, pounding, thudding against my skull.

If they drummed any harder, the whole band was going to burst right out of my head.

I pressed my forehead against the cold, hard floor beneath me, trying to make it stop, but the band drummed on.

I tried to open my eyes, but there was fabric pressed against the bridge of my nose to my eyebrows, and it rubbed against my eyelashes when I blinked.

Blindfolded.

I wriggled my hands behind my back, but rough rope cut into my wrists, chafing more with every movement.

Bound.

I tested my ankles, but they moved freely, no rope or metal cuffs digging into my skin.

It shouldn't have surprised me to find myself on *Signore's* basement floor, but this wasn't how it was supposed to happen.

I moved my legs just a little, searching for the reassuring brush of the holster around my thigh.

My thigh was bare beneath my skirt.

He'd taken my knife, the only weapon I had.

You'll find a way, I tried to reassure myself, but it didn't stop my body from trembling. It didn't make it any easier to chase the air with fast, shallow breaths that wouldn't fill my lungs.

How had I even gotten here?

I'd made the call to *Signore* and then kept walking, but everything that happened after was blurry like those old drunk driving commercials.

There'd been a car, but I couldn't see who was in it. The pungent odor of exhaust. The opening click of a car door. And then nothing.

Nothing but this pounding headache that was turning my stomach.

Someone must have knocked me unconscious. It hurt like hell, but at least it was making it difficult to focus on anything else.

Until a door creaked open somewhere behind me and heavy footsteps thudded across the cold, concrete floor.

I froze, the shallow breath in my lungs trapped.

The sound wasn't right.

It should have been the scrape of a door at the upper landing and then fourteen footsteps down wooden stairs that creaked and groaned beneath *Signore's* weight.

The footsteps stopped right behind me, then silence.

One, two, three.

The hard toe of a boot nudged my hip.

More silence.

One, two, three.

"Give it up, Ella. Unconscious girls breathe," a deep, gruff voice spoke from somewhere above me. A deep, gruff, and *familiar* voice.

Signore had put me somewhere in the basement I'd never been, somewhere smaller, if the cloistering, stagnant air was any indicator.

I let out the breath I'd been holding but stayed silent, trying to puzzle out what was coming next.

If *Signore* had sent someone in his stead to punish me, what did that mean?

Before I could fathom a guess, hands grasped me beneath the arms.

I fought the urge to struggle. I'd done this to myself. I'd put myself here. The struggle was futile.

Not for the first time, terror ripped and clawed at my insides.

Just think about Leo.

I'd done this to keep him safe. No regrets, even if I had lost my knife. There was no possibility of backing out now.

I just had to find another way.

The big hands pulled me up off the floor, almost gently, not digging his fingers in so deep it would leave bruises. Cold, hard wood cradled my butt and thighs as he sat me back onto a chair, my hands still trapped painfully at my tailbone.

"If I untie you, are you going to be a good girl?" he asked, grazing a finger around my wrists, just above the rope.

The girl I'd once been tried to bubble to the surface, ready to snap and scold, but I bit my lip and nodded.

"I never liked the silent treatment, Ella. Use your words," he instructed, tipping my chin up with two fingers.

I resisted the urge to yank my chin from his grip. "Yes, I'll be good."

"*Perfetto,*" he said, then his fingers worked at the ropes around my wrists, plucking and yanking until the scratchy fabric fell away.

My fingers tingled and pricked as blood rushed back to them.

I plopped my half-numb hands down on my lap, clenching and relaxing my fists until circulation had been restored.

Without making any further demands, his fingers moved to the back of my head, fiddling with the knot of the blindfold. It fell away, but the sudden light was too bright, blinding. My eyes squeezed shut reflexively, but I forced them open enough to look around.

The man standing in front of me was no surprise.

I skipped right over him to take in the rest of my surroundings.

Bare concrete walls and floors. An old drop-tile ceiling. No hooks or cuffs, no whips or gags. There was even a window, mostly shrouded by thick orange curtains. It was an ordinary unfinished basement, not something I'd ever imagined in *Signore's* home.

In fact, with each passing second, it was becoming clearer to me that *this* was not *Signore's* home.

"Where am I, Riccardo?"

Riccardo smiled and followed my perusal around the room. "You don't like it? It seemed a step up to me from that dungeon he kept you in."

The tone of his voice and the furrow between his brows made it seem like he was genuinely disgruntled by my reaction.

I dug my teeth into my bottom lip.

Riccardo had always been, if not nice, then indifferent toward me, but now, it felt like there was a human time bomb standing in front of me, ready to detonate any second.

"It's much better," I lied.

A prison was a prison.

But something was off here.

Riccardo seemed *bigger*, more connected to and in command of this small concrete space.

"Good." He sighed as he turned and wandered casually around the room.

I had a feeling I wasn't at liberty to do the same.

I watched him through my lashes as he leaned a shoulder against the wall on the opposite side of the room and glanced at his watch. Outwardly calm, but the pinch at the corners of his eyes gave him away.

He was nervous. *Anxious.*

When I'd gleaned all I could from watching him, I turned my attention back to the room.

The concrete was older, evident by the thin cracks that broke up the smooth surface. There was no lock on the door he'd come in through, but *Signore's* men were probably standing guard outside it.

"You know, Ella, it surprised me to hear you arguing with that lover boy of yours," Riccardo said, glancing at his watch again. "If someone was offering to take out the son of a bitch who'd tortured me for years, I would have gladly jumped on board." He laughed then crossed the room and reached behind me, grabbing something from the floor. It was my bag. He opened the flap, ripped open the inner seam, and held it out in front of me. A tiny, round disc was stuck to the inside fabric. "One little bug, and I could hear everything. That ridiculous bird carrier has one too." He shrugged.

"You've been listening to me? To everything?" I felt violated in a whole new way. All the intimate moments I'd shared with Leo flashed through my mind. My cheeks flamed, and angry tears blurred my vision. Those moments were *mine*. They didn't belong to him or anyone else. "What do you want, Riccardo?" I ground out between clenched teeth.

Riccardo had never toyed with me before.

A dark cloud passed across his gaze before he glanced down at his watch again. "We'll get to that," he said then dropped the bag next to my feet. "We're just waiting for the rest of our party to arrive."

So, this was just another one of *Signore's* games.

Chapter Forty

Leo

My father sat at the head of the mahogany table, his fingers steepled.

The adrenaline in the air was so thick, it was hard to draw a full breath. Even my father was affected by it; his shoulders taut, his hands pressed together so hard, the pads of his fingers had turned white.

"What makes you so certain this 'Riccardo' has her?" he asked while I did my best not to fly out of my seat and out of the house. "I already have men searching for an address on Riccardo."

"I ran into him at the hotel. He's the one who came looking for Ella and said something that didn't stand out at the time, but it does now."

His cocky attitude, the itch beneath his skin I could almost feel—it should have stood out then. Riccardo was a man looking to claw his way out of his current role, looking to climb up the ladder. I wanted to hit myself for missing it.

"What did he say?" Greta asked, absently rubbing her bruised jaw. My sister really had an arm on her.

"Not all men are fortunate enough to have powerful alliances. Some men must rely on their cunning and wit.' I'd thought he was talking about Avalone, but he'd been talking about himself."

Gabe nodded. "I can see that. He fits the mold. But what does that have to do with Ella?"

"Avalone used her to collect secrets—any information he could use to stay ahead of the game. If Riccardo has just toppled Avalone, he'll want any info he can get."

All I could do was hope that was all he wanted from Ella. *Fat fucking chance.*

"All right, I'm on board," Nico said, nodding his approval. "I say the minute we have the address, we go."

"You got it, boss," Salvatore—Nico's right-hand man—said. He looked like he was rubbing his hands together in his mind, raring for a fight.

Dante laughed. "Just remember, it's your turn to get your ass blown up this time, Salvatore."

They'd fought side by side when we'd rescued my sister, and Salvatore had dragged my brother's burned ass away from an explosion.

"Looking forward to it," Salvatore joked. At least, I thought he was joking. There was a crazy light in his dark eyes that made me wonder.

"How are we doing on that address, my friend?" Brute asked my father from where he hovered in the doorway.

It was the first time Brute had said a word since walking into that basement. He was the only man not seated, and I couldn't blame him. This wait was going to kill me.

My father's phone rang before he could answer.

I was on my feet in a flash.

We were armed, prepared, and I was ready to get out of here.

"Ella's going to be okay, Leo," Raven said, squeezing my arm.

"Damn right, hot stuff," Greta added from across the table. "From what I've heard, the girl survived hell. She *will* survive this." She spoke with so much conviction, I could feel it brushing against my skin, trying to seep beneath the surface. Trying, but not quite succeeding.

My father was scribbling an address onto a piece of paper in front of him, the phone pressed to his ear. A furrow formed between his brows, and he scribbled down another address. Then he hung up the phone without a word and stared at the paper in front of him.

No more than a few seconds passed, but it felt like an eternity. "Where is he?" I asked, trying to swallow the growl in my tone.

"He has a condo in the city under his mother's maiden name," my father said, "and an old piece of property outside of Manchester, New Hampshire, that belonged to his father."

"He didn't take her to a condo," I said with absolute certainty.

"He would have known it would be harder for us to track down the condo," Dom said. "So, how can you be sure?"

I clenched my jaw hard, hating the answer, not wanting to speak it out loud and give it life. "Because he's going to have to make her scream to get what he wants out of her head," I ground out. "We need the jet ready to go."

I pushed past Brute and headed for the front door while the urge to tear Avalone's goon apart limb from limb pumped hot and heavy through my veins.

I made it to my car in a red haze, but by the time I'd revved the engine, I had it in check. Maybe I was no poster boy for good mental health, but I knew how to compartmentalize, shove it all into a box so I could do what needed to be done.

As I shifted gears, Gabe hopped into the passenger seat, a gun in one hand, and a grim smile on his face.

It was a good thing we didn't have to go through security at the airport. The metal detectors would be lighting up like the Fourth of July.

"Your father's making arrangements for the flight. Let's go," he said, looking ready to pedal the car Flintstones-style if I didn't get my ass moving. "That asshole's got my cousin, and with everyone else dead, Riccardo is my only hope of finding out the name of the ship before it fucks off completely."

"You're kind of big on the rescuing thing, aren't you?"

I wasn't complaining. He'd just been pretty vague about what he was up to and why he'd been scoping out Avalone.

Gabe shrugged. "I missed out on the big heroic rescue last time," he said just as vaguely and making light of the fact he'd been taken by Diego Berlusconi too, cuffed to the same pole as my sister. In the end, he'd been the one to put the bullet between Berlusconi's eyes. "Besides, can't a guy have a thing for rescuing damsels in distress? Do I not look like an ideal knight in shining armor?"

I laughed, looking at the two of us dressed all in black. "You and me both, *amico.*"

I turned the car around and started up the driveway as the cars behind me filled with our men and Costa's, Brute leading their way directly on my tail. Halfway up the drive, two black vehicles turned off the main road and into the driveway. Two black BMWs.

"Fuck," I cursed.

"What the hell is this?" Gabe asked, switching off the safety on his gun.

The Russians stopped, right there in the driveway.

A lone man got out of the passenger side. Tall, midtwenties, sandy blond hair, and well-dressed. He closed the passenger door and stood there, hands at his sides.

If he was on a suicide mission, then he'd come to the right place.

The urge to plow right through him had me pressing down on the gas pedal.

These Russians could all go get fucked and die, for all I cared.

But two cars to take on every man on the Luca estate? That just didn't make any sense.

I eased off of the gas.

They'd been after me ever since I picked up Ella, had come at me with four vehicles when it was just me and Gabe.

They wouldn't come here now, seriously lacking in man power unless…

I hit the brake, and the row of cars behind me screeched to a stop. At least if I was wrong about this, there were plenty of men here to kill the Russian.

"What the hell are you doing, Leo?" Gabe hissed as I got out of the car, my Glock in hand, but I kept it pointed at the ground.

"If you're some sort of kamikaze driver, you should know, you're a shitty one," I said to the lone passenger as car doors opened and closed behind me.

"I'm here to help," the man said, holding his arms out, hands empty. He spoke with a bit of a Russian accent, but it was heavily watered down.

"While I appreciate the thought, blocking our driveway isn't as helpful as you might think."

I could feel every second ticking by, every second away from Ella, every second I had no idea what was happening to her.

"Riccardo Bianchi is not working alone," the Russian said, taking a step toward me.

I raised a brow.

"How do you know that?" Dom asked. He'd come up from behind and now stood beside me, his gun at his side, but his finger was on the trigger.

The Russian looked at Dom and held his hands open wider like he was reminding us he was unarmed then turned his gaze back to me. "Fiorenzo Avalone's men turned on him tonight, but they were not alone."

"Who helped them?" I asked.

"I don't know. I did not recognize them, but they were not all Avalone's men."

"Then I guess I just have the ten-million-dollar question left for you: Why are you telling us this?"

"My grandfather, he doesn't trust you. He believes you took Ella against her will, and until this evening, I believed it too. He thinks you will hurt my cousin, just like Fiorenzo Avalone."

"Ella's your cousin?" Nico said, an undercurrent of disbelief in his tone. He'd sidled up on the other side of me, a gun in one hand and a knife in the other. The man really did love his knives.

The Russian nodded.

I recalled Ella climbing up inside herself when I'd asked about the Russians.

"What's your name?" I asked him.

"Nikolai Volkov, son of Dimitri Volkov, and nephew of Mikhail Volkov, Ella's father."

Gabriella Moretti had run off amid some sort of family altercation with the Volkovs, but it wasn't over a forced marriage like I'd suspected. It was over a forced *separation*.

A Moretti and a Volkov—I had a feeling neither family had approved of *that* union.

"He's telling the truth," I told Dom and Nico, but unless Nikolai had more intel, it was time to leave. "We know where she is. You need to get out of the way right now."

Nikolai nodded but didn't move. "I'm coming," he said, straightening his spine, his gaze passing from Dom to me to Nico.

"Leo, do you trust this guy?" Dom asked.

"About as far as I can throw him." I did believe he was Ella's family, so I was willing to give him the smallest benefit of the doubt. "She's in New Hampshire. If you can get there, it's a free country." I shrugged. "But I suggest you leave your goons at home, *capisce?*"

I turned around and got back inside the Lambo before Nikolai could respond.

It was time to fucking *go*.

Chapter Forty-One

Ella

A breeze blew, rustling the orange curtains on the only window in the room.

A *breeze*.

The window was open.

Riccardo had left me alone in here.

How soon would he be back?

There was no clock in the room, but I could hear one ticking in my head.

Tick, tick, tick.

Every second thrust me closer to *Signore*.

He was coming.

Any second now…

And yet, the fear that had festered in my veins endlessly for years was subdued. Not gone, but quieter. No one had forced me here; no one had taken away my choice. No matter what *Signore* did to me, this was *my* decision. And no matter what he did to me, his days were numbered.

I wasn't going to be the one to break this time.

I crept to the window, my footsteps soundless on the concrete floor.

I had no intention of escaping, but to feel the breeze against my skin, the soft brush, would feel like freedom even here, trapped in this concrete box.

I didn't have to stretch up to pull the curtain aside. The heavy orange fabric glided smoothly across the vinyl rod, revealing the early gray light of dawn and the thick steel bars on the outside of the window. The bars were a disappointment, but not surprising.

I closed my eyes to block them out and let the cool dawn air waft across my face, whispering through the wisps of hair at my brow.

The doorknob turned.

I kept my eyes closed and focused on the breeze.

Two sets of footsteps entered the room, then stopped.

The door closed. More footsteps.

I fought against the ingrained urge to kneel and focused on the wind. The freedom.

"You really are exceptional, my dear." The voice was wrong.

My eyes flew open.

The man had dark hair, sprinkled with silver along his brow. Deep lines etched his eyes and mouth. A face I'd seen before, but what was he doing here?

"The most beautiful girl I've ever seen, I think." He smiled, revealing a mouth full of too-white teeth. "No wonder Fiorenzo got away with his game for so long," he said in Italian.

There was no uncertainty in his eyes; he knew I could understand him.

"*Buongiorno, Signor* Belemonte," I said, turning away from the window.

I could have played stupid. Or I could have tried to explain to him that I'd had no choice. But I was done cowering.

Riccardo reclined against the door, blocking it with his massive frame while Belemonte stared at me. He was eerily still, his keen, dark eyes the only part of him that moved, wandering down to my toes and back up twice before his gaze stopped on mine.

"I was angry when Riccardo told me what your master had been up to all this time," *Signor* Belemonte said, clasping his hands behind his back. "But I can be a reasonable man, Ella. I understand you had no say in the matter." He gave me a sympathetic grin that looked out of place on his face. "So," he said, clapping his hands once, "just like that, you are forgiven, my dear."

"*Grazie,*" I said, not believing him for a second.

"But I want you to know..."—the grin fell away, and his eyes turned ice-cold—"...that if you ever attempt to deceive me again, I will wash the entire city with the blood of the people you care about. Do you understand me?"

I fought the urge to shiver and kept my eyes locked on his. "What did you do to *Signor* Avalone?"

"We'll get to that. For now, I think you'll find it more important to worry about me and what I want."

"And what is it you want?"

Signor Belemonte laughed. "Information, of course... among other things." His eyes grazed downward, lingering on my breasts before continuing on.

My stomach threatened to revolt, flooding my mouth with saliva, but I dared not to swallow and risk it making me retch.

"What information?" I asked, trying to focus on the cracks in the wall, the grain on the wooden door, the texture of the concrete beneath my feet.

"All of it, my dear. Every last bit you've got floating around in that pretty head. I have survived, I have *thrived*, because I learned a valuable truth early on: Information is power."

"And then?" I asked, just trying to buy time.

Signor Belemonte had not been part of the plan.

He took a step toward me, and then another, closing the distance between us.

My muscles came alive with the urge to flee, but with the concrete at my back, there was nowhere for me to go.

Signor Belemonte leaned in close until his breath tickled my cheek.

"You know what comes next, my dear," he said, stroking his finger down my neck to my clavicle. His touch felt like slugs across my skin, leaving cold, sticky slime in their wake. "But," he said, stepping back enough that every breath didn't feel like it had been filtered through his lungs. "Business first, then pleasure. Where are my manners? Please, take a seat," he said, motioning to the only chair in the room.

It wasn't a request, it was a *command.*

I obeyed.

Whatever had happened to *Signore*, this man was in charge for the time being.

While I knew *Signore's* mind and how it worked, this man was a new kind of evil, the kind that made the devil run and hide and threw all my plans into chaos.

Signor Belemonte and Riccardo followed me to the chair, Riccardo against the wall beside me and Belemonte directly in front of me. He stood tall with his shoulders back and arms crossed over his chest.

"I'm going to start simple, my dear. I want you to tell me what information you have on the Russians who've been visiting our fine city."

"I don't have any information on the Russians."

Riccardo's hand shot out, cutting across my cheek with a stinging slap.

My eyes watered, but I bit my tongue, refusing to give either of them the satisfaction.

Belemonte was shaking his head disapprovingly, but his gaze was directed at Riccardo. He took a step forward and grabbed the strap of my dress, shoving it down to reveal an expanse of my back and shoulder. "You think a girl who withstood this is going to crumble beneath your hand?"

The scars across my back prickled beneath their gazes.

"You've got a better idea?" Riccardo barked.

"I always do," Belemonte said, stepping back and retrieving a phone from his jacket pocket. Without a word, he turned it on and shoved the screen in front of my face. "Do you recognize this place, my dear?"

A gasp slipped out before I could stop it.

My heart pounded, mimicking the violent thud in my head. Of course, I recognized it. I'd worked there for months.

"Answer me, *per favore.*"

"Yes, I recognize it," I forced the words out.

"Good. I'm going to give you a small demonstration, just so you understand that I'm not a man who plays games or uses idle threats."

"No, don't. Please." My breath came faster, making my throbbing head spin.

I recognized the men in the bar, the men I'd watched tipping back drinks and telling stories of their youth. The tough guys in leather, so many of whom wore their hearts on their sleeves.

Belemonte ignored me. He pressed a button on the phone without turning the screen away from me.

The wall of liquor behind the bar exploded, sending alcohol and broken glass flying in all directions, and all over the men nearest to it. There was no sound coming from the phone. It all happened in eerie silence.

Men jumped back, cuts appeared, welling with blood. A shard of glass flew at Old Mike. His mouth opened in a silent roar as his tattooed hands flew to his face.

My hands trembled.

I wanted to grab the phone and… and… *damn it.* There was nothing I could do to help them. This wasn't supposed to happen.

I'd gone back to *Signore* to save them—all of them.

And it had been for nothing.

"A single explosive, hidden in an innocuous shipment of scotch." Belemonte shrugged and turned off the phone.

"No. Turn it back on, please," I cried.

He shook his head. "There are four more explosive devices in and around the bar. Tell me what I want to know, or I will detonate another one every thirty seconds. Starting… now."

"I don't know anything," I sobbed. Angry tears welled in my eyes.

"Twenty-six, twenty-five, twenty-four..."

I wracked my brain for something. The things I knew couldn't have anything to do with the Russians here now. It wasn't possible.

"Nineteen, eighteen, seventeen..."

"I'm Russian," I blurted out.

"Is that so?" he asked, his head cocked to the side.

"Yes! My father, he was Russian."

Belemonte was silent, staring at me while my heart beat hard against my ribs.

Then he laughed. "So, she ran off with a Russian," he said, slipping his phone back into his jacket. "I always wondered if the rumors were true. Gabriella covered her tracks so well, not even I could find her."

The gleam in his eyes was like a child who'd just discovered a buried treasure trove of candy.

I was about to ask how he knew Gabriella was my mother, but then I remembered the device Riccardo had shown me.

They'd both been listening.

They'd both heard *everything*.

"The spawn of mafia and Bratva, I bet. That's a lot of powerful blood running through your veins. I wonder what kind of price that would fetch?" His gaze traveled over me from head to toe, leaving ice in its wake. "No," he said, shaking his head. "I think I like you right where you are. All the information in your head will be worth more than enough. And of course, we both know how easy it is for you to use your cunt to collect more."

I cringed. When he put it so bluntly, it made me sick.

"But we'll get to that. For now, I need you to understand that I will punish you for defying me," he said, nodding to the jacket pocket where he'd put his phone. "But that's not what I want, Ella. I want to reward you."

He nodded to Riccardo who then heaved himself off the wall and left the room. Seconds ticked by in silence until the door handle turned again.

"And to prove just how much I want to reward you, I'm going to give you this." Belemonte took a step back and looked toward the door as it swung open.

My jaw nearly hit the floor.

Chapter Forty-Two

Leo

Flying at a cruise speed of Mach 0.71—or roughly five hundred and forty-one miles per hour—used to feel like one hell of a fast trip to anywhere.

Forty-thousand feet above the ground. No obstacles from here to kingdom come. Right now, though, it felt like we were crawling through the sky at a snail's pace.

"*Papà* arranged for transportation on the ground," Dante said, clapping me on the back. "Five minutes to go, *fratello.*"

"*Si, lo so.*"

I'd felt the air pressure in the cabin begin to change fifteen minutes ago—the signal our pilot had begun his descent.

Five more minutes.

Five more minutes of picturing what was happening to Ella. Five more minutes of worrying whether I'd get to her in time, of wondering if I'd screwed up completely because she wasn't even in New Hampshire.

Compartmentalizing only worked when I had something else to do, something worthwhile to focus on.

Flying around in a souped-up tin can wasn't it.

I looked around the cabin, at the men and woman sitting at the edges of their seats. There were ten of us—the super midsize jet's maximum capacity.

We looked like a team of mercenaries, dressed in black, armed to the teeth—and then some—and bristling with pent-up adrenaline.

It was kind of incredible. Not so long ago, it was every family for itself. Members of three different families and a biker gang all in one plane would have guaranteed a bloody slaughter. They would have been scraping our gray matter off the walls and scrubbing our guts out of the cream leather seats.

I much preferred the seats gut-free.

Brute kind of looked ready to redecorate the plane's interior with my guts, though—or at least throw a few Molotov cocktails at me. He'd been silent the whole flight, sitting on his own at the back and glaring daggers at me.

We were going in as a team, so it was time to clear the air. If he needed to throw a few punches, better now than on the ground.

"Is there something you want to say to me, Brute?" I said, keeping my voice low enough to keep the conversation between the two of us.

He pressed his lips together, and his hands gripped the armrests so tight, it was a wonder they didn't break right off.

"I'm angry, my friend. I'm angry with you, with Avalone, with this pussy, Riccardo." He let go of the armrests and cracked his knuckles. "But mostly, I'm angry with myself."

I'd expected him to throw punches, not words, so this was progress.

"Ella, she reminds me a lot of someone, probably why I took to watching over her." Brute heaved a sigh and sat back in the chair. "My sister."

I didn't know Brute had a sister. Actually, it was kind of scary to picture a girl the mammoth size of Brute.

"Long, dark hair, big eyes that you just knew were seeing more than they should be," he said, his eyes losing focus. "Anyway, she's been gone nine years."

I sat down in the seat opposite him and waited.

"I came home one day, and my dad said she was gone," he said, shrugging. "Not dead, not run off. Just... *gone*. I tried looking for her, roughed up a whole lot of people, searching for answers, but I never got any. I asked him one last time, right before I killed him, but he was determined to take that secret to the grave. When Ella showed up, well, it was like fate was giving me a chance to do better this time around, you know?"

"This isn't your fault, Brute. It's mine, and we both know it," I said quietly.

Brute laughed, but it didn't reach his eyes. "What you and me both know is that girl is stubborn. You could have locked her up on the moon, my friend, and she would have found a way to do whatever she'd set her mind to doing."

Brute wasn't wrong.

Shame on me for ever thinking Ella had a weak bone in her body.

"We're going to find her, Brute," I said just as the landing gear touched down. "We're going to get her back. Right. Fucking. Now."

Chapter Forty-Three

Ella

The man who had starred in every one of my nightmares for half a decade stood in the basement doorway.

His shoulders were hunched, and his face was pale.

Dark bags hung beneath his bruised and red-rimmed eyes.

Tears dripped off his chin.

I'd never seen him like this, but none of it was nearly as disturbing as the blood that dripped from his mangled fingers. They didn't even look like fingers; swollen stubs that stuck out every which way.

Riccardo had hold of him by the back of his tattered jacket, holding him up and shoving him forward. Closer.

Signore moaned and stumbled along in front of him.

"What did you do?" I whispered, my voice trapped beneath layers of shock and disgust.

"You don't look happy, my dear," *Signor* Belemonte observed, frowning at me. "But I think you'll find, thanks to me, *Signor* Avalone won't ever raise a hand to you again." He chuckled under his breath like he'd made a clever joke. "Release him," he told Riccardo.

Riccardo complied, his lips pressed together, his eyes narrowed into slits as if the order grated on him like nails across a chalkboard.

No longer supported, *Signore* stumbled. He threw out an arm to catch himself until his mutilated hand made contact with the concrete wall. He screamed as his body convulsed, clutching his hands to his chest like he could cradle the pain away, draw it into himself and make it disappear.

I stared at him, waiting for the wash of relief, even pleasure, at the sound of his tortured cry.

I'd waited for it for so long, imagined him suffering as much as he'd made me suffer so many times.

But I felt no pleasure, no relief. Nothing but cold. Nausea. Revulsion.

Signor Belemonte, on the other hand, was grinning like the Cheshire cat. "*Signor* Avalone had his sights so narrowly focused on the Lucas, he didn't even see me coming, did you, Fiorenzo?"

"Us," Riccardo piped up, the muscles in his jaw twitching. "He never saw *us* coming."

"Of course," *Signor* Belemonte acknowledged without looking at him.

I'd stood up at some point since the door opened, and now I took a step back, wanting no part of whatever this was.

"It's all right, my dear. Fiorenzo can't hurt you. I'm offering you a gift here," Belemonte continued.

"I don't understand," I stuttered.

The light glinted off the long, jagged blade that had appeared in Belemonte's hand. "Revenge, my dear, you must want it."

I nodded, no more able to stop it than I could the tremble in my hands because I didn't just want it.

I'd dreamed of it, *fantasized* about it.

Signor Belemonte smiled. "Then take it." He held out the knife, the hilt toward me, balancing it on two fingers. "It's yours."

My hand moved of its own volition.

I watched as my fingers wrapped around the hilt and *Signor's* Belemonte's hand fell away.

Revenge, my soul breathed.

Every lash that scarred my body flared to life.

The mark on the back of my shoulder burned.

The memories beat down like a monsoon.

The whole world disappeared behind it.

There was nothing but the blade in my hand and the broken man who stood sniveling in front of me.

He was smaller than I remembered him, almost human.

In my mind, he'd been a gargantuan, malevolent being with hellfire in his eyes. But he was just a man. A man I'd let rule me with fear even after I escaped him. I'd let him lead me back to him, terrified of his unholy wrath.

What a fool I'd been.

"Come now, my dear. The man tormented you, used you like a common whore. His family is dead; his men are dead; he has nothing to live for. Really, you'd be putting him out of his misery."

"His family is dead?"

Belemonte had killed them? A child? Of all the nightmarish things *Signore* had done, he'd never murdered a child in cold blood.

My heart hurt for the child I'd never met.

Belemonte didn't answer, but a tear trickled down Avalone's cheek. A human's tear.

"I… I want something else," I said, lowering the knife to my side.

Belemonte smiled. "Is that so? I'm not really in the business of doling out favors, but you can try your luck."

"Leave the Lucas and their men alone. Please." I met his cold gaze.

He chuckled, rubbing his fingers over his lips. "That is quite an admirable favor, my dear, but I'm afraid it is one I can't possibly grant," he said with a shrug. "The Lucas' influence has grown too big and too fast. They are the link between families who have no business aligning themselves with one another. It's just not the way things are done."

He wasn't going to change his mind.

I could take it or leave it.

Revenge was the only "*gift*" he intended to offer.

I shifted the knife in my hand until it rested comfortably, just like my father had taught me so many years ago. I was ten the first time he'd put a knife in my hand and showed me how to attack and gut the bag of corn strung up in the barn. How mundane it had seemed then.

Now, I was grateful.

"I suggest you take the gift I've offered you before my well of generosity runs dry," Belemonte said, a growl of impatience poorly concealed in his voice.

I reached for the numbness that had swathed me the day I'd dragged a steak knife across a man's throat. It steadied my hand and cleared my mind.

Signore didn't flinch as I raised the knife. Those cold, black eyes stared back at me, red-rimmed now, but just as lifeless as they'd ever been.

Out the corner of my eye, I could see Belemonte's lips curving up and up.

He *wanted* this, perhaps as much as I did.

I drew in a breath, and on the exhale, I pivoted and thrust the jagged blade into Belemonte's gut, burying it to the hilt.

His smile fell away, and his eyes widened in surprise. His mouth opened in a silent scream.

I had a second, maybe two, before the shock passed and Riccardo made a grab for me, so I used it wisely, yanking the blade out and driving it back in.

Belemonte could not walk away from this.

I would not bow to a new master.

I would not stand idly by while he threatened Leo's life.

"No," I whispered as Belemonte gasped and clutched at his stomach. I savored the taste of the word on my tongue, relishing in the truth of it, its meaning honoring the essence of it.

I yanked the knife out at the same time Riccardo barked out a laugh.

He didn't move. He didn't try to grab the knife or help Belemonte.

"I told you giving this girl a blade was a dumb fucking move," he said, grinning as Belemonte dropped to the floor, curled around his bleeding abdomen. So much blood. The jagged knife had done irreparable damage.

Signore staggered sideways, dropping down in the chair I'd vacated not long ago. His face was ghost-white, but I thought it had more to do with pain and blood loss than watching Belemonte bleed out on the concrete floor.

Did he wonder if he was next? Or maybe he hoped for it. *Go ahead and hope.* God knows he'd made me pray for death more times than I could count.

"You've had your fun now, Ella. Give me the knife," Riccardo said at the same time an ominous click sounded.

The gun was aimed directly at my head.

Chapter Forty-Four

Leo

"End of the line, *amicos*," I said, standing on a strip of gravel and dirt that passed for a road, abandoning the rental cars for the time being—black BMWs. I wasn't sure if that was fate's twisted sense of humor or my father's.

The half mile distance left to the house, we'd have to travel by foot. There was no access road or driveway to the property—not that I could see, nor were there any signs of one on the map. If there was a way in by vehicle, we'd waste too much precious time searching for it.

The woods in front of us were nearly silent. No birds tweeting, no animals scurrying. There wasn't even a single cricket chirping. A bad sign. Something had them seriously spooked.

The last time we'd crept up on an enemy, we'd had the cover of darkness and the element of surprise on our side.

This time, we had neither.

Broad daylight. Nothing but trees to hide our advance, any of which could be concealing Riccardo's men—and the men of a mystery player, if Nikolai Volkov was right. *Fucking awesome.*

"A walk in the park, right?" Gabe quipped while his eyes scanned the trees and brush in front of us.

"If by 'park' you mean 'minefield', then absolutely," Greta said, double-checking the guns in her holsters.

"All right, we go by twos, a hundred feet apart, and converge on the house," Dom announced, and all heads nodded.

Dante and Salvatore headed up the dirt road first, taking the furthest point south. Greta sidled up next to Brute, and they took off to the second furthest point together. Then Nico and Marco, and Dom and Vito Agossi—Greta's uncle. The pairings weren't random. They were morbidly strategic, guaranteeing that no one family bore the brunt of the losses in the case of an ambush.

Gabe and I ventured into the forest, guns and knives drawn— if we could kill these fuckers quietly by slitting their throats, all the better.

As we walked, I listened for the crunch of leaves, the snap of a twig, or the creaking of a branch above us. Anything that would give away Riccardo's men.

They were here, hiding somewhere.

I could feel it in the pit of my stomach and in the prickling at the back of my neck, so strong I'd swear I could close my eyes and find them by instinct alone—not that I was going to be the dumbass who closed his eyes in enemy territory.

Every step was a battle of brain versus heart. The slower we went, the easier it was to keep our approach silent, but no matter how much I focused on what needed to be done, she was still there, in the core of me, ripping apart my heart while the tattered remnants pounded against my chest.

A hundred yards.

Two hundred yards.

It was so quiet and so still.

No sign of Riccardo's men.

No gunshots reverberating through the treetops to suggest any of our men had stumbled upon them.

Fucking nothing.

What if I was wrong? What if she isn't here?

The thoughts scraped across my brain, over and over again, wearing away the layers of certainty and bleeding out doubt and dread in equal measures.

Four hundred yards in, I saw him.

He wasn't out in the open.

He was hidden behind a balsam fir forty feet ahead, but the flat needlelike leaves were too thin to shroud the dark crouched shape of the man.

A glance at Gabe confirmed he saw him, too.

I motioned for him to keep going, then I dropped and veered off course, taking a wide berth around, far enough I could approach the guy from behind without him any the wiser.

Adrenaline pumped through my veins, feeding my muscles while it patched up the layers in my brain.

Ella was here.

So *close*.

I had my knife in hand.

It hadn't been that long since I'd crept through the dark toward the man who'd kidnapped my sister. My fingers were alive with memories, aching to drag the knife across flesh, to feel the smooth glide of the blade through veins and cartilage, to watch the life dissipate from a man's eyes while his blood spilled out around him. It was barbaric.

But when the man dying beneath the blade was a cruel son of a bitch, it was one of the greatest highs life had to offer.

I crept closer, approaching the man from directly behind now.

He had his gaze fixed on Gabe, swiveling to the left and right every few seconds, probably trying to figure out where I'd gone.

He had a gun in his hands, tracking Gabe through the balsam's branches.

I could now see the sweat trickling down the back of the man's neck and the radio in his hand.

He'd called for backup; they'd be on us any second.

I leaned in and grabbed him by the hair, yanking his head up to expose his stubble-covered neck.

The man didn't have time to shout, to beg for his life.

I dragged the knife across his throat with all the pent-up rage in my veins, cutting so deep, the blade severed his trachea.

He thrashed for a few seconds, pumping blood from his carotid artery and jugular vein onto the leaves of the balsam fir like some morbid Christmas scene.

And then he was gone—his eyes lifeless, his soul on its way to hell where it belonged.

And then the sound of a gunshot pierced the forest's silence.

Chapter Forty-Five

Ella

I'd never stood on this side of torment before.

I'd always been directly beneath it, the screams torn from my own throat, the smell of my blood permeating the air.

Riccardo dragged the knife down Belemonte's arm, from the bullet hole he'd put in his shoulder to his wrist, slicing through fabric and skin.

The man screamed. *God, he screamed.* So loud, I didn't think the sound was ever going to stop.

Signore mewled from the chair where he'd collapsed. He couldn't cover his ears even if he'd had working hands; Riccardo had tied him to the chair.

"You really did me a favor, Ella," Riccardo said, pausing with the knife dug into Belemonte's wrist. "There was no way I could have taken down Avalone all on my own. Belemonte was so eager to get to all the shit in your head, it was easy to get him on board. But once he swooped in, he thought he ran the fucking show." He laughed and turned his attention back to the man bleeding on the floor. "You're not running shit anymore, are you, asshole?" he said then spat in Belemonte's face.

I'd started this.

If I hadn't stabbed Belemonte, this wouldn't be happening.

But I'd just wanted him gone, not able to hurt me or Leo anymore. Not *this*.

"Just… just put him out of his misery, Riccardo." I had nothing left in my stomach, but that didn't stop it from trying to heave uselessly.

"You," he barked, pointing the gun in his other hand at me, "have no say here."

Seemingly just to prove his point, he aimed the gun at Belemonte's foot and pulled the trigger.

Belemonte howled.

I covered my ears with my hands, but the sound tore right through my fingers and burrowed into my brain.

I tried to remember what he'd just done to the men at Brute's bar.

What about before when *Signore* had given me to him?

The vise of his hands around my throat, the blood on his fingertips.

Belemonte wore a suave exterior, but he was a sadist underneath.

"He deserves it," I whispered under my breath.

For all he'd done to me, for all he'd done to others. For all he would do to Leo and his family.

Another gunshot reverberated off the concrete walls.

Another bullet hole, this time in Belemonte's thigh.

The ringing in my ears.

The shrieks.

"Stop!" I screamed.

Riccardo looked up at me. "Did you know that the stupid little shit who tried to save you three years ago was my brother?"

The dark-haired young lackey whose brown eyes were too kind for this black world. The young man who no longer looked human by the time *Signore* had finished with him.

"He knew," Riccardo barked, jerking his head in *Signore's* direction. "My little pissant of a brother was stupid, but he didn't deserve to die, not like that. Do you remember, Avalone?" He looked directly at *Signore*. "Do you remember making me clean up my own brother's mutilated body after two fucking days of letting him rot?" he roared.

Signore made a strangled sound in his throat. He sat there looking half-dead.

Riccardo was shaking; the barrel of the gun clattered against Belemonte's belt, but he turned his attention back to me and some of his trembling subsided.

"Right then, I decided how this would end," he said with a shrug. "I get rid of Avalone, and I take over his empire. And you, Ella, will spend the rest of your miserable life spreading your legs, just like you always have. You'll use that cunt to make up for what you did—for frying my brother's brain so he couldn't think with anything but his dick."

"Why did you kill Johnny to help me escape?" I asked, my voice low.

He laughed. "I killed good ol' Johnny to get you away from Avalone. There was no way I could have taken you from under his nose. Out there, though..."—he nodded toward the window—"...it was just a matter of time before I found you again... until you ended up with the Lucas." He growled. "I had no choice but to take on Belemonte to get to you. I knew he wouldn't be able to resist. All that information in your head, it was like crack to him, wasn't it, Belemonte?" He looked down at the bleeding, broken man like he was dirt on the bottom of his shoe.

Belemonte wheezed, his mouth opening and closing, but no words slipped out.

With his attention on Belemonte, I let my gaze flicker over to the door.

"Don't bother, Ella. You wouldn't make it two steps. The building is filled with Avalone and Belemonte's men." He laughed. "I suppose they're my men now."

Belemonte coughed and choked out a laugh. "Lucas... coming," he wheezed.

Riccardo froze, even his lungs stopped drawing breath, but then he shook his head.

"All they would have found at Avalone's was dead bodies," he said dismissively.

"Except yours." Belemonte smiled gruesomely. "They're coming," he almost sang in a breathless voice. "And I have... a surprise for you," he panted and untucked his uninjured arm from where he'd held it against him. He had a phone in his hand. "My gift to you... my dear," he said to me, nodding weakly to the message on the phone.

There was one word on the phone's screen.

Five letters Belemonte had managed to type into his phone and send off without Riccardo noticing.

Five letters that turned Riccardo's face beet red and made his heart pound so hard, I could see the pulse of his veins in his temples.

"*LEAVE,*" the message read and had presumably been sent to all of Belemonte's men.

Riccardo's hand shook as he shoved the gun in Belemonte's face and squeezed the trigger so many times I lost count.

Every loud crack jolted through me.

I pressed my hands over my ears so hard, it felt like my head was in a vise, but still, the sound tore through my eardrums.

Riccardo kept shooting even after the bullets had been spent and every pull of the trigger made a useless clicking sound.

With Belemonte and Avalone down, I realized with a sinking feeling that there were no other targets left.

I was next.

Chapter Forty-Six

Leo

Fuck stealth.

I ran through the forest, heedless of the crunch of twigs and leaves beneath my feet.

The gunshots hadn't come from our men.

They'd come from straight ahead of me.

Every muffled crack had pierced my chest and fractured my heart.

And the sound of a woman's scream...

The trees in front of me blurred behind gruesome images.

Images of her blood-covered lifeless body I'd never be able to forget.

A gunshot sounded closer.

White-hot heat tore across my left arm, but I barely felt it.

I spotted the shooter a split second later.

Gabe and I both fired on him, filling him with enough holes to turn him into a sieve.

Gabe looked at me out the corner of his eye as we moved forward. "You good, Leo?"

"*Sí*," I lied, putting one foot in front of the other, stupidly clinging to the hope that she was alive.

I'd made it hundreds of yards before running into a single shooter. We weren't facing enough resistance.

Another gunshot cracked in the air which went wide, ricocheting off a nearby tree.

I followed the trajectory back without stopping and fired two shots just before the shooter managed to slip back behind a tree for cover. He dropped to the ground thirty feet away.

I spotted the ordinary-looking two-story redbrick house in a clearing between the trees, just fifty yards away.

A strange noise slipped out of my throat, half growl, half cry.

"Go, Leo. I've got your back," Gabe said, nodding toward the house.

I took off like a bat out of hell, straining to see beyond the images in my head.

Blood.

Lifeless green eyes.

Pale skin.

Blue lips.

Gabe was close on my heels, his footsteps landing in tandem with mine.

As I made it out of the trees, into the overgrown lawn beyond them, I saw Brute breaking through the trees and brush thirty yards to my right, barreling toward the house, Greta close on his heels.

It was the back of the house, I realized quickly.

There was no back door, and all of the windows looked like they'd been boarded up.

Without slowing down, I circled around toward the front of the house, ahead of Gabe.

The second I turned the corner, sunlight glinted off the gun in some oversized goon's hand. I slammed to a stop ten feet from him.

I had my gun aimed and ready. Unfortunately, I was going down too. *I failed.* It would be up to my brothers and the others here to avenge my death, but at least this way, I'd die never knowing. I'd take my last breath with the hope she was still alive.

A gunshot went off somewhere in front of the house. Not my gun. Not the goon's.

A bullet tore right through the goon's head, ear to ear, right in front of me, and he dropped to the ground.

A figure emerged from the overgrown brush fifty feet away.

Tall, sandy blond hair, a rifle in his hand.

"*Grazie,* Nikolai." It was the first time I'd ever thanked a Russian.

Nikolai nodded. "Next time, skip the cars and take a boat," he motioned behind him, presumably in the direction of the river. "It's a much more direct route."

With Gabe, Brute, and Greta caught up, the five of us proceeded to the front door.

It wasn't guarded. No men on either side of it.

"We had almost no resistance all the way here. Is anyone else finding this a little too easy?" Greta asked, looking around.

I nodded. "Aside from nearly ending up with a bullet in my head, yeah, I was thinking the same thing."

"A dozen men headed for the river two minutes ago," Nikolai whispered, nodding in the direction he'd been hiding. "She wasn't with them, but something definitely sent them running."

"Sounds like something spooked them," Gabe said, peering inside the open front door.

"Cowards," Greta muttered under her breath.

A muscle was twitching in Brute's jaw.

I had a feeling he really would have liked the opportunity to fill the dozen cowards with bullets.

I half-expected to find a mammoth creature with razor-sharp claws and teeth in the front foyer.

Inside, the house was quiet. *Too* quiet.

No gunshots. No screams. No creature. Nothing but silence.

Dom and the others appeared from around the side of the house and caught up.

"That was too fucking easy," Nico said. He looked seriously disappointed.

Dom nodded. "We only ran into two men the whole way."

I stepped inside, listening over my heartbeat jackhammering in my ears.

Dom and Nico fanned out to my left and right while I heard Greta's footsteps sound somewhere behind me.

I made a beeline through the house, looking for the door to the basement. That's where he would have taken her.

Gabe, Brute, and Nikolai were close on my heels, each with their guns raised, watching for threats from a different direction.

It only took seconds to find the door, but it felt like an eternity.

There was no lock on the basement door.

I pulled it open slowly, but the hinges squeaked like they hadn't seen oil in a century.

"I'll keep watch," Nikolai said at the top landing while Gabe and Brute followed me down.

The stairs creaked just like they had at Avalone's, and the knots in my stomach twisted up tighter with every step.

My blood pumped harder.

My vision clouded with a red haze.

The tension in the air around us sparked and snapped like a live wire.

All three of us had stood in Avalone's basement just hours ago.

I had no doubt Gabe and Brute were imagining the walls down below, lined with every kind of torture device known to man.

When I reached the base of the stairs, I held my breath.

The concrete walls of the big, open room were empty. No whips or chains, no O-rings in the floor. No cages in the corner.

No Ella.

There was nothing here.

Nothing but a door on the far side of the room.

Without a word, we surrounded it, me in front of it, and Gabe and Brute on either side.

There was no way to know what we'd find in there, but my mind conjured plenty, carving out my soul a little more with every heart-wrenching image.

Gabe started the silent countdown, counting on his fingers with the hand that hovered over the doorknob.

Five...

Four...

I gripped the gun tighter, ignoring the blood that dripped from my forearm.

Three...

Two...

I envisioned Riccardo on the other side, imagining where I'd bury the first bullet.

One...

Gabe turned the handle and threw open the door.

Ella was alive.

My heart soared for a fraction of a second, and then it plummeted, slamming into the ground with the force of a Mack Truck.

Ella stood ten feet inside the dark room, her back pressed tight against Riccardo's body, his meaty arm wrapped around her chest.

And the barrel of his gun pressed against her temple.

Chapter Forty-Seven

Ella

Riccardo had turned off the light.

The only light spilled in from the open doorway where Leo, Brute, and Gabe stood, guns drawn.

"Let her go," Leo snarled as all three of them took aim.

The same glint of cold steel flashed in their eyes.

None of them fired.

If they did, Riccardo's gun would go off reflexively.

"I suggest you all stay very still," Riccardo said as a wave of terror crested inside me.

But it was fury that rode in on its trough—white-hot, violent, and numbing.

I was aware of Riccardo's arm around me, pressing so hard my ribs strained beneath the pressure.

The cold steel of the barrel of his gun bit into my temple.

But I felt nothing.

The men in this room—*Signore,* Belemonte, and Riccardo—had taken everything from me.

My freedom, my fight, my dignity.

But they were done taking.

Belemonte was dead.

Signore was circling death's door.

Leo, Gabe, and Brute just needed a clear shot at Riccardo.

It was my fault they were here, so it was my responsibility to give them that.

"Let her go," Brute hissed, "or you'll wish you were fucking dead."

Brute stood up tall, his shoulders back like he was trying to take up as much space, draw as much attention toward him as possible. He wanted Riccardo to see him as the biggest threat.

I loved him for that.

It was just built into him to try to protect those around him.

Riccardo shifted, pressing the gun harder against my head.

The look in Leo's eyes turned feral, inhuman.

I could see it in his twilight blue irises as he tore Riccardo apart in his mind, shredding him until he was nothing but ribbons of bloody bone and flesh.

Gabe and Leo inched closer, but Riccardo didn't notice; all of his attention was fixed on Brute as the hand holding the gun against my temple shook with indecision.

Keep his leverage and risk the crazed biker's next move?

Or risk Leo and Gabe's wrath and take him out?

The shaking stopped. "I don't think so, Old Dog. I let her go and you... How did you explain it, Leo? Turn me into a human sieve?" Riccardo chuckled darkly and shook his head. "I would suggest you check up on your friends, though, Brute. You never know what can happen when you leave those Dogs unattended."

Brute's expression didn't change.

I cringed, knowing what awaited him at his bar.

More people hurt because of the monsters in this room.

They wouldn't be the last if I didn't do something.

"How do you think this ends, *amico*?" Leo asked in a tone that belied the violence in his eyes. "There's no scenario where you walk out of here."

Gabe nodded. "Do yourself a favor, and let her go. Maybe then, we'll show mercy and kill you fast." There was nothing in his expression that looked the least bit merciful.

Riccardo didn't budge. He'd wrapped himself in a calm and cool outer shell, but I could feel the manic energy vibrating beneath his skin. Any second now, it would burst free, and there was no telling in which direction it would explode.

Toward Gabe, whose veins were filled with the same blood as mine?

Toward Brute, who'd been like a father to me?

Or toward Leo, who carried my heart in his chest?

"If you're ever in a bind," my father had told me nearly a decade ago as he'd wrapped his arms around me from behind. *"You jab your elbow into the guy like you're trying to make it go right through him,"* he'd explained, thrusting *my puny elbow back into his solar plexus in demonstration. "And just to be safe, slam your foot down on his like you're trying to crush it into the ground. Got it, princess?"*

It had taken me four months to get a shot in, and another year after that before I even managed to leave him winded. My father was fast, and he didn't believe in letting me win. *"False victories give you a false sense of security, Ella. You've got to earn it, and I know you can do that."*

His lessons had seemed so pointless back then, tucked safely away on my parents' small farm. And useless with *Signore* because he'd always been careful not to put himself in a vulnerable position.

But Riccardo hadn't been so smart. He just didn't know it yet.

I looked directly at Leo.

I couldn't tell him what I was planning, but I hoped like hell he could read it in my eyes.

I forced my muscles to loosen beneath Riccardo's grasp, willing his to follow suit like a mirror. Just a little. Just enough that I could shift like… *Yes, just like that.*

I shuffled my foot to the right under the guise of righting my balance and breathed deep to gauge the range of motion my shoulder could get. It wasn't much, but it was enough.

It would be challenging to duck my head out of the path of the gun and jab him at the same time, but I could do it.

Even if I couldn't, it would leave Leo clear to take the shot.

I looked at Leo once more.

It wasn't the first time my life had hung in the balance.

Thanks to the monsters in this room, the feeling had become disgustingly familiar. But this time was different.

It wasn't about me.

It was about Leo.

For the first time, I was truly grateful he'd brought me back, he'd reawakened my comatose heart and made me care.

The only thing worse than dying was living with nothing to die for.

I took one more deep breath while I shifted my weight ever so gently to my left foot.

Leo's eyes flared with protest.

Brute shook his head, almost imperceptibly, when they realized what I was doing.

But it was too late to stop now.

No stopping.

No more cowering.

I ducked my head, shot my elbow up and back, and slammed my heel down on the most vulnerable spot on Riccardo's foot, just above his shoe.

Riccardo gasped.

And the gun went off.

Chapter Forty-Nine

Leo

Ella stood turned away from Avalone with her back to me.

The only sound in the room was her breathing, a little too slow, a little too deep.

Seconds passed.

Nobody moved.

Every eye was fixed on Ella, not a single glance spared for the dead monster.

The strap of her dress had fallen off her shoulder, exposing some of the scars Avalone had left behind. The proof that she'd had every right to her retribution, and yet, she'd chosen to be merciful.

Brute took a step toward her.

I think he thought she was falling to pieces, but I went with my gut and put an arm out to stop him and shook my head. I couldn't say how I knew, but something inside me screamed that she needed this; this moment to put herself back together in a world where there was no one left to harm her, no more demons to slay.

It felt like an eternity, but really, it was only seconds. Seconds until she turned around, her eyes bright with a fresh sheen of tears, but none had spilled over.

I closed the distance between us, watching her body language, trying to fathom what she was feeling, but damned if I could stop myself from enveloping her in my arms.

This girl was steel and silk; light and dark; so small, and yet, her presence filled the room; everything I hadn't known I'd been missing all my life.

"I'm really... *free?*" she said, her voice rife with confusion.

"Of course, you are, pretty girl," Brute said with a gentle smile that almost seemed out of place on the crazy Old Dog.

Gabe and Greta nodded, adding their assurance.

"Damn right," Nico added with a rare smile that had no steel behind it. "Now that you've got Costas and Lucas—"

"And Old Dogs," Brute piped up.

"And Lucianos," Greta added with a sly smile.

Nico rolled his eyes then cleared his throat. "Now that you've got every family in a thousand-mile radius in your life, no one like that," he said, nodding to Avalone's corpse, "will ever get near you again."

Though he'd remained silent, the same sentiment flared in Nikolai's eyes. He was still staring at Ella like she was a mythical creature come to life. And maybe he wasn't wrong; she was unlike any woman I'd ever met.

Gabe was nodding, but he had a hand over his mouth in a poor attempt to hide a smile. Nico wasn't really the type to give grand speeches—the guy barely smiled before he met Raven.

"*Grazie,*" Ella said quietly.

Her gaze swung back to mine, the question still blaring in her eyes because she wasn't really asking if she was free; she was asking what that meant.

My heart ached to know it had been so long that she didn't really know what freedom looked like.

"It means you decide where you go and what you do, *gattina*. And who you do those things with," I forced out the last part, though a very big part of me didn't want to give her that choice.

Mine, it cried like a caveman.

Her eyes flared, knocking away some of the confusion in her gaze. "I don't care about the *where* or *what*, Leo."

I raised an eyebrow, feigning a cockiness I wasn't quite feeling at the moment.

What if, after having no say in the matter for so long, she wanted to experience life on her own for a while? Could I really fault her for it? The caveman in me said, *hell, yes,* but my conscience screamed *no*.

"I only care about the *who*, Leo, and that will always be you." A little more of the confusion fell away and the corners of her lips turned up in a heart-stopping smile.

I gathered her against me, reveling in the warmth of her skin and the knowledge this was right where she wanted to be.

"I'm proud of you, pretty girl," Brute said, coming up from behind and resting his big hand on her shoulder.

Ella froze. "Oh god, Brute, I'm so sorry. The bar—"

"I already know. Tate's dealing with the girl who stocked those shelves. Seems someone bribed her to look the other way. But it's okay, pretty girl, nothing those boys couldn't handle," he said, gripping her shoulder reassuringly.

She melted into me as a lone sob slipped out. "Thank God," she whispered against my chest.

I held her tighter, kissing the top of her head as Dante walked into the room. It didn't escape my notice the way his eyes skipped over the dead men and went straight to Ella. Damn lucky for him that he had a concerned look on his face and he seemed to be searching for injuries.

"She's okay, *fratello*. Thanks for asking," I said, glaring just a little.

He grinned like the Cheshire cat before his attention was drawn downward to the faceless corpse. "Has anyone else noticed the dead guy on the floor?"

Ella blew out a ragged breath. "It's Harry Belemonte," she said. She was looking at me but spoke loud enough for everyone to hear. "I stabbed him."

Dom whistled, clearly impressed.

Nico's lips turned up in a smile that was all steel. "Damn, I would have liked to have been here to see that, *cugina*." Cousin—it was still hard to believe she was related to a man like Nico, but then, there was a whole lot more steel in her than I'd given her credit for.

"He detonated an explosive in Brute's bar," she went on, her eyes fixed on mine like she owed me an explanation. "And he threatened you and your whole family. I couldn't just..."

"He needed to die, *gattina*. I'm sorry you had to be the one to do it."

She shook her head, and finally, a single tear slipped free. "I stabbed him, but he didn't die, Leo. Riccardo, he..." She pressed her lips together, and I covered them with one finger. She didn't need to say more. The gory picture Riccardo had painted was quite clear.

Dante slipped off his jacket and laid it over what was left of Belemonte's face then nodded to Ella.

She mouthed the words *"Thank you"* and nestled herself closer against my chest.

"I'm sorry I didn't get here sooner," I whispered, hating that she'd had to see that.

She laughed quietly. "How about no more apologies, okay? We're alive, we're together. That's all that matters, right?"

"I couldn't have said it better myself," I said and sealed it with a kiss.

***

Flames danced inside the redbrick tomb, little by little stretching outward, slowly engulfing the walls, floors, and the bodies of the three men who'd been given a one-way ticket to hell.

Surprisingly, Brute had played no part in prepping for the fiery show. He'd stayed right beside Ella, his big hand enveloping hers as I held her against my chest, still not ready to let her go.

I probably wouldn't ever be ready.

She'd insisted on staying here until the fire was well under way.

Everyone else was free to head back to the plane, but they'd stayed, Nico and Gabe on either side of her, and Brute, a constant shadow behind me and her.

I think it was a funeral pyre for her—bidding farewell to the life she'd lived for too many years. There were no tears in her eyes. She stood stoically, staring as the first lick of fire breached the open front door. Her shoulders sagged, and I could feel her deep exhale against me. She'd finished with whatever goodbyes she'd needed to bid.

"Are you ready, *gattina?*" I whispered against her ear.

Ella nodded against my chest, but her gaze flickered to the Russian. It wasn't the first time; it was hard to miss his attentive stare. He'd stayed quiet, though, giving her a chance to grieve with the family she already knew.

With her demons finally laid to rest, her attention lingered this time rather than swinging back to the burning house.

I wondered if she could see the similarities between herself and the blond-haired man.

They were faint; Ella had taken much more after her mother than her father, it seemed, but it was there in the winged arch of their eyebrows, the shape of their lips, and the high sweep of cheekbones.

"Ella, this is Nikolai Volkov," I told her, motioning to the Russian.

Her breath caught in her throat.

"I'm your cousin, Ella. I've been looking forward to meeting you for a very long time. My father knew about you even before you were born, but your father had sworn him to secrecy. He didn't learn of your father's death until years after it happened. We've been trying to find you—"

"Volkov?" she whispered, her gaze flicking up to mine and then back.

I understood now why my questions about the Russians had distressed her so much. But her family were Volkovs, not the Sokolovs—not that it would have mattered. She could have had the blood of the devil himself running through her veins, and it wouldn't have changed a thing.

"Ha! Those pigs are gone, and good riddance," Nikolai said. "Isn't that right, Mr. Hastings?" His gaze swung to Brute.

Brute sighed, his chest deflating. "Leo, I—"

"Brute?" Ella interrupted, her brow furrowed and panic widening her eyes.

Dom's gaze swung back and forth between Nikolai and Brute.

"It's all right, pretty girl," Brute said, patting her shoulder. "I saw you there that night at the cemetery. I appreciate you keeping quiet all this time, I really do. But it's about time I man up." He dropped his hand from her shoulder and turned to face me.

"My father and his Dogs were in trouble with the Aliyev family—some pretty powerful Russians, back in the day. The Sokolovs came to him, offering assistance with that particular problem in return for his help with another family. Your family," he said bluntly. "Since he'd wanted the Lucas gone too, he saw the opportunity in teaming up with them. I'd been away from the Old Dogs for a long time, searching for my sister... I didn't have the kind of sway I needed to stop them, so I..."

I had a feeling I didn't want to hear this.

"The day of the attack, I steered them and the Russians in the wrong direction. Your direction, Leo..." Brute continued. "If they got their hands on Dominic, they may very well have won. But you... I figured, at your age, you wouldn't have known much about Luca business, and I thought... I thought they would have taken it easy on a kid. I was wrong, and I'm sorry, Leo."

As much as I hated to admit it, he'd made the right call—the call to protect the Luca family as a whole. The same call I would have made.

"Goddamn it, Brute," Dom seethed, his hands bunched in fists.

Ella whimpered, ripped herself out of my arms, and threw herself in front of Brute, glaring daggers at my brother.

Brute smiled at her, but he took her by the shoulders and shifted her out of the way, back into my arms. "You've done enough, pretty girl. The Lucas have a right to whatever vengeance they need."

"Dom, wait," I said.

Dom didn't have a gun in his hand; I wasn't sure he'd actually kill Brute, but he kind of looked like he wanted to throw a few good punches. He stopped moving and cocked an eyebrow at me.

"Your father was murdered shortly after, wasn't he?" I asked Brute.

Brute nodded once.

"And several of the Old Dogs, if I remember correctly."

Another nod.

"There was rumor that it was an inside job," I mused, connecting the dots by the fierce shine of satisfaction in his eyes. "You killed your father and the men who were loyal to him."

Dom's fists loosened just a little.

"He was an evil man, Leo. What he tried to do to your family was wrong, and he wouldn't have stopped. I had to stop him," Brute said plainly.

"Then we're good, *amico*," I said.

I meant it. Thanks to Ella, I'd already made peace with my past.

"Leo?" Dom prompted, not quite ready to let bygones be bygones, it seemed.

"Brute sent them at me to protect the Luca family as a whole, *fratello*. You can't fault him for that. Gun to the head, any one of us would have made the same call—because it was the *right* call, and you know it." He could glare at me all he wanted; I was right. "So, how about you two shake hands so we can get the fuck out of here?"

Dom sighed, but hard-ass or not, he knew it was the right thing to do. He stuck out his hand.

Brute hesitated but then he took Dom's hand and shook it. "You're good people," he said to Dom then nodded to me.

"Apparently," Dom said flatly, though the corners of his lips twitched with humor. He drew his hand back, but he clapped Brute on the shoulder. "I'll see you back at the house, *amico*. I hear the bar's in no condition for a victory toast."

I kept my arm around Ella the whole walk back to the cars, trailing further and further behind the others until only Brute and Nikolai remained beside us.

I wanted her all to myself, but it seemed they weren't quite ready to let Ella out of their sights yet. I couldn't blame them, even if I was kind of wishing the ground would open and swallow them up—just for a little while.

With every step further away from the redbrick tomb, the air around us had grown lighter. Freer. Until we reached the BMW I'd left parked at the side of the road, and it started to buzz with excitement.

Ella's eyes flared just a little, and I could almost hear the way the car called to her.

"Do you want to drive, *gattina?*" The BMW wasn't as pretty as my Lambo, but I had a feeling she'd like it just fine.

"Yes," she said while the life in her eyes flared brighter, making something in my chest explode like fireworks. Her smile, the light in her eyes, her delicate and dangerous hands; every part of her was like a drug, and I was hopelessly, irrevocably hooked.

"Then be my guest," I said as I opened the driver's side door. Truth be told, my arm was fucking killing me.

Brute and Nikolai stared with their brows knitted in confusion. They both knew she'd been held captive by Avalone for years—no chance of driver's ed. training in that hell.

I smiled, closed the door, and circled around to the passenger side.

Brute and Nikolai got in the back, both their expressions wary.

"Just wait, *amicos,*" I said as Ella shifted gears and maneuvered around the car ahead of us and back onto the road.

"Not bad, pretty girl," Brute said, easing back a little more comfortably in the seat while a slow smile crept up Nikolai's mouth.

Ella's lips turned up in a devious smile.

"Hold on, boys," she said as she shifted through the gears, gaining speed these roads had never seen.

I had a feeling every minute with Ella was going to be one hell of a wild ride.

Epilogue

Ella

I stood on the docks, dressed in black, squinting to see the dark shadows ghost across the ship's deck.

I couldn't see much, but they were there, moving like avenging apparitions in the night.

Lucas, Costas, Lucianos, and Nikolai Volkov.

Family. Every one of them. Maybe not all by blood, but it didn't matter. They were tied together by something bigger, and now I was a part of it, too.

"Pretty impressive, huh?" Raven said, sidling up next to me.

I nodded.

Her and I were "on the benches" for this one—both Dom's and Nico's orders. She hadn't been impressed until Nico promised to let her in on the action next time. Me, I probably should have stayed back at the house, getting it ready for what was coming.

Let's face it: I was far from combat ready. But something inside me needed to be here, even if all I could do was stand on the sidelines.

"I know about Berlusconi," Raven said, leaning back against the side of one of the black vans we'd rented.

My heart beat faster, and I could feel my cheeks warming with shame. "I'm sorry, Raven."

She shook her head. "Don't be. I didn't bring it up to freak you out. I just wanted you to know there's no bad blood between us. You didn't know me. You didn't even know what Berlusconi was planning. And I see the way Leo looks at you. He's crazy about you, and he's a darn good judge of people—he sees *more*, you know?"

I nodded. There was no arguing with that.

Raven shrugged. "I figure you've got to be pretty damn amazing for my brother to look at you the way he does."

"Thank you, Raven."

"Hey, the way I see it, if I can keep you with Leo and land a girl for Dante, we'll finally outnumber the guys." She waggled her brows but then frowned. "Since I brought Nico into the fold, I guess we won't really outnumber them anymore, but who knows, maybe we'll find two girls for Dante. I don't think he'd mind, do you?"

I laughed. "I doubt it."

Just like that, my last secret was gone, out in the air and drifting away into nothingness.

I'd handed the rest of them over to Leo, all for one low price. One favor.

While some of my intel was probably outdated, the Lucas and their alliance were now likely the most powerful and well-informed men in the country. Politicians, cartel *capos,* businessmen, crooked cops; *Signore* had been thorough, digging for information in all the right places.

"Here they come," Raven said, pointing to the dark figures approaching from the boat.

My breath caught in my throat as I squinted to see, to make out one shape from another. All of them tall, some of them with bound figures in front of them or heaved over their shoulders.

As they got closer, I could make out the dark outlines of faces I recognized.

Dante and Dom, Nico and Salvatore, Nikolai and Marco.

Where were the others?

We're too late.

And where the hell was Leo?

My heart thumped heavily against my chest as I scanned the darkness.

There he was! Behind the others, Leo and Gabe hauled a ginormous mountain of a man between them.

My lungs remembered how to breathe as I watched him coming closer. And closer. From twenty feet away, I could see the purplish bruise that marred his jaw, but he appeared otherwise uninjured.

"The others still on the ship are knocked out and tied up. We're all clear," Gabe announced as he and Leo heaved the unconscious mountain into the back of one of the vans along with the roped-up men the others had deposited in there.

I didn't envy those men, but I didn't pity them either.

They weren't going home; they would never see their homes again.

They were bound for a basement in a club called Onyx where Leo, Dante, Nico, and Gabe intended to get answers. Answers that would, hopefully, stop more girls from being taken.

Leo winked at me. "Come on, *gattina.*" He nodded toward the boat.

This was why I was here, why I'd had to come no matter how useless I was to this mission. "Are they…"

"Greta and Vito are working on getting the container open now."

I couldn't feel my legs as I let Leo take my hand and lead me onto the ship.

My chest felt cold, every breath my lungs drew made it colder.

Somewhere on the boat, there were girls just like me. It was like approaching a mirror after a brutal beating.

I wasn't sure I was ready to see my reflection in their faces.

I focused on the quiet lap of waves against the boat as I followed Leo, ignoring the puddles of blood on the deck and the occasional unconscious hog-tied body.

When I spotted Greta up ahead, I kept my eyes on her as she yanked a long length of chain off the giant container's door.

I was five feet away when she stepped back, and Vito grabbed hold of the door and pulled it open, the loud grinding of steel against steel piercing the quiet night.

"You're up, Ella," Greta whispered, flashing me a reassuring smile. She rested a hand on my shoulder then nudged me forward.

Inside, the container was dark, but I could feel them there.

Dirty and bruised, tired and frightened.

Every one of them was me.

I was them.

It felt like there was an invisible web running through the air, connecting all of us together.

Rather than shining flashlights into the container and scaring them, Vito set a lantern on the ground, just inside the door, illuminating us just as much as them.

Them. Two dozen girls, maybe more, all cowering at the far side of the container, knees drawn up, huddled together.

Over the past several days, I'd tried to rehearse this moment, but if I'd come up with any words, they escaped me now.

The girls stared up at me with wide eyes, the dirt on their cheeks streaked with tear tracks.

Damn it, just say something, Ella.

"You're safe." It was the first thing that came to mind. "And I'm not going to let anything happen to you," I said with so much conviction I could feel it seeping out my pores. "We're going to take you all somewhere safe. If you have families, we can help you contact them. If you don't, then you do now," I said, holding out my arms and encompassing all the people behind me—*my family.*

It started small; one hiccupping sob, and then another.

Then the silence erupted with cries.

Not cries of terror. Or pain.

They were cries of relief, of *hope.*

My shoulders shook as my own sobs of relief joined theirs.

***

The scent of chamomile and vanilla filled the kitchen as I poured hot water into the blue and gold Bernardaud teapot on the counter.

I could still hear Riccardo and Johnny arguing, their voices echoing off the cherrywood cabinets. It would probably be a long time before I stopped hearing the ghosts in this house, but one day, I'd walk through it and the walls would be silent.

"Are you okay, *gattina?*" Leo asked, walking in and wrapping his arms around me from behind.

He'd been gone for seven hours, doing what needed to be done at Onyx while the rest of us had helped to get the girls settled here.

"I am now," I said, spinning around in his arms and looking him over.

He'd changed clothes, and his skin looked squeaky clean.

I didn't even want to imagine how much blood he'd scrubbed off before leaving Onyx.

"I still don't understand why you chose this place," he said, tipping my chin up and kissing my forehead, my nose, and then my lips.

"Yes, you do." Leo's sixth sense was uncanny. "I'm done letting fear rule me, and to avoid this house, to hide away from it... I couldn't do that. I planned to burn it down—you know, face my demons and watch them burn. But I didn't just want to face it. I wanted to turn this place into something good."

A place for healing, not hurting.

"It's more than good, *gattina*. It's incredible. But you do know I would have bought if for you with or without your secrets, right?"

I nodded.

Leo would have given me the whole world on a silver platter if I'd asked for it. But I needed to own it, to take control of it.

While I had no money, there was no doubt that the secrets I had were a worthwhile barter.

"You do know I would have told you all my secrets with or without this house?" I quipped.

Leo smiled and grazed his lips down my neck, suckling and nipping to the base of my throat. "We both know I have ways of making you talk if I'd wanted to."

"No doubt," I said, savoring the tingle and sting of every kiss and nibble.

"How long do you think they'll stay?" he asked when he'd worked his way back up to my lips, nodding toward the front parlor where most of the girls had congregated.

"I don't know. Most of them have no families to go back to, and I'm hoping they'll feel comfortable enough to stay here until they decide what they want to do next."

It seemed the majority of the girls had been kidnapped from Mexico and the border states, most of them with no real families to return to, no one who would have missed them or mourned them. Orphans, foster kids… They were like me in more ways than one.

"All right, well, if we're going to have a full house for a while, I should probably see about arranging for more supplies," he said, kissing my forehead.

I smiled a devious smile and pulled out my phone. It was Brute's phone, actually. I still liked keeping it with me. I turned on the screen.

"Nikolai looked into my parents," I said, holding up the screen for Leo to see. "I guess they left me something," I said while his eyes perused the offshore bank account with a good number of zeroes in it.

He laughed. "And I have a feeling you're going to insist on using it to fund this."

There wasn't an ounce of doubt in his voice. He knew me well.

I shrugged. "I don't need the money. I have you, and there is nothing in the world I want more."

His lips touched mine just as Raven walked into the kitchen.

"I think that's it," she said, letting out a tired sigh. "A little undernourished and dehydrated. Some cuts and bruises, but nothing long-lasting."

"Thank you, Raven," I said with every ounce of sincerity in me.

Raven had worked tirelessly for the past seven hours, putting her nursing skills to work and examining all the girls. Thank God there were no serious injuries, not physically, at least.

Hopefully, with enough time and support, the deeper injuries—the ones nobody could see—would heal.

She squeezed my hand then turned her attention on Leo. "I do have a question for you," she said, leaning a hip against the counter. "You do realize that if word gets out about what we're doing here, it might hurt your big, bad reputation as mafia men, right? Providing sanctuary for kidnapped girls? Not a good bad-boy look."

Leo laughed, as unperturbed as ever. "Maybe, but if word gets out about what we do with the men who kidnapped them, I think it might just redeem us as the scary motherfuckers we are."

"Fair enough." Raven grinned.

"I need to borrow Ella for a while," Leo said. "Do you think you could handle this?" He motioned to the teapot and teacups on a tray on the counter.

"A while?" she asked, waggling her brows. "And just how long is 'a while'?"

He waggled his right back. "If we're not back in a few hours… wait longer."

Without waiting for an answer, he winked at Raven and tugged me along, outside and through the hedges off to the side of the property.

Leo stopped as we came out the other side of them.

There was a blanket laid out on the ground with a bottle of champagne and two glasses on it, and a bouquet of wildflowers in the center. Not trimmed and tamed; a cacophony of leaves and stems and vibrant color. It was perfect.

"I thought you deserved a victory toast," he said, leaning down to scoop up the bottle.

I looked around at the maples and pines that bracketed the property, remembering every brown in their ridges, from rich chestnut to deep mahogany. I could still feel the cold, wet grass beneath my feet, and if I listened closely enough, I could hear the crack of Riccardo's gunshot reverberating all around me.

"I ran this way the night I escaped."

Leo froze. "I'm sorry, *gattina*. Would you rather—"

"No, it's perfect." I smiled as the echo of the gunshot faded away into nothingness, the first of the ghosts to disappear. "It was the night I started running to you, Leo… I just didn't realize it at the time."

He laughed. "Ella, you might have started running to me that night, but I've been waiting for you my whole life."

"Well," I said with a shrug, "now that you have me…" I slipped the straps of my dress off my shoulders and let it drop to the ground. "What are you going to do with me?"

A groan and a growl rumbled up his throat as his eyes filled with heat that told me everything he intended to do with me.

Whoa.

A few hours was definitely not going to be enough time.

* * *

Kiana Hettinger

THANK YOU FOR READING: MAFIA KINGS:
CORRUPTED BOOK 3: CORRUPTED PROTECTOR

DON'T MISS THE FREE SIZZLING BONUS CHAPTER

EXCLUSIVE FREE BONUS CHAPTER

"Well, gattina, what do you think?" I asked as Ella closed the distance between us and peered inside through the open cabin door, looking around at the pale wood floors, sage green walls, and white fabric on the windows and furniture.

"I think it's perfect." Her smile lit up her eyes.

"Me too," I said, looking at the woman, not the room.

Ella had paint splotches on her bare arms, a dirt smudge across her forehead, and her dress had caught on a nail somewhere, ripping it across her hip.

Fucking perfect.

She wrapped her arms around my neck and leaned up on her toes to kiss me. What kind of dumbass would I have been to not take full advantage of that? I hoisted her off the floor and dragged her up my body.

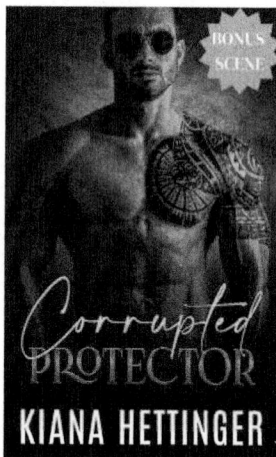

Can't get enough of Leo and Ella? Download the <u>free bonus scene</u> for one more steamy chapter.

Download the FREE bonus chapter here -
https://geni.us/corruptedpbonus

What's Next?

Wow! I hope you enjoyed *Corrupted Protector!* Your support means the world to me.

The next book in the <u>Mafia Kings: Corrupted Series</u> is <u>Corrupted Obsession.</u>

Calling all Kittens! Come join the fun:

If you're thirsty for more discussions with other readers of the series, join my readers' group on Facebook, Kiana's Kittens! – facebook.com/groups/KianasKittens

CAN YOU DO ME A HUGE FAVOR?

Would you be willing to leave me a review?

I'd be over the moon because just one positive review on Amazon is like buying the book a hundred times! Reader support is the lifeblood for Indie authors. It provides us the feedback we need to give readers what they want in future stories!

Your positive review would mean the world to me. You can post your review on Amazon or Goodreads. I'd be forever grateful, thank you from the bottom of my heart!

Printed in Great Britain
by Amazon